WEDDING KING'S CONVENIENCE

BY
MAUREEN CHILD

AND

BEDDING THE SECRET HEIRESS

BY
EMILIE ROSE

MILLS & BOON

"Why're you here?"

"You mean, why am I standing in the rain in front of a hardheaded woman who isn't honoring the contract she signed?"

"Your people are littering the street in front of my house at this very moment," she challenged, "so I'm thinking I'm honoring what was between us a good deal more than you have."

"You know," he said, "I've been back in Ireland about an hour and in that short amount of time, I've been rained on, had a flat tire, got mud in my shoes and been insulted by everyone I've spoken to. So I'm not in the mood to listen to more obscure references to what a bastard I am. If you've got a problem with me, then tell me what it is so I can fix it."

Her eyes narrowed on him. She crossed her arms over her chest, lifted her chin and said, "I'm pregnant. Fix *that*."

WEDDING AT KING'S CONVENIENCE

BY
MAUREEN CHILD

All the characters in this book have no existence outside the imagination of
the author, and have no relation whatsoever to anyone bearing the same name
or names. They are not even distantly inspired by any individual known or
unknown to the author, and all the incidents are pure invention.

Published in Great Britain 2010
Harlequin Mills & Boon Limited,
Eton House, 18-24 Paradise Road, Richmond, Surrey TW9 1SR

© Maureen Child 2009

ISBN: 978 0 263 88181 3

51-1010

Harlequin Mills & Boon policy is to use papers that are natural, renewable
and recyclable products and made from wood grown in sustainable forests.
The logging and manufacturing processes conform to the legal environmental
regulations of the country of origin.

Printed and bound in Spain
by Litografia Rosés S.A., Barcelona

Maureen Child is a California native who loves to travel. Every chance they get, she and her husband are taking off on another research trip. The author of more than sixty books, Maureen loves a happy ending and still swears that she has the best job in the world. She lives in Southern California with her husband, two children and a golden retriever with delusions of grandeur. Visit Maureen's website at www.maureenchild.com.

To Kate Carlisle

A great friend, a terrific writer, and the one person I want to share a latte with before RWA meetings!

Can't wait to see your first Desire™ book in print, Kate!

Dear Reader,

Thank you so much for coming along for the ride in this latest from the KINGS OF CALIFORNIA series! I can't tell you how much fun I'm having with the Kings and I'm delighted you're enjoying them, too!

In this third book, you'll meet Jefferson King. He's the head of King Studios in Hollywood, but he's not a man to sit behind a desk every day. He prefers going out into the field, scouting locations for the movies his company produces.

And it's on a location hunt that he meets Maura Donohue, owner of a sheep farm in County Mayo, Ireland. Maura is his match in every way and Jefferson is more intrigued than he wants to admit even to himself.

Sparks fly and passion simmers as these two hardheaded people are forced to find common ground.

Ireland is one of my favorite places in the world. And this little slice of that country, in County Mayo, is where my husband and I stayed the last time we visited.

The country's as beautiful as its people are warm and welcoming, and personally, I can't wait to go back! I really hope you enjoy this latest KINGS OF CALIFORNIA book—just as I hope you love the peek at Ireland!

I would love to hear from you—to e-mail me just go to my website at www.maureenchild.com or, if you prefer, my mailing address is PO Box 1883, Westminster, CA 92684-1883.

And happy reading!

Maureen

One

"You think I'm charming," Jefferson King said with a smug smile. "I can tell."

"Charming, is it?" Maura Donohue straightened up to her full, if less-than-imposing height. "Do you believe I'm so easily swayed by a smooth-talking man?"

"Easily?" Jefferson laughed. "We've known each other for the better part of a week now, Maura, and I can say with certainty there's nothing 'easy' about you."

"Well now," she countered with a smile of her own. "Isn't that a lovely thing to say."

She was pleased. Jefferson read the truth on her features. No other woman he'd ever known would have been complimented by knowing that a man thought her difficult. But then, Maura Donohue was one in a million, wasn't she?

He'd known it the moment he met her.

In Ireland scouting locations for an upcoming movie from King Studios, Jefferson had stumbled across Maura's sheep farm in County Mayo and had realized instantly that it was just what he'd been searching for. Of course, convincing Maura of that fact was something else again.

"You know," he said, leaning one shoulder against the white-washed stone wall of the barn, "most people would be leaping at the chance to make some easy money."

She flipped her long black hair behind her shoulder, narrowed sea-blue eyes on him and countered, "There you are again, using the word 'easy,' when you've already admitted I'm not a woman accustomed to taking the easy way."

He sighed and shook his head. The woman had an answer for everything but damned if she wasn't intriguing enough that he was enjoying himself. As the head of King Studios, Jefferson was more accustomed to people falling all over themselves to accommodate him. When he rolled into a town looking to pay top dollar for the use of a location, those he dealt with were always eager to sign on the dotted line and collect their cash.

Not Maura, though.

For days now, he'd been coming to the Donohue farm to talk to its stubborn owner/operator. He'd plied Maura with compliments, tempted her with promises of mountains of money he knew damn well she could ill afford to turn down and in general had tried to make himself too amiable to resist.

Yet she'd managed.

"You're in my way," she said.

"Sorry." Jefferson stepped aside so she could walk past him carrying a sack of God-knew-what. His every instinct told him to snatch the heavy load out of her arms and carry it for her. But she wouldn't accept or appreciate his offer at help.

She was fiercely independent, with a quick wit, sharp tongue and a body that he'd spent far too much time thinking about. Her thick black hair fell in soft waves to the middle of her back and he itched to gather it up in his hands to feel its sleekness sliding across his skin. She had a stubborn chin that she tended to lift when making a point and a pair of dark blue eyes fringed by long, inky-black lashes.

She was dressed in worn jeans and a heavy Irish knit sweater that covered most of her curves. But winter in Ireland meant damp, cold weather so he could hardly blame her for bundling up. Still, he hoped she invited him into her house for a cup of tea, because then she'd strip that sweater off to reveal a shirt that gave him a much better peek at what she kept hidden.

But for now, he followed her out of the barn into an icy wind that slapped at his face and stung his eyes as if daring him to brave the Irish countryside. His ears were cold and his overcoat wasn't nearly warm enough. He made a mental note to do some shopping in the village. Buy a heavier coat if he could find one and a few of the hand-knit sweaters. Couldn't hurt to endear himself to the local merchants. He'd want everyone in the tiny town of Craic on his side as he tried to sway Maura into renting King Studios the use of her farm.

"Where are we going?" he shouted into the wind and could have sworn he actually *saw* the wind throw his words back at him.

"*We're* not going anywhere," she called back over her shoulder. "*I'm* going to the high pasture to lay out a bit more feed."

"I could help," he said.

She turned and looked him over, her gaze pausing on his well-shined, expensive black shoes. Smirking then, she said, "In those fine shoes? They'll be ruined in a moment, walking through the grass and mud."

"Why not let me worry about my shoes?"

Lifting that stubborn chin of hers, she said, "Spoken like a man who needn't worry about where his *next* pair of shoes might come from."

"Is it all rich people you don't like," Jefferson asked, an amused smile on his face, "or is it just me?"

She grinned back at him, completely unabashed. "Well now, that's an interesting question, isn't it?"

Jefferson laughed. The women he was used to were more coy. More willing to agree with him no matter what he said. They didn't voice opinions for fear he wouldn't share them. He hadn't enjoyed himself this much in way too long.

And it wasn't just the women, either, he mused. It was everyone he knew back in Hollywood.

Came from not only being a member of a prominent family, but from being the head of a studio where dreams could be made or shattered on the whim of an executive. Too many people were trying too hard to stay on his good side. It was refreshing as hell to find some-one who didn't care if he *had* a good side.

Maura slammed the gate of her small, beat-up lorry, then leaned back against it. Folding her arms over her chest in a classic defensive posture she asked, "Why are you trying so hard, Jefferson King? Is it the challenge of winning me over that's driving you? Are you not used to hearing the word 'no'?"

"I don't hear it often, that's true."

"I imagine you don't. A man like you with his fine shoes and his full wallet. Probably you're welcome wherever you go, aren't you?"

"You have something against a full wallet?"

"Only when it's thrown in my face every few minutes."

"Not thrown," he corrected. "Offered. I'm offering you a small fortune for the lease of your land for a few weeks. How is that an insult?"

Her mouth worked as if she were fighting a smile. "Not an insult, to be sure. But your stubborn determi-nation to win me over is a curiosity."

"As you said, I do love a challenge." Every King did. And Maura Donohue was the most interesting one he'd had in a long time.

"We've that in common, then."

"Shared ground at last. Why not let me ride with you up to the high pasture? You can show me the rest of your farm."

She studied him for a long, quiet moment as the wind buffeted them both. Finally, she asked, "Why do you want to come with me?"

He shrugged. "Honestly, I've nothing better to do right now. Why is it you don't want me along?"

"Because I don't need help," she pointed out.

"You seem pretty sure of yourself," he told her.

"And I am," she assured him.

"Then why should you care if I ride along and help out if I can? Unless you're worried that you're going to be seduced by my lethal charisma."

She laughed. Threw her head back and let loose a loud, delighted roll of laughter that touched something inside him even as it poked at his pride. "Ah, you're an amusing man, Jefferson."

"Wasn't trying to be."

"Which only makes it that much more funny, don't you see?"

Hunching deeper into his overcoat against the cold, Jefferson told himself that she was no doubt trying to reassure herself that he wasn't getting to her. Because he knew he was. She wasn't nearly as distant as she had been the first time he'd driven onto the Donohue farm. That day, he'd been half expecting her to pull out a shotgun and force him off her land.

Not exactly the picture of Irish hospitality.

Thankfully, he'd always been the patient one in the family.

Trying a different tack now, he said, "Look at it this way. While you drive me around your place, you can have the chance to elaborate as to why you don't want to take me up on my offer to rent your farm for an already mentioned *exorbitant* amount of money."

She cocked her head to study him and her black hair

danced in the cold wind like a battle flag. "Fine then. Come along if you must."

"A gracious invitation, as always," he muttered.

"If you want gracious," she told him, "you should head down to Kerry, go to Dromyland Castle. They've fine waiters, lovely food and neatly tended garden paths designed to make sure their visitors' fine shoes don't get ruined."

"I'm not interested in gracious," he told her, heading for the side of the car. "That's why I'm here."

After a moment, she laughed shortly. "You give as good as you get, I'll say that for you."

"Thanks."

She joined him at the door of the truck. "But if you don't mind, I'll drive my own lorry."

"What?" Jefferson realized he'd gone to the right side—what should be the passenger side—but in Ireland, the steering wheel was on the right. "You do realize you guys have the wheel on the wrong side of the car."

"It's a matter of perspective, now isn't it?" She shooed him off and he rounded the front of the small truck, walking to the other door. "Wrong side, right side, makes no difference, as they're both *my* side."

Jefferson leaned his forearms on the roof of the truck. "Believe it or not, Maura, I'm on your side, too."

"Ah now," she said, grinning, "that I don't believe, Jefferson King, as I'm thinking that you're always on your own side."

She hopped in, fired up the engine and Jefferson moved fast to climb in himself, since he was sure she'd have no qualms about driving off and leaving him standing where he was. She was hardheaded. And beautiful. As stubborn as the hills here were green.

Watching the big American striding across a sheep-dung-littered rainy field on a blustery day was a fine thing, Maura mused. Even here, where he was so clearly out of his element, Jefferson King walked as if he owned the land. The edges of his gray overcoat flapped in the wind like a ghost's shroud. His thick black hair ruffled as though spirits were raking their cold fingers through it and his delicious-looking mouth was twisted up into a sneer of distaste. And yet, she thought, he continued on. Carrying sacks of feed across muddy ground to tip and pour the grain into troughs for her sheep.

As the feed hit the bottom of the troughs, the black and white creatures came scampering ever closer, as though they'd been starved for weeks. Greedy beasts, she thought with a smile as they nudged and pushed at the great Jefferson King.

To give him his due, he wasn't skittish around the animals as most city people were. They tended to look on mountain sheep as they would a hungry tiger, wondering if the beasties were going to turn on them with fangs and the taste for human flesh. For a rich American, he seemed oddly at home in the open country, though for some reason, the man refused to wear stout boots instead of his shiny, no doubt hideously expensive shoes.

He laughed suddenly as a head butt from the sheep nearly sent him sprawling face-first into the muck. Maura smiled at the sound of his laughter and told herself to ignore the swift, nearly debilitating rush of heat that swamped her. An impossible order to obey, she thought as she watched the wide smile on his face lighting up his features.

Her knees went wobbly and she knew her body was not listening to her mind.

Jefferson King was a man meant to be ogled by women, she thought, eyeing his fine physique. Broad shoulders, narrow hips and large hands with more calluses on them than she would have imagined a Hollywood type to have. He had long legs, muscular thighs and a fine ass if anyone were to ask her opinion.

And he was only a temporary visitor to the lovely island she called home. She had to remember that. He'd only come to Ireland looking for a place to make a movie. He wasn't here on the Donohue Farm because he found her fascinating. He was here to rent her land, nothing more. Once she'd signed his bloody papers, he'd be off. Back to his own world that lay so very far from hers.

Well. She didn't like the thought of that.

And so, she continued to draw out the negotiations.

"They act like they haven't eaten in weeks," Jefferson said as he walked toward her.

"Aye, well, it's cold out. That'll make for heartier appetites."

"Speaking of," he hinted broadly.

They'd fallen into a routine of sorts since his arrival. Maura had hardly noticed it happening, but there it was. Jefferson spent most of the day at her farm, following her about, touting the merits of the deal he was trying to make her and then they ended the afternoon over a bowl of soup and some hot tea in her kitchen. Strange how she'd come to look forward to that time with him.

Still, she said, "You could ask the sheep to share their meal with you if you're that hungry."

"Tempting," he said, pushing one hand through his hair to sweep it back off his forehead. "But I'd prefer some of that brown bread you gave me yesterday."

"Fond of soda bread, are you?"

He looked down at her from his great height and she could have sworn she saw actual sparks glittering in his pale blue eyes. "I'm fond of a lot of things around here."

"Oh, you've a smooth tongue on you, Jefferson King." And her knees wobbled even more as she thought of the many uses that smooth tongue of his could be put to.

"Do I?"

"And well you know it," she told him, plucking two long strands of her hair out of her eyes. "But you're wasting your time trying to wheedle me into signing that contract of yours. I will or I won't and nothing you can say will sway me in either direction."

"Ah, but it's my time, isn't it?"

"It is indeed," she said and was silently glad he hadn't given up just yet.

In truth, she'd been considering his offer seriously since the moment he'd made it. Her mind had raced with possibilities. With the money he was offering her, she had tried to imagine what she could do to the centuries-old farmhouse that had been in her family for forever. Not to mention the changes she could make to the farm itself.

She already had a paid worker coming a few days a

week, but with Jefferson King's money, she would be able to hire someone full-time, to help ease the workload. And even with all that, she'd still have money left over to make a fine cushion in her bank account.

But she wasn't entirely ready to agree to his terms just yet. He'd already sweetened his offer once and she'd no doubt he would do so again. Yes, he could find another farm just as suitable for his needs, but he wouldn't find a prettier one, Maura told herself. Besides, he'd already told her he thought the Donohue land was perfect.

Which meant he wouldn't be withdrawing his offer. And Maura, coming from a long line of wily horse traders, was going to make sure she got the very best deal she could. It wasn't greed motivating her, either. Just think what a movie crew would do to her well-ordered life, not to mention her home and land. She'd need some of the money he would pay her just to put to rights the sorry mess they would no doubt leave behind.

While she stared at him, his gaze moved past her, scanning the surrounding countryside. As she'd grown up on Donohue land, and knew every inch of it as well as Tarzan knew the jungle, she didn't have to look to know what he was seeing. Green fields as far as the eye could see. Stone fences rising up from the ground like ancient sentinels. The shadow of the Partry Mountains looming behind them and the whole of Lough Mask stretching out in front of them, its silvery surface looking on this gray day like molten steel frothing in the wind. Across the way, a tumbled ruin of an ancient castle slept as if only waiting for the clang of a sword to wake it. Sheep wandered these hills freely as they had for centuries and would, no doubt, for centuries to come. The Irish wind kissed the land and the rain blessed it and those who lived here appreciated every single acre as no outsider ever could.

The village of Craic was only two kilometers down the long, twisting road and dotted along the way were B and Bs, a few more farmhouses and even one palatial mansion belonging to one Rogan Butler and his wife, Aly, who now spent most of their time in Dublin.

But here in the middle of her own fields, she and Jefferson might as well have been the only two people on the planet. A latter-day Adam and Eve, without the fig leaves, thanks very much, and surrounded by bleating sheep.

"Did I tell you," he said, shattering the quiet between them, "that my great-grandmother was Irish?"

"You mean Mary Frances Rafferty King who was born in County Sligo and met your great-grandfather when he was taking a tour of Ireland? He saw her in a pub. On a Tuesday, wasn't it?" Maura smiled. "Aye, you might have mentioned her once or twice."

He grinned at her. "Didn't mean to bore you."

"Did I say I was bored?"

"No." He stepped closer and she felt the heat of him reaching for her, charging the icy air. "But let me know if you feel yourself nodding off and I'll try harder to enchant you."

"You mean to say you've got to *try* to be appealing?" she quipped, taking a quick step or two back from him. "I'm disappointed. Here I thought you were just a born charmer."

"Did you?" he asked, closing the distance between

them again with a single, long step. "Now, isn't that interesting?"

"I didn't say your charm was *working* on me, mind you," Maura told him, enjoying their sparring far too much. It had been a long time since she'd met a man who appealed to her on so many different levels. A shame, she reminded herself, that he was only here temporarily. Better that she keep that thought in mind before her body and heart became too involved for their own good.

"You can't fool me, Maura. I'm wearing you down."

"Is that right?"

"It is," he said. "You haven't threatened to throw me off your property in almost—" he checked his watch "—six hours."

Still smiling, she said, "I could remedy that right now."

"Ah, but you don't want to."

"I don't?" That smile of his should be considered a lethal weapon, she told herself.

"No," he said, "because you actually like having me around, whether you'll admit to it or not."

Well, he was right about that now, wasn't he, she thought. But then what single woman in her right mind wouldn't enjoy having a man such as Jefferson King about the house? It wasn't every day a rich, gorgeous man showed up on her doorstep wanting to rent her farm. Could she really help it if she was enjoying the negotiations so much that she was rather dragging the process out?

"Admit it," he said, his voice low enough that it was barely more than a breath. "I dare you."

"You'll find, Jefferson," she said softly, lifting her eyes to meet his, "that if I want you...*around,* I'll have no trouble admitting it. To you or to myself."

Two

In the village of Craic, Jefferson King was big news and Maura had half the town nagging her to sign his silly papers so they could all "get famous." Not a moment went by when she didn't hear someone's opinion on the subject.

But she wasn't going to be hurried into a decision. Not by her friends, not by her sister and not by Jefferson. She'd give him her answer when she was ready and not before.

She should have thought twice about suggesting to him they go to the village pub for supper. Should have known that her friends and neighbors would pounce on the opportunity to engage Jefferson in conversation while managing to give Maura a nudge or two at the same time. But, the truth was, she had been feeling far too…itchy to trust herself alone in her house with him. He was a fine-looking man after all, and her hormones had been doing a fast step-dance since the moment she'd first laid eyes on him.

Now, Maura had to wonder if coming into the Lion's Den pub for a meal hadn't been a bad idea after all.

Of course, she was surrounded by villagers, so there was no chance at all her hormones would be able to take over her good sense. But the downside was, she was surrounded by villagers, all of whom were vying for Jefferson's attentions.

In early December, the interior of the pub was dim, with lamplight gleaming dully on paneled walls stained with centuries of smoke from the peat fires kept burning in a brazier. The floor was wood as well, scuffed from the steps of thousands of patrons. There were several small round tables with chairs gathered close and a handful of booths lining two of the walls. The bar itself was highly polished walnut that Michael O'Shay, the pub owner, kept as shiny as a church pew. And beside the wide mirror reflecting the crowd back on itself, there was a television perched high on a shelf, displaying a soccer game with the sound muted.

Michael sauntered up to their table with a perfectly stacked pint of Guinness beer for Jefferson and a glass of Harp beer for Maura. As he set them down, he gave a swift, unnecessary swipe of the gleaming table with a pristine bar rag. Then he beamed at them both like Father Christmas. "I'll have your soup and bread up for you in a moment. It's potato-leek today. My Margaret made it and you'll enjoy it I'm sure. When your movie folk arrive," he added with a grin for Jefferson, "I'll see that Margaret makes it by the boatload for you."

Maura sighed. Hadn't taken him long to get Hollywood into the conversation.

"Sounds good," Jefferson said, taking a sip of his thick black beer.

"Has your Rose had her baby yet, Michael?" Maura asked, then said in an aside to Jefferson, "Michael and Margaret are about to become grandparents."

"We are indeed," the pub owner said and gave Maura a knowing look, "so the extra money made when your film crew arrives will be most welcome."

Maura closed her eyes. Clearly, all anyone wanted to talk about was the notion of having a film made in their little village. Michael had hardly left to bustle back to his bar when three or four other locals found a reason to stop by the table and talk to Jefferson.

She watched him handle the people she'd known all her life with courtesy and she liked him for it. Surely a man like him didn't enjoy being the center of attention in a village less than a third the size of the town he called home. But rather than being abrupt, he seemed to almost encourage their chatter.

Maura listened with half an ear as Frances Boyle raved about her small traveler's inn and the good service she could promise King Studios. Then Bill Howard, owner of the local market, swore he'd be happy to order in any and all supplies Jefferson might require. Nora Bailey gave him her card and told him again that she ran a full-service bakery and would be happy to work with his caterers and finally Colleen Ryan offered her skills as a seamstress, knowing that being so far from Hollywood, his costume people might be needing an extra hand, fine with a needle.

By the time they wandered off, each of them giving Maura a nudging glare, Jefferson was grinning and Maura's head pounded like a badly played bodhran drum.

"Seems as though you're the only one who doesn't want my business," he said, then took another sip of his beer.

"Aye, it does at that, doesn't it?"

"So why are you holding out?"

"Holding out?" Maura pretended surprise. "I've not promised you a thing, have I?"

"No," he said, smiling. "You haven't. You've just sat by and let me talk and wheedle and eventually raise my offer a bit each day."

True enough and she had hopes he'd go a bit higher yet before the deed was done and the bargain struck. If her friends and neighbors could curb their enthusiasm a little.

"The whole town wants this to happen," he said.

"Aye, but the whole town won't have the disruption of a film crew camped out on their land during the height of lambing season, will they?" She considered that a point well made and rewarded herself with a sip of her beer.

"You said yourself that most of the sheep give birth out in the fields. We'll be filming mostly at the front of the house. Outdoor shots of the manor—"

She snorted. "It's a farmhouse."

"Looks like a manor to me," he countered, then continued quickly, "There may be a few scenes around the barn and the holding pens, but we won't get in the way."

"And you can promise that?" She eased back in the booth and looked at him across the table.

"I'll promise it, if that's what it takes to get you to sign."

"Desperate now?" She smiled and took another soothing drink. "Might make a woman think you'd be willing to sweeten your offer a bit."

"You drive a hard bargain," Jefferson told her with a nod of approval. "But I might be willing to go a little higher yet, if you'd make up your mind and give me your decision."

She smiled to herself, but kept it small so he wouldn't see the victorious gleam that had to be shining in her eyes. "As well I might, depending on how much higher you're talking about."

He gave her an admiring tip of his head. "Too bad your sister's not the one making this deal. I have the distinct feeling she'd be easier to convince."

"Ah, but Cara has her own priorities, doesn't she?" Smiling at the thought of her younger sister, Maura could admit to herself that she would have eventually accepted Jefferson's offer even if he hadn't paid her for the use of her land. Because he'd agreed to give Cara a small part in the movie. And since her sister dreamed of being a famous actress, Cara had been walking in the clouds for days now.

"True," he said. "If she were doing the bargaining, she might have wangled herself a bigger part."

"She'll do fine with what she's got. She's very good, you know." Maura leaned forward. "For a few weeks last year, Cara was on one of those British soap operas. She was brilliant, really, until they killed her off. She had a lovely death scene and all. Made me cry when she died."

His mouth quirked, just high enough to display a dimple in his left cheek. "I know. I sat through the tapes."

"She is good, isn't she? I mean, it's not only that I'm her sister and love her that makes me think so, is it?"

"No, it's not. She's very good," Jefferson told her.

"She has dreams, Cara has," Maura murmured.

"What about you? Do you have dreams, too?" he asked.

Her gaze met his as she shook her head. "'Course I do, though my dreams are less lofty. The barn needs a new roof and before long, my old lorry's going to keel over dead with all four tires in the air. And there's a fine breed of sheep I'd like to try on my fields, as well."

"You're too beautiful to have such small dreams, Maura."

She blinked at him, surprised by the flattery and, at the same time, almost insulted to be told that her dreams were somehow lacking in imagination. She'd once had bigger dreams, as all young girls do. But she'd grown up, hadn't she? And now her dreams were more practical. That didn't make them less important. "They're mine, aren't they, and I don't think they're small dreams at all."

"I just meant—"

She knew what he meant. No doubt he was more accustomed to women who dreamed of diamonds or, God help her, furs and shiny cars. He probably saw her as a country bumpkin with her worn jeans and fields full of shaggy sheep. That thought was as good as a cold shower, dousing the fire in her hormones until she felt almost chilled at the lack of heat.

Before he could speak again, she glanced to one side

and announced, "Oh look! The Flanagan boys are going to play."

"What?"

Maura pointed to the far corner of the pub where three young men with dark red hair sat down, cradling an assortment of instruments between them. While Michael finally made good on his promise and delivered their bowls of steaming potato-leek soup and soda bread hot from the oven, the Flanagan brothers began to play.

In moments, the small pub was filled with the kind of music most people would pay a fortune to hear in a concert hall. Fiddle, drum and flute all came together in a wild yet fluid mesh of music that soared up to the rafters and rattled the window panes. Toes started tapping, hands were clapping and a few hearty souls sang out the lyrics to traditional Irish music.

One tune slid into another, rushing from fast and furious to the slow and heartbreaking, with the three brothers never missing a beat. Jefferson watched the energized crowd with a filmmaker's eye and knew that he'd have to include at least one pub scene in the movie they would be filming here in a few months. And he was going to put in a word with his director about the Flanagan brothers. Their talent was amazing and he thought the least he could do was display it on film. Who knew, maybe he could help more dreams to come true.

Once he finally got Maura to sign his damned contract.

Jefferson's gaze slid to her and his breath caught in his chest. He'd been aware of her beauty before now, but in the dim light of the pub with a single candle burning in a glass jar on the table, she looked almost ethereal.

Insubstantial. Which was a ridiculous thought because he'd seen her wrestle a full-grown sheep down to the ground, so a fragile woman she most definitely was not. Yet he was seeing her now in a new way. A way that made his body tighten to the point of discomfort.

You'd think he'd be used to it, he thought. He'd been achy for nearly a week now, his body in a constant state of unrequited readiness that was making him crazy. Maybe what he needed to do was stop being so damn polite and just swoop in and seduce Maura before she knew what hit her.

Then a whirlwind swept into the pub and dropped down at their booth, nudging her sister over on the bench seat.

"Oh, soup!" Cara Donohue cooed the words and reached for her sister's bowl with both hands. "Lovely. I'm famished."

"Get your own, you beggar," Maura told her with a laugh, but pushed her soup toward her sister.

"Don't need to, do I?" Cara grinned, then shot a quick look at Jefferson. "Have you convinced her to sign up yet?"

"Not yet," he said, putting thoughts of seduction to one side for the moment. Cara Donohue was taller and thinner than Maura, with a short cap of dark curls and blue eyes that shone with eagerness to be doing. Seeing. Experiencing. She was four years younger than her sister and twice as outgoing, and yet Jefferson felt no deep stirring for her.

She was a nice kid with a bright future ahead of her, but Maura was a woman to make a man stop for a second and even a third look.

"You will," Cara said with a bright, musical laugh. "You Americans are all stubborn, aren't you? And besides, Maura thinks you're gorgeous."

"Cara!"

"Well, it's true and all," her sister said with another laugh as she finished Maura's soup, then reached for her sister's beer. She had a sip, then winked at Jefferson. "It does no harm to let you know she enjoys looking at you, for what breathing woman wouldn't? And I've seen you giving her a look or two yourself."

"Cara, if you don't shut your mouth this minute…"

Maura's threat died unuttered, but Jefferson couldn't help smiling at the sisters. He and his brothers were just the same, teasing each other no matter who happened to be around to listen. Besides, he liked hearing that Maura had been talking about him.

"There's no harm in it, is there?" Cara was saying, with a glance at first her sister, then Jefferson. "Why shouldn't you take a good look at each other?"

"Pay no attention to my sister," Maura told him with a shake of her head.

"Why?" he asked. "She's not wrong."

"Maybe not, but she doesn't have to be so loud about it, does she?"

"Ah Maura, you worry too much," her sister told her and patted her arm.

The music suddenly shifted, jumping into a wild, frenetic song with a beat that seemed to thrum against the walls and batter its way into a man's soul. Jefferson found himself tapping his fingers on the tabletop in time with the quickening rhythm.

"Oh, they're playing 'Whiskey in the Jar!' Come on, Maura, dance with me."

She shook her head and resisted when Cara tried to pull her to her feet. "I've worked all day and I'm in no mood for step dancing. Most especially not with my big-mouthed sister."

"But you love me and you know it. Besides, it'll do you good and you know you adore this song." Cara grinned again and gave her sister's arm a good yank.

On her feet, Maura looked at him, almost embarrassed, Jefferson thought, then with a shrug she followed her sister into the cleared-away area in front of the tables. A few people applauded as Cara and Maura took their places beside each other, then, laughing together, the Donohue sisters leaped into action. Their backs were arrow straight, their arms pinned to their sides and their feet were *flying*.

Jefferson, like most everyone else in the world, had seen the Broadway show with the Irish dancers and he'd come away impressed. But here, in this tiny pub in a small village on the coast of Ireland, he was swept into a kind of magic.

Music thundered, people applauded and the two sisters danced as if they had wings on their feet. He couldn't tear his eyes off Maura. She'd worked hard all day at a job that would have exhausted most of the men he knew. Yet there she was, dancing and laughing, as graceful as a leaf on the wind. She was tireless. And spirited. And so damned beautiful, he could hardly draw a breath for wanting her.

Without warning, Jefferson's mind turned instantly

to the stories he'd heard about his great-grandfather and how he'd fallen in love at first sight with an Irish girl in a pub just like this, on one magical night.

For the first time in his life, he completely understood how it had happened.

Cara left the pub soon after, claiming she was going to drive into Westport, a bustling harbor city not five miles from the village of Craic.

"I'll be at Mary Dooley's place if you need me," she said as she left, giving Jefferson a wink and her sister a kiss and a smile. "Otherwise, I'll see you sometime tomorrow."

When her sister was gone in a blur of motion, Maura looked at Jefferson and laughed shortly. "She's a force of nature," she said. "Always has been. The only thing that came close to slowing her down was our mother's death four years ago."

"I'm sorry," he said quickly. "I know what it's like to lose your parents. It's never easy no matter how old you are."

"No, it's not," Maura admitted, feeling the sting of remembrance and how hard it had been for her and her sister in those long silent weeks after their mother had passed away. Smiles had been hard to come by and they'd clung to each other to ease their pain.

Eventually though, life had crowded in, insisting it be lived.

"But my mother had been lonely for my father for years. Now that she's joined him, she's happy again, I know."

"You believe that."

A statement, not a question, she thought. "Aye, I do."

"Are you born with that kind of faith, I wonder, or do you have to work to earn it?"

"It just…is," Maura said simply. "Haven't you ever sensed the presence of one you lost and felt better for knowing it?"

"I have," he admitted quietly. "Though it's not something I've ever talked about before."

"Why should you?" She smiled at him again. "It's a private thing, after all."

Jefferson looked at her for a long moment and she tried to read what thoughts might be rushing through his mind. But his eyes were cool, shadowed with old pain, so she was forced to wait until he spoke.

"Ten years ago, my parents died together in a car accident that nearly killed one of my brothers, too." He finished the last of his beer in one swallow, set the glass down and said, "Later, once my three brothers and I had lived through the grief, we all realized that if they'd had a choice, our folks would have elected to go together. Neither of them would have been complete without the other."

"I know just what you mean." Maura sighed through a sad smile. Music played on in the background and dozens of voices rose and fell in waves of conversation. Yet here in the shadow-filled booth, she felt as if she and Jefferson were alone in the room. "My father died when Cara was small and my mother was never the same without him. She tried, for our sakes of course, but for her, there was always something missing. A love like that, I think, is both blessing and curse."

He lifted his beer glass in a toast. "You might be right about that."

He smiled, too, and she thought how odd it was that they would find this mutual understanding in memories of pain. But somehow, sitting in the near dark with Jefferson, sharing stories of loss made her feel closer to him than she had to anyone in a long time.

"Still," she said, her voice soft and low, "even knowing your parents were together, it must have been hard on you and your brothers."

"It was." A slight frown creased his features briefly. "I'd finally recovered from…" He stopped, caught himself and said instead, "Doesn't matter. The point is, when we needed it the most, my brothers and I had each other. And we had to help Justice recover."

She wondered what he'd been about to say. What he'd thought better of sharing with her. And wondered why, if it was so many years ago, that thought could have left a shadow of pain flashing in his eyes. His secret, whatever it was, had hit him deeply, cutting him in his heart and soul. So much so that even now, he didn't talk about it.

Maura buried her curiosity for the moment and said only, "Justice? An interesting name."

"Interesting man," Jefferson told her with a quick smile that was filled, she thought, with a bit of gratitude for her ignoring his earlier slip of the tongue. "He runs the family ranch."

Delighted by the image, she smiled. "So he's a cowboy, then?"

"Yeah, he is." He grinned suddenly, though sorrow

still glittered in his eyes. "And he's married now, with a son and another baby on the way."

"Lovely," she said, envying him his large family. "And your other brothers?"

"The youngest, Jesse, is married, too. His wife just had a baby boy a few months back." He stopped and grinned. "Jesse passed out during the delivery. We love to remind him of that."

"What a wonderful story," Maura said. "His love and worry for his wife making him faint. He must be a lovely man."

"Lovely?" Jefferson thought about it and shrugged. "I'm sure his wife Bella thinks so."

The sorrow in his eyes was fading, the longer he talked about his brothers, and Maura realized she thought even more of him now that she knew how close he was to his family. "And your other brother?"

"Jericho is in the Marines. He's serving in the Middle East right now."

"That's a worry for you." She saw the truth of that in the way his jaw clenched briefly.

"Yeah, it is. But he's doing what he loves, so…"

"I understand." Maura drew a fingertip through the ring of damp her beer glass had left behind on the table. "When Cara first left home to go to London and be an actor, I wanted to lock her in the closet." She laughed, remembering how panicked she'd been at the thought of Cara alone in the big city. "Oh, it's not the same kind of worry you must feel, I know, but at the time I thought for sure she'd be eaten alive by all manner of terrible monsters in that city."

"Worry's worry, Maura," he told her, "and it probably drove you nuts to be so far away from her."

Maura nodded and laughed to herself. "I shouldn't have bothered making myself crazy, of course. Cara sailed ahead, claiming the city as her own and making a good start to the career she wants."

"What about you?"

"What about me?" she asked.

"Your career," he said, his eyes locked on her. "Did you always want to be a sheep farmer?"

Maura gave him a half grin. "Well now, what little girl wouldn't dream of sheep dip and shearing time and lambing emergencies. It's the glamour, you see, that drew me."

Now he laughed and she thought it a wonderful sound. She was glad to see that the sadness in his eyes had all but disappeared, as well.

"So then, what made you choose to be what you are?"

"I like my life being my own. I've always worked the farm. I answer to no one. No clock to watch, no boss to kowtow to. No harried rushing about to drive into the city."

He nodded as if he understood exactly what she was saying. But that couldn't be, because the man made his living in one of the busiest cities in the world. He'd no doubt schedules to keep, people to answer to and hordes of employees clustering about him.

"I can see the appeal of that," he admitted.

"Oh, sure you can," Maura teased. "Look at yourself. Flying all around the world, looking for places to put your cameras. I'd wager you've never spent a full day away from a telephone or an Internet modem in years."

"You'd be right about that," he said with a grudging smile. "But to the travel, I do it because I enjoy it. Take Ireland for example…"

"Why don't we?"

Still smiling, he said, "The studio has location scouts, but I wanted to come here for myself. I've always enjoyed travel, seeing new places. It's the best part of the job. So I had my scout find two or three suitable properties online, then I flew over to check them out."

"Two or three?" she asked, curious now. "And which was the Donohue farm? Where did I figure on your list?"

"You were the second place I looked at—and I knew the minute I saw your farm that it was the one I wanted."

"Which brings us back to your offer."

"Isn't that handy?"

She had to give it to him. He was as stubborn as her, with a mind that continually returned to the goal no matter how many distractions got in the way. She could admire that.

Just as she could admit silently that it was time to act. To accept his offer, sign his contract and let him be off, back to his real life before she became so attached her heart would break at his leaving. Besides, she'd gotten her sister's warning glare earlier and knew that Cara would never forgive her if Maura didn't sign on the dotted line, allowing her sister to earn a small part in a big-budget American movie.

"So what's it going to be, Maura?" he asked a

moment later. "Are we going to strike a deal or am I going to have to revisit those other properties?"

In the sudden silence, Maura gave a quick look around the Lion's Den. But for Michael behind the bar and a few straggling patrons nursing a final beer, she and Jefferson were alone. The crowd had gone off and the Flanagans had packed up their instruments and left for home and she hadn't even noticed. She'd been so wrapped up in talking with Jefferson, watching his smile, listening to the rumble of his voice, the whole world could have come to an end and she'd have sat through it all without a care.

Which told her she was in very deep danger of losing her heart to a man who wouldn't be interested in keeping it. Yes, best all around to have their business be done so he could leave and her life could settle back into its familiar pattern.

She held her right hand out to him then and there. "We've a deal, Jefferson King. You'll make your movie on my farm and we'll both get what we want."

He took her hand in his, but instead of shaking it as she'd expected, he simply held on to it, stroking his thumb across her slender fingers. Her stomach jittered and her mouth went dry. Suddenly, she wished she'd ordered another beer because something cool and frothy would no doubt ease her parched throat.

"I have the papers at the inn," he said. "Why don't you come to my room now and we can get them signed."

She slipped her hand from his and chuckled. "Oh, no thank you. If I'm seen going into your hotel room at this hour, the village wags will be talking about us for weeks."

"How would anyone know?"

"In a village, there are no secrets," she told him. "Frances Boyle runs a tight ship at her inn. Believe me when I tell you she knows every person that steps across her threshold."

"Okay," he said, "then why don't we order another round, I'll go to the hotel, gather the papers and bring them back here for you to sign?"

Maura considered it, chewing at her bottom lip. She did want the deed done, but it was already late and she'd have to be up with the sun and—

"I thought you said you didn't have to run your life by the clock," he reminded her.

"Touché," she said with a nod, amused that he'd rightly guessed what she'd been thinking about. "All right then, I'll order the beer while you get your paperwork."

When he left, Maura's gaze dropped to his behind and she gave herself a stern talking-to. *You'll have a drink, sign his papers and say thanks very much and goodbye. There'll be no loitering in the moonlight, Maura Donohue. He's a man you can't have, so there's no point in wishing things were different. Don't be a fool about this, Maura, or you'll surely regret it.*

All very rational, she thought. Too bad she wasn't listening.

Three

He wasn't gone long.

The truth was, Jefferson hadn't wanted to leave her at all. He'd hoped to get her back to the hotel where he could try to slide her into his bed and seal the deal in a way that would ease the ache he'd been carrying for the last few days. But typically enough, Maura had managed to shatter his quickly thought-up plan with a simple "no." So, adjusting his plan on the fly, he thought he could maneuver her into letting him take her home and maybe he could slide himself into *her* bed instead.

When he walked into the quiet pub, Michael the barman gave him a nod of welcome, then went back to watching the news on the television. There was only one other customer left at the bar and Maura at the table where he'd left her. The single candle flickering on their table threw dancing shadows across her face and its faint light seemed to shimmer in the rich thickness of her hair.

The need he'd been carrying around inside him burst into flame. Instantly, his mind filled again with the image of her dancing. Her smile. Her regal yet somehow wild bearing. The rhythm in her body, the fast fury of her small feet, and he wanted with a desperation he'd never known before.

"That was quick," she said when he stopped at the edge of their table.

"No point in wasting time, is there?"

"None at all," she agreed, sliding out of the booth to stand beside him. "But I think we should go back to the farm so Michael can close the pub and go home. I've some wine in the fridge. We can toast the signed contract if you like."

Jefferson was silent for a moment, simply because he couldn't believe she'd suggested the very thing he'd been about to recommend. She seemed to be one step ahead of him and that was an unusual enough happening that he could enjoy the sensation. He wondered, though, if she wanted what he did. Was she simply being nice, or was she as anxious as him for them to be alone together?

He'd find out soon enough.

"Good idea." He laid one hand at the small of her back and guided her across the room. When she called out good-night to Michael, the barman merely waved a towel at them.

Then they were outside, in the stillness. The village was quiet—houses dark, streets empty. There was a hush in the air that felt as if the world had taken a breath and held it.

Or maybe, Jefferson told himself, his time in Ireland had been enough to make any man—even *him*—fanciful.

The trip to the Donohue farmhouse was a quick one, yet it felt like forever to Jefferson. With Maura beside him in the car, her scent seemed to wrap itself around him, taunting him, arousing him to the point where simply sitting still became an act of torture.

At the house he parked the car in the driveway, what Maura would call "the street," and walked beside her in silence to the front door. Neither of them had much to say, mainly he thought, because there was too *much* to say. So where was a man supposed to start?

Sign the contract?

Take off your clothes?

He knew which he'd prefer, but he had a feeling it wouldn't be that easy.

Inside the house, Maura flipped light switches on as they moved through the silent rooms to the kitchen. There, she tossed her keys onto the table and walked to the fridge. Looking at him over her shoulder, she said, "Will you take down a couple of glasses from the far cupboard?"

"Sure." Jefferson laid the envelope containing the contract on the table and went for the glasses. A moment later, she was filling them with a cold, straw-colored wine that shone almost gold in the overhead light.

He'd been in this room before, though those visits had been in broad daylight. The old kitchen was clean and tidy, its ancient appliances gleaming with the care she took with them. The counter was bare of all but a set of canisters and a teapot and the wood floor was scarred from wear but polished to a high shine.

"I suppose I should sign the papers first," she was saying and Jefferson turned his attention to her.

"Good idea. We take care of business first."

"First. And then what?" Her blue eyes glittered as she turned them up to him and Jefferson's body stirred like a hungry dog on a short leash.

"Then," he said, "we'll toast to the success of our joint venture."

A smile tugged at her lips. "Venture, is it? A fine word for it, anyway."

She took the pen he offered her and sat down to read through the short contract. He liked that about her, too. He thought a lot of people might have just taken him at his word and signed where he indicated. Not Maura though. She was careful. Not going to take his word for it that her interests were being looked after.

Was there anything sexier than a smart woman?

Her teeth pulled at her bottom lip as she read and he heard the ticking of the wall clock behind him in the strained quiet. Her head was bent over the paperwork and he had to force himself not to touch her. Not to stroke his fingers through the shining black hair that was only inches from him. *Soon,* he promised himself, reaching for the self-control that had always been a part of him.

But even as that thought rattled through his mind, he had to smile. His self-control had been mostly absent since the first moment he'd seen Maura. She tripped something inside him. Something he hadn't even been aware of in years. Something he hadn't felt since—

The scratch of a pen on paper broke the silence and

he came out of his thoughts in time to watch her put the pen down and pick up the now-signed contract.

"It's done," she said.

"It'll be good doing business with you, Maura."

"Ah, I'll wager you say that to all of the people you rent locations from."

"No," he said, sliding the contract back into the envelope then tossing them on the table. "I don't. You're…different."

"Is that so?" She picked up the wineglasses, handed one to him and took a sip of her own. "And how might that be?"

"I think you know the answer to that."

"I might at that," she mused and set her glass down again to take off the cream-colored Irish sweater she wore. Pulling it up and over her head, she shook her hair back and smiled up at him.

Jefferson sucked in a gulp of air, then chased it with a swallow of cold, crisp wine. All she'd been wearing under that sweater of hers tonight was a white silk camisole that clung to her skin and displayed her pebbled nipples with fine clarity.

"You must have been freezing tonight," he muttered.

"A bit," she admitted, "though inside the pub was warm enough and I'll admit, I thought perhaps we might end up back here tonight and I wanted to see the look on your face when I took off the sweater."

"And was it worth it?" he managed to ask.

"Aye, it was." She reached up, hooked one hand behind his head and threaded her fingers through his hair. "I've been wanting you, Jefferson."

His body jumped into overdrive, his erection painfully pushing against his slacks. "Have you?"

"I have. I think you've been wanting me, as well," she added, moving in closer to him.

"Aye," he mimicked. "I have."

Her fingers at the back of his neck felt seductive and sure and he suddenly wanted that touch all over him. He needed to feel her hands on him, to get his hands on her.

He set his glass down and reached for her. Holding her pressed tightly against him, he felt her nipples pushing into his chest and damn near groaned. Then he had to smile. "You know, I'd planned to seduce you tonight."

She grinned up at him. "Well, isn't it a fine thing indeed when two plans come together so nicely?"

"Indeed," he murmured and bent his head to take a kiss. The first of many. His mouth covered hers and she sighed into him, parting her lips eagerly, hungrily. She matched his need and as their tongues twisted and danced together, the flames they built erupted into an inferno.

He wrapped his arms around her, holding her pressed tightly to him and still it wasn't close enough. Couldn't feel enough of her. He needed her naked. Needed to feel skin to skin, rough to smooth. He needed to slide his body into hers and feel her heat surround him.

And he needed it *now*.

Quickly, he swept her up, turned around and plopped her down onto the kitchen counter. She whooped in surprise, but recovered quickly enough. Wrapping her legs around his middle, she clung to him, her tongue tangling with his, their breaths combining into a symphony of sighs that filled the quiet of the old house with the desperate sounds of passion.

Again and again, he kissed her, long, deep, short, fast. He loved the taste of her. Richer than any wine, headier than any intoxicant could be. She was all. She was everything. The world spun about her and he was pulled into her orbit with the deliberate tug of a gravity too fierce to fight.

He yanked up the hem of that silken camisole, tore it up over her head, then tossed it behind him without missing a beat. Her breasts were bared to him and he inhaled sharply as he fed the need to admire her. Full, ripe breasts with dark pink nipples, peaked now as if just awaiting his pleasure.

Jefferson cupped those milk-white globes in his hands and sighed himself with her whispered approval. His thumbs and forefingers tweaked and pulled gently at her nipples and when she writhed into him, he dipped his head, taking first one, then the other into his mouth. He licked, he sucked, he nibbled and the sounds she made urged him on, encouraged him to take all he wanted.

Her hands fisted in his hair and held his head to her breasts as if she were worried he'd stop. But stopping wasn't in the game plan. In fact, he couldn't have stopped now if his life depended on it. God help him if she were to suddenly change her mind and show him the door. He'd never live through it.

He pulled back, looked up into misty blue eyes and returned the grin she had aimed at him.

"Let's have your shirt off, Jefferson," she said. "I've a need to feel your skin beneath my hands."

He obliged her quickly, tearing off his own sweater and the shirt he wore beneath it. Then he groaned as her palms swept over his shoulders and along his back. The warmth of her touch slid into him and sent bolts of fresh need shooting through his system. Her short nails scraped at his skin. Her breath came in hard, brief pants and when she slid her hands down his arms, they were both gasping for air.

"Help me with these," she said, her voice low and tight as though she'd had to force the words from her throat.

"What?"

"My jeans, man." She had them unsnapped and was whipping the zipper down as she spoke. She'd already kicked off her shoes. "Help me out of them before I lose my mind for the wanting."

"Right, right." His head was full and spinning. All he could think about was the next touch, the next kiss. So he helped her out of her pants, lifting her off the counter so she could scoot around and free herself of both jeans and white cotton bikini underwear.

Jefferson had one shining moment of clarity when he realized that her simple, plain panties were more erotic than any scraps of black lace he'd ever seen. Then the moment was gone and he was lost in the glory of looking at her. Her milk-white skin was soft and smooth and he ached to touch her all over. Explore every curve, every line of her body until he knew her more intimately than any other man ever had.

"Now yours," she said, reaching for his belt buckle.

She grinned, tossed her hair back over her shoulder and met his eyes with her own. She was strong and sure of herself, and the sexual ache he felt went a notch higher. "I've a powerful need for you, Jefferson, and I'm not a patient woman as you might have noticed."

"Believe me, I'm grateful to hear it," he muttered, stepping out of his clothes and standing naked in front of her. His body leaped to attention, hard and thick and aching to ease itself inside her. But Jefferson had one more quick moment of reason show itself, so he said, "We should go upstairs. To your bedroom."

"Later," she countered, reaching for him, wrapping her arms around his neck even as she parted her legs and scooted forward to the counter's edge. "If I don't have you inside me this moment, Jefferson King, I'll not be responsible for what happens next."

"My kind of woman," he growled with a smile. "I knew it the moment I saw you."

Her hands cupped his cheeks again. "Then fill me, Jefferson, ease the ache."

He did.

She was hot and wet and so ready for him he almost exploded the moment he entered her. Only his immense self-control kept him from hurtling too soon over an edge he craved like a dying man wished for a few more moments of life. She threw her head back, baring her throat for him and he kissed her there, along the line of her lovely throat, lips and tongue sliding across her skin until she shivered in his arms.

He pushed himself deep as her legs locked around his hips, then pulled out and did the same again. Over and over, as he set a rhythm she raced to follow, their bodies came together, melding, meshing, sliding into a dance they had been building toward for what seemed like forever.

Her soft pants and muted sighs fueled him, fed the images in his mind, the sensations in his body. Never before had Jefferson so lost himself in a woman. He wasn't sure where he ended and she began and he knew with a blinding flash of insight that it didn't matter.

All that mattered was this moment. This one heart-stopping, mind-numbing moment in time.

Pulling his head back, he watched her as he moved one hand to the spot where their bodies joined and touched the pad of his thumb to the most sensitive flesh at her core. She gasped, trembled in his arms and shrieked out his name as her body whipped into a frenzied release.

And no more than a heartbeat later, Jefferson gave himself up, at last, to the crashing need and surrendered himself into her keeping.

Hours later, Maura stretched out on her bed and felt blissfully languid. Every cell in her body was replete. Satisfied. And even as she lay there, just an arm's reach from her lover, she felt hunger begin to stir inside again.

She turned her head on the pillow to look at Jefferson and smiled to herself. He'd been well worth the agonizing wait, she told herself even as a small voice in the back of her head warned her against feeling too much. Wanting too much.

Outside, a storm was building. She heard the first taps

of rain against her window as a cold wind rattled the panes. But here, in the cozy master bedroom of the farmhouse, a peat fire burned in the corner hearth and she lay on sweet-smelling sheets beside a man who touched her as she'd never been touched before.

Instantly, that nagging, annoying voice started up again. *Careful now, Maura,* it warned, *he's not the forever kind of man. He's not staying—neither here in your bed nor even in Ireland. He'll be off now that he has what he came for. So don't be a fool and fall in love.*

So she wouldn't take the fall. But she couldn't help feeling for the man.

He would go home remembering her and this night as something magical.

Seemed only fair, since so would she.

"I think I may be dead," Jefferson murmured.

Her thoughts crashed to a halt as he looked at her, his eyes the pale blue color of cornflowers in summer. There was the shadow of a beard on his jaws and his black hair was nearly standing on end. Not surprising considering how they'd spent the last few hours.

Maura's heart turned over in her chest. Soon, very soon, he'd be walking out her door. And as she considered it, she knew she had to have him again. One last time before he became nothing more than a sweet, tender spot in her soul.

Laying one hand on his abdomen, she slowly slid her palm lower and lower. His breath caught in his chest as she wrapped her long fingers around him and felt that hard, eager part of him leap into life again. "Not so very near death, I'm thinking," she said with a teasing smile.

He hissed in another breath, blew it out and said, "You could rouse a dead man, Maura. You've just proved it."

She grinned, feeling a delicious sense of female power rise up inside her. To know she had this effect on a strong man was a heady thing indeed. To know that he was watching her, waiting for her to make her next move, only enhanced the sensation.

Her fingers moved over him, the hard, silky feel of his skin pulsing beneath her own. Then she reached farther down and cupped him, gently rubbing, stroking until he lifted his hips off the mattress and into her touch.

"You do want me dead, is that it?" he managed to wheeze.

"Oh, no," she answered, shifting position to straddle him, "I want you alive, Jefferson King. Alive and inside me."

His hands came down on her upper thighs and she smiled at him, scooping her arms under her hair and lifting them high, displaying her breasts for his pleasure. Her hair fell down around her shoulders in a tangle, her nipples peeking through the black strands. And when his eyes narrowed, she knew she had him. Rising up onto her knees, she looked down at him as if he were her captive.

He reached for her, his hands moving over her body with a greedy touch and she nearly purred at the feel of him against her. But she wanted more. She wanted another time with him. She wanted to ride him and look down into his eyes and know that no matter where else he went in his life, he would take this mental image of the two of them together with him. Always.

She took his hard length in her hand, held him poised just at the entrance to her heat and rubbed the head of him against her until they were both at the ragged edge of control. Then finally, she lowered her body onto his, taking him, inch by glorious inch, inside her.

Maura groaned as he filled her so deeply, she felt him touch her heart and when they were firmly joined, connected as deeply as two people could possibly be, she moved on him. Riding him, her body sliding up and down atop him, setting a pace that started out slow and then became frantic. She swiveled her hips against him and leaned over so that he could cup her breasts and pull at her aching nipples.

Her gaze locked with his, she kept moving, tirelessly, ceaselessly, laying claim to his body as she couldn't his heart. And when the expectant rise of glory slammed home and shattered her, she called his name out loud. When she felt him release an instant later and heard him shout for her, she knew the echo of it would ripple through her life forever.

Dull gray light slid through the wisp of white curtains hanging at her windows and Jefferson knew the night was over. Maura was curled into him, one leg across his, one arm tossed over his chest. Her every breath dusted his skin and the scent of her hair was in every lungful of air he claimed.

He hadn't slept, yet he was more awake than he could ever remember being. For hours, he'd made love to his wild Irish woman. And when she'd finally fallen into exhausted slumber, he'd remained awake, just watching her sleep.

His time there was over and he told himself that was a very good thing. He'd become…comfortable in Ireland. In this house. With this woman. He'd begun to structure his days around seeing her. Arguing with her. Watching her laugh.

And that simply wasn't in his plan.

Jefferson didn't want to care about her. Didn't want to ever go down that road again. He would retain control at all costs to avoid the pain he'd once suffered.

Carefully, he slipped out of bed, amused more than anything else when Maura simply snuggled deeper beneath the handmade quilt they'd drawn up over themselves during the night. She muttered something unintelligible, then pulled that quilt over her head.

When they'd finally come upstairs the night before they'd carried their discarded clothes with them, so Jefferson snatched his slacks and shirt off a delicate-looking chair and drew them on. Once he was dressed, he was more in control. He felt his life slide back into place and knew that it was the best for all concerned.

One spectacular night with an intriguing woman wasn't going to change him. He was what he was and his life wasn't in Ireland, no matter how tempting the thought might be. Besides, no one had said anything about permanent. He'd deliberately avoided even thinking that word. What he had with Maura was fun. Uncomplicated. Best to leave it at that.

"You're leaving, then?" Her voice was muffled, since her head was still beneath the quilt.

"Yeah," he said. "I've got to get back to work. I've been gone longer than I planned already. And, now that the contract is signed, there's really no reason to stay any longer."

"Ah yes, the contract."

She pulled the quilt down and her sleepy, dark blue eyes pinned him. For one awful moment, he was afraid she might ask him to stay. He hoped to hell she didn't, because it wouldn't take much convincing to have him going along with that idea, and all that would do was prolong the inevitable. Make this harder—on both of them.

But she surprised him again.

Pushing her hair back out of her face, she nodded and sat up, letting the quilt pool at her waist. His mouth went dry and his body stirred, requiring all of his focus just to get it under control again. Completely at ease with her own nudity, she scooted off the bed, walked right up to him and went up on her toes. Linking her arms around his neck, she gave him a long, luscious kiss, then looked up at him. "Then I'll say goodbye, Jefferson King. Have a safe trip."

His hands rested on her bare hips and his fingers burned with the heat of her. Nothing quite like a warm, naked woman pressed up against you to make a man think of a long, lazy day spent rolling around on her bed. But he had a King jet waiting for him and a business and a life to get back to.

She smiled and he asked, "That's it? No, 'Please stay, Jefferson'?"

Shaking her head, she rubbed her fingertip across his

mouth, then stepped back from him. "What would be the point in that? We're neither of us children. We wanted each other and we had each other. It was a lovely night. Let's keep its ending just as lovely."

Apparently, he'd been worried for no reason. She wasn't going to beg him to stay. She wasn't going to cry or say how she'd miss him or ask when he was returning. None of the things he'd hoped to avoid were happening.

So why was he irritated?

"I'll see you off, shall I?" She stepped over to her closet, grabbed a dark green terry-cloth robe and slipped into it. Her body was covered now, but the imprint of her was still etched firmly in his mind. Hiding what he'd already spent hours exploring wasn't going to change anything.

"You don't have to go downstairs with me."

"Oh," she said, leading the way out to the landing and then down the stairs. "'Tisn't just for you. I'm off to brew some tea and then get to work myself."

His eyebrows rose. So much for the fond farewell. His leaving was no more than a by-product here. She was picking up the threads of her everyday life and so was he, he reminded himself. So again, why the flicker of irritation?

She opened the front door and held it wide for him. She smiled, reached up and cupped his cheek briefly. "Fly safe, Jefferson."

"Right." He stepped onto the porch and the Irish wind howled around him. "Take care of yourself, Maura."

"Oh, I always do," she told him. "And you, as well. Not to worry about your film crew, either. All will be here when they arrive."

"Fine."

"All right then." She gave him one last smile, then shut the door, leaving him no choice now but to walk to his car and leave.

With her back to the closed door, Maura wrapped her arms around her middle and held on. After a few steadying breaths, she heard his car engine fire up and she leaned toward the nearest window to catch one last glimpse of him.

He steered his car out onto the road and in a moment, he was gone, as if he'd never been. Even the echo of his car was nothing more than a hush on the wind.

"Well, now," she murmured, swiping away the tears running down her cheeks. "It's best this way and you know it, my girl. No point in laying out your heart for him to stumble over on his way out of the country."

She wasn't the first foolish woman to fall for the wrong man entirely. No doubt, she wouldn't be the last, either.

"Doesn't matter now anyway as he's gone." She headed through the quiet house toward the kitchen and a morning pot of tea. Best to get back to her life. The life she knew. The animals and the land and the world that was hers. "You'll get over him," she promised herself firmly. "Won't take long at all."

Four

She wasn't over him.

It had been two months and she still thought of Jefferson King nearly every day. Her only hope was that he was being haunted by memories, as well. That would make this whole thing more fair.

The problem was, she had too much alone time, she told herself. Too much empty time to spend in thoughts she shouldn't be indulging in anyway. But with Cara off making a film in Dublin, Maura was alone at the farmhouse with nothing more to talk to than the dog she'd recently acquired.

Unfortunately, King, named for a certain man she was still feeling fondness for when she purchased the dog, was not much of a conversationalist.

Now, along with her wild thoughts, her misery at

missing the man she never should have let into her heart, the work building up to lambing season and her new dog, she was also feeling a bit off physically. Her stomach was queasy most of the time and she'd been so dizzy only that morning in the barn, she'd had to sit down before she fell down.

"I was right, wasn't I? It's the flu, I know it," Maura told the village doctor as he walked into the examination room. "I haven't been getting enough sleep and there's so much work to be done. I'm run down is all. I thought you could give me a little something to help me sleep."

Doc Rafferty had been in the village for forty years. He'd treated everyone for miles around and he had delivered both Maura and Cara himself. So he knew them far too intimately to pull any punches, so to speak. And as he was a forthright man in any case, he met her gaze and told her the truth of the matter.

"I've got the results of your test," he said, checking the papers he held in his hand as if to be sure of what he was about to say. "If this is the flu, it's the nine-month variety, Maura. You're pregnant."

A beat of silence fell between them as those last two words of the doctor's repeated over and over again in her head. Sure she'd misheard him, Maura laughed shortly.

"No, I'm not." She shook her head. "That's impossible."

"Is it now?" The older man sat down on a rolling stool and shifted his pale green eyes up to hers. "You're telling me you've done nothing to produce such a condition?"

"Well I—" He'd examined her from head to toe too

often for her to try to persuade him she was a virgin, and why would she care to? But this? No. It couldn't be.

Maura stopped, frowned and started thinking. Odd, but she'd been paying no attention at all to her period and hadn't even noticed until now that it hadn't shown up in quite some time. Quickly, she did a little math in her head and as she reached the only conclusion she could under the circumstances, she let out a breath and whispered, "Oh my God."

"There you are, then." Doc Rafferty reached out, patted her knee. "You'll be feeling fine again soon. The first couple of months are always the hardest, after all. In the meantime though, I want you to take better care of yourself." He scribbled a few things down on a pad and then tore off the top sheet and handed it to her.

Maura couldn't read it through the fog blocking her vision.

"Eat regular meals, cut back on the caffeine and I'll have Nurse Doherty give you a sample bottle of vitamins." He stood up, looked down at her through kind eyes and said, "Maura, love. You should tell the baby's father right away."

The baby's father.

The man she'd sworn to put firmly in her past.

So much for that fine notion. He would surely be a part of her future now, wouldn't he?

"Yes, I will." Tell Jefferson that he was going to be a father. Well, wouldn't that make for a lovely long-distance conversation?

"Will you be all right with this, Maura?"

"Of course. I'll be fine." And she would. Already, the

first shock of the news was passing and a small curl of excitement was fluttering to life inside her.

She was going to have a baby.

"Do you need to talk about anything?"

"What?" Maura's gaze lifted to meet his. Kindness was stamped on his familiar features and she knew he was worried for her. And though she appreciated it, he needn't be.

"No, Doctor," she told him, scooting off the examination table. "I'm fine, really. It was a bit of a shock, but…" She stopped and smiled. "It's happy news after all, isn't it?"

"You're a good girl, Maura, as I've always said." He gave her a nod of approval and added, "I'd like to see you once a month now, just to keep a check on you and the baby. Make the appointment on your way out. And, Maura, no more heavy lifting, understand?"

When he left the room, she was alone with her news. Although…

"Not as alone as I was when I arrived, am I?" she whispered and dropped one hand to her flat belly.

Awe rose up inside her.

There was a child growing within her. A new life. A precious, innocent life that would be counting on her. But Maura was a woman used to responsibility, so that didn't worry her. The fact that her child would grow up without a father was a bit of a hitch. When she'd imagined the day she would become a mother, she'd had hazy, blurry images of a faceless man standing at her side, rejoicing with her at the birth.

Never once had she considered being a single mother.

Heaven knew she hadn't planned on this. Had, in fact been taking precautions—well, the over-the-counter precautions. It wasn't as though she had sex often enough to warrant anything permanent.

Of course, she should have insisted Jefferson wear a condom, that would have been the intelligent thing to do. But neither of them had been thinking straight that night, she admitted silently. For herself, she'd been in such a hunger to have Jefferson over, under and in her, she hadn't wanted to wait for anything.

Now, it seemed, there would be consequences.

But such wonderful consequences. All penances should be this happily paid.

A child.

She'd always wanted to be a mother.

Maura turned, looked out the window and watched as thick, pewter clouds raced across the sky. A storm was brewing, she thought, and wondered if it was a metaphor for what was about to happen to her life.

"We'll be just fine, you and I," she told her child, still keeping one hand tight to the womb where her baby slept. She would see to it that her child was safe and well and happy.

As soon as she got home, she'd call Jefferson. She'd keep the conversation brisk and as impersonal as she could, considering the situation. She'd tell him because it was right. But she'd also tell him she had no need for him to come rushing back. She wasn't over him just yet and had no wish to see him again, stirring up things that had yet to settle down.

One phone call.

Then they'd be done.

Two months later...

"Mr. King said there would be no problems."

Maura glared at the little man standing on her porch. He was short, bald and looked as though a stiff wind off the lake might blow him into Galway city. She showed him no mercy. "Aye, your Mr. King says a lot of things, doesn't he?"

He took a deep breath as if trying for patience. She understood that feeling very well as she'd been trying for weeks and still hadn't found any.

"We do have a contract," the man reminded her.

She looked past him out to the film crew setting up tents and trailers and cameras with banks of lights surrounding them. Somehow she hadn't expected the whole mess to be quite so...intimidating. As it was, she had dozens of people trampling the grass in her front yard and the complaining bleats from the sheep were as sharp as nails against a chalkboard. Swallowing her irritation as best she could, she said, "We do indeed and I'll stay to the very letter of the contract."

"Meaning?" the little man asked, his small tight mouth flattening into a grim slash across his narrow face.

"Meaning, I said you could be on my property, but nowhere near the lambing sheds."

"But Mr. King said..."

"If you've a problem with me," Maura told him, "I suggest you phone your I'm-so-busy-I-can't-bother-to-return-a-message King and deliver your complaints to him." Just before she slammed the front door, she added, "And I wish you good luck getting him on the bleeding phone as I haven't been able to manage that no-doubt miraculous feat in the last two months."

Jefferson King was juggling what felt like thirty different projects at once. It helped to stay busy. Thankfully, his position at King Studios ensured that he remained that way.

There were currently three films under production and each of them presented different headaches. Dealing with producers, directors and, worst of all to his mind, the actors, was enough to make a man wonder what he'd first enjoyed about this business. He had deals rolling with agents, a couple of smaller studios he was looking to absorb and he was in the middle of buying the rights to a bestselling romance novel to turn it into what would be, he firmly believed, a blockbuster summer hit.

So yeah. Busy. But he preferred it that way. Busy meant his thoughts were too distracted to drift toward memories of Ireland that came only a dozen times a day now. Images of deep green fields, smoky, music-filled pubs and, mostly, thoughts of Maura Donohue.

Which was just as well because every time a picture of that blue-eyed woman rose up in his mind, he was filled with a wild mixture of emotions that were so tangled and twisted into knots inside him it was impossible to figure out which had prominence.

He tossed his pen onto the desktop and scowled at the wall opposite him. Of course he remembered the passion. The chemistry between them that had built slowly and inexorably until it had finally exploded on their last night together.

Yet he also recalled clearly the calm, cool look in her eye as she walked him to the door that last morning. He gritted his teeth as he saw her face in his mind. Clear blue eyes, luscious mouth curved in a half smile. She hadn't cried. Hadn't asked him to stay. Had, in fact, acted as if he were nothing more than an annoying guest keeping her from her work.

Fresh aggravation rose inside him at the memory, so he pushed it away and grabbed his pen again. Thumb flicking madly at the pen top, he told himself it wasn't that he really *cared,* it was the principle of the thing. Women didn't walk away from Jefferson King. No matter the situation, it was *he* who did the walking. Always. But she'd thrown him off. Caught him off balance and kept him that way and a part of him wondered if that hadn't been her plan all along.

Had she been teasing him, leading him along sexually until she got the offer just the way she wanted it, and then took him to bed to seal the deal? Was she that manipulative and he simply hadn't seen it? He'd hate to think that. Went against the grain to consider it, but why else had she been so casual about a night that had damn well hit him harder than he had expected it to?

What kind of woman spent the night with a man and then turned him loose the next morning so easily?

And why the *hell* was he still thinking about her? The deal was done; it was time to move on. "Well past time," he muttered, since there was no one else in his office to overhear him.

"That's perfect," he added under his breath, "now she's got me talking to myself and the woman probably hasn't given me a single thought."

Which really fried his ass if truth be told. Damn it, Jefferson King was *not* forgettable. Women usually crowded around him, clamoring for his attention. Not just the wannabe actresses who littered Hollywood's streets every few feet, either. But women with wit and intelligence. Women who looked at him and saw a successful man, sure of himself and his own place in the world.

Women who weren't Maura.

Still grumbling, Jefferson flipped through the stack of papers on his desk, and made a few scattered notes. He was buying up an independent film company, thinking of branching King Studios out into documentaries. But it was a stretch to say his mind was focused on that particular task at the moment.

No, like it or not, he was still thinking about *her*.

But why? After all, it wasn't as if either of them had wanted or counted on a relationship. They'd had some good times together, capped by one amazing night of mind-blowing sex. So why was he so disgusted at her casual goodbye the next morning? It wasn't as if he'd been planning to stay anyway.

It had to be ego, pure and simple.

His had taken a slap and that was something he wasn't used to. How had Maura slipped under his well-honed defenses to leave such an indelible image on his mind?

"Doesn't matter," he said aloud, hearing the determination in not only the words but his tone. The memories would fade, eventually. But that wasn't much comfort in the middle of the night when he woke up with dreams of her raging through his mind.

But a man couldn't be held responsible for what his unconscious mind dredged up, could he? He pushed away from his desk and walked to the window overlooking Beverly Hills and Hollywood. The streets were jammed with cars and in the distance he could see the stalled traffic on the freeway. Smog hung low over the scene, a hazy brown blanket covering a city with millions of people all hurrying through their lives. And for just a moment, he let himself imagine the cool green fields of Ireland. The warm welcome of the pub.

The narrow road to Maura's farmhouse.

Irritated with himself and the memories that were still far too vivid, he scrubbed both hands over his face and turned away from the window. He didn't have time to waste indulging in thoughts of a woman who'd no doubt already moved on.

His phone rang and he grabbed at it with the eagerness of a drowning man reaching for a life preserver. "What is it, Joan?"

His assistant said, "Mr. King, Harry Robinson's on line three for you. He says they're having problems on location."

Harry was directing the Irish epic shooting at Maura's farmhouse. Frowning, Jefferson said, "Thanks, Joan. Put him through."

The line clicked over and he asked, "What seems to be the problem, Harry?"

The other man's voice was sharp and filled with both static and disgust. "The problem is, nothing's going right over here. It's a nightmare."

"What? What happened?"

"What hasn't?" Harry countered. "That inn you told me about? Suddenly it has no vacancies. The local caterer's prices have gone up three times in the last week and the coffee's always cold. The guy at the pub even insists he's run out of beer whenever we walk in."

Jefferson turned around and stared blankly out at the city view again. His own reflection stared back at him from the sun-drenched glass. He looked just as confused as he felt. "Run out of beer? How is it possible for a pub to run out of beer?"

"Tell me about it."

That mild swell of irritation he'd felt earlier began to bubble and churn inside him. "That doesn't sound like Craic to me."

"Yeah, well, it doesn't exactly match the description you gave me of the place, either." In an aside to someone else, Harry said, "Well, move the trough out of the shot. No? Fine. I'll be there in a minute." Then he refocused. "That's an example of what we're dealing with. There's a feed trough I want to move and Ms. Donohue refuses to cooperate."

Jefferson tugged at the tie that felt as if it was strangling him. "Go on."

"Yesterday," Harry told him, "the owner of the market

told us he wouldn't be selling to us at all and we could just go into the city for whatever we needed."

"He can't do that."

"Seems he can. I don't have to tell you that Westport's a much longer drive and it's eating up time we don't have."

"I know." What the hell was going on?

"Oh, and the market guy said that if I spoke to you I should tell you, and I quote, 'There'll be no peace for you here until someone does his duty,' end quote. Do you have any idea what he was talking about?"

"No." Duty? What someone? What duty? What the hell had happened in Ireland to turn an entire village against his film crew? The citizens of Craic had been nothing but excited about the prospect a few months ago. What could possibly have changed?

"What about Maura?" he asked suddenly. "Hasn't she been able to help with any of this?"

"Help?" Harry laughed. "That woman would as soon as shoot us as look at us."

"Maura?" Jefferson was stunned now and even more in the dark than he had been before. All right, she hadn't been as thrilled with the prospect of a film crew being on her land as her friends and neighbors had been. But she'd signed the contract in good faith and he knew she had been prepared for all of the confusion and disruption. Her own sister was *in* the movie, so if nothing else, that should have garnered her cooperation. So what had changed?

"Yes, Maura," Harry snapped. "She lets her sheep run wild through shots, her dog chews everything it can get its paws on—"

"She's got a dog?" When did she get a dog?

"She says it's a dog. I say it's part pony. The thing's huge and clumsy. Always knocking things over. Then as if that wasn't enough, one of the cameramen was chased by Ms. Donohue's damn bull."

All right, something was definitely wrong. Whatever else he could say or think about Maura, she was nothing if not meticulous about caring for her animals and the farm itself. She'd shown him the bull, and had warned him away even though the animal was an old one. "How'd the bull get out?"

"Damned if I know. One minute we're shooting the scene, the next minute, Davy Simpson's nearly flattened under the damn bull. Good thing Davy's fast on his feet."

"What is going on over there?" Frustration spiked with temper and twisted into an ugly knot inside him.

His mind raced with possibilities and none of them were flattering to the woman who'd signed his contract. Was she after more money? Was she trying to back out of the whole deal?

Too damn bad to either of those scenarios, he told himself. He had her signature on a legal document and he wasn't about to let her off any hook, nor was he going to be extorted for more money. Whatever she was up to, it seemed she'd gotten the whole village to back her play. What other reason would they have for acting as they were?

Well, it wasn't going to work.

Jefferson King didn't bow to pressure and he sure as hell didn't walk away from trouble.

"That's what I'd like to know," Harry muttered and

the words were almost lost in the static of a bad connection. "The way you talked about this place, I thought it would be an easy shoot."

"It should've been," Jefferson insisted. "Everything was agreed on and besides, we've got a signed contract allowing you access to Maura's farm."

"Yeah, the production assistant tried to remind her of that the other day. Got the door slammed in his face."

"She can't do that," Jefferson told him.

"Uh-huh. I know that. You know that. I don't think she does. Or if she does, she doesn't care."

A hard punch of irritation shot through him again and this time it was brighter, fiercer. "She damn well should. She signed the contract willingly enough. And cashed the check. Nobody forced her to."

Harry huffed out a breath. "I'm telling you, Jefferson, unless things get straightened out around here soon, this shoot is going to go way over budget. Hell, even the weather's giving us a hard time. I've never seen so much rain."

This didn't make any sense. None of it. He'd thought everything was settled. Clearly, he'd been wrong. Looked like he was going to be heading back to County Mayo whether he had planned to or not. Time to have a little talk with a certain sheep farmer. Time to remind her that he had the law on his side and he wasn't leery about using it.

"All right," he said. "The rain I can't do anything about. But I'll take care of the rest of it."

"Yeah?" the director asked. "How?"

"I'll fly over there myself and get to the bottom of

it." Something inside him stirred into life at the thought of seeing Maura again, though he wouldn't admit that, even to himself. This wasn't about his fling with Maura Donohue. This was about business. And she'd better have a damned good reason for being so uncooperative.

"Fine. Hurry."

Jefferson hung up, shouted for his assistant and grabbed his suit jacket out of the closet. He'd already scheduled a trip to Austria to meet with the owner of an ancient castle to talk about filming rights. He'd just work Ireland into the trip.

Shouldn't take long to fix whatever had gone wrong in Craic. He'd stay in the village, talk to everyone, then remind Maura that they had a damn deal. If she was playing games, they were going to stop.

Women were notoriously inconsistent, he reminded himself. God knew the actresses and agents he worked with could drive a man insane. Their moods could change with a whim and any man in the vicinity was liable to be flattened.

Besides, seeing Maura would probably be a good thing in the long run. Give him a chance to look at her without the haze of great sex as a filter. He'd see her for what she was. Just a woman he was doing business with. They could meet, talk, then part again and maybe then he'd stop being hounded by his own memories.

His assistant, Joan, an older woman with no-non-sense green eyes and a detail-oriented personality, hustled into the office.

"What's going on?" she asked.

"I'm going to need you to contact the airport. Tell the

pilot we're making a pit stop in Ireland before we head to Austria."

"Sure, Ireland, Austria. Practically neighbors."

"Funny. Something's come up." He was already headed for the door. "I'm going by my house to pack. Tell the pilot I'll be there in two hours. Have the plane prepped and ready to go."

One of the perks of being a member of the King family was having King Jets at one's disposal. His cousin Jackson ran the company, renting out luxury planes to those who willingly paid outrageous amounts of money for comfort while traveling. But the King family always had the pick of the jets whenever they needed them. Which made all the travel Jefferson did for work a lot easier to take.

Because of that, he could be in the air before dinnertime and in Ireland for breakfast.

"I'll tell him," Joan said as he walked past her. "The jet will be ready. Should I fax you those papers on the McClane buyout while you're in the air or wait until you return?"

He thought about it for a moment, then shook his head. J. T. McClane was the owner of an actual ghost town just on the outskirts of the Mohave desert. Jefferson had the idea to do a modern-day western-gothic film set in what was left of that town. But the man had been dickering over the price for weeks. Wouldn't hurt to remind the man that King Studios was going to remain in charge of the negotiations.

"Just hang on to them until I get back," he said

finally. "Won't hurt to make McClane sweat about this deal for a while."

Joan smiled. "Got it. And, boss…"

"Yeah?"

"Good luck."

Jefferson smiled and nodded as he left, and kept his thoughts to himself. No point in telling Joan that the only one who was going to need luck around here was Maura Donohue.

Five

Jefferson stopped in the village to book a room at the small inn that he'd stayed in on his last trip. He was jet-lagged, hungry and well past the breaking point. So when the innkeeper, Frances Boyle, was less than welcoming when she opened her bright red front door and gave him a grim glare, Jefferson's hackles went up.

"Well," she said, crossing her thick arms over a prodigious chest covered by a shawl the color of mustard. "If it isn't himself, come back to the scene of the crime."

"Crime?" One black eyebrow lifted. "Excuse me?"

"Hah! A fine time to be beggin' pardon and if it's pardon you're asking I'm not the one it should be aimed at."

He closed his eyes briefly. The older woman's brogue was so thick, and she spoke so quickly, he'd thought for a moment she was speaking Gaelic. Then her words sunk in and he realized he was being *scolded* as if he were a five-year-old who'd thrown a rock through her window.

"Mrs. Boyle," Jefferson said, gathering the reins on his simmering temper and trying for a charming smile. "I've just spent too many hours on a jet, then driven here from the airport in a rental car that blew a tire on the road and now—" he paused to toss a hard stare at the lowering gray sky "—I'm getting rained on. I'm happy to listen to whatever your complaints might be after you rent me a room so I can change clothes and get settled."

"Humph."

Her snort was caught between a snide laugh and a jolt of outrage. "Used to giving orders, aren't you? No doubt your lackeys jump to attention when you snarl. Well, I'm no one's lackey, boyo, and I've no time for the likes of you, Jefferson King."

Lackey? He didn't have lackeys.

"The likes of—" What the hell had happened to this place in a few short months? Had he stepped into an alternate universe? He pushed his wet hair out of his eyes, blinked the raindrops off his lashes and asked, "What did I do? I haven't even been here in months!"

She huffed out a breath. "So you haven't, when you should've been, I say. You're a sad disappointment to me, *Mister* King."

"Disappointment?" Seriously, he felt as though he needed a translator. It was as if the older woman was speaking in code. "What the *hell* is going on around here?"

"A *decent* man would already know the answer to that question." Her features were hard as stone and her normally placid eyes were glittering. The toe of her practical black shoe tapped against the linoleum. "And I don't appreciate you swearing at me in my own home."

"I'm not in your home," he pointed out, as a cold drop of rain sneaked underneath his shirt collar and rolled icily down his spine.

"And not likely to be any time soon, either."

So, he was getting a firsthand lesson in what his film crew had been experiencing. He couldn't understand this. When he'd been here the last time, Frances Boyle had been warm, funny, *friendly*. He wasn't used to being treated with outright disrespect.

But whatever her problem was with him, he'd deal with it later. All he wanted at the moment was a room, a change of clothes and a meal. Once he was warm, dry and fed, he knew he'd be in better shape to handle not only Mrs. Boyle, but anything else that awaited him in this picturesque village.

Then he'd be ready to head off to Maura's farmhouse to settle whatever bug she had up her— He cut that thought off abruptly and tried one last time. "Mrs. Boyle. I just need a room for a couple of days," he said tightly.

"A shame for you as I'm full up."

"Full? It's not even tourist season."

She sniffed and her voice was cold enough to drop frost on her words. "Be that as it may."

Then she closed the door on him with a sharp crack of sound. So much for charm. Fine. He'd just stop at a B and B somewhere along the road. As he recalled, there was one not far from Maura's farmhouse.

Still, it stung. Hardly the welcome he'd been expecting. Jefferson turned around on her porch and looked up and down the narrow Main Street of the village. It looked like a postcard, even in this miserable weather. Sidewalks were thin strips of cement that rose up and down as the road willed it. The shops were a rainbow of colors, and smoke drifted upward from chimneys to be caught by the ever-present wind. Doors were closed against the rain currently pummeling him and early-blooming flowers in pots bent with the water and wind.

Scraping one hand across his face, he stepped off the porch and headed for the Lion's Den pub. At least there, he'd be able to get a meal and something hot to drink. Then he'd face the rest of the drive to Maura's. As he jogged across the empty street, he told himself that Mrs. Boyle's attitude was probably just a case of women sticking together. He already knew Maura was angry about something and the innkeeper was just showing solidarity. God knew every female he'd ever known would be willing to take the side of a fellow woman against a man no matter what the argument might be.

Jefferson stepped into the warmth of the pub and paused a moment to enjoy the glow of the fire in the hearth and the rich scents of beer and some kind of stew simmering in the kitchen. Then he nodded vaguely at a couple of men seated at a table, before taking a spot at the bar for himself. He'd barely settled himself when Michael came out of the kitchen, took a look at Jefferson and came to a sudden stop. His wide, genial face flushed dark red and his blue eyes flashed with trouble.

"We're closed," he said.

Jefferson muffled a groan. This he hadn't expected at all and if he were to be honest about it, he could admit to himself that he felt a bit betrayed at the moment. He and Michael had become friends the last time he was here. And now, the look on the man's face said he'd happily plant one of his meaty fists on Jefferson's jaw.

"Closed?" Jefferson jerked a thumb in the direction of the two men, each sipping a freshly stacked Guinness beer. "What about them?"

"We're not closed to them, are we?"

"So, it's only me."

"I didn't say that." Michael picked up a pristine bar rag and idly polished a bar that already shone like a dark jewel in the overhead light.

"Yeah." Jefferson swallowed his anger because it wasn't going to do him any good here anyway. Until he knew exactly what he was accused of, he couldn't fight it.

He pushed off the stool, leaned both hands on the bar and met Michael's heated stare with one of his own. "When we first met, you struck me as a fair man, Michael," he said. "I'm sorry to be proven wrong."

The man inhaled so sharply, his barrel chest swelled up to massive proportions. "Aye and you struck me as a man to do his duty."

"Duty?" He threw both arms wide. "Is everyone in the village nuts all of a sudden? What're you talking about?"

Michael slapped the bar with his palm. "What I'm talking about is you being nothing more than a rich American taking what he wants and never paying a mind to his leavings."

Jefferson straightened up like someone had shoved

a poker down the back of his shirt. He was trying to be reasonable here, but a man could only be pushed so far. "What leavings?"

"That's not for me to say but for you to know."

Great, he thought, disgusted. More code.

"Look, we obviously don't know each other as well as I thought, Michael," Jefferson told him, "so I'm going to let that insult go. But I can tell you I've never shirked my duty in my life—nor do I know anything about any 'leavings'—not that I owe you any explanations."

"Oh, on that you're spot-on," the big man muttered. "It's not *me* you're owin', Jefferson King."

"What's that supposed to mean?"

"It's time you found out, don't you think?"

"And just who should I ask?" Even as he said the words though, he knew what the answer would be.

Sure enough, a moment later, Michael said, "Talk to Maura. She'll tell you or not as she pleases. But don't come into Craic looking for friends until you do."

The men at the table behind him muttered agreement, but Jefferson paid them no attention at all. Why was the town one step short of a mob threatening to tar and feather him?

And why was he still standing there when he knew where he could go to get some answers?

"Fine. I'm here to talk to Maura anyway. I'll settle this with her and then you and I are going to have a talk."

"I look forward to it."

He left the pub at a brisk walk and headed straight for his rental car. The rain pelted at him as if Heaven were throwing icy pebbles down just to elevate his misery. He felt the stares of dozens of people watching him as he went and realized that he'd fully expected to solve this problem with ease.

He'd had friends here, damn it. What could have happened to change that so completely? And why was Maura the key?

He fired up the engine and steered the small sports car down the narrow road leading out of town and toward Maura. It was time to get some answers.

The muddy track was familiar, and despite the carefully banked anger inside him, there was something else within, too. A curl of anticipation at the thought of seeing Maura again. He didn't want it. Had fought the very memory of her for months. But being here again fed the flames he'd been trying to extinguish.

Now wasn't the time for that, though. He wasn't here to indulge in his desire for a woman who'd made no secret of the fact that she wasn't interested. He wasn't going to walk blindly back down a path he'd already traveled.

Besides, he was wet, tired and just this side of miserable when he pulled the rental car into Maura's drive. Through the heavy mist and low-hanging clouds, the manor house sat like a beacon of light. Its whitewashed walls, dark green shutters and bright blue door belied the gray day and the jewel-colored flowers bursting from pots on either side of the door valiantly stood against an icy wind.

On the far side of the yard, three RVs, a tent and the equipment that made up a film shoot were staggered. People bustled about, though Jefferson knew the actors would be tucked inside their trailers, waiting out the weather. Between the rain and the delays caused by an uncooperative Maura and friends, Jefferson could practically hear money being flushed down the drain.

Frustrated with the entire situation, Jefferson opened the car door to a fresh wall of wet, and once he was standing on the sodden gravel drive slammed the door closed again.

Heads turned. Worker bees, the PA, Harry the director, all looked at him, but when Harry made to walk toward him, Jefferson held him back with one upraised hand. He wanted to talk to Maura before he got any more information.

"And she'd better have some damn answers," he muttered, soles of his shoes sliding on the wet gravel.

With anger churning in his gut, he started for the house. He didn't notice the charm of the place now. Paid no attention to the half-dozen or so spring lambs chasing each other through the fenced front yard.

He didn't even slow down when someone shouted a warning, so he was taken by surprise when a black dog as big as a small bear charged from the corner of the house and made straight for him.

"Jesus Christ!" Jefferson's shout of surprise was raw and hoarse, scraping from his throat loud enough to carry over the deranged barking filling the air.

Instantly, the front door flew open. Maura stepped into the rain and said sharply, "King!"

The dog skidded to a stop on the gravel, its momentum carrying it into Jefferson, who swayed, but held his ground against the heavy impact. Still startled, Jefferson looked down into a smiling dog face, complete with sharp black eyes and a tongue the size of a flag lolling out the side of its mouth.

The dog's huge head was waist high on Jefferson, and the dog had to weigh at least a hundred pounds.

"It *is* a pony," he said, remembering Harry's comment.

"Irish wolfhound," Maura told him, then added, "He meant no harm. He was only greeting you, as he's a baby yet and a poor judge of character."

He ground his back teeth together and shifted a look at her. "His name's King? You named him after me?"

Her mouth twisted into a brief sneer. "Aye, I did as he's a son of a bitch, as well."

Jefferson wasn't amused. He looked into her dark blue eyes and saw a river of emotions shining out at him. They were shifting, changing even as he watched, so that he wasn't sure if she was going to throw something at him or rush into his arms, however belatedly. A moment later, he had his answer.

"Why're you here?"

The music of her accent didn't soften her words any. She faced him down as the wind lifted her long black hair into a dance about her head. She was beautiful and stubborn and the most fascinating woman he'd ever known.

Because of her, he'd hopped a plane and flown thousands of miles only to be treated like a leper by people he'd considered friends.

"You mean, why am I standing in the rain in front of a hardheaded woman who isn't honoring the contract she signed?" He snapped the words out and noticed she didn't so much as flinch. "I've been asking myself the same thing."

"Your people are littering the street in front of my house at this very moment," she challenged, "so I'm thinking I'm honoring what was between us a good deal more than you have."

"You know," he said, shoving the monstrously huge dog off his legs so that he could stalk toward the porch. And her. "I've been back in Ireland about an hour and in that short amount of time, I've been rained on, had a flat tire, got mud in my shoes and been insulted by everyone I've spoken to. So I'm not in the mood to listen to more obscure references to what a bastard I am. If you've got a problem with me," he added, stopping just short of the porch, "then tell me what it is so I can fix it."

Her eyes narrowed on him. She crossed her arms over her chest, lifted her chin and said, "I'm pregnant. Fix *that*."

Six

She slammed the door an instant later.

Eyes wide, heart pounding in her chest, Maura leaned back against the door and tried to catch her breath. She shivered slightly and couldn't be sure if it was the bitter spring weather or the ice in Jefferson's pale blue eyes that had made her feel cold down to the bone. She only knew that seeing him again had shaken her. Shaken her so badly she couldn't afford to let him see it.

Bad enough he'd shown up on her doorstep without so much as a phone call in warning. "But then," she murmured aloud, "the man obviously doesn't know how to *use* a bloody phone now, does he, since I've been calling him for more than three months now with no success."

And yet here he was.

At her front door, looking half-drowned and furious

with it and still so tempting everything in her wanted to shout for glee at seeing him again. Even though she knew better, Maura felt that familiar need for him rise up inside her. She should have been prepared for this. Somehow, she should have known.

Of course he'd come back to Ireland. If not to see her, then to check on his blasted movie people. Yet, even if she had expected to see him, she doubted she would have been prepared for the delicious licks of want and desire that swept through her with just a single look into the man's eyes.

"He had the right of it. He is a bastard." She leaned her head back against the closed door and waited for him to start pounding on it.

Jefferson wasn't the kind of man who'd hear the news she'd just delivered and then disappear as quickly as he could. Oh no, he'd be demanding entry in another moment or two. And then he'd be righteous and full of himself and expecting explanations and details.

Though she'd been trying for months to give him exactly that, right now, she was in no mind to speak with him at all.

Mostly because her stomach was still spinning from that first sight of him. And because her hands itched to slap or hold she wasn't sure which and mostly, because he was *Jefferson*.

God help her, it didn't seem to matter that she was furious with him. Her heart was still full of him and she couldn't seem to dig him out despite how hard she tried. Which only made her even *more* furious with herself than she was with him.

And who would have thought that possible?

A heartbeat later, several loud thuds came from right behind her head. She knew without looking out the window that he was using his fist to batter at her door. Her heartbeat quickened and low in her belly something stirred, buzzing awake feelings that had been lying fallow for weeks now. Like a limb waking from a deep sleep, there were pinpricks of awareness tingling across every inch of her skin.

"Damn it, Maura, open the door!"

She might have if he hadn't ordered her to. As it was, the anger she'd been carrying around for months suddenly swamped her and she pushed away from the door. "Go away, Jefferson!"

"Not gonna happen!" he shouted back. "Now, do we have this conversation loud enough for everyone to listen in or do we talk in private?"

Private.

That got her moving. She wasn't interested in having half of Hollywood listening in on her private business. Maura flung the door open and stepped back as Jefferson marched inside, followed by King, who promptly shook the rainwater off his coat and onto everything else.

"For heaven's sake," she muttered as the dog sprinted off the long hallway toward the kitchen and his bed.

Wiping water off her face, she stared up into Jefferson's eyes and almost took a step back from the glittering wrath shining there. Then she remembered just which of them had the right to be angry.

"You've nothing to be snippy about," she told him before he could speak.

"Snippy?" He pushed both hands through his wet hair, shrugged out of his suit jacket and tossed it onto the umbrella stand beside the door. His white dress shirt was soaked as well, clinging to the muscled contours of his chest and abdomen in a way that made Maura's mouth water, though she wouldn't have admitted it even with a knife to her throat.

"I'm way more than snippy," he told her. "What the hell do you mean you're pregnant?"

She forced herself to calmly close the front door before she turned to answer him. "Just how many things could I mean, do you think, Jefferson?" Oh, she'd imagined this scene too many times to count and the reactions she'd given him in her mind had been wide and varied. But in none of them had he looked as though someone had hit him over the head with a stick.

He was stunned, pure and simple, which told her flat out that no one had given him the countless messages she'd left over the last couple of months. Why did the man employ so many people if none of them could be trusted to pass on a message?

Her temper built steadily as she met his shocked gaze. "It's easy enough to understand. I'm *pregnant*. With child. Carrying. Bun in the oven." She tipped her head to one side. "Shall I draw you a picture?"

A tension-filled second or two ticked past, the only sounds in the house that of the rain battering at the windows and the wind whistling beneath the eaves. Finally, he spoke and his voice was tight with controlled emotion.

"If you think you're being funny, you're mistaken. And if you're really pregnant why the *hell* didn't you tell me?"

"Really pregnant?" She repeated the words, spitting them back at him. "Instead of only a bit pregnant, is that it?"

"That's not what I meant. Why didn't you tell me?"

"Hah! You've quite the nerve asking me that question, I'll say." She closed the space between them with two quick steps and poked her index finger against the center of his chest. "With me calling and calling that bloody studio of yours, leaving messages both long and short with that crowd of people standing between you and the public?"

"You called?"

"Repeatedly and I'll tell you now, the Pope would be easier to ring up."

"I never got any message from you," he said, pulling his tie off and opening the collar of his shirt.

Was that true? She wondered if she'd been wrong all this time. For weeks now, she'd been harboring a snarling fury toward him. She'd thought he'd been getting all of her messages and simply ignoring them. Choosing to distance himself from a woman he no longer wanted and a child he had no interest in. She'd thought him the lowest sort of man and she'd been hurt and furious with herself that she hadn't seen him originally for the snake he'd turned out to be.

Now…she had to rethink everything. She had to consider that perhaps he really hadn't known about the baby. And if that was true then what did it mean for all of them? Ah God, she needed time to think, without him standing within arm's reach of her and looking good enough to bite.

Irritated beyond measure, she snapped, "It's hardly my fault that you didn't get messages I left, now is it?"

He tossed the tie onto his suit jacket. "You're pregnant."

"As I've said."

Shaking his head, he looked as though he wanted to say something, but he bit the words back before they could escape. Instead, he swiped one hand across his face, stared at her as if he'd never seen her before, then muttered something under his breath that she didn't quite catch.

He took a few steps down the polished wood hallway, then stopped and turned around. "Does everyone in the village know about this?"

Maura sighed. It hadn't taken long at all for her secret to become public knowledge. "Nurse Doherty has ever had a flapping tongue."

"That means yes, I take it."

"It does."

"You ought to sue her," he mumbled. "Doctor-patient privilege."

She laughed shortly. "Isn't that just like an American? Lawsuits the answer to all problems? Well, what good would it do me to sue a woman who's known me since my mother was carrying me?" Maura sighed again and explained, "It wasn't Doc Rafferty who spilled the news. Trying to quiet Patty Doherty would be like holding back the tide by building a wall of sand."

She'd known the moment she left the doctor's office that fine day that within hours, word of her pregnancy would be spread across all of Craic. Not that she was ashamed of her situation. But if Maura had even guessed beforehand that she might be pregnant, she'd have visited a doctor in Westport, to keep her business her own.

"Are you well?" he asked quietly. "The baby?"

"We're both fine," she assured him.

And weren't they being civilized, Maura thought vaguely. Just two adults who'd made a child, standing in a dimly lit hall speaking to each other like strangers. The cold she'd felt earlier dropped into the freezing range.

When he'd first come to Ireland, there'd been heat. Heat that had burned bright and hot between them, ending in the inevitable. Now though, Maura thought that if he had looked at her then the way he was now, they wouldn't be in the position they were in.

It wasn't lust he was showing her now. It was…less and more at the same time. Confusing to both of them, no doubt.

All around them, a storm raged, yet here in the house where she'd lived her whole life, there was a stillness that ate at her nerves and chewed at the edges of her heart. Was he wondering what to do with her? How to keep his affair with a sheep farmer a secret from the press?

Why the devil wouldn't he *say* something?

"Must you just stand there staring at me as if I've grown two heads?"

He inhaled sharply. "It's a lot to take in."

"Oh, aye," she agreed. "What to do about Maura? Must be bloody difficult to think of the right thing to say."

He ignored that. "So, the reason the film crew's having so much trouble…the reason I couldn't get a room at the inn or a beer in the pub…" His voice trailed off, but Maura could see him thinking and knew from the expression on his face he didn't much care for what was in his mind.

"They're angry on my behalf," she told him, her voice soft, her words sharp. "Everyone in the village knows I'm pregnant and that you've done nothing about it."

"I—" He took a step toward her and stopped again. "How in the hell could I have done anything about it when you didn't bother to tell me?"

"I've already explained that I bloody well tried to tell you, didn't I?"

Maura stormed out of the hall into the main room. Through the bank of windows, she saw the gray skies, the green field where lambs played and the wide, pewter stretch of the lake. She didn't turn around to know he'd followed her into the room. She didn't have to. She would have sensed him even if she hadn't heard his footsteps.

"How hard did you try, Maura?" He grabbed her upper arm and turned her around to face him. "A man's got a right to know when he's going to be a father."

"Aye, he does. And along with that right," she countered, refusing to be cowed by the flash of indignation in his eyes, "comes a responsibility to return calls left so that he might discover what a body's trying to tell him."

"I never got any messages."

"So you say, though I left dozens. Maybe hundreds." Doubt crept in and battered at the anger she'd been carrying for weeks.

"With whom?"

"With anyone I could get on the phone, blast you!"

She yanked free of his grasp and whipped her hair back behind her shoulders. "Mostly I called your office and never got past your secretary. Oh, she was polite and all and told me how nice it was that I wanted to stay in touch, but that you're a busy man and so I was to be sure and let her know if I had any problems in the future."

"Joan. Did you tell her about the baby?"

"I did. She congratulated me as nice as you please and said she was sure Mr. King would be happy for me. *Happy* for me." She folded her arms across her chest. "I assumed you wanted nothing to do with me *or* my child."

"*Our* child."

She nodded. "As you say. So when I heard nothing from you for weeks, I put you out of my mind entirely."

Liar, her brain screamed silently. He'd never been out of her thoughts. Or her dreams. Even with the hurt and disappointment and anger, she'd thought of him, remembered that night with him and torn herself up with regrets for what had been lost.

Blast if she'd let him know that, though.

"So it seems, Jefferson, that once your contract is signed, you've no need to be polite to those you've already won over."

"I can't believe Joan knew and didn't say anything."

"Get a lot of those messages, does she?" Stung, she snapped, "Believe me or not, it's your business to be sure."

"I don't mean I didn't believe you. I meant—" His voice trailed off. Shoving both hands into his pockets, he shook his head and said, "I've had people call after the contract was signed, trying to up the amount of money they agreed to. Or to get more out of me in other ways.

Joan—my assistant—knows that and weeds out people she thinks might be causing trouble."

"Well, I might see how she could think that when, after the first few tries I made, I might have lost my temper with her...."

"Might have?" he asked, one corner of his mouth lifting.

"All right, *did,* but I had my reasons, didn't I?"

"Yeah, you did. She should have told me you called."

Jefferson blew out an unsteady breath. This was all happening so fast he could hardly think. He'd never even considered the possibility of leaving Maura pregnant. Which made him a complete ass. He hadn't worried about contraception— had just given himself over to the heat of the moment. Something he had never been careless about. But damn it, he couldn't be faulted for not acting on something he hadn't even known about.

The important thing to focus on was the fact that he was going to be a father.

Everything in him trembled. Not the kind of news a man got every day. Not hard to understand why his brain was having a tough time computing it all. He hadn't known. For four months, she'd been alone with this knowledge, thinking that he didn't care. Thinking he wanted nothing to do with her. No wonder she was spitting fire at him. Guilt roared up, took a bite of him, then Jefferson shoved it back down. Damned if he'd take the blame for something he hadn't even known about.

"I'll have a talk with Joan when I get back. Make it clear that I want to see all of my messages, not just the few she decides are worth my time." It infuriated him

that Maura had been trying to get hold of him for months unsuccessfully. Still in his own defense, he said, "A lot of people call me, Maura."

"Women, I suppose," she said with a sneer.

Yes, women, he thought, though there hadn't been any since he'd last been here. Hell, he hadn't been able to look at another woman without seeing dark blue eyes and a wide, luscious mouth. His thoughts had been with Maura even when he hadn't wanted it that way.

"I saw a picture of you in one of those celebrity magazines a month or so back. You looked very handsome in your splendid tuxedo with an empty-headed blond on your arm. Yes, you were very busy."

He enjoyed the scorn in her voice. "Jealous?"

She snorted. "Indeed not. Just observant."

That might be what she was telling herself, but he was glad to know she'd been keeping tabs on him anyway. "That was the lead actress in our latest movie. I escorted her to the premiere."

"Aye, she looked the 'escort' type."

He laughed shortly. "It's my job, Maura."

"And you do it so well," she told him, dropping into a chair that looked worn and comfortable.

In fact, the whole house looked cozy, he thought, giving the room a quick going over. It had stood there for centuries and the interior of the farmhouse had the softly shabby look that spoke not of neglect, but comfort. Familiarity.

He stood over her. "You're taking shots at me. I get that. My point, though, was that a lot of people leave messages for me. It's not that surprising that yours got lost or misdirected or—" He threw his hands up in frustration.

"And how many of those messages were from women telling you they're pregnant?" She glared up at him with sparks flashing in her eyes. "Because if there's a line of us, you can tell me now, Jefferson. I won't be part of your herd. And my child won't be one of dozens of your bastards."

"Stop it." He leaned down, planting both hands on the arms of the chair, caging her neatly. The scent of her drifted to him and he inhaled it deeply. God, he'd missed her more than he'd wanted to admit, even to himself. Now, her eyes were wild with rage, but there was hurt there, too, and that bothered him.

"There's no one else. I don't have any other children. I didn't know about your pregnancy. If I had, I would have been here. Would have talked to you. Done—"

"What?" she asked, a little less battle-ready now. "What would you have done?"

"I don't know. Something."

She looked up into his eyes for a long second or two, then finally nodded. "I believe you. You didn't get the messages. You didn't know."

"Thanks for that, anyway." He pushed up and off the chair and moved away from her.

He was going to be a father. A hard thing for a man to consider. To accept. There was anticipation inside him, even excitement. But there was also uncertainty. He had to make plans. *They* had to make plans. Hell, he didn't even know where to start.

"Now I know how Justice felt," he mumbled.

"Justice?"

"My brother. The one on the ranch." He glanced at

her and gave her a wry smile. "His wife, Maggie, didn't tell him they'd had a son together until Jonas was six months old."

"Why not?"

"Because she thought Justice wouldn't believe her." To stop her from asking why again, he said, "It's a long story. The point is, at the time, I thought Justice over-reacted to what Maggie had done. He was furious with her and I thought he should just get over it, deal with the new reality. But now I get it."

"Is that right? So now you're furious, are you? Well, join the club."

"No." He laughed out loud, enjoying her mercurial nature. Had there ever been another woman like her? Smiling one minute and fierce the next. She was a tangled web of emotions that a man had to be crazy to want to explore. Well, sign him up to be committed. "I'm not furious. Just…wondering where the hell we go from here, that's all."

"Well then, when you're finished doing your wonder-ing, you know where to find me, don't you?" She stood up out of the chair and headed for the bank of windows overlooking the front yard.

"Maura, I'm not leaving until we settle this."

"I don't want you here."

"Too bad." She could push him away all she liked, he was going nowhere until he was good and ready. And that wasn't going to happen anytime soon. "I'm staying until we figure this out."

"There's nothing *to* figure out." She looked at him briefly over her shoulder before turning her face back to the window and the view beyond. "I'm pregnant. You're not. Go home."

"No."

She lifted one hand and laid her palm on the rain-streaked pane. "Tell your movie people they'll have no more trouble from me or the village. I'll see to it."

"Thanks. That takes care of one problem."

She stiffened. "I'm not a problem, and neither is my child."

"I didn't say that, either." God, she was a minefield and he was walking through it blindfolded.

"You might as well have. It's in your mind. Your heart."

"So you read minds now, too?"

"Yours is easy enough," she told him.

He caught her reflection in the glass and hated that her eyes were shining with unshed tears. He realized he'd never seen Maura cry and he damned well didn't care for the fact that he was behind those tears now.

"Go away," she said softly. "Please."

Jefferson heard the click of nails on wood, so wasn't surprised when her huge black dog entered the room and walked toward her. Automatically, she dropped one hand to the dog's head and stroked her fingers through its fur. The two of them looked like a painting together.

At the moment, Jefferson thought, there was no place for him there. Maura had drawn a line to close him out. Maybe he couldn't blame her.

That didn't mean he was going to let this go, though, and she'd better get used to that idea real fast. But for now, he'd leave, gather his forces and come back when he had things settled in his mind. He knew what needed to be done. From the moment he first heard about the baby, he'd known.

But he needed time to work out the details.

Then he'd be back and Maura Donohue would see that a King never walked away from his responsibilities.

With that thought in mind, he turned to leave, as she'd asked him to. Before he walked out of the room, though, he promised, "This isn't over, Maura."

Seven

A few hours later, Cara asked, "Then what did he do?"

"He left." Maura lifted a week-old lamb, cradled it against her chest, then held a baby bottle out for it. Instantly, the tiny, black-and-white creature latched on to the rubber nipple and began tugging at it. Maura smiled even as she tried to ignore her sister's interrogation.

Naturally, Cara wouldn't leave the thing alone even when Maura insisted she didn't want to speak about it. The only thing she could do now was hope to finish the conversation as quickly as possible.

"He just left? He didn't propose?"

Maura laughed at that notion, more to cover up her own disappointment than anything else. Until that very afternoon, she'd had dreams. Fantasies you might say,

during the weeks when she was trying so futilely to get
hold of the Great One himself. She'd imagined him
going down on bended knee, here in this very barn.
She'd pictured him proposing and, in her frustration
with his ignoring her or so she'd thought, she'd pictured
herself telling him no. After all, he'd been ignoring her
for months, so she'd imagined the stunned surprise on
his face as she told him what he could do with his
belated proposal.

Then he'd shattered that lovely dream by not even
bothering to give her a duty proposal. She frowned to
herself and realized just how hard it was to love a man
who had no idea how she felt.

"No," she said tightly. "He didn't propose and it's not
likely to happen anytime soon."

"Why ever not?" Cara wanted to know. "He's given
you a baby, the least he can do is make you a wife."

Maura chuckled in spite of the situation. "You know,
for someone who claims to be a very modern woman
of the world, you sounded remarkably like an old grand-
mother just then."

Cara frowned. "Being modern is one thing. Watching
my sister be a single mother is another altogether.
Besides, Maura, you love him."

Maura's gaze snapped to her sister, who was looking
tired and near half-asleep. And why shouldn't she? Cara
was balancing a waitressing job in Westport while
coming back to the farm nearly every day to film her
small role in Jefferson's movie. Her sister was smart,
talented and far too knowing about some things.

"I'll thank you to keep that piece of news to yourself," Maura told her. "Besides, I'll not have his pity and that's all it would be if he pretended to love me now. Or worse yet, if he were appalled at the notion. So mind your tongue, Cara."

Clearly insulted, Cara drew her head back as if she'd been slapped. "As if you need tell me. I'm your sister, aren't I? Would I side with a Yank against my own blood?"

Mollified a bit, Maura nodded and put her attention back to the task at hand. She could learn to forget him, she told herself. She would content herself in the future with her farm and her child and one day, the man she loved would be no more than a fond memory she indulged in on lonely nights. For now though, Jefferson had work and so did she. And hers, she thought, was more pressing than contracts or actors or the placement of a camera.

She had a total of six lambs so far this season who needed to be hand-fed. There were two pens holding the little ones, who snuggled together to sleep in a pile beneath heat lamps that kept the spring chill away. A few had been abandoned by their mothers for whatever reason a sheep might deem reasonable. Happened every year, a ewe would give birth and simply stroll away from the lamb, ignoring its bleating calls.

The others were simply too small to be left alone with their mothers, so the ewes were penned nearby so the lambs could nurse as well as get extra nutrition from a baby bottle. The tiny, warm bodies were a constant wonder to Maura. They were so small, so helpless when new that it was difficult to remain detached, as she must. Since most of the lambs would be sold off and—

"You should be the one to tell him at any rate," Cara said and reached for one of the lambs. Grabbing up an extra bottle, she cuddled the pure white baby and smiled at the hungry sounds it made as it fed.

Her sister might have her sights set on acting, but Cara was born and bred a farm girl and knew what needed doing without being told. And for a few minutes, the two sisters enjoyed the stillness. Outside, the storm had passed, leaving only the sound of water dripping from the roof edges and the ever-present wind rattling the shingles.

"He's staying in one of the trailers, you know."

"What?" Startled, Maura looked her sister in the eye.

"I said, Jefferson is staying in one of the trailers."

Maura threw a look at the closed barn doors as if she could see through them to the yard outside. "You mean now? He's living out there? In the street?"

"In one of the trailers, yes." Cara smiled and stroked the lamb as she fed it. "Everyone else left hours ago, headed off to the B & B and some into Westport. But Jefferson is staying here. Said he wanted to be close. Why's that, do you think?"

She didn't know. And couldn't guess. Oh, she didn't like that. She'd hoped he'd be off to the city and give her some breathing room. How was she supposed to relax into her routine if she knew he was less than a hundred feet from her own front door? Her insides were fluttering and she knew it wasn't the baby moving as that hadn't happened yet. No, it was her child's father setting off swarms of butterflies in the pit of her belly.

"He can't stay there."

"Of course he can." Cara tipped her head to one side and studied her older sister. "They're his trailers, after all. And you did give him leave to park them there."

"Not to *live* in!"

Cara laughed. "Look at you. Just knowing he's close by has put color in your cheeks and a shine in your eyes."

"That's just anger is all."

"It's not, no," her sister said. "Honestly, Maura, must you be so stubborn at all times? You're flushed over him and you say you don't want him? You're having his baby, for goodness' sake. Why shouldn't you be married to the man?"

"She will be."

Both women jolted at the sound of the deep voice. They turned as one and stared at Jefferson as he stepped into the warm barn and closed the door behind him. He wore black jeans, a dark red pullover sweatshirt and heavy black boots that were as scuffed as the floor of the barn. His hair was windblown across his forehead and his mouth was a firm, grim line. The overhead lights were harsh and bright and cast unforgiving shadows over his face until he looked like some pirate with danger on his mind.

Maura's heart did a slow roll in her chest and a deep, throbbing ache set up shop low in her body. Would he always have this kind of effect on her?

"She will be what?" Cara asked.

"I said, your sister will be marrying me." Jefferson walked toward them, sidling past idle machinery and stacks of baled hay on one side of the barn. As he neared the closed-off area, one of the ewes scuttled nervously in her pen. He looked at all of the animals crowded together, then shifted his gaze back to Maura. "As soon as we can manage it."

Amazing how quickly fire could turn to ice. Here then was her "proposal." A demand from a man who clearly expected her to jump through hoops when ordered to.

"No, I'm not," Maura told him, wishing the barn were bigger. Wishing she were back in the house behind locked doors. Wishing Jefferson had never returned to Ireland. What a sorry mess.

If he thought *that* was a proposal, he was sorely lacking. Step into her barn and issue commands as though he actually *were* a king. Was he so full of himself that he expected her to fall in line with whatever he wanted? Did he really think her such an easy woman as all that?

It didn't matter, really, Maura told herself. His decisions would have no impact on her. And though her heart was galloping in her chest, she wouldn't be saying yes. She wouldn't have a man who didn't love her and she knew bloody well Jefferson King was not in love.

"Argue if it makes you feel better." Jefferson looked down at her, their eyes locked and she read pure determination in those pale blue depths. For all the good it would do him.

"And you make all the decisions you like," Maura countered briskly. "It appears you enjoy doing it no matter that nothing will come of it."

"It's all arranged." He sniffed at the mingled scents of hay and wet sheep. "Or it will be soon. My assistant's taking care of the details, but with the time difference, it'll probably take a couple of days."

"What exactly," Cara asked, when it became clear Maura had no intention of asking the question herself, "is it that your assistant is so busily arranging?"

"A marriage license, a venue." His gaze fixed on Maura. "I told Joan I thought you'd prefer to be married in the village church, but we can change that if you'd rather. Westport maybe? Dublin? Hell, we can wait and get married in Hollywood if you want."

"Hollywood?" Cara asked, saying the word a bit wistfully.

"Doesn't matter to me," Jefferson said. "As long as we get married, I don't care where we do it."

"How very thoughtful," Maura managed to choke out.

"It's not thoughtful," he countered. "It's expedient."

"And quite romantic," Maura sniped. "Why, my heart's just weeping with the joy of it all."

"This isn't about romance," he said.

"That'd be plain to a blind man."

"It's about what's right."

"Oh, and I suppose you're the one to be deciding what right is?"

"Someone has to," he said with a barely restrained snarl.

"Well then," Cara announced, effectively interrupting the argument, "I can see you two have a lot to talk about, so I'll be going, shall I?"

Maura jolted. She didn't want to be alone with Jefferson. Not now. Not yet. "Don't you dare leave this barn, Cara...."

Giving her a wink, her sister stood up, handed the lamb and its bottle to Jefferson and announced, "I wish you luck in your dealings with my sister. She can be a bit hardheaded, as I'm sure you've noticed."

"So much for family loyalty," Maura murmured.

Cara ignored her and spoke only to Jefferson. "Mind though, make her cry and I'll make your life a living misery."

"Fair warning," Jefferson said with a nod as he settled the lamb more comfortably against him.

"Good."

"Cara, blast you for a traitor, don't you leave me here with him—"

"I'll take myself off back to Westport," Cara said, lifting her voice to carry over Maura's. "I'll stay with Mary Dooley again since I've an early shift at the café tomorrow anyway. You two have a good night," she added, then looked at Jefferson. "Mind the lamb drinks the whole bottle now."

She was gone a moment later and the only sounds in the barn were those made by the restive sheep.

"I've never fed a lamb before," Jefferson said, taking a seat on an upturned crate. He looked down at the small animal in his arms and added, "I've hand-fed calves though. Shouldn't be too different, though if you tell Justice I said that, I'll deny it."

Maura swallowed hard, then realized her lamb was through feeding. She set him down in the pen, reached for the next one and began the process over again. They were too intimate here. Too crowded together in too small a space. She couldn't draw a breath without taking in the scent of him. It was fogging her mind, but not so much that she'd give way to a bully trying to force his decisions on her.

"There's no reason for you to stay," she said.

"I'm helping," he told her.

"I don't need your help just as I don't need to be told I'm getting married."

"Apparently," he said, "you do."

"I won't marry you."

"Why the hell not?" He lifted his eyes from the lamb, who was feeding as if it were the last bit of milk it might ever see. "It's the right thing to do and you know it. You're pregnant with my child. In my family, kids have parents who are married. Besides, my child is going to carry my name."

"So this is nothing to do with me," Maura argued. "It's all what you think should be done. Your rights. Your responsibility. Your child. Well go and have *your* marriage. Just don't expect me to participate."

"If you'll quit being so damn stubborn about this, you could think rationally. For the sake of the baby we made, we have to get married. Our kid deserves two parents."

"And he'll have them."

"He?" Jefferson asked.

She sighed. "No, I don't know what sex the baby is and don't want to know."

"Good," he said with a nod. "I like the surprise, too."

A part of her melted at that until she reminded herself that a man who cared for his child wouldn't necessarily care for the child's mother. This was all wrong. All of it. It broke her heart, but damned if she'd sentence either of them to a life without love.

"Do you really think I'll marry you because you think you owe me your protection?" She shook her head and scoffed at the notion. "I'm a grown woman. And this isn't the nineteenth century, Jefferson. Even in Ireland a woman alone can raise her child in peace. And the name Donohue will suit *my* child nicely."

"*Our* child," he corrected, "and there's no reason for you to be alone. I accept my responsibilities, Maura."

"Well, don't I feel warm and treasured. A responsibility. Surely that's a word every woman longs to hear from a man."

"Not five hours ago, you were pissed at me because I *wasn't* taking responsibility. Now I am."

"I don't want you to."

"That's a shame."

The ewes scuttled uneasily in their pens again as if picking up on the tension in the air.

"And," he continued, "once we're married, I'll take you back to Los Angeles. Buy you a big house in Beverly Hills."

That gave her a start. For all her idle dreams of proposals, she'd never once considered leaving the home she loved. But of course he wouldn't want to stay here. He had a life and a business in the States. She suddenly felt bereft for a dream that hadn't had a chance to come true in the first place. "I've a home right here."

"You can sell the farm," he said offhandedly. "You won't have to work so hard anymore. You can sleep in instead of running out in all weather taking care of sheep. You can have a life of luxury. Do whatever you want to do. Travel. Shop."

He seemed so pleased with himself. Didn't he hear how empty the life he described sounded? If she didn't have her farm, her work, who would she be?

"So I'm to give up my home," she said, her voice low, soft, barely making more than a hush in the quiet. "Sell the land my family's worked for generations. And then I'm to go off to Hollywood and spend your money. Is that it? Is that the life you've planned for me?"

Something in her tone warned him. Wary now, Jefferson watched her as she gently set the lamb down in the pen beside her and just as carefully picked up the last one. Her features were blank, but her eyes were glittering darkly.

Jefferson didn't see the problem. He was offering her the kind of life thousands of women would kill for. But maybe it would just take her a minute to see the beauty of it. So he gave her an easy smile and painted an even rosier—to his mind—picture than he had before. "Think about it, Maura. Lazy days sitting by a pool. Going out to lunch with your friends. Having time to play with the baby as much as you want. As my wife, you won't be expected to work every day. You can take it easy for the first time in your life."

"Take it easy. Just live to serve you, is that it?" she asked, tenderly stroking the head of the lamb suckling at the bottle she held.

In the glare of the lights, her features were in sharp relief. She looked calm, which Jefferson knew was a lie. Her eyes were bright and a flush of color filled her cheeks. No matter how tranquil she might appear, she was reining in a temper he'd seen in full force before, up close and personal.

"I don't know what you're getting all worked up over. You're not going to be serving me, for God's sake," he said, wondering why she couldn't see the simple beauty in his plan. "Maura, you're deliberately putting words in my mouth and making this harder than it has to be."

"Oh, am I? So selling my farm, my *home* should be easy? Leaving the life I love, my friends, my family, my *country,* should be a lark?" She shook her head and kept her voice low, not for his sake, he knew, but for the sake of the baby animal she held in her arms. "I'm sorry to tell you, but I've no interest at all in moving to Hollywood, with you or without you. And I can tell you now, you won't be after changing my mind about this no matter what you have your assistant 'arrange.'"

He put a lid on the frustration beginning to churn inside him. It wouldn't help a thing to just hammer back at her. Instead, he had to try to smooth her into seeing things his way. "Just think about it, all right? Before you dismiss it out of hand. You can pick out whichever house you want. It doesn't have to be in the city. We can buy something in the mountains. With some land. Whatever you want. I'll even buy you some sheep if you want and you can hire someone to do the work. I can make your life a hell of a lot easier than it's been so far. What's so wrong with that?"

Silently, he congratulated himself on being able to lay the facts out so tidily. Surely she'd see now exactly what kind of life he could offer her.

"This is how you think to convince me?" she asked, shaking her head in disappointment as she looked at him. "Am I supposed to be impressed with your station?"

"My what?" Confusion bloomed in his mind.

"You use your money so easily. Are people so eager to be purchased by you that you expect it from everyone?"

"Purchased?" he echoed. "I'm not trying to buy you, Maura, I'm trying to give you—"

"Is your life so much better than mine?" she demanded, interrupting him as she put the lamb back in the pen and stood up. "Is this the prince offering the pauper a peek at the finer things in life? Should I be awed? Grateful? Is that it?"

"Prince? Where'd you get that?" This really wasn't going at all well and damned if he could figure out how he'd blown it. But looking into dark blue eyes that were flashing with insult and anger, he knew he had.

"You're speaking to me as you would to a child you're offering a special treat. You with your money and your fine houses and your jets. Did you really think I'd be pleased to have you swoop in and throw money at me?" She lifted the lamb from his arms, returned it to the pen with the others, then snatched the empty baby bottle from him. "Well, I'm not. My life is just exactly that. *My* life. I don't care two spits about your money, just so you know. If you put a torch to it, I wouldn't so much as warm myself by the blaze."

Completely baffled, he only stared at her. "How did this get to be about money?"

"You started it, with your list of temptations, thinking to seduce me away from the home I love." Her eyes were wide and bright and her mouth was set into a furious line. "You with your fine education, pretty suits and private jets. Like all rich men, you wield power however it suits you no matter who is in the way. You've no idea at all how real people live, do you?"

"Real people?" That was enough. He stood up and looked down at her. "I don't have a damn clue what you're talking about. I'm trying to do the right thing here. The right thing for you *and* the baby."

"And I'm to fall in line, am I?"

"This is crazy," he said and grabbed her shoulders, holding her still when she would have bolted. "You're not going to make me feel guilty for offering to give you and my child a better life."

"And who's to say which life is better? You, I suppose?"

"Not better," he corrected. "Easier."

"The easy way isn't always the best way. When I marry, *if* I marry, it'll be for love, Jefferson King—and I've not heard *that* word out of you."

He let her go as if his fingers had been burned. "This isn't about love."

"And that's my point."

He pushed his hand through his hair, then scrubbed that hand across the back of his neck. Finally, when he'd eased the tension in his own chest, he looked at her and said softly, "We weren't in love when we made that child. Why do we need to be in love to raise it?"

She pulled in a slow, deep breath then let it slide from her lungs. "What we shared, neither of us thought to be a permanent thing. It was heat and passion and want. Raising a child is more than that, Jefferson, as well you know."

"There was more to that night than simple desire and you know that."

A long minute slipped past before she nodded. "I do, yes. There was caring between us, I admit that. But affection isn't love."

He couldn't give her what she wanted. He'd done love once before and when it ended, he'd sworn off. Love wasn't in his future plans. Wasn't even on his horizon. Yes, he felt something for Maura, but it wasn't love. He'd been in love before and what was now crowded in his chest, squeezing his heart, was nothing like he'd felt back then.

"There's nothing wrong with affection, Maura. Plenty of marriages have started with less."

"Mine won't," she said simply. Then she squared her shoulders and looked him dead in the eye. "You've done your duty, Jefferson King. You can go back to your life knowing you tried to do the right thing. But I tell you here and now, I won't be marrying you."

Eight

Two days later, Maura felt like a caged animal. Oh, she had the run of the farm, but she remained under the watchful eye of Jefferson King. He was everywhere she turned. She hadn't had a moment to herself since he'd arrived during the last storm. If she stepped outside the house, there he was. If she was feeding the lambs, he turned up to help. If she walked into the village, he went with her.

She'd reached the point now where she was looking for him, expecting him. Blast the man, that had most likely been his plan all along.

Though she'd set the village to rights and her friends and neighbors had once again opened their businesses to the film crew, Jefferson remained in the trailer parked outside her home. He didn't go back to the inn. Didn't move to a comfortable hotel. Oh, no. He stayed in that too-small trailer so that he could badger Maura and tell her what their future was going to be, like it or not.

"What kind of world is it when a woman has to sneak out of her own house?" she murmured to herself as she quietly closed the back door, wincing at the click of the door shutting. All she wanted was some time alone. To think. To feel sorry for herself. To do a little damn whining in private. Was that too much to ask?

Being around Jefferson was wearing on her. Love for him was caught up in her chest and strangling her with the effort to express itself. But how could she profess her love for a man who thought "affection" was enough to build a life on?

She snapped her fingers for King and the dog came running. He sprinted past her, out into the fields behind the farmhouse, chasing his own imagination and the rabbits he continually hoped to find. Maura only smiled. She'd made it. Gotten clean away and so she took a deep breath of the chill spring air. It was a fine day, and no sign of another storm yet, though she knew the good weather wouldn't last. But while it did, she wanted to be outside, with the sunshine spilling down on her and the soft wind blowing through her hair.

And as she walked, she asked herself if she could really have given up this life. Her gaze followed the sweep and roll of the green hills and fields. Stone fences and trees twisted by wind and storm stood as monuments to the only life she'd ever known. Could she have walked away?

If Jefferson had actually meant that proposal. If there had been love rather than duty prompting it. Could she have sold her farm, moved thousands of miles away and given up the cool, clear beauty of the fields for the tangled crush of people?

The answer, of course, was yes. For love, she would have tried it. She might not have sold the farm, but she could have leased the land to a nearby farmer. She could have come back to visit, though the thought of leaving tore at her heart enough to make her stagger a bit. Yes. For love she would have made the effort.

For affection, she would not.

"Are you all right?" a too-familiar deep voice called out from behind her.

She sighed. So she hadn't escaped after all.

Maura didn't turn, didn't slow down, just shouted, "I'm fine, Jefferson, just as I was the last time you asked that question an hour ago."

He caught up with her in a moment's time, her much-shorter legs no match for his long strides. Falling into step beside her, he tucked his hands into the pockets of his jeans and lifted his face to the sun. "Feels good to actually see sunlight for a change."

"Spring's a stormy season," she muttered and told her jittery stomach to calm down. Much to her own chagrin, it wasn't just his constant presence that was making her feel trapped. It was her body's, her heart's reaction to him that was eating away at her.

Even now, her heartbeat was quickening. Being near Jefferson set her blood to boiling and her nerves dancing. His scent. His voice. His nearness. All combined to make her want with an ache she knew would never really leave her.

And to have him always close by was nothing less than torture.

"Where are you off to?"

"Just a walk," she told him with a wave. "Up to the ruins and back."

"That's at least a mile," he pointed out.

"At least." She glanced up at him and smiled at the concerned frown she saw on his face. "I'm used to the exercise, Jefferson. And I don't need a bodyguard here on my own land."

He grinned suddenly. "But I enjoy guarding your body."

She flushed as he'd meant her to and the nerves already scampering through her system went on a rampage. It was probably hormones, she thought. She'd always heard that pregnant women were needier than usual. So it wasn't entirely her fault that at the moment she wanted nothing more than to feel his arms come around her. To have him roll the two of them to the sweet-smelling grass and bury himself inside her.

She took a shallow breath. No. Not her fault at all.

"Shouldn't you be working with your people?" she asked, hoping against hope to convince him to stay at the farm.

"The director knows what he's doing. I don't butt in on his job."

"But you're comfortable butting into mine," she said, smiling to take the sting out of the words.

"You're not working. You're walking."

"You're an impossible man, Jefferson King."

"So I've been told." He bent down, broke off the stem of a wild daffodil and held it out to her.

Charmed in spite of herself, Maura took it and twirled the dainty flower in her fingers. "How long are you staying in Ireland?"

"Eager to see me go?"

No. Of course she didn't say what she was thinking. "There's no real need for you to stay."

"I say there is." He stopped, turned her to face him and deliberately let his gaze slide down to her belly.

He couldn't see the small bump because she was wearing one of her thick Irish sweaters. But she felt him watching her, and felt the possession in that steady gaze and it thrilled her. In some elemental part of her heart and soul, Maura loved the way he looked at her. At the child they'd made.

But even as she admitted that, she had to also admit that it meant nothing. He was concerned for her and their baby. But he didn't love them.

Need without love was an empty thing she wanted no part of. Especially now that she had more than just her own feelings to think of.

"Don't you have work to do, Jefferson? Worlds to buy, movies to make?"

He grinned again and the sudden sweep of emotion on his face was another staggering blow to a woman already distinctly off balance.

"I've been working."

"In your trailer?" She started walking again and looked into the distance for King. She spotted him then, a black blur, racing across the open fields, and she smiled.

"With technology, I could work in a tent," Jefferson told her. "All I really need is a computer, a satellite phone with Internet and a fax machine, which I'm going to be buying today in Westport. You won't mind if I connect it in your house, will you?"

"I don't know if that's a good idea—"

"Good, thanks."

She muttered something under her breath about him being far more stubborn than she could ever hope to be. But a part of her relished what he was doing. Though she had no intention of being nothing more than a problem for Jefferson to solve, it salved her pride some to have him working so hard to persuade her.

"So, how'd the bull get out?"

His question brought a quick stop to her thoughts and it took her a second to realize what he was talking about. She cringed slightly, remembering. "Oh. You heard about that, did you?"

"Davy Simpson's still telling the story," Jefferson said, his grin spreading. "And with every telling, he runs a little faster, the bull gets bigger and meaner and the danger is more desperate."

Maura laughed at the image. "He sounds Irish. We love nothing more than a good storyteller."

"Uh-huh. The bull, Maura. Did you turn it loose on purpose?"

"Of course not!" She might have thought about it, but she never would have done it. In fact, she'd been terrified when the bull escaped, worried that it might actually hurt someone. "No, 'twas an accident entirely. I had Tim Daley in to help me that day. Tim's but sixteen and his mind is forever wandering to Noreen Muldoon."

"I know what that's like," he muttered.

"What was that?"

"Nothing," he said. "Go on."

"There's not much more to the tale. After feeding the bull, Tim, with his mind still on Noreen, forgot to latch the gate behind him and…" She shrugged. "It was an accident, and thankfully no one was hurt. Took me more than an hour to get the bull set away again."

"You put the bull away?" He goggled at her.

"And who else?" she asked. "'Tis my bull, after all."

"Your bull." He dropped his head forward, chin to chest, as he sighed.

"Aye, and his escape was a mistake, though I'll admit that the sheep running mad through your set was not."

He lifted his eyes to her. "That doesn't surprise me."

"I was angry. You were ignoring me."

King bulleted back to them through the grass, gave a happy bark, then spun around and took off again.

"You had a right to be angry," Jefferson said, "but now you're being stubborn just to spite me."

She stopped in the field, with wild daffodils blooming all around her. The sky was a soft blue, with clouds scudding its surface like sailing ships on a placid sea. The wind blew and the grass danced and in the distance, King barked, delighted with his life.

"Is that what you think?" she asked, turning her face up to his so that their eyes met and there could be no secrets between them on this. "Do you believe I'd punish you, myself, my baby all for the sake of spite?"

"Wouldn't you?"

"You don't know me as well as you think, Jefferson, if you believe me capable of that." She plucked windblown hair out of her eyes and stared at him. "I'm doing what's best. For all of us. I won't be a pity wife."

He gaped at her. "Pity wife? Where the hell did that come from?"

She smiled and shook her head. "We both know you've no interest in acquiring a wife. It's the baby worrying you and that speaks well of you. But marrying me is nothing more than feeling sorry for what you see as my 'difficult position.'"

"It's not *pity*," he told her. "It's concern. For you *and* our child."

"Doesn't really matter. I won't leave my home, Jefferson, and try to make myself into the kind of person who would belong in your world. Can't you see it would never work?"

Instinctively, she reached out, laid one hand on his chest and felt the pounding of his heart beneath her palm. "I don't belong in your world any more than you do in mine. We'd make each other miserable inside a year and that would be a punishment on a child who deserves only love."

"That's a great speech, Maura," he said and caught her hand in his. "But it's bull and you know it. This isn't about you not belonging in Hollywood. You know damn well that you'd fit in anywhere if you made your mind up to it."

She flushed and tried to pull free of his grip.

"This isn't about us, anyway. This is about our baby. I won't be an absentee father, Maura." His fingers folded around her hand, holding it fast. "I won't see my own child once a month or for summer vacations."

Clouds covered the sun and the wind sharpened.

"I'm not leaving, Maura. I'm not going to walk away so you'd better get used to the idea of having me around."

"It'll do you no good, Jefferson. I won't change my mind."

"Don't be so sure," he told her with assurance, "and don't say anything you'll have to take back later. It'll only make it that much harder on you."

Astonished at his raw nerve, she said, "You've an ego the size of the moon."

"It's called confidence, babe," he said with a smile that softened his words. Then he bent his head to hers and whispered, "And confidence comes from *always* getting what I want. Trust me when I say, I will have you, Maura. Just where I want you."

Aggravated with him and furious at the way her body was humming with a near-electrical charge, she said, "Why you miserable, softheaded—"

He cut off her diatribe with a kiss that stole her breath, fogged her mind and sent her body sliding away into a sort of dazed confusion. His tongue tangled with hers and Maura groaned at the invasion. It had been too long. Too many empty nights had passed. Too many dreams of him had haunted her.

She surrendered to what she'd missed so sorely. It didn't mean she was changing her mind. It only meant that sometimes, a bit of what you wanted was better than nothing at all.

She wrapped her arms around his neck and gave herself up to the taste of him. The feel of him pressed against her. She'd longed for this. Dreamed of this. And now that it was here, she didn't care if it was only making the situation more difficult. For this one brief moment, she would have him in her arms.

A heartbeat later, though, they jolted apart, with each of them staring down at the slight curve of her belly.

"Did you feel that?" she asked.

"I felt...something." Awed now, Jefferson came closer, laid one hand on her abdomen and Maura covered his hand with her own. She'd thought it was too soon to feel the baby move. But the doctor had told her it would be any day now and that she'd know it when it happened.

And so she had.

A flutter, then a twitch as if her child had wanted to make its presence known while both of its parents were handy. Maura was thrilled, and, looking at Jefferson, she could see he felt the same. It was magic, pure and simple. Life stirring. A life they'd created. What a gift it was to be able to share this moment with the man who'd given her the child. And how sad for each of them that they wouldn't share more.

"It's not moving anymore," Jefferson said in a worried hush. "Why did it stop? Is everything all right? We should go to the doctor—"

She shook her head and smiled. "No doctor, just wait a moment..." She was whispering, as if afraid to have the baby within hear her and stop moving deliberately.

"Maybe...*there!*" A more solid movement this time, with a sort of rippling sensation to accompany it.

Awed, humbled, Maura turned amazed, shining eyes up to his and Jefferson grinned like a fool.

"He moved."

"Aye, she did." Still caught up in the enchantment of

that moment, Maura took a second to notice the change in Jefferson's eyes. They'd gone from amused to aroused and now, they were filled with a dark determination.

"I won't lose this, Maura. Make up your mind to it." He gave her belly a possessive pat, then pulled his hand back. "Whatever it takes. That baby is a King and he'll grow up as one. Whether his mother likes it or not."

"The problem is," Cara was saying, "you're going about this in all the wrong ways."

Jefferson nodded, sat back in his chair and let his gaze scan the interior of the pub. Dark, noisy, with soft lamplight and a dark red glow of the peat fire in the hearth, the place smelled like beer and wet wool. It was raining again, so the Lion's Den was busy. Locals gathered there to have a beer with friends and listen to music. To get out of their own homes for a while. And Jefferson was surrounded by a group of them who were now, it seemed, completely on his side of the situation. All it had taken was for them to find out that he'd proposed and Maura had turned him down.

Just remembering her refusal was enough to churn his guts and have him gritting his teeth. Not once had he imagined that she would say *no*. Should have known Maura would do the unexpected.

"Maura ever was a stubborn girl," Michael said thoughtfully, waving away a customer clamoring for another beer.

"Nonsense," Frances Boyle put in, taking a sip of her tea. "She's a strong little thing is all and knows her own mind."

"She does," Cara said, "but she's also one to take a stand and then not move from it whether or not she should."

"True, true," Michael agreed, with a sad shake of his head. Then he pointed his index finger at Jefferson. "She's a fine woman though, mind, no matter what we who love her say."

"I know." Jefferson was still working on his first beer as advice swarmed around him like ants at a picnic.

It seemed everyone in the village had a theory on how he should be handling the situation with Maura. Not that he was listening to any of them. Since when did a King need help getting a woman?

Since now? a sneaky, annoying voice in the back of his mind whispered to him and Jefferson grumbled under his breath in response. He'd never had to work this hard for anything. Always, when Jefferson King set out to do a thing, it got done. He'd never before run into a solid wall like the one Maura had erected between them and damned if he could figure out how to knock it down.

An ancient-looking man on one of the bar stools offered, "Buy her a ram. That'll do it. A sheep farmer will appreciate fine stock."

Jefferson snorted. Was the way to this woman's heart through her sheep? He didn't think so. Yet as he considered it, he felt a quick stir of something remarkably like anxiety flicker through him. He wasn't trying to get to Maura's heart, was he? No. This wasn't about love. This was about the baby they'd made together, plain and simple. Telling himself that eased him a bit. "I don't see how buying her a new ram for her flock will win me any points."

"It'll win you lots of points with the ewes," someone shouted from the back of the pub.

Laughter erupted at that and Jefferson could only scowl at the whole damn room. Good to know that everyone in the village was having such an entertaining time.

"Great, that's great." What the hell was he doing here? Thousands of miles from home, from family, from sanity. He was sitting in the middle of an Irish Brigadoon trying to make sense of a woman who defied logic at every turn.

What woman in her right mind would turn down a proposal that offered her luxury? Every wish granted? He'd offered her a life of comfort and ease and she'd tossed it back in his face as if he'd insulted her.

Money and power, that's what she'd said, he reminded himself. As if having contacts and financial independence were a bad thing. He didn't understand *real people.* He *was* real people. His brothers were real. What, did she think just because a man had money, he was less than worthy?

"She's the snob," he muttered as the crowd around him continued the argument without his input, "not me."

He'd never judged anyone on the size of their bank balance. He had friends who were mechanics as well as friends who were movie stars. And though his family had money, he hadn't grown up with a silver spoon in his mouth. He'd had to work, just as his brothers had. They'd worked the ranch as kids and as they got older, their parents had told them if they wanted something, they'd have to earn it. So they'd each worked part-time jobs so they could afford secondhand cars and the gas and insurance that went with it.

Hell, he had friends who weren't nearly as well off as his family had been and their parents had paid for everything. The more Jefferson thought about Maura's accusations and generalizations, the angrier he became. He didn't need to excuse his life or make apologies for the way he lived it just because she was being self-righteous.

"You could buy her a new house," someone shouted.

"Or a new roof for the old house. It leaks something fierce in the winter," Frances said.

"Pay them no mind," Cara told him, and drew her chair closer to his. Leaning her forearms on the table, she said, "I can tell you how to win my sister."

He glanced at her and caught the brilliant smile she had aimed at him. Cara, he thought, was the reasonable Donohue sister. She knew what she wanted—to be rich and famous doing what she loved doing—and went after it. She didn't sneer at him for having money. Why would she? It's what she wanted for herself.

With an inward sigh, he asked himself why it hadn't been Cara who made his blood heat. Life would have been a hell of a lot easier.

Instead, he'd become involved with a woman whose head was as hard as the stones in her fields. Just thinking about it irritated him. Damned if he'd take it. Maura thought he was an arrogant, rich American. So he'd prove her right. If she was going to damn him for his money, he might as well make it worth her while.

His mind raced with possibilities. With ideas, notions and plans. And he liked every one of them. Time to pull off the gloves, he told himself. He'd never yet lost an acquisition he was determined to have and this wouldn't be the first time.

"Jefferson? Are you listening?" Cara gave his arm a nudge. "I said, I've a way for you to win my sister round."

"Thanks," he said and stood up. Digging into his pocket, he came up with a sheaf of bills and tossed a few of them onto the table, paying not only for his and Cara's drinks, but for most of those in the bar. "I appreciate it. But this is between me and Maura. And I've got a few ideas of my own."

He left then and never saw Cara shake her head and murmur, "Luck to you, then. I've a feeling you're going to need it."

Nine

Bright and early the next morning, Maura stepped outside, braced for the next confrontation with Jefferson. She glanced around and blew out a breath that misted in front of her face in the cold damp. Dawn was just painting the sky with the first of a palette of colors. Gray clouds rolled in from the sea and she smelled another storm on the air.

"Maybe the coming storm will keep him in the trailer," she told herself, even though she didn't believe it for a moment, and truth be told, she didn't wish for it, either. Even as annoying as the man could become, she liked having him about. Which only went to prove she really was a madwoman.

What woman in her right mind would torture herself so willingly by being around a man she couldn't have?

But what choice did she have? It wasn't as if asking him to leave her be had gotten her anywhere. Jefferson would stay until he left. Period. Nothing she could say would move him along any faster.

He'd made that clear enough.

There would be no way to escape his company and as long as that were true, she could admit, if only to herself, that she was storing this time up in her memories. Etching each moment with him on her brain so that she could draw the images out later, when he really was gone from her.

So she was prepared to have him riding as a passenger in her battered old lorry as she drove up to the high pasture. She'd even thought of a few things to tell him during the long, sleepless night. She was going to be reasonable, patient and firm. The only way to handle a man like Jefferson King. Temper wouldn't do it as the man was immune to her shouts and curses. So she'd use practicality as it was his normal weapon of choice. She could explain to him simply and deliberately that he was wasting his time staying on at the farm. She wouldn't be coerced or convinced to do something she'd no intention of doing.

She smiled to herself, called for King and stepped out of the way when the big dog raced down the hallway and out the back door.

The film crew was already busy in the front, according to the low rumbles of conversation and the sounds of engines and generators. Maura had become so accustomed to the sounds of the film crew that she had the oddest feeling she might actually miss all of the clatter and din they created each day. As she would soon be missing Jefferson, as well.

Her heart ached at the thought, but what else could she do? She couldn't marry him knowing he had no interest in loving her. She couldn't be a man's duty. His *penance*. Her blood ran cold at the thought. What kind of life would that be? For any of them?

King was barking from the far side of the barn where she'd been parking her lorry since the arrival of the film crew. Musings shattered, Maura quickened her steps, wondering what it was that had set her dog off.

She rounded the corner of the barn and stopped dead. Her battered lorry was gone. In its place sat a gloriously new and shiny truck, bright red in color, boasting a massive white bow on its roof. "What? How? When?"

"All very good questions," a deep voice rumbled from nearby.

Maura shot a look at Jefferson, leaning back against the side wall of the barn like a man well pleased with himself. The broad smile on his face told her he was responsible for this—as if she hadn't been able to guess.

"What've you done?"

"I should think that's fairly obvious."

"Where's my lorry?"

"You mean that chunk of rust with wheels?" He shrugged. "I had it towed away an hour or so ago. Surprised you didn't hear it."

She had heard more general clatter than usual this morning to be sure, but she'd become so accustomed to disregarding the hubbub caused by the film crew that she'd paid it no mind at all.

"You—" Maura looked at the new truck and felt herself being seduced by the shining paint and the large, sturdy tires—and even as her heart yearned, she closed herself off to it. "You'd no right."

"I've every right, Maura." He pushed away from the wall and walked toward her. When he was close enough, he ran the flat of his hand over the roof of the new truck and smiled, satisfied. "You weren't just trusting your own life to that accident waiting to happen, remember. You're carrying my baby. No way do I let you ride around in that old truck."

"Let me?" She gasped, pulled in air and prepared for battle. "You don't *let* me do anything, Jefferson King. I don't want your shiny new toy here—"

He smiled knowingly. "Yes, you do."

Oh, it was a hard thing to know that he could read her so easily.

"The nerve you have," she muttered darkly and stepped around him. Her gaze raked the area, hoping that he'd lied and that she'd find her old truck still here, worn and weary from too many years of work. But it wasn't. All that remained was the shiny, tempting lorry, complete with unpatched tires, uncracked windshield and—she peered in the window surreptitiously—lovely black leather seats. Wasn't it a lovely thing?

Not that it mattered, she thought as she straightened up to glare at him again. "What made you think I would be happy about this?"

"Oh, believe me," he said, opening the driver's-side door for her, "I never once thought you'd be *happy*. In fact, I knew you'd look daggers at me. You'll notice it didn't stop me."

He dangled the keys before her as he would a cookie in front of a recalcitrant toddler. "But you're too intelligent to not admit that you needed this truck, Maura."

She glared at him, then the keys and back again. Her shoulders slumped in defeat. "Clever, aren't you? Flatter me so that to turn you down makes me seem like a complete fool."

Clearly pleased with himself, he grinned. "Bottom line is, Maura," he said, "I'm going to take care of you and the baby with your approval or not. So you might as well get used to it."

Was it so wrong, she wondered, to allow him to take care of her? Was it wrong to wish for more? She'd wanted him to acknowledge their child. But she now wanted something she couldn't have. She wanted love. The fantasy.

"And if I don't?"

"You will." He cupped her cheek in his palm.

Maura shivered right down to her toes. How was it that the simple touch of his skin to hers could cause so many different sensations to course through her? And how was it that he didn't share them? That he could shut himself off from the threads of connection that bound them?

He bent his head to hers until his mouth was just a breath away. "You might be stubborn, but you're an intelligent woman and you'll eventually see that I'm right about this."

She sighed and gave him a resigned smile. "So, I'm

intelligent to agree with you and foolish to have my own opinion."

"Pretty much."

That slight curve of his mouth was a weapon, she thought. One he wielded expertly. And she was a willing victim. For heaven's sake, the man had purchased her a lorry and tied a huge bow to it. How was she to argue or stand up against a man who surprised her, not with diamonds or fancy clothes, but with the one thing he knew she not only wanted, but needed?

"You're making this difficult for me."

"Glad to hear it. Now, do you want to take her out for a spin?"

Those keys dangled in front of her face and this time, Maura snatched them. Who was she to fight the inevitable? Besides, if she was to admit the truth, at least to herself, she could say how grateful she was to have a vehicle she felt confident driving. "If you're coming," she told him with a grin, "get in and buckle up."

He did, managing to tear the white bow off the roof as he went and once they were settled, Maura fired the truck up and hooted with glee at the pantherlike snarl of a well-tuned engine. "Isn't she a beauty, then?"

"Yeah," Jefferson said, and when she glanced at him, saw that he was staring right at her as he said, "she really is a beauty."

Jefferson had the marriage license. Now all he needed was the bride. But Maura was showing no signs of weakening. He'd even moved to a hotel in Westport, to give her some space. To prove that he could be as sensitive as the next guy. But did she appreciate it? Hell no. The only thing being "sensitive" had gotten him was three days of missing the woman more than he would have thought possible.

He even missed her damn dog.

Something had to break and it had to happen soon. He couldn't stay in Ireland indefinitely. He had a life, work, waiting for him.

"Which is the only reason I was willing to try Cara's plan," he said into the phone.

"Cara," his brother Justice asked. "Who is she again?"

Jefferson gave an impatient sigh. "Maura's sister. I told you."

"You've been rattling off names of everyone in the village for the last half hour, how'm I supposed to keep them all straight? So Cara is Maura's sister and Maura's the one who turned you down."

Jefferson scowled both at the phone *and* at his younger brother on the other end. "Yes, thanks for reminding me."

Justice laughed and he sounded as if he were in the next room, not sitting at his ranch in California. "Pardon me for enjoying this, but I seem to remember you getting a charge out of watching Maggie make me miserable not so long ago."

"That was different," Jefferson said and walked to the balcony of his suite. Looking out over the river, glistening like quicksilver in the moonlight, he only half listened to the jumble of music drifting to him from a nearby pub. This harbor city, though it was nowhere near as big as L.A., was a far cry from the village of

Craic and the otherworldly quiet that he'd become so used to. Realizing that didn't put him in a better frame of mind. "That was you being miserable. This is *me*."

"Right," Justice said, still laughing, then to someone else added, "He says he *did* propose the right way." He sighed, then said to Jefferson, "Maggie doesn't believe you."

"Tell her thanks for the support." Naturally his sister-in-law would come down on Maura's side. Female solidarity at work again. He'd about had his fill of strong women lately. Especially strong women who were currently making him insane.

"So tell me again," his brother said, "what was Cara's plan?"

Jefferson frowned out at the city. Westport was awake and partying. Lovers walked along the Carrowberg River, pausing now and then for a desperate kiss beneath old-fashioned streetlamps.

It was a great view, he admitted silently. But it wasn't the one he wanted. He preferred the view of the lake out Maura's bedroom window.

Damn it.

Months, he thought, since he'd touched her. Except for that one kiss interrupted by the movement of his child. And that kiss haunted him, waking and sleeping. Need was a clawing, vicious beast crouched inside him, tearing at him constantly. The only way to assuage the beast was to be with her and the only way to be with her was to promise her something he couldn't.

He was a man caught in a web that twisted more tightly about him every time he tried to escape it.

"You still there?" Justice demanded.

"Yeah, I'm here." Jefferson turned his back on the view and said, "What were we talking about? Oh, right. Cara's plan. Well, right about now, she's telling Maura that I'm going to fire her from the movie unless Maura agrees to marry me."

"Are you nuts?"

Since he'd just thought the same thing himself, that was a statement hard to argue with. Jefferson muttered a curse and dropped onto the edge of the bed. "No. Maybe. I don't know."

"Let me get this straight," Justice said in his slow, thoughtful style, "you're planning to use extortion to get the mother of your child to marry you. That about cover it?"

Somehow, this idea sounded worse when Justice said it. "Yeah. That's the plan."

"And you think this move is going to endear you to her?"

He stood up again, feeling a swirl of something that he might have thought was panic if he'd been the kind of man to feel that particular emotion. "I never said that's what I was going for. This isn't about that at all."

"Good thing," Justice murmured.

Jefferson had thought that Justice, of all of his brothers, would understand because of his well-developed sense of honor and loyalty. "This is about marrying the mother of my baby. It's the right thing to do and you know it."

"Sure, if you love her."

Exasperated now, he demanded, "Who said anything about love?"

"I think I just did."

"Well, knock it off." Jefferson paced his bedroom and when he didn't have enough room, left to stride back and forth across the living area. "This isn't about love, Justice, and since when did you become the touchy-feely brother?"

A laugh barked into the phone. "I'm not. I'm only saying that marrying someone *just* because of a baby is a bad idea."

"That's what Maura keeps saying."

"Smart woman." Then to his own wife, Justice added, "Not smarter than you, honey." Then he was back and saying, "Jeff, don't dig yourself a hole you're not gonna be able to climb out of. You can be a part of your kid's life without being married to his mother."

Yeah, he could. Logically, Jefferson knew his brother was right. But he didn't want that. He didn't want to be a part-time father. Be one of the weekend dads that he saw all over Los Angeles. He wanted the same kind of relationship with his own kid that Jefferson himself had had with his father. He wanted a damn family for his child. That made him a bad guy? In whose book?

What was so wrong with wanting to be with his child's mother?

"That's not how it's going to be," he said firmly, feeling his resolve settle in. He'd outmaneuvered studio heads, business moguls and financial wizards. He had no doubt that he could outdo one beautiful sheep farmer.

"Your call," Justice said, "but I've gotta say, I think you're asking for trouble."

"Wouldn't be the first time," he answered ruefully.

Maura was going to be furious. But he'd had to get her here. To talk to him. And Cara's plan had been the only way.

There was a knock at the door and Jefferson's head snapped up like a wolf picking up the scent of its prey. Had to be Maura. No one else would be coming here to see him. And knowing she would show up, he'd left her name at the desk, clearing her for the elevator to his floor. "Can't talk now," he said softly. "She's here."

"I sure hope you know what you're doing, brother," Justice told him. "Let me know what happens."

With Justice's less-than-hopeful words ringing in his ear, Jefferson tossed his cell phone onto the coffee table and walked to the door. He hardly noticed the lush room. It was much like every other suite in every other hotel he'd ever stayed in. Crystal vases filled with colorful flowers standing on gleaming tables. Comfortable chairs drawn up to a gas-fed hearth where carefully monitored flames leaped and danced.

He moved quickly, but even with that, three sharp, impatient knocks sounded out again before he reached the door.

When he opened it, Maura rushed right past him, anger radiating off her in thick waves. And all he could think was, *God, she's beautiful.*

She wore dark-wash jeans and a red sweater beneath a black coat she peeled off and tossed across a chair the moment she was in the room. Her long black hair was windblown and there was hot color in her cheeks.

"You lying, sneaky, treacherous, no good…"

"Hello to you, too." He closed the door and faced her,

determined to play this out. He'd set his course with Cara, so he'd hold true to it until he got what he wanted.

Maura's complete surrender.

"Don't you hello me, Jefferson King," she shot back, lifting one hand to shake her index finger at him. "How can you stand there looking so smug and proud of yourself? What kind of man is it to do what you've done?" Briefly, she threw both hands up in disbelief. "I don't even have the words for it. How could you? How could you be so hard? So mean? So…"

"Cruel?" he helped out. "Callous? Uncaring?"

"Aye," she snapped. "All of those and more, though 'tis clear to me you've not the decency to be ashamed of it."

She was more furious than he'd ever seen her before and that gave him pause to wonder if maybe Justice hadn't been right. But it was too late now, he told himself. He'd set a course and he wasn't a man to back off just because the road got a little bumpier than expected.

"I see Cara gave you the news."

Maura bristled. Since the moment her sister had come to her at the farm, crying over an opportunity lost, Maura had been able to think of nothing else but coming here and facing Jefferson with what he'd done. She'd driven into the city like a madwoman, steering the lorry he'd given her down the familiar roads in a blind rage. The desk clerk had taken one look at her and had pointed out the elevators, obviously unwilling to take a chance on trying to stop her. A wise choice on his part.

Now that she was here, the fury riding within was bubbling to the surface. Jefferson's casual attitude wasn't soothing her any. He looked smug and sure of himself as he watched her. So much so she felt a distinct urge to kick him. Hard. And only barely resisted. Her entire body was shaking with temper and disappointment and hurt.

He'd shown a side of himself she'd never guessed at. How had she not seen what he was capable of before? How had she trusted this man? Given herself to him? Thought herself in love with him?

She looked up into pale blue eyes and saw only cold distance glittering back at her. As if he were standing right in front of her, a part of him was sealed off from this confrontation. As if his mind and heart had taken a step aside, leaving only the ruthless businessman in their place. For the first time since she'd known him, Maura saw his fierceness. The steely resolve of a powerful man who would do whatever he must to ensure he got exactly what he wanted.

Tension coiled and crackled in the air between them. She could hardly draw a breath for the iron band tightening around her chest. Her heart.

"You've gone too far," she told him, her voice hardly more than a scrape of sound.

"I don't know what you mean."

"Don't pretend ignorance. It insults us both," she said and tossed her purse atop her coat. "You've fired Cara from your movie."

He shrugged and walked past her toward one of the twin couches set in the middle of the luxurious room. "She wasn't working out."

She watched him go, vaguely noticing how at home he was in the lush surroundings. How this place, this life seemed to suit him and how it also seemed to mark the difference between them. But Maura pushed that thought aside and concentrated on her reason for being there.

"That's a lie. You told me yourself you thought Cara a fine actor. So it's not her work you've a problem with. It's *me*. You think to use my family to get my cooperation. That's the mark of a small man, Jefferson King."

"You're wrong," he said, whirling back around, returning to her, coming close enough that she could see his eyes were now shining with an inner light that blazed with banked temper and conviction. "It's the mark of a man who goes after what he wants any way he has to. I warned you I wouldn't give up. I'm Jefferson King. And a King does what he must to get what he wants."

"No matter the cost?" She searched his eyes for some sign of the man she'd fallen in love with, but he wasn't there.

"I told you going in, Maura. You're carrying my child. I'll do whatever it takes to make sure he's taken care of."

She knew, logically, that his determination to care for his child was a good thing. After all, not every man would care, would he? But Jefferson used his wealth and privilege as a club, swinging it wildly, knocking aside whoever might stand in the way of his goals and that she didn't understand. Or forgive.

"You've no right to draw Cara into this," she said, silently congratulating herself on the calm, reasonable tone of her own voice. "It's between us, Jefferson. No one else."

"You brought her into this," he said, "when you wouldn't see reason."

"And because I don't agree with you, out come the bully tactics?"

He winced, or she thought he had. The expression was gone so quickly, she couldn't be sure. "You wanted this the hard way, Maura. Not me."

"I only want—"

"What?" He grabbed her, big hands coming down on her shoulders, holding her in place. "What is it you *really* want, Maura?"

Something he had no interest in hearing, she thought sadly, staring up into his eyes and finally, *finally,* seeing the man she knew and loved looking back at her. He was as torn up by all of this as she was, Maura knew that. She felt his frustration as surely as she did her own.

And oh, what a tricky question he'd asked her. *What did she really want?* She wanted the fairy tale. What she wanted was to love him and be loved in return. To marry Jefferson King and make a family. She wanted it so badly, in fact, that she was ashamed to admit even to herself that she'd recently begun to actually reconsider his pitiful proposal. If she married for the sake of her child, it would be foolish, she knew. But oh, the temptation of saying yes. Of living with him. Being with him.

Yet even in the midst of wild dreams, she knew also that if she allowed herself to weaken on that point, she would, eventually, regret it.

So she kept those wants locked away inside her and said only, "I want you to give Cara her job back."

"And you'll do what for me in return?"

Temper drained away to be replaced by a sorrow that went soul-deep. She lifted her hands to his, linking them, as she looked into his eyes. "Not what you're hoping. I won't marry you for the sake of the child, Jefferson. I can't do that. Not to myself *or* to you. Sentence all three of us to half a life? What would be the good in that?"

He dropped his forehead to hers. "You're as thick-headed as I am," he murmured.

"We are the pair, aren't we?"

Lifting his head again, he met her gaze and said, "She has her job back."

"Thank you," she said, mildly surprised that it was taken care of so easily. Over so quickly. Her body was still buzzing from a combination of anger and desire and now…she had to leave.

But his hands on her shoulders were hard and tender and warm. Heat from his skin seeped into hers, chasing away the chill she'd been carrying for what felt like forever. She'd held strong against her own wants and needs, thinking that to be with him now would only make the parting that much harder.

Yet she was deceiving no one. Their parting would devastate her no matter the circumstances. Would one more night together really add to the pain? Or would it be an easing of sorts?

As if he could read her mind, he pulled her closer, wrapping his arms around her, burying his face in the curve of her neck. His lips on her skin sent ripples of awareness coursing through her. His hands running up and down her spine caused every cell in her body to jump up and shout for joy.

Her heart ached, her body burned and her mind knew it could never stand against heart and soul and body, so it quietly closed up shop and allowed Maura to only *feel*. For this, she didn't want to think. Didn't need to think.

This, what lay between them, was good and strong and so powerful the only thing either of them needed was their instincts, drawing them together.

"I've missed you," he said, lifting his head again, kissing her forehead, her cheeks, the tip of her nose. "I didn't want to," he admitted next, "but I did. You're in me, Maura, and now I need to be in you."

"I need that, as well." She sighed, lifting her mouth for his. He claimed a kiss, moving his mouth over hers with an aching tenderness that made her want to weep with the beauty of it.

There was a gentleness in his touch that took the hard edge off the need pulsing between them. Maura felt his quiet control and sighed for it.

Here was home, she thought, her mind sliding into a wonderfully hazy oblivion as emotion and sensation took the forefront. Here was where she wanted to be. Yearned to be. In his arms. Always.

He skimmed one hand up, into her hair to the back of her neck. He held her head steady while his mouth plundered hers and she gave herself up to the amazement flooding her system.

How had she thought she could go the rest of her life without feeling this? Experiencing this? How had she lasted months without the caress of his hands on her skin? And how would she make it through the rest of her life without him?

"Be with me," he whispered, already leading her through the seating area to the bedroom beyond.

He moved her as if they were dancing, one arm around her waist now, one hand holding hers close to his heart. She looked up into his eyes as the room slowly whirled around her and knew she'd dance anywhere with him.

"Be with me." She repeated his words to her and his swift intake of breath, coupled with a flash deep in his eyes, were all that told her how she had touched him.

Ten

In the bedroom, she saw the balcony doors were open, a soft, cold breeze sliding into the room, ruffling lacy white sheers. From the street below came the muted sounds of pub music, riding the wind. One lamp in the room was on, spilling enough golden light to chase away shadows.

Then he stopped alongside the wide bed and helped her out of the sweater she wore. Beneath was a plain white shirt that he quickly unbuttoned and tossed aside. He unhooked her bra with a surprising agility and then dispensed with her boots, jeans and underwear. In moments, she was unclothed before him and feeling just a bit hesitant about her changing body.

He hadn't seen her naked since the night they'd made their child. And since then, she'd gained a little weight and her belly was rounded with the growing baby.

She watched him as he gazed at her and she saw his eyes soften when he looked at her abdomen. Suddenly uneasy, she said, "I've changed, I know."

"Yes," he said, lifting his gaze to hers even as he laid the flat of one hand against the mound of their child. "You're even more beautiful."

"Oh," Maura told him, a smile curving her mouth, "you've the gift of the Irish for saying exactly the right thing at the right time."

He smiled, too, then said, "You're shivering. I'll close the window."

"No, don't," she told him. "The weather isn't what's making me tremble, Jefferson. It's need, is all. Need for you."

He swallowed hard and reached past her to pull back the quilt and sheets covering the bed. "Get under the covers anyway," he said and waited until she had.

Then hurriedly, he stripped out of his own clothes and joined her under the down comforter. Maura moved into him and instinctively aligned her body with his. The slide of his skin against hers felt so right. So perfect. She sighed in contentment, shifting her hands over his broad, muscled back, up to encircle his neck and then plunging her fingers into his hair, drawing his head to hers.

Lips met, tongues entangled and breath was exchanged for breath. They came together as silently, as magically as if they'd been born for this and only this.

Sensations rose up and crashed inside her and Maura could only hold on to him as he covered her body with his. He parted her thighs, she lifted her hips to welcome him and in the soft light of that luxurious room, he claimed her as he had before. He slid into her heat, her depths and in the taking, gave. In the giving, took. Hearts beat as one. Bodies moved together in perfect rhythm and sighing groans filled the air like blessings.

He kissed her as the first wave of completion caught her and she cried out his name as her soul shattered under his tender hands. Only moments later, she held him to her as his body released into hers and he collapsed atop her.

In the quiet stillness, minutes or hours could have gone by.

All Maura knew was that she didn't want this night to end. Didn't want to lose Jefferson. Yet, she couldn't think of a way to keep him. Not and keep her pride, as well. Could the man not see that he loved her? She felt it in his touch. Saw it in his eyes. Sensed the gentleness beneath the passion and knew that it didn't come only from desire. From lust. There was feeling there—and it was more than affection.

Yet, he pulled back from the mention of three small words. Held himself safely distanced from the risk of love. What was it, she wondered, that made him so determined to avoid giving his heart?

As she struggled with troubling thoughts, Jefferson rolled to one side, drawing her with him, cradling her closely against his body. Her head on his shoulder, his arms around her, he lay in the lamp-lit dark and said nothing.

How long could they go on like this? she thought desperately. How long before they tore each other's hearts to shreds and there was nothing left for either of them?

He trailed one hand idly down the length of her until

he could cover her abdomen with his palm. She sighed at the gentleness of his touch even as she remembered the fire in his passion. He rested his hand on her, fingers splayed, and she felt him take a breath and hold it—waiting for his child to move again.

As if to please its father, the baby obliged with a tiny kick that brought a smile to Maura's face despite unshed tears burning her eyes.

"He's strong already," Jefferson mused and she could hear pride ringing in his tone.

"Aye, soon he'll be trying to kick his way out," she said, surprised at the thickness of her voice.

Jefferson turned his head to look at her. "You're crying. Why are you crying?"

"'Tis foolish, never mind."

He levered himself up on one elbow and looked down at her. His eyes were the palest blue and in the darkness, they almost seemed to glow with some inner light. Maura stared up into them, then lifted her hand to smooth his hair back from his forehead.

"Are you all right?" he asked. "I didn't hurt you or the baby, did I?"

"You didn't, no," she told him, easing the fear she saw in his gaze. "I'm feeling a bit weepy these days is all."

"That's not it," he said, his mouth firming, a muscle in his jaw twitching as he gritted his teeth. "Don't lie to me, Maura."

"'Tisn't a lie," she countered, pushing at his chest to shove him away. But it was like trying to push at the walls of her barn. "I *am* weepier these days. A woman's hormones are all over the place when she's carrying."

"Fine, not a lie. But not the complete truth."

"Ah, Jefferson," she said on a sigh, "what difference does it make?"

"The difference is, we at least owe each other honesty, don't we?"

"You're right," Maura mused. "Honesty would be best. Especially now."

"So tell me why you're crying."

This time when she gave him a little nudge, he yielded and Maura pushed herself up into a sitting position on the bed. Tugging the quilt and sheets up over her breasts, she glanced out the window at the shining night beyond. When she spoke, her voice was hushed.

"I was only thinking of how much I'll miss you when you go."

"You don't have to," he said and he, too, spoke in a whisper. "You can come with me."

"We've been over this," she said, pushing her hair back from her face with both hands. "The baby is not a reason to wed."

"That's not what I'm saying this time," he told her and instantly won her full attention.

Maura stared at him and tried to read what she saw in his eyes, but the shadows in the room were too deep. "What are you saying, then?"

"I've been thinking about this, Maura," he told her as he edged off the bed, snatched up his jeans and tugged them on. He didn't bother to button them, just stalked across the room to her side of the bed and stood there, looking down at her. Arms folded across his chest, legs braced as if for battle, he said, "What just happened between us sort of solidified those thoughts. We're good together. Right. And you know it."

"I do," she agreed, wondering where he was going with this. Trying not to hope, but failing miserably, she clung to the dream in her heart and waited for him to continue.

"Good. I'm glad you can see that. It'll make what I have to say that much easier."

"What is it you're getting to?"

"In a minute," Jefferson said, wanting to get everything between them out in the open now. "We said we'd be honest—"

She only waited.

He blurted a truth he hadn't planned on telling her. "I didn't fire Cara."

"What?"

"It was her idea," he said quickly, giving her a smile he hoped would head her temper off before it got a foothold. "The idea was to make you so angry that you'd agree to marry me so that I'd take her back on the film."

She hissed in a breath. "Of all the low, despicable…"

"I know. I've heard them all." He leaned down to kiss her, quick, hard, cutting off her thread of insults before she could really get going. Then, easing back, he said, "Now, continuing with the honesty vein…marry me, Maura."

Clearly still angry over the deception, she narrowed her eyes on him. "We've been over this until the path is beaten down, Jefferson. I won't marry you for the child's sake."

"Hear me out at least. This isn't about the baby. This is about us."

"It is?"

He had her attention now, he told himself, judging by the interested gleam in her eyes. And as he relished the fact that he was back in charge, he warmed to his theme. He'd faced down hostile mergers before. This was no different. He'd convince her that he knew what was best and they'd go on with their lives.

Deliberately, Jefferson slid one hand down her warm, curvy body and settled his palm atop their child in a possessive move she couldn't miss. That simple action linked them, made the three of them a unit. As they should be.

He had to convince her. Had to make her see. He wouldn't lose this. Wouldn't lose her because of her own stubborn pride or unwillingness to listen to reason. Being with her again had brought it all home to him. He'd lay it all out for her, exactly as it had just popped into his mind and then she'd see that he was right.

The perfect solution.

"What is it you have in mind, then?" she asked.

"I'm proposing a marriage of convenience," he started and when she opened her mouth to speak, he hurried on, determined to have his say completely. "We're good together and you've already admitted it, so there's no point in denying it. The sex is great and we actually like each other."

"Like," she repeated.

"Exactly." He smiled at her. "Marrying is just a good business decision. Everyone wins this way, Maura. You. Me. The baby. We know going in exactly what kind of marriage we have so there're no misconceptions. No room for hurt feelings or shattered illusions."

"Convenience," she said softly. "Marriage as a convenience."

He didn't like the hesitation in her voice, but chalked it up to the fact that she hadn't had time to fully realize all of the advantages he was offering her. Well, she was a smart woman. She'd work it out and come to the same conclusion he had, given enough time. "Just think about it for a minute."

"Oh, I am," she assured him with a small shake of her head. "And while I'm thinking, perhaps you can tell me, Jefferson, just where does love come into this arrangement between us?"

Everything in him went cold and still. He felt himself shutting down, closing off. Hadn't he couched his proposal in terms that would guarantee love wouldn't be able to rear its ugly head? He couldn't have been more clear about it. Irritation flowed through him, but he couldn't look away from her eyes, swimming with emotion.

"Why does it have to come into it at all?"

"Marriage without love would be a cold and empty sort of thing, don't you think?"

"It doesn't have to be," he argued.

Why was she making this more difficult than it had to be? Damn it. He'd laid it out for her. Explained how he felt and what they could have. But instead of being reasonable, she was going to make him confess everything. Force him to hurt her by telling her exactly why he couldn't give her what she wanted.

He blew out an impatient breath and stood up, turning his back on her to walk to the balcony and stand in the breeze still rushing in. He'd stayed too long in this place, Jefferson thought. If he'd left a couple of weeks ago, he could have avoided this. Could have spared both of them this.

But he hadn't been able to leave her. Now they'd both pay for that indulgence. He stared out at the night for a long moment before finally turning his gaze back to her.

She looked ethereal, there in his bed. Her hair a wild tangle, her mouth still swollen from his kisses. Lamp-light and shadow played on her features and her eyes shone as she watched him. He steeled himself against the well of emotion threatening to choke him.

"I can't love you, Maura," he finally said softly.

"Can't? Or won't?"

"Can't." He folded his arms across his chest in a classic pose of self-defense. "I was married before."

She went absolutely still.

He didn't like thinking about it. Didn't like remembering old pain. But there was no choice but to speak of it.

"Her name was Anna and she was the love of my life," he said, needing to have this said aloud, so that Maura could understand what was keeping him from her. "We were too young to get married, but we did anyway." He smiled a bit at the memories rushing into his mind. They were soft now, hazy with time and distance, but there was still an innocence and sweetness to them that tugged at his heart.

"What happened?"

"She died."

"I'm sorry."

He nodded. "She was only twenty-one. I was a year older. It was a stupid accident. Anna was painting our bedroom. She fell off the ladder. Hit her head." He was quiet for a moment or two, recalling how she'd brushed it off, said she was fine. "She seemed all right. Wouldn't go to the doctor. Said it was silly to make a big deal over a little bump. She died in her sleep that night. The autopsy found a hemorrhage in her brain."

"That's terrible, Jefferson," Maura said softly. "I'm so sorry for you and for her."

Mentally, he pulled away from the past and said briskly, "When she died, I swore that I'd never love another woman the way I loved her."

She drew in a long, deep breath but still remained silent. He hoped she understood. Hoped she could now see that what he was offering her was the best he had inside him. This was it. Take him as he was, or they would have nothing.

Walking back to her, he stood beside the bed and said, "I want to marry you, Maura. Not just because of the baby, either. I like being with you. I like having you beside me at night. I think we could make a good life together."

Still she was quiet and the shadows had deepened so that he couldn't even read her eyes now.

"I'm offering you my name," he told her. "I'm offering to build a life with you and raise our child. But don't expect love from me, Maura, because I won't love you. Ever."

The distant music from the pub on the street below sounded overly loud in the strained silence. Time ticked past in long, drawn-out seconds.

"Without love, we have nothing," she finally said and Jefferson's hopes crashed and burned at his feet.

Instinctively, he reached for her, but she scooted off the opposite side of the bed, avoiding his touch. Moving quickly, she gathered up her clothes and started pulling them on.

"Maura," he said, giving himself points for the calm restraint he heard in his own voice, "if you'll just be reasonable about this…"

"Reason," she muttered, buttoning up the front of her shirt with shaking fingers. "The man wants reason when what he's speaking is nonsense."

"Nonsense?" He came around the edge of the bed and took her upper arm in a hard grip. "I'm trying to be honest with you. To tell you exactly who and what I am so that there'll be no more misunderstandings. I don't want to hurt you anymore, Maura. Can't you see that?"

She yanked herself free of him, stepped into her boots and shook her hair back from her face. "You're not being honest, Jefferson. Not with me or yourself, come to that. You're hiding from the future by staying in your past. And that's cheating not just me, but yourself of what you might find if you'd open your eyes."

"I'm not hiding," he said in a snarl, insulted that she would take what he'd offered and throw it back at him. "I don't hide from anything."

"And the truly sad part?" she asked quietly. "It's that you actually believe that."

She pulled her sweater over her head, scooped up her hair and drew it free to lie on her shoulders. Jefferson's hands itched to touch it. His whole body yearned to have her back in that bed. Back to where they'd been together just a few short minutes ago.

She stalked from the bedroom into the living area and Jefferson was just a step or two behind her. "Where are you going?"

She sighed. "I'm going home, Jefferson. As you should."

"What?"

Maura turned to look at him and she knew her aching heart had to be shining in her eyes, for the pain was staggering. She'd had hope, until tonight, that he might wake up and see that love was staring him in the face. She'd hoped he might let himself take the tumble. See what they could have together if only he'd allow himself to love.

Now, that hope was ground into dust. The man was just thickheaded enough to cling to a promise made by a heartsick boy so long ago. And if she couldn't have all of him, she'll not have him at all.

"Do you think this is what your Anna would have wanted for you?"

"We'll never know that, will we? Because she's *dead*." His voice was tight and hard.

"And so are you, inside, dead as your lost love," Maura told him. "The difference is, I believe if she were given the choice, your Anna would choose *life*. You've chosen to stay in the shadows and there's nothing anyone but you can do about it."

His features were as remote as if his face had been carved from granite. "You wanted honesty. I gave it to you."

"So you did. I thank you for your offer, Jefferson King, but I won't marry without love. Or at least the hope of it."

"Maura, you're being ridiculous."

"I don't think so," she told him, keeping her voice even and steady despite her urge to shout the roof down and howl out her misery. "I'm sorry for you, Jefferson. I truly am."

"I don't want your pity," he snapped.

"That's a shame, for you have it." She picked up her coat, slung her purse over one shoulder and said, "If you won't let go of your past, what chance do we have of making a future? No, Jefferson, 'tis better this way, you'll see."

"How is this better?"

She walked to the front door, put her hand on the knob and paused for one last look at him. Instead of answering his question, she said, "You can come and see our child anytime you're able. You'll always be welcome, though you won't have me."

"Maura, think about what you're doing."

"I have. And I also think you should go home now, Jefferson. Back to Los Angeles and the empty life you're clinging to with such steadfastness."

"My life's not empty," he countered as she opened the door and stepped through. "But you're right about one thing, Maura. It's time for me to go home."

She watched him walk toward her, his features a study in blank isolation. Maura curled her fingers into fists to keep from holding out a hand to him. It would change nothing, only prolong this wretched ending to all of their possibilities.

Maura wanted to brace herself for the pain that was building within but all she could do was wait for it.

Impossible to prepare for a crippling misery that she knew would be with her for the rest of her life. But damned if she'd let him see that he had so much power over her heart, her mind, her very soul.

He wouldn't learn from her that she loved him and always would. No, she'd send him back to his life, his world, as cleanly as she had before. And as before, she would take comfort in knowing that he would think of her—and their child—often.

His eyes were cool as glass as he looked down at her. "I'll be by in the morning to see you before I leave."

How businesslike he sounded. As if they were no more than acquaintances who'd happened upon each other. Already he was stepping away from her, closing the door on all they'd found, all they might have shared. And she wondered how it was she could love a man so bone-deep foolish.

"That'll be fine," she told him smoothly. "I'll expect you then."

"Good night, Maura," he said and shut the door as she stood there.

"Goodbye, Jefferson," she murmured as the first tears fell.

The pain lasted a week.

Maura had cried until she'd no more tears left in her body. She'd wallowed in her despair until even her sister, Cara, had lost all patience with her. She'd watched the last of the film crew pack up and leave when their work was done, severing that final thread connecting her to Jefferson.

Every night she dreamed of him and every day she missed him. Finally though, anger jostled her out of her self-pitying stupor. She hadn't actually believed he would *leave*. Maura had left the hotel convinced that when he came to say goodbye, they would instead have a good clearing-the-air fight, followed by spectacular sex and pledges of eternal love.

Instead, the tricky man had come to her home cool, detached, handed her a bloody sheaf of papers, then walked away, as calm as you please. He hadn't even looked back at her, the low skunk of a man, she thought with a hearty stomp in the mud.

The fury that had been growing inside her for the last couple of days seemed to explode all at once. Blast Jefferson King, she saw him everywhere she went. His voice haunted her home. His smile chased her across fields and even driving into town was no escape, as she was sitting in the bright red lorry he'd purchased for her.

He'd invaded her life, upset the balance and then disappeared. "What kind of man does that?" she asked aloud of no one.

Automatically, she checked the latch on the barn door where the ewes and their lambs were safe from wind and rain. Then continuing on toward the house, she asked King, "Am I that forgettable, then? Is it so easy to make love with me, then say 'thanks very much, bye now'?"

The dog whined in response and she appreciated the support. "No, you're right. I bloody well am not forgettable. The man's crazy for me and doesn't even know it."

She remembered everything about that last night with Jefferson and hoped to Heaven he was remembering, too. And hoped it was tearing him apart. But even if she were sure that he was being tortured by the memories of what he'd tossed away, it wouldn't be enough to ease the emptiness inside.

"How does he dare turn his back on me? On *us*?" She muttered dark and vile curses, all aimed at his handsome head, as she stomped through the farmyard, King dancing at her heels. "What gives him the right to say 'tis over? Am I to listen to him and go away quietly, like some schoolgirl afraid of punishment?"

The dog barked and Maura nodded as if the beast had agreed with her. She crossed the yard, ran up the short flight of steps to the back porch and kicked off her Wellington boots. As if in sympathy with her dark emotions, it had been raining steadily for the last few days and the farm was hardly more than a river of mud. King loved it, of course, which was why she also kept an old towel and a tub of water by the back door.

"In you go," she ordered and the big dog daintily stepped through the water and out the other side. Maura dried his paws, tossed the towel over the porch railing, then opened the door, letting them both into the warmth of the kitchen.

"Thinks I'll just sit with my mouth shut, does he? Accept what he says as a declaration from the mount and go on with my life?"

She took the teakettle to the sink, filled it with water and set it on to boil. As the flames licked at the base of the copper pot, she tapped her fingers impatiently against the stove top. "And why shouldn't he think that, Maura, you great idiot? Didn't you walk away, as well?

Didn't you let him slip through your fingers without ever once telling him that you love him?"

Lowering to admit as it was, Maura had to concede that she'd allowed her own pain and disappointment to color her responses to Jefferson on that last night. If she hadn't been so stunned by his announcing that as he'd loved once he couldn't love again, she might have stood her ground. She might have told him exactly what she thought of a man too afraid to love. She might have—

"And this is doing no good at all. Not for either of us. What good is it to shout the ceiling down when he's not here to listen?"

He had to listen, she thought. She had to *make* him listen. Her thoughts slammed to a stop and she whirled around, staring at the yellow phone on the counter.

Before she could think better of it, she walked directly to the drawer by the telephone and pulled out the four sheets of paper Jefferson had left with her.

Phone numbers and addresses of everyone he could think of, all neatly typed and printed out. He was nothing if not efficient, her Jefferson—and he *was* her Jefferson—the stubborn mule of a man.

She looked at the list. His cell-phone number, numbers for his brothers, his cousins, his office, his home, his vacation home in the mountains and even for the places he kept in London and Paris. He'd said that last morning that he didn't want her to have trouble contacting him again.

The man was a font of information when he wanted to be, she mused, running the tip of one finger down the list.

She wouldn't be calling Jefferson directly though,

she told herself. No. What she had to say to him could only be said in person so that she could knock some sense into his head if need be. So that left her with at least three choices. She picked the one whose name seemed the most familiar and dialed his number.

When a gruff voice answered, she said, "Hello. Is this Justice King, brother to Jefferson?"

A long pause, then, "It is. I'm guessing from your accent that you must be Maura."

"I am," she said, grateful to know that at least the dunderheaded man she loved had spoken of her to his brothers. "I've something to say to that great lout of a man, personally. I was wondering if you could help me."

There was a low, deep chuckle that rumbled through the phone line and then Justice answered, "You planning a trip to L.A.?"

"I am, yes," she said, plans forming in her mind even as she spoke. "As soon as I can get a plane ticket."

"No need for that," Justice told her. "When can you be ready to leave?"

Steam shot from the spout of the teakettle and Maura walked to turn off the stove. While she did, she decided on whom she would ask to take care of the farm for a few days and when she had it set in her mind, she said, "I can have things arranged by tomorrow night."

"Then pack a bag, Maura," Justice said. "I'll have a King jet waiting at the airport for you. All you'll need is a passport."

She gasped, surprised at the generosity of the offer. "'Tisn't necessary," she told him, "I was only calling

you to see if you could arrange to have Jefferson somewhere we can talk."

Justice laughed and she enjoyed the sound, feeling
as though she had an ally in this oh-so-personal battle.

"Maura, trust me. Sending the jet is a selfish move.
My brother's been in a black mood since he got back
from Ireland. My wife tells me there's a reason for it and
she thinks it's you."

She grinned now, knowing that Jefferson was as miserable as her. "Isn't that a lovely thing to say," she
murmured.

Justice laughed again. "Oh yeah, you and my Maggie
are going to be great friends. I can see it already." There
was a pause and then he said, "So, once we get you here,
what's your plan?"

Maura leaned back against the counter and told Jefferson's brother exactly what she had in mind. Between
the two of them, they refined their strategies. By the
time she hung up, Maura felt her self-assurance slide
back into place, for the first time in days.

"Jefferson King, you've no idea what's in store for
you."

Eleven

"What was so damned important I had to come all the way out to the ranch?" Jefferson slammed his car door and faced down his brother.

"Just a few things we need to discuss," Justice told him. "But first, I've got to get that yearling back in his stall."

He followed Justice out to the paddock and watched as his brother hopped the rail fence and loped across the dirt enclosure without so much as a limp. Months after the accident that had brought Justice and Maggie back together again, his brother's leg was as good as new.

"Hey, you're here!"

Jefferson turned around to spot his youngest brother, Jesse, headed toward him. A former professional surfer, Jesse was a successful businessman now, running King

Beach, surf and sportswear. And by rights, he should have been in Morgan Beach. So what was he doing at the ranch? Suspicion flitted through Jefferson's mind, but he couldn't quite put his finger on what the trouble might be, so he let it go. For now.

"What are you doing here?" Jefferson asked, shifting a glance to Justice, who was taking a young horse by the bridle and leading him off to the barn.

"Bella wanted to visit with Maggie, so I tagged along. What are you doing here?" Jesse grinned as he said it. "Who's making movies if you're out wandering the ranch?"

"I'm not wandering. Justice said he needed to talk to me about something. And where are Maggie and Bella?"

Jesse shrugged. "Shopping?"

Wariness had him turning for the barn. Something was definitely up. The wives were gone. Both of his brothers here. Grinding his back teeth together, Jefferson headed for the barn. Stepping into the shadowy interior, with Jesse right on his heels, Jefferson called out, "Justice, are you going to tell me what you wanted to see me about?"

Justice ignored him as he led the horse into a stall. Once the task was finished, though, he faced him and smiled. "Jesse and I thought it was time we got you out here to talk about what the hell is wrong with you."

"I knew you were up to something the minute I saw Jesse here." He looked from one brother to the other in disgust. "This I wasn't expecting. You're trying to tell me this is an intervention?"

"Call it whatever you want," Jesse told him, slapping

his back. "The time has come, big brother, to stop acting like a bastard and tell us what's going on."

"Screw this," Jefferson said, turning on his heel to walk to his car. "I'm going back to the office. You two can sit around and psychoanalyze each other."

"No one at the office wants you there," Justice told him in his slow, patient voice.

That stopped him. Jefferson glared at each of his brothers in turn. "You're telling me they were in on this setup?"

"Joan thanked me," Jesse said on a laugh. "Seems you've been miserable to deal with since you got home."

He couldn't argue with that, Jefferson thought, pushing one hand through his hair in a gesture fraught with frustration.

Back a week now and nothing was the same. He'd expected to come home, slide into work as if he'd never been gone and pick up the threads of his life. But that hadn't happened. He was restless. Dissatisfied. He felt it and couldn't find a way to combat it.

His mind continued to drift toward Ireland. The green hills, the farmhouse.

Maura.

Compared to what he'd left there what he'd returned to was lacking. That he hadn't expected. He'd always liked his life, damn it. So why then did Los Angeles and the job he loved seem suddenly to be nothing more than plastic and illusion? Why did he feel alone surrounded by hundreds of people? Why was he waking in the middle of the night, reaching for Maura?

He knew why, of course. The simple truth was he

wasn't the same man anymore. The bright sunlight and hot Santa Ana winds felt alien to him and his heart yearned for what he'd lost.

"So." Justice stopped for a private word with his foreman before steering Jefferson to the ranch house. "You going to talk to us about this or what?"

"Yeah," he said. "Yeah, I'm coming."

Justice's study was a man's room. Leather chairs, shelves lined with books and a massive desk against one wall. Of course, the toys strewn across the floor marked the fact that his son, Jonas, spent plenty of time in the room, too. The three brothers settled into chairs, each of them holding a cold beer from the bar refrigerator.

After a couple of long moments passed, Justice finally asked, "So what is it? What's crawled into you and died?"

Jefferson smirked. "Very nice."

"Not interested in being nice. We want to know what's going on."

Jefferson stood up, took a swallow of icy beer and then began to pace. Nervous energy pumped through him, feeding his steps, stoking a temper that seemed to be continually on the boil lately. "Damned if I know. I feel wrong, somehow. As if I made a bad turn on a highway and now I'm lost."

"Easy enough to turn around again," Jesse commented.

"Is it?" Jefferson stared at him. "When turning around changes everything, is it really so easy to do it?"

"Depends on what you gain and what you lose with the effort," Justice mused, giving their youngest brother a hard look demanding patience. "So, where'd you make the wrong turn, Jeff? Was it Maura?"

"I'm starting to think that leaving her was the mistake I made. But what the hell else could I have done? She wouldn't give an inch. A more stubborn woman I've never known."

"She sounds perfect for you," Jesse offered and received a glare for his trouble.

Jefferson looked at Justice. "I told you she's pregnant."

"Yeah, you did."

"I asked her to marry me." He took a swig of the beer.

"So you screwed up the proposal?" Jesse asked. "That's easily fixed."

"That's not it." He took a breath, then studied the label on the beer bottle as if the printing there held the answers to every question he had. "She wants a real marriage."

"Imagine that," Jesse mused.

Jefferson's gaze shot to their youngest brother and seared him to his chair. "If you can't help, then be quiet."

"You don't need help," Jesse countered. "You need therapy. Why the hell can't you give her a real marriage?"

"Because I've already been in love. Anna."

Instantly, both of his brothers went quiet. Not so full of answers now, were they?

"Don't you get it? If I admit to loving Maura now," he said, "I'm essentially saying that Anna didn't count. That what we shared was replaceable."

Justice shook his head, stretched out his legs in front of him and balanced his beer bottle on his flat abdomen. "That is the *dumbest* thing I've ever heard." He shifted a look at Jesse. "How about you?"

"Oh yeah," he agreed. "It's right there with the top

three." Then to Jefferson, he said, "What, you're only allowed to love one person in your life?"

"No," Jefferson muttered, realizing just how foolish that statement sounded when said aloud. "That's not what I meant."

"What did you mean, then?" Justice asked. "Are you saying Anna would want you alone and lonely for the rest of your life to prove that you loved her?"

Jefferson thought about the young woman he'd loved and lost so long ago. "No," he admitted, "she wouldn't have."

Odd, but for the first time, he realized that the mental images he had of Anna and their time together had grown hazy. To be expected, he guessed, since time had a way of dulling the edges of pain or grief. Leaving behind only the vaguest feeling of guilt for having to live on. To keep breathing while the one you loved was gone.

"Jefferson," Jesse said softly, "if you had a child already, would you be able to love the one Maura's carrying?"

"That's a stupid question," he shot back.

"Is it?" Jesse laughed at him. "You're standing there telling us that you can't love Maura because you already loved Anna. How does that make sense?"

It wasn't just loving Maura that made him feel as though he were somehow betraying Anna, Jefferson thought with a glaring flash of insight. It was the fact that what he felt for Maura was so much more than what he'd once known. But he couldn't tell his brothers that. They already thought he was crazy.

While it was hard, he realized that the love he'd had for Anna had been a young man's love. Innocent in its way and it had ended before it could be tested. But he could love more now, deeper now, because he'd lived longer, knew more, had experienced more. His life had made him more than he had been at the time, so he was capable of feeling more than he'd been able to at twenty. Was it really that simple? Had he missed this revelation somehow because he'd been so determined to give Anna the loyalty he'd thought she deserved?

Justice was right. Anna wouldn't have wanted him to be alone and empty for the rest of his life in some bizarre tribute to her. A heavy load slid off his heart as he drew a deep, easy breath for the first time in weeks.

"God knows I'm no expert," Justice was saying. "Took long enough for me to realize what an ass I'd been in letting Maggie go. But I wised up in time. Are you gonna be able to say the same?"

Jefferson's hand tightened around the beer bottle. He knew what he wanted now, but would he be able to make Maura believe him?

"Yeah, I am," he said aloud, imagining the look on Maura's face when he showed up on her front porch at the farmhouse. "I'm going back to Ireland."

"For how long?"

He looked at Jesse. "Permanently."

"What about the studio?" Justice asked.

"I can handle it by phone and fax," Jefferson said, setting his beer down onto the closest table. "And I can be back here easily enough if I have to handle something in person."

"You? On a farm?" Jesse asked with a broad smile.

"Me on a farm," he repeated, already mentally arranging his move to the country, the woman he loved. "Why's that so hard to believe? Hell, we grew up on a ranch! Maura would never be happy anywhere else and I can work from anywhere. Besides," he added with a wide smile, "I have to get back. Find out if Michael's grandchild has been born. See if Cara's moving back to London. And it's lambing season, so Maura will be shorthanded…"

"Lambs?"

Jefferson laughed at Justice's horrified expression. "I know. You're a cattleman to the bone, but you're going to have to come visit our sheep."

God, he felt like he could climb mountains, run all the way to Ireland with his feet never even touching the water. He knew what he wanted. And he wouldn't settle for less than all. If Maura didn't agree right away, he'd just kidnap her, haul her in front of the village priest and marry her whether she liked it or not.

"I've gotta go," he said, checking his watch and mentally calculating the time he would need to tie up some loose ends and then get to the airport.

Jesse and Justice exchanged a glance and ordinarily, Jefferson would have been curious. But at the moment, he was too busy planning his reunion with Maura. He left the house, his brothers right behind him. But when he got to his car, he stopped.

"What the hell happened?"

All four tires were flat. The small, sapphire-blue sports car was practically resting on its rims in the dirt of the drive. Jefferson looked at his brothers. "Do you know something about this?"

"Hey," Jesse said, lifting both hands, "don't look at me."

Justice scrubbed one hand across his jaw and muttered, "I told the man *one* tire."

Before Jefferson could say anything to that, the throaty purr of an expensive engine rolled toward them. He looked up to watch a King family limo, all shining black paint and chrome, glide up the drive. "What the…"

Justice clapped one hand to Jefferson's shoulder. "This is why the flat tires. We had to keep you here. Although, Mike was a bit more thorough than I'd planned."

"What are you talking about?" His gaze was still fixed on the limo as the driver hopped out, opened the rear door and Maura stepped from the car, looking straight at him.

"Don't screw it up," Jesse muttered.

Justice shoved him and said, "We'll be in the barn. You two take your time."

Jefferson never even saw them leave. His gaze was fixed on the woman he loved and he couldn't have looked away if his life had depended on it. He wasn't betraying Anna by moving on. He knew that now. The living had to live. And he had no interest in doing that without Maura.

From the moment she'd stepped foot onto the King family jet, Maura had felt as though she were walking into a fairy tale. Surrounded by luxury, she'd flown halfway across the world for this moment. She'd slept in a bed thirty thousand feet in the air. At her arrival in Los Angeles, she'd been swept into the private opulence of the limousine and driven off down freeways choking with more traffic than she'd seen in her lifetime. And through it all, she'd had one thought in her mind. Getting to Jefferson. Making him see all that he was giving up when he turned his back on what they'd found.

When the limo turned into the long, winding drive of the King ranch, she had felt a slight stirring of nerves. Anxious, she had worried that going with her instincts might not have been the best idea. But she was committed to her plan and she wouldn't back out now that the moment had arrived.

Yet when she stepped out of the car, all she could do was look at Jefferson. He looked wildly handsome in his white shirt and black slacks with the wind ruffling his hair across his forehead. Even the baby inside her jumped and kicked, feeling the excitement of being with its father again.

Maura felt the hot, dry wind tug at her hair and burn her eyes. Surely that was the reason her vision was blurring with unshed tears. The King family ranch was a lovely place, what she noticed of it, but her gaze locked unerringly on Jefferson.

"Maura," he said, taking a step toward her.

"No. Stay there, if you please." Instantly, she held up one hand to keep him at bay. If he came too close, she might give in to her urge to run into his arms, when what she needed to do was stand her ground and speak her heart. "I've come all this way to have my say, Jefferson King, and you'll do me the courtesy of standing there to listen."

"You don't have to say anything," he said.

"That's for me to decide," she told him and paid no

attention as the driver of her limo discreetly slipped off in the direction of the barn. "I've spent the last several hours thinking of exactly what I want to tell you and now I will."

"Fine," he said, stuffing his hands into the pockets of his slacks. "Have at it."

"Good then. Where to begin?" She took a deep breath, met his eyes and said the first thing that came to her mind. "You're a bloody fool to walk away from me, Jefferson King."

"That's what you wanted to tell me?" he asked, smiling. "You came all this way to insult me?"

"That and more. I'll say this to your face as it's not something a woman wants to tell a man over the telephone." She walked toward him then, steel in her spine and fury in her steps, despite her earlier hesitation to be too close. "The reason I refused to marry you when you offered me a cold, empty marriage for the sake of our child or for convenience's sake was because I *love* you, you great ape of a man."

He gave her a slow smile. "You love me."

"I did. I do. But don't hold that lapse against me." Sputtering now, as thoughts crashed through her mind in a kaleidoscope of images and words, she wondered where her carefully rehearsed speech had disappeared to. Then she gave it up and spoke from the heart. "Though I love you, I won't marry a man who won't love me back."

She glowered at him, seeing him now through her tears and anger and wanting nothing more than to throw herself into his arms and taste his kiss on her lips again.

"So I've come to tell you that refusing to love another out of loyalty to your first wife is a foolish waste—though I'll say it speaks well of you to remember her and care for the memory."

"Thanks," he said, then added, "God, I love you."

She rolled right over his words, intent on telling him everything that was inside her. "Still, the living must live, Jefferson. Denying your heart is just another kind of death. I won't do that. And I hate that you're willing to. I'll tell you now, I will love you till I die, but I won't stop living. I'll be there, in Ireland, when you come to your senses."

"Maura," he said, "I love you."

"I've not finished," she told him sternly. Why couldn't the man be silent and let her get this said? "You'll miss me, Jefferson, and the life we could have had. You'll pine for me and I swear you'll regret ever walking away. And when, in your misery, you finally realize that loving me is what you were meant to do, remember it was I who told you. 'Twas me who came here to look you in the eye and give you one last chance. And blast it all, remember it was *love* that brought me here."

"I said I love you."

"What?" She whipped her head back to shake her hair out of her eyes and blinked up at him as if he were suddenly speaking Gaelic. "What was that? What did you just say?"

"I said, *I love you.*"

She looked up into his eyes and read the truth of his words shining back at her. A bright burst of light exploded in the center of her chest and Maura thought

FREE BOOKS OFFER

To get you started, we'll send you
2 FREE books and a FREE gift

There's no catch, everything is **FREE**

Accepting your **2 FREE** books and **FREE** mystery gift places you under no obligation to buy anything.

Be part of the Mills & Boon® Book Club™ and receive your favourite Series books up to 2 months before they are in the shops and delivered straight to your door. Plus, enjoy a wide range of **EXCLUSIVE** benefits!

 Best new women's fiction – delivered right to your door with FREE P&P

 Avoid disappointment – get your books up to 2 months before they are in the shops

 No contract – no obligation to buy

We hope that after receiving your free books you'll want to remain a member. But the choice is yours. So why not give us a go? You'll be glad you did!

Visit **millsandboon.co.uk** to stay up to date with offers and to sign-up for our newsletter

2 **FREE** books and a **FREE** gift

D0JIA

Mrs/Miss/Ms/Mr   Initials

BLOCK CAPITALS PLEASE

Surname

Address

Postcode

Email

MILLS & BOON

MILLS & BOON®
Book Club

**FREE BOOK OFFER
FREEPOST NAT 10298
RICHMOND
TW9 1BR**

NO STAMP
NECESSARY
IF POSTED IN
THE U.K. OR N.I.

with those words ringing in her ears, she wouldn't have need of a plane to get back home. She'd simply float across the Atlantic.

"You love me."

"I do," he said, grinning now as he reached for her.

She went willingly, throwing herself at him as she'd longed to do from the first moment she stepped out of that long, elegant car. Her arms came around his neck and she clung to him as she muttered thickly, "Well, why the devil didn't you say so?"

He laughed out loud and, arms wrapped around her waist, he lifted her off her feet and swung her in circles around the drive. "Who could get a word in when you're on a rant?"

"True, it's true. I've a terrible temper, I know, but it's just that I hurt so badly and I wanted you to be as miserable as I was feeling," she whispered into the curve of his neck, inhaling his scent, feeling the hard, solid strength of him pressed against her.

"I was," he confessed, his strong arms crushing her to him. "Without you, there's nothing. I know that now."

"Oh, Jefferson, I've missed you so."

"I was coming to you," he told her, his voice husky and filled with emotion. "I'd just decided to go back to Ireland and convince you to marry me, even if I had to abduct you."

She laughed a little, relief and wonder tangling up inside her. "I'm almost sorry to have missed that."

"I'll make it up to you," he promised. "I want to live in Ireland, with you and our baby, at the farm."

She pulled her head back to stare up at him in

wonder as the last of the dream slid into place. "You'd live in Ireland?"

"It's not a hardship," he told her. "I think I love the place almost as much as you do."

"You're a lovely man," she said on a sigh. "Have I mentioned that lately?"

He grinned. "Not lately, no."

She'd come so far, hoped and dreamed so much and now that she had everything she had ever wanted in the circle of her arms, she could only hold on to him, reeling at the happiness coursing through her. Finally though, he set her on her feet, but left his hands at her waist as if he couldn't bear to let her go.

"I'll still have to do some traveling at times," he was telling her, "but you and the baby can come with me. We'll have so many adventures, love. Our life will be full and happy, I promise you."

"I believe you," she said, lifting one hand to cup his cheek.

"Maura," he said softly, staring into her eyes like a man who'd just awakened from a long sleep to find his heart's desire landing at his feet. "I'm going to ask you again. The right way this time. I want you to marry me. For real. Forever."

"Ah, Jefferson, now I'm going to cry," she said, and felt the tears sliding along her cheeks.

"Don't," he whispered, bending to kiss her briefly, hungrily. "Don't cry." He smoothed her tears away with his thumbs and smiled into her eyes. "I'm really not worthy of you at all, am I?"

She laughed and leaned into him, relishing the sound

of his heartbeat beneath her ear. Wrapping both arms around his middle, she said, "Oh, you darlin' man…if every woman waited for a man who was worthy of her, there'd be no marriages, would there?"

He laughed aloud and pulled her tightly against him. "You're the one for me, Maura. The only one."

"And you for me, Jefferson. I will love you always."

"I'm counting on it," he told her, and gave her a soul-searing kiss that promised a lifetime of love more powerful than either of them had ever imagined.

And when that kiss ended, they parted to the sound of hearty applause and sharp whistles. Looking toward the barn, Jefferson grinned, took Maura's hand in his and said, "Come with me. I want you to meet my family."

"*Our* family," she corrected and laid her head against his shoulder.

Then together, they walked away from the past and into the future.

* * * * *

"You like playing with fire." Gage's deep, quiet voice rumbled over her.

"Apparently so do you."

He turned in his chair, his knee branding her thigh. "If we go upstairs now, I'm going to strip you down, take you to bed, and not let you out... before morning."

She gulped at the image he painted with his candor.

Should she go against wisdom and take a risk? Or play it safe? Either way, she was pretty certain she was damned if she did and damned if she didn't.

BEDDING THE
SECRET HEIRESS

BY
EMILIE ROSE

Published in Great Britain 2010
Harlequin Mills & Boon Limited,
Eton House, 18-24 Paradise Road, Richmond, Surrey TW9 1SR

© Emilie Rose Cunningham 2009

ISBN: 978 0 263 88181 3

51-1010

Harlequin Mills & Boon policy is to use papers that are natural, renewable
and recyclable products and made from wood grown in sustainable forests.
The logging and manufacturing processes conform to the legal environmental
regulations of the country of origin.

Printed and bound in Spain
by Litografia Rosés S.A., Barcelona

Bestselling Desire™ author and RITA® Award finalist
Emilie Rose lives in her native North Carolina with her
four sons and two adopted mutts. Writing is her third
(and hopefully her last) career. She's managed a medical
office and run a home day care, neither of which offers
half as much satisfaction as plotting happy endings.
Her hobbies include gardening and cooking (especially
cheesecake). She's a rabid country music fan because
she can find an entire book in almost any song, and is
currently working her way through her own "Bucket
List", which includes learning to ride a Harley. Visit her
website at www.emilierose.com. Letters can be mailed
to PO Box 20145, Raleigh, NC 27619. E-mail her at
EmilieRoseC@aol.com.

This one's for LaShawn.
Thank you for teaching me to dance like
nobody's watching.

Dear Reader,

Putting myself in my characters' shoes is a great way to do research. I did that for this book and had a blast. I bought a Harley and I had my newly licensed pilot son fly me to lunch. I visited Knoxville and Daytona, and literally traveled in my heroine's shoes. Not every book allows me to do that, and the ones that do are a gift.

But I've noticed when I travel I usually discover a lot more than just the sights. That's what happens for Lauren Lynch when she travels to Knoxville to meet the half-siblings she hadn't known she had. And, of course, there's the little surprise of her half-brother's friend, Gage Faulkner. Sit back and watch the sparks fly.

Happy reading!

Emilie Rose

One

Here we go again.

Lauren expelled an exasperated breath and punched the elevator button for the top floor. Getting called to her half brother's office was a lot like the way she imagined getting called to the principal's office might have been if she'd ever dared to get into trouble in school.

Trent didn't want her here—an opinion he'd made abundantly clear in the six weeks since their mother had used her position as president of the board of directors and the company's largest stockholder to force him to hire Lauren as a pilot for Hightower Aviation Management Corporation.

Trent couldn't fire her, but he'd done everything in his power to make her quit. He seemed to relish personally doling out lousy assignments no one else wanted: the obnoxious clients, red-eye flights and landings at substandard airports. Today's summons was bound to deliver more of the same. But he'd soon learn she could handle anything he dished out.

The elevator stopped on the third floor and two suit-clad women boarded. Security badges labeled them HAMC employees. Their cool gazes raked Lauren's clothing, making her wish she'd taken time to don her pilot's uniform, but she could hardly ride her Harley in a skirt. And if these two had received a memo from her half brother ordering them to make her work life a living hell, they'd discover she didn't care.

She'd never had anyone hate her before, but besides the chill factor from other employees, she had three of her four newly discovered half siblings wishing she'd disappear. Who could blame them? She was a walking, talking reminder of their mother's infidelity, the child Jacqueline Hightower had borne to her pilot lover while still married to their father, an embarrassing dirty secret Jacqui had managed to keep tucked away in another state for twenty-five years.

The door opened on the tenth floor and the sour-faced women disembarked. As the doors closed again Lauren fought the urge to hit the down button, go back to Florida and forget her new family. Too bad the Hightowers, bless their cold, moneygrubbing hearts, were the only relatives she had left. For her father's sake, for Falcon Air's sake, she'd suck it up and deal with any and all unpleasant attitudes until she had the information about her father's death that only her mother could provide.

Had he committed suicide or had his crash been an accident? Her mother had been the last to talk to him. If he'd been considering something so desperate, surely he'd have given Jacqui some clues? But, damn her, Jacqui wasn't talking. And until the Federal Aviation

Administration, the National Transportation Safety Board and the insurance company finished their investigations Lauren's hands were bound by red tape.

She didn't want to believe her father had deliberately ended his life, but the alternative was even more horrific. She'd helped him build the experimental plane he'd crashed. If his accident had been caused by an equipment failure, then she could be partly to blame.

Grief and guilt squeezed her lungs and burned her throat. She swallowed the caustic emotions. The elevator doors opened to the executive floor. She took a deep, bracing breath and readied herself for yet another battle.

Only for you, Daddy.

Tucking her riding gloves into the motorcycle helmet dangling from her fingertips, she stepped out of the compartment. Her lug-soled Harley boots sank into thick carpeting, another reminder that she wasn't in Daytona anymore. The luxurious Hightower high-rise was a far cry from the concrete floors and drafty metal hangars she'd grown up in.

She stretched her lips into as big a smile as she could muster and unzipped her jacket as she approached "The Sphinx's" desk. Getting her brother's administrative assistant to crack an expression—*any* expression—had become a mission. No success this time, either. The woman should play poker for a living.

"Hi, Becky. The boss wants to see me." Becky—a warm and friendly name for a cold woman. Talk about irony.

Becky looked pointedly at her watch. "I'll inform him you've *finally* arrived."

Lauren bit her tongue. Trent was lucky she'd answered her cell phone once she'd recognized his office number on caller ID. But she *was* making an effort to be civil.

She studied the fresh-cut flower arrangement on the credenza while Becky did her thing. The massive bouquet had probably cost as much as an hour's worth of jet fuel. Pretty, but a total waste of money, in Lauren's opinion.

"You may go in." Becky's stiff words pulled Lauren's attention away from the cloying blooms that reminded her of her father's funeral.

Such formality. Back home Lauren had knocked and entered her father's and Uncle Lou's offices at Falcon Air without playing the stupid Simon Says game. They'd had no secrets...or so she'd thought.

"Thanks." Lauren pushed open the heavy six-panel door of what she'd come to call the throne room. Her half brother sat behind his football field–size desk in his massive leather chair looking as arrogant and unwelcoming as ever. "You called?"

Darn straight he had. He'd interrupted her motorcycle ride along Knoxville's back roads. He couldn't know how much she'd been enjoying blowing away her tension by cruising along the curvy, hilly terrain after a lifetime of Daytona's flat, straight streets. She'd be damned if she'd let him know he'd ruined her day.

His upper lip hitched in disapproval as he took in her riding gear.

The back of Lauren's neck pricked. She turned quickly to her right. A raven-haired thirtysomething man rose from the visitor chair. Alert dark eyes lasered into hers before his gaze taxied over her black leather jacket, pants, boots and back to the helmet hanging from her left hand. He had a power and charisma thing going that she would have found attractive in other circumstances.

While he assessed her, she cataloged his above-average height, his wide shoulders and a don't-mess-with-me stubborn jaw. From the perfect fit of his black suit she guessed he was an HAMC customer. And if he was here for her, then he was probably also an arrogant jackass no matter how handsome he might be. Big brother had yet to assign her any other kind of client.

Taking the initiative, she offered her hand. "I'm Lauren Lynch. And you are…?"

"Gage Faulkner." His hand engulfed hers in a firm, warm grip that made it difficult to inhale. She wondered how he'd managed to squish the air from her lungs with a handshake and how to abort that little trick. She blinked and gently tugged her arm, but he didn't release her.

There was no welcome in his expression as he looked beyond her shoulder to her half brother. "She looks too young to be a commercial pilot."

"You know I'd never set you up with someone who wasn't qualified," Trent replied.

Irked at being talked about as if she wasn't there, Lauren gave her wrist a quick twist and hard yank, breaking Faulkner's hold the way she'd been taught by an airport security guard she'd once dated. "I'm twenty-five. I've been licensed since my sixteenth birthday, and I've logged more than ten thousand hours."

Faulkner's cool gaze found hers again, and she noted flecks of gold in the brown of his irises. A tight smile twitched his lips. Nice lips. Kissable lips.

Client.

The warning flashed in her brain like airfield lamps, shutting down that runway. Getting involved with a client was grounds for firing. Was Trent setting her up with a gorgeous guy to take her down? She wouldn't put it past him since all his other strategies had failed.

She cut her brother a suspicious look. Did he think she

couldn't resist an attractive face? Knucklehead didn't know she'd been fending off men since puberty. Not that she was beautiful or anything, but she wasn't ugly, and the man-to-woman ratio at small airports left a lot of men lonely and looking. She'd had her father and Uncle Leo as growling watchdogs, but they hadn't always been around. She'd learned a few lessons the hard way.

Trent hit her with his usual joy-killing glare. "Gage, please excuse Lauren's attire. I assure you HAMC has a dress code."

Her spine snapped erect. "It's my day off. I wasn't sitting at home in my uniform waiting for your call. When you said urgent I came straight in instead of making you cool your jets while I went home to change."

Faulkner choked a noise that sounded a lot like a laugh. She shot him a warning look. He wiped his jaw, hiding his mouth, but his eyes glimmered with amusement. For some reason that irritated Lauren even more. Their family feud was none of his business.

"Sit down, Lauren." Trent's superior tone set her teeth on edge. One of these days someone was going to knock the landing gear out from under his ego. She hoped she'd be around to witness him biting the asphalt. Unlikely she'd have the pleasure since she planned to vacate Knoxville and abandon her polar bear relatives as soon as she got what she needed from her mother.

Lauren sat in the guest chair beside Faulkner's. A subtle but pleasant trace of his spicy cologne teased her nose. She focused on her brother, the arrogant butt-head in charge. "What's so urgent it couldn't wait until I clock in tomorrow?"

"Gage needs a pilot. You're it."

That was her job, the job of any HAMC pilot, for that

matter. So why did that telling itch crawling up her neck warn her that this wasn't a regular assignment?

"What and where will I be flying?"

Probably an albatross to some mosquito-infested, potholed, mud runway or an unheated cargo carrier to the frozen tundra, if her half brother continued true to form.

"Gage will use a variety of aircraft, depending on the length of his trip and the size of the team accompanying him. The majority of the time you'll fly a small to midsize jet, but occasionally a helicopter or Cessna."

Excitement gurgled through her before she could dam it. The job description sounded too good to be true—especially since Hightower Aviation limited its pilots to flying only one type of aircraft so they'd be familiar with the controls. That had been her primary grievance since she'd arrived. She lived for variety and loved testing the abilities of different airplanes.

Her half brother was being nice *and* bending company policy. Had his conscience finally kicked in? She studied his impassive face, not buying altruism as his motive for one second.

"Trent assures me you can handle whatever I need."

Faulkner's velvety voice snagged her attention, winching her gaze back to him. He meant flightwise, didn't he?

Her stomach did a weird flutter thing that made her question the sanitation grade of the roadside diner she and her neighbors had stopped at for lunch.

"I'm certified to fly almost anything civilian with wings or rotors. Mastering different aircraft is kind of a hobby of mine." *More like an obsession.* "What's the catch?"

Did she imagine a quick stiffening of those broad shoulders? The slight hesitation as he pursed that attention-getting mouth? "If you fly for me, you'll be on call 24/7, beginning tomorrow morning at five."

Again, standard procedure for HAMC pilots. They all flew on four hours notice or less. Something wasn't right here. "And?"

"You'll be working exclusively for Gage."

Trent's statement had her head whipping his way as the meaning of his bombshell sank in. "You're taking me off rotation?"

"I'm giving you a special assignment."

The bully was farming her out to someone else, and there wasn't one thing she could say about it in front of the client, unless she wanted to get fired for insubordination. She refused to mouth off and give Trent the satisfaction of an easy way out.

Gritting her teeth, she fought her seething anger. Being cut from the schedule was like being sent to her room or put in time out. And damn it, she hadn't done anything wrong to earn such shoddy treatment. Working for only one client would limit her hours and her pay. Her mother would never allow—

No. She wouldn't go to her mother. Their relationship was too new, too tentative and too volatile for Lauren to ask Jacqui to choose sides between her oldest son and her youngest daughter, and Lauren couldn't afford to alienate her mother yet. This turf war was between her and Trent, and Lauren refused to let him win.

Tightening her grip on her helmet strap rather than around her half brother's thick neck as she'd prefer, she stared him down. "I'll be the pilot-in-command instead of first officer?"

Her idiot brother had limited her to flying as first officer instead of the pilot-in-command. She hadn't flown in the copilot seat in years, and the pilots he'd made her fly with often had fewer qualifications than she did. But she'd accepted the entry-level position while she earned her certifications in the models and equipment new to her. She could endure any indignity as long as it benefited her in the end—even playing nice with her mother.

Trent tossed his pen onto his blotter. "None of the aircraft Gage has requested require a copilot."

He threw her a sweet bone of concession to offset the bitter deal he was forcing down her throat. "None of your other HAMC pilots is assigned a one-on-one job."

"My other pilots don't have your...varied experience." He made the comment sound like an insult instead of the compliment it would have been coming from any other employer.

Don't let him rattle you. You know that's what he wants. "How long is the assignment?"

"For as long as Gage needs you. Becky has your immediate schedule and plane assignments." Trent rose and indicated the door, dismissing her.

She'd learned early on that arguing with Trent was a waste of time. Eager to escape the blockhead's presence as well as see what and where she'd be flying, Lauren sprang to her feet. The upside was HAMC had some sweet planes that her brother had yet to let her touch. Maybe she'd get behind the controls of a few.

Faulkner unfolded his long body beside her, making her aware of his height and the smooth, athletic way he moved. He towered over her as he offered his hand. "I look forward to flying with you, Lauren."

His chilly tone belied his words and made her wonder if Trent had poisoned yet another mind against her. She reluctantly put her hand in his. That same breath-stealing surge shot through her again, and something flickered in his eyes, making her wonder if he felt it, too—whatever *it* was. Didn't matter. That wasn't a trip she'd be taking.

"I'll do my best to deliver smooth, punctual flights." Ripping her hand free, she spun on her heel and hustled her boots out of the throne room. Killjoy Trent shadowed her to The Sphinx's desk.

"Lauren, Gage is a close personal friend." He pitched his voice low enough not to carry back through the open door of his office. "Don't blow this or you're out of a job."

Ah. The catch. She rocked back on her heels. Trent had assigned her to work for a spy—one who would help him find grounds to get rid of her.

Wasn't that a show of brotherly love? She bit back the urge to tell him to kiss her butt. But she'd deal with Trent's tricks until she got what she needed. Then she'd tell him what he could do with his big head and bad attitude.

"Piece of cake, big brother. I'll treat your buddy like precious cargo."

The obvious grinding of his teeth when she called him *brother* nearly made her laugh out loud. Score one for baby sister. But she knew better than to let down her guard. This battle was far from over.

Angel or badass?

Gage's gaze tracked Lauren Lynch out of the room. The woman was a walking contradiction with her big teal eyes, flawless honey complexion and the black leather biker gear hugging her lean curves.

The bone-jarring effect of her touch had been an unwelcome surprise. Even if she weren't Trent's sister, she was too young for him, and he had no time or inclination for complications—not when he was this close to reaching his goal of having Faulkner Consulting be the best in the industry and having six million in secure investments.

"Your announcement was a bit premature," Gage said the moment Trent closed the office door. "You haven't convinced me to fly with Hightower Aviation yet."

"I will."

Maybe. Maybe not. But he'd give Trent a chance to state his case. He owed him that much. "Lauren gives you a hard time."

"But she's smart enough to keep from crossing the line and giving me grounds to fire her. She has my mother wrapped around her little finger."

"Are you sure? Jacqueline's pretty sharp. You have to give her credit for keeping Hightower Aviation from going under after her father died and yours dropped the ball. She even managed to take HAMC international by convincing her jet-setting friends to employ your services on their pleasure jaunts."

Trent sat behind his desk. "Mom's been hoodwinked this time."

"How does this involve me? Your message said you needed my help, but you left out the details."

"Eighteen months ago Mom flew to Daytona. Shortly thereafter she began making large cash withdrawals of between twenty and thirty thousand on a regular basis. She's returned to Daytona bimonthly since then."

"Is it company money?" Embezzlement would be bad news.

"No, it's my mother's personal funds, but her accountant called me with a heads-up. I ordered him to alert me to any unusual transactions. Remember my father's stunt? And yours?"

Gage's gut tightened. "I remember."

He might have only been ten when his father over-extended himself, borrowing against his business and their home until he'd lost everything, but living in the family car for six months wasn't something Gage would ever forget. Trent was the only one Gage had ever trusted with those details.

"Why would Jacqueline suddenly go off the deep end now?"

"That's what I'm trying to figure out. If Mom's judgment is faulty or if she's getting senile, then I need to get her off the board of directors before she does serious damage."

"You're going to need more than speculation to unseat her."

Trent glanced at the papers on his desk. "Mom's spending and visits to Daytona escalated a few months before Lauren moved to Knoxville. Lauren is from Daytona. My guess is she discovered her birth mother had deep pockets and decided to cozy up and dip her hands into them."

"Lauren doesn't look like a con artist."

"Don't let those big blue eyes and her innocent girl-next-door look fool you. If I didn't have good reason to suspect she's tapped my mother's financial vein, I wouldn't have called you."

Trent, like Gage, wasn't the type to ask for help. That his friend had called meant he was desperate. "If your mother is channeling money to your baby sister—"

"*Half* sister," Trent corrected. "And the only reason I believe that is because I had a DNA test done during her employment screening process."

"Is that legal and does Lauren know?"

"I doubt she knows, but she signed a waiver allowing us to test for whatever we wanted when she took the job. I tested for everything."

"She came up clean?"

"Unfortunately. Ditching her would have been much easier if her drug tests or background check had revealed even a hint of something questionable. Hell, even her credit history is clear."

Trent really had it in for the girl, but he'd never been the type to overreact or jump to conclusions. Because of his family's wealth Trent had always been a target for gold diggers, and his radar for them was unmatched. He must have good cause for his suspicions about Lauren.

"You've asked your mother about the cash?"

Trent nodded. "And she locked up tighter than Fort Knox. If she has nothing to hide, then why keep secrets?"

"I hear you." But Gage lived by the opposite theory. He didn't believe in revealing anything unless required. "What about Lauren? Did you ask her why she relocated?"

"Lauren gave me some bullshit about her father wanting her to meet her Hightower siblings as a reason for her move to Knoxville, and she claims she knows nothing about the money."

"Why wouldn't your mother have given Lauren money sooner? Why wait twenty-five years?"

"Maybe Mom didn't know where Lauren was or she could have been giving her smaller amounts over the years that didn't catch the accountant's notice. But we never heard a whisper about Mom's little mistake until she showed up on our doorstep, pilot credentials in hand and expecting to waltz into a job. Do you know how selective Hightower Aviation is in hiring?"

"Lauren doesn't meet your standards?"

Trent's scowl deepened. "Other than her lack of a college degree, she exceeds them. But, Gage, she's too damned young to have the résumé she's claiming. I just haven't been able to prove she's lying. Hell, I've checked and rechecked her credentials and put her through a battery of physical and mental testing, looking for any reason to reject her. I even forced her to sit through hours of training in a flight simulator before allowing her in a real cockpit. But the little smart-ass aced all the tests and refused to quit."

That earned her a dose of grudging respect. "Maybe she's simply a good pilot."

"Nobody's that good at that age."

"You were."

Trent's entire body tensed and Gage regretted his words. Trent had practically been raised in a cockpit. He'd been eager to join the Air Force as a pilot after college, but his father had nearly destroyed HAMC by incurring gambling debts that had jeopardized the company. Trent had been forced to abandon his military career plans to clean up his father's mess. By the time he'd dug HAMC out of the negative spiral Trent's dream had been supplanted by the necessity of remaining CEO of HAMC.

"I apologize. I shouldn't have brought that up."

"Forget it. It was a long time ago. I'm over it." Trent cleared his throat. "Here's what I know. My mother hid her pregnancy then gave Lauren up for adoption to her natural father rather than tell my father she'd gotten knocked up by one of her lovers."

"Your father must have known. As Jacqueline's husband he would have been Lauren's legal father despite her biological paternity. He would have had to agree to relinquish."

Trent raked a hand through hair a shade lighter than his half sister's dirty blond. "Dad claims he doesn't remember the 'incident' or signing any forms. My guess is he would have done anything to keep my mother funding his gambling addiction. Remember, HAMC was a smaller operation back then, and the majority of Hightower money came from my mother's family. Consequently, Dad turned a blind eye to all her affairs. My grandfather probably greased the wheels to keep things quiet."

"All valid points." But despite her biker gear and attitude, Lauren didn't give off the greedy bitch vibe. "Lauren doesn't look like a woman being showered with gifts from a wealthy benefactress. She's not wearing jewelry, makeup or designer clothes."

"She drives a twenty-thousand-dollar motorcycle, a sixty-thousand-dollar truck and flies a quarter-million-dollar airplane. What does that tell you?"

That she'd fooled him. But hadn't he learned the hard way that women often promised one thing and schemed to get something else altogether? Gage's anger stirred. "She's damned good at hiding her avaricious nature. But I repeat, what does this have to do with me?"

"Until I can get the cash flow dammed I need you to keep Lauren out of my hair and away from my mother."

"And from your phone message I gather you believe I can do that by using Hightower Aviation's services for free."

Trent nodded. "Flying a private jet rather than a commercial airline will save you time. You've canceled our last three dinners because you claimed you needed to be in two places at once due to two of your team members being out on parental leave."

"Right." Yet another reason why Gage would never

have children. They were a distraction. Recent family additions had turned two of his best consultants—one male, one female—into babbling, sleep-deprived fools. He wasn't letting anyone get between him and a steady, secure income. And he didn't want anyone depending on him.

"I can help you, and in turn, you can help me," Trent added. "If I don't cut off the money leak, then Mom could be tempted to dip into Hightower Aviation funds the way my father did. For the next two or three months you'll be out of town more than in. If Lauren is your pilot, she will be, too. That works for me."

Gage's collar suddenly felt like a noose. As convenient as having a plane at his beck and call might be, he'd never been comfortable with the freeloader role— a circumstance Trent knew only too well. "Faulkner Consultants can afford HAMC's services. Draw up a contract."

"No way. We both know how you feel about large capital expenses. I explained on the message machine before you came in. This one's on me."

"You laid out a sketchy plan, but there's more involved here than you let on."

"Damn it, Gage, get the chip off your shoulder. How many times do I have to tell you that you don't owe me or my family anything? Trust me on this. If you can occupy Lauren for a couple of months, *I'll* owe *you*. Keeping the parasite away from my mother is going to save me more money in the long run than you leasing a plane or buying fractional ownership in one is going to generate."

Gage's molars ground together. He'd swallowed more humble pie than he could handle in a lifetime. Never again. "Trent—"

"I need your help, man. Don't make me beg."

Gage ran a hand over the tense muscles of his neck. "Then we do it my way. Draw up a short-term contract. If it saves me time and money, then I'll renew when the term ends. If not, I'll at least know I paid my way."

Trent's jaw jacked up. "That's not necessary."

"It is for me."

Trent's mouth opened, but closed again without further argument. "Fine. If you can manage to find out Lauren's intentions while you're at it, that would be even better."

Gage recoiled. He'd been waiting thirteen years for an opportunity to repay the debt he owed his former college roommate, but there were some boundaries he wouldn't cross even for his best friend. "I won't be your snitch."

"I'm not asking you to sleep with her or marry her to get information. Just find out how long she intends to be a boil on my ass."

"If Lauren is the mercenary bitch you claim, then I'll tell you what you need to know to protect yourself and your assets. But that's it. Nothing more."

Trent's brow creased as he considered Gage's offer. "Deal."

Two

The rasp of a suit-clad leg brushing her shoulder shattered Lauren's concentration. She looked up from entering data into the navigation screen as Gage squeezed through the narrow opening between the cockpit and passenger cabin.

"Mr. Faulkner, we're about to take off. Please go back to your seat and buckle in."

"Call me Gage, and I prefer sitting up front." He folded into the copilot chair on her right.

"I'd rather you stay in the passenger cabin."

He reached for the seat belt and clicked it in place. "Are you afraid I'll see you skip a step in preflight preparations, Lauren?"

Her teeth clicked together. He'd been an aggravation from the moment he'd insisted on carrying his own bags on board. The HAMC rulebook stated that her job as pilot was to greet each passenger and personally carry on and properly stow any weighted objects they brought along. The last thing she needed to do was give her half brother a stupid infraction to use against her.

"I never skip steps."

"Good. Do you have a spare headset?"

The mercury in her mental thermometer climbed and her ears burned. "We're flying a Cessna Mustang because you wanted to work on the way to Baton Rouge in the luxury of a spacious cabin. You even requested no flight attendant on board so you wouldn't have interruptions."

He kept his gaze leveled on hers, not giving an inch. An odd tension seeped into her midsection.

"I awoke hours before my alarm went off this morning and accomplished what I needed to do before I left for the airport. I'd rather sit up front where I can see."

Disliking the invasion of her space and the breach in protocol, she grappled for patience and stretched her lips into a smile. "There are six windows in the back. Besides, on an overcast day there's not a lot to see from thirty thousand feet. I'll be flying above the cloud deck."

"I'll take my chances."

She counted to three, trying to rein in her temper. "The seats in the cabin are larger, more comfortable and they recline. You could catch up on your missed sleep during the flight."

"Not necessary."

Her knuckleheaded half brother had probably asked his spy to annoy her as much as possible, and judging by the gleam in Faulkner's dark eyes and the stubborn set of his jaw he knew he was getting under her skin like a splinter.

"If you'd mentioned your preference for sitting up front earlier, we could have cleared it with the office and conserved fuel by taking a smaller plane rather than fly five empty seats."

"That would have cost us speed and time."

She couldn't argue with facts. A smaller plane would have flown slower and lower than HAMC's smallest jet. "Allowing passengers in the cockpit is against HAMC protocol."

"Call your brother."

"Half brother. I can't. As you no doubt know, he's tied up in a board meeting all morning, and his dragon lady won't put calls through."

"Then I guess you're stuck with me in the copilot seat."

But she would take this up with Trent when she returned home. Her father's number one rule echoed in her head. *The customer is always right—unless safety is involved.* Resigned to Faulkner's unwanted company, she conceded, "There's a spare headset beneath your seat."

Most pilots, including her, brought their own equipment, but Hightower Aviation always provided extras. She hated to admit it, but HAMC went first-class all the way by providing luxuries for its passengers and crew that Falcon Air couldn't afford.

Gage removed the gear from the bag and plugged the headset into the appropriate jack as if he'd done this before, then sat back in his seat with his long-fingered hands relaxed on his thighs.

Muscular thighs, not desk jockey thighs.

Client.

She diverted her stray thoughts, assumed her strictest flight instructor persona and met his gaze. "If you have sunglasses, put them on. Don't speak until I tell you I've finished with the control tower, and don't touch anything that doesn't belong to you. You may not need to concentrate during the flight, but I do if you want me to keep this baby in the air."

The corners of his lips twitched, and she almost smiled back. "That would be preferable to the alternative."

Of crashing. Like her father.

The swift stab of pain caught her off guard. She squelched her grief and focused on entering her flight plan data into the computer. It took twenty minutes to finish her preflight check, get clearance and put the plane in the air—twenty minutes during which Gage silently observed her every move like an eagle waiting to strike.

When she was in the cockpit she was all business all the time. Her father had taught her that was the only way young pilots lived to become old pilots. An airplane was the one place she knew she was good—*damned* good. But Gage made her second-guess her actions instead of doing them instinctively. Before him, no other passenger or pilot had ever disrupted her concentration.

She hated being conscious of each shift of his body in the leather seat, the rise and fall of his chest and the spicy tang of his cologne. And while she couldn't hear him moving and breathing through her noise-canceling headphones, she could feel his presence in the close quarters of the cockpit.

His steady regard made her very aware of her scraped-back hair, lack of makeup and unpainted, short-clipped nails. He made her feel feminine. And lacking. Not a pleasant combination.

Once she reached cruising altitude, she glanced at him and straight into those dark eyes. Her stomach swooped as if she'd hit an air pocket and the plane had dropped. "You can talk now. If you must. Speak in a regular tone of voice. I'll hear you loud and clear through the headphones."

"Why flying?" he fired back without hesitation.

A familiar question. She shrugged. "I grew up around airports and never wanted to do anything else."

"What did you do before joining Hightower Aviation?"

Her half brother had probably asked Gage to grill her. Careerwise, she had nothing to hide, nothing that she hadn't put in her résumé. Still, unsure of his agenda, she chose her words carefully. "Fifty percent of the time I'm a flight instructor. The rest of the time I fly charter jets for Falcon Air."

"What's Falcon Air?"

He certainly had a talent for faking genuine interest while pumping her for information. "My father's charter plane company."

"Is he running it while you're gone?"

She flinched as the unintentional arrow sank deep into her chest. Would the pain ever stop? "No. He recently…died. My uncle is acting as general manager."

"My condolences." Cool words devoid of emotion.

"What is it you do exactly, Mr.—Gage?" Not that she cared, but she'd rather talk about him than herself and risk inadvertently revealing something she shouldn't. If word got out that her father might have committed suicide, then Falcon Air would lose business. Their clients would not be inclined to hire a company that flew faulty planes—or worse, engage a pilot who might take a deliberate header into the Everglades with them on board. And finances were iffy enough already.

"I'm a business consultant. I assess companies and make recommendations for improvements, specifically targeting ways to make them financially secure by eliminating waste and increasing productivity."

"You do that internationally?"

"Yes. Did you decide to search for your birth mother after your father's death?"

She stifled her frustration as he volleyed the topic back to her. "No. She came to me."

"You must have been surprised to meet her."

"Meet her? I don't know what Trent told you, but I've known Jacqui all my life. I wasn't aware my father's on-again-off-again girlfriend was my mother until my eighteenth birthday when she and my father decided to share the information. I didn't know Jacqui was married until after my father's funeral when she told me my father wanted me to meet my sib—her other children."

His eyes narrowed. "You've known Jacqueline for years?"

"Yes."

"What kind of mother was she? A generous one, I'll bet."

More innuendo. She rolled her eyes and then scanned the sky for traffic. She'd had a load of the same attitude from all but one of her half siblings. They seemed to think she was looking for handouts and a free ride, but what she wanted was something Jacqui could give her without putting a dent in the Hightower heirs' inheritance.

"I just told you Jacqui wasn't a mother at all. And no, she didn't shower me with expensive gifts. My father wouldn't have allowed it. Nor would I have accepted them."

The disbelief written all over his face ticked her off. One, because this stranger had judged and assumed the worst of her, and two, because Trent had probably filled Gage's ears with lies. It was one thing for her half brother to resent her and hate her guts, but it was low and crass of him to spread his poison professionally. She knew he had. Otherwise, the other HAMC employees wouldn't give her the cold shoulder.

"Jacqueline wanted you to join Hightower Aviation?"

"This is a temporary gig. Jacqui knows I'm going back to Falcon in a few months."

"Why a few months?"

"Why twenty questions?" she countered.

"I'm curious. Most people wouldn't willingly walk away from the level of luxury associated with the Hightower name."

"I'm not most people, Mr. Faulkner, and I'm not a Hightower. If we're going to work together, you'd better get used to that. And if Trent put you up to this interrogation, then please tell him he'll have to come to me himself for answers."

Not that she'd ever reveal the full truth behind her presence in Knoxville. Her reasons for being here were no one's business but hers, and she'd be damned if she'd feed Gage Faulkner anything he could carry back to Trent to be used against her. If she did, it could destroy Falcon Air, and then she'd have nothing to return home to.

Gage's gut told him Lauren was hiding something, and his gut was never wrong.

She'd clammed up as soon as the conversation about her mother had become interesting, and no amount of questioning, subtle or otherwise, had gotten her to open up again during the flight. But getting answers was his specialty.

He flashed the ID badge Hightower Aviation had provided for him at the security guard. The man waved him through the doors to the tarmac. "Have a good trip, sir."

Gage nodded his thanks, exited the terminal of the

small suburban airport and approached the jet. Trent had been right. Traveling via private carrier was a lot less hassle than flying a commercial airline. Faster in, faster out allowed for more time on the job and less in transit. Gage had to admit he liked the efficiency.

Tired, but satisfied with the preliminary information he'd gathered on the project he'd come to Baton Rouge to assess, he checked his watch. Because of the security check-in time savings he was an hour early. When he'd left Lauren seven hours ago she hadn't seemed concerned at being stranded with nothing to do for the majority of the day. In fact, her eyes had sparkled and her body had practically vibrated with excitement as if she couldn't wait to be rid of him. Not a common occurrence for him. Women—when he made time for them—enjoyed his company.

But not Lauren.

She'd given him her cell number and asked him to call when he finished his business and headed toward the airport, claiming it would allow her to prepare the plane for takeoff before he arrived. He hadn't called. Arriving early fit in with his plan to catch her doing whatever it was she did to fill her day. Her activities might give some clue as to her intentions.

The door to the Cessna stood open and the stairs were down as if waiting for visitors on this warm October day. He climbed on board, and the plane rocked slightly under his weight. Lauren abruptly sat upright in one of the plush leather passenger seats and lowered the feet she'd had tucked under her to the floor. She had a laptop computer resting on her thighs. "You're back."

"Did I interrupt something?"

"No. I was just…killing time."

But not in a relaxed way, judging by the tension around her mouth and eyes.

The setting sun streamed through the window behind her, painting coppery streaks in the slightly disheveled dark blond curtain hanging past her shoulders. Her uniform hat rested on a nearby table and her jacket draped a seat back. She hastily closed the open top button of her shirt, covering a V of pale honeyed skin.

"You were supposed to call so I could get the pre-flight done and get you into the air faster."

She seemed flustered. Was she hiding something?

"My mind was on work." Not a lie, just not the entire truth and a necessary omission if he were going to play sleuth. He stowed his briefcase in the compartment she'd shown him earlier.

Her eyes narrowed as if she didn't believe him, and then she typed a few keys. A few seconds later her eyebrows and the corners of her lips dipped. "Jacqui says hello."

Alarms sounded in his brain. "You were online with your mother?"

"Yes." A flicker of irritation crossed her face. "Instant messaging."

Lauren closed her computer, tucked it into a leather bag by her feet and rose. She twisted her hair up, clipping it into place then she snatched up her hat and set it on her head. "She remembers you from your college visits with Trent."

Jacqueline would. The Hightower family had often included Gage on vacations—probably because Trent had told them that Gage had nowhere else to go when the dorms shut down for the holidays. He couldn't exactly join his father because his parent was usually living in a homeless shelter or on the street. Gage had no idea where his mother had gone. The old humiliation still burned his pride.

"I wouldn't have pegged Jacqueline as the instant messaging type."

"You'd be wrong. She's quite techno-savvy."

That translated into trouble. He could physically keep the women apart, but he couldn't prevent them from connecting via cyberspace when all of HAMC's planes had wireless access. That was something neither he nor Trent had anticipated. The situation would require reevaluation and a new strategy.

Lauren stowed her computer case in the compartment behind the pilot's seat and locked it down. "I refueled after we landed, but I'll need about thirty minutes to get ready for takeoff."

"No rush. In fact, why don't we have dinner first?"

Lauren's crisp, economical movements stopped abruptly with her uniform jacket half-on. Her eyes turned wary. "Dinner?"

He needed to find out exactly how tight she and her mother had become. "I passed a Brazilian steak place on the way to the airport that looked interesting."

She licked her lips as if tempted, and his gaze involuntarily followed the sweep of her pink tongue. The muscles in his gut tightened. He dammed the reaction. Lauren might look as fresh-faced as the proverbial girl next door, but the intelligence in her eyes and her quiet confidence as she operated the multimillion dollar aircraft belied her being uncomplicated.

She finished putting on her coat and buttoned it up to her neck. "I'm more than happy to delay takeoff until after you've eaten. It'll give me time to prepare for—"

"Join me, Lauren."

She shook her head. "Fraternizing with clients is against HAMC rules."

"I'll call Trent and clear it."

She blinked. Why had he never noticed her long lashes before? "Thank you, but I've already eaten."

He didn't believe her. "What did you have?"

She hesitated. "A sandwich from the airstrip cantina."

"Then I'll have the same. Keep me company." At least that would keep her from hooking up with her mother again while he was out of sight.

A stubborn expression shut down her face. "No thank you, Mr. Faulkner. I'll prepare the plane while you eat."

He had the distinct impression she didn't want to be alone with him. He had every intention of finding out why and what she had to hide.

The crunch of a shoe behind her in the misty, dark parking lot kicked Lauren's adrenaline into high gear. She spun around, ready to gouge an assailant with her keys if necessary.

Trent stepped into the murky light of a lamppost and stopped two yards away when he saw her aggressive stance.

Lauren's hammering pulse slowed, but her irritation rose. After a full day's flying and dealing with Gage's scrutiny, she was too tired for a backbiting confrontation. She needed to get home and call her mother and then her uncle. For five full seconds she debated ignoring her half brother, climbing into her truck and driving off. But she'd never been one to back down from a bully.

She lowered her keys. "You need better lighting in

your parking area. If I were trigger-happy and had pepper spray, you'd be on your knees howling by now."

Trent's gaze went from her to her truck and back. "I'll mention your concerns to security."

Sure he would. Impatient, she tapped her toe. "Did you need something?"

"Lauren, if Gage wants to sit in the cockpit he can. If he asks you to eat dinner with him, do it. Do whatever he says."

His my-word-is-law tone raised her hackles and sent a trickle of unease through her. "Exactly how far do you expect me to go to keep the customer happy?"

His head jerked back and his nostrils flared. "I'm not asking you to do anything illegal or immoral."

"You're asking me to violate HAMC rules. I want you to spell out your expectations—in writing. Preferably signed and notarized."

"What? You don't trust me, little sister?"

"Half sister." She shouldered her flight bag. "You've made it clear from day one that I'm unwelcome here. I'm not handing you a blank check to write me out of the picture."

"Would a blank check work?"

His audacity took her breath. "Could you possibly be more of a jack—"

The scrape of a shoe on asphalt drew her attention to another approaching male. Gage. Great. Two headaches. "I'll talk to you tomorrow."

"There's nothing you can't say in front of Gage. He's like family."

The statement only irritated her more. "Unlike me who actually *is* family. I admire your loyalty. To your friends at least."

"What's your price, Lauren?" Trent asked.

She wanted to kick the knucklehead in the kneecap, but she'd encountered and dealt with worse than him before without resorting to assault. "You can't buy me off, *big brother.* You've had our mother for thirtysome-thing years. It's my turn to spend a little time with her. Don't worry. I'll give her back."

"You've known her all your life."

A gurgle of disgust bubbled up her throat. She cut a look at Gage, who stood by Trent's side. "I see your spy has debriefed."

Gage frowned. "Lauren, our conversation wasn't confidential."

"Don't waste your breath, Faulkner. I knew where your loyalties lay before we ever set foot on an airplane together."

Trent squared his shoulders, trying to intimidate her by towering over her. Too bad it didn't work. "If you've known our mother all your life, why are we only now hearing about you?"

"Because apparently *our* parent wanted to keep us all in the dark. She never told me about you, either." She turned away then turned back. "Did you know my father was one of the founders of Hightower Aviation?"

The men's breath whistled in stereo.

Trent scowled—his usual expression around her. "I've heard no such claim."

"And neither had I until I started clearing out my father's old papers. Your father and mine were in the Air Force together. I found pictures. They started HAMC after they got out. They were scraping along, strapped for cash when our grandfather Bernard Waterman came on the scene and offered them money in return for one-third ownership. I'm not sure how our mother plays into the picture."

"I'll have to verify your story."

"Good luck with that. Jacqui's not talking." But why? And why had her father kept the secret? "Don't sweat it, boss. I'm not demanding a percentage of the stock. My father sold out to our mother while she was pregnant with me, and as far as I can tell he got a fair price. He took that money and started Falcon Air with my uncle Lou, who also used to work here."

Suspicion narrowed Trent's eyes. "Your uncle?"

"Oh, for pity's sake, relax. He isn't a blood relative. You won't have another relative crawling out of the woodwork, showing up and asking for a job."

Gage shoved his hands in his overcoat pockets. "Trent and I are going to have a drink. Do you want to join us and tell us more about this history of HAMC?"

Trent stiffened as if Gage's invitation had surprised him.

Obviously they'd decided to tag team her out of a job. She hit the remote to unlock her door, opened it and slung her bag inside. "Nice try, Faulkner. But I have to fly in the morning and any alcohol within twelve hours of flight time gets me fired. Company policy."

"Nice truck," Gage said behind her. "Big engine."

"For a girl, you mean? I need ten cylinders to tow airplanes around back home." The Dodge SRT Ram was her pride and joy and had been a true labor of love shared with the people she cared most about. It would also be the last project she, her father and Uncle Lou would work on together.

"Look, if you guys are through with the interrogation, I need some shut-eye. I've been here since four this morning, and I'm due back at the same time tomorrow for our flight to Lancaster."

Trent nodded. "Good night."

"Go ahead," Gage told him. "I'll catch up with you at the restaurant."

After a moment's hesitation Trent strolled toward his BMW, leaving her alone with Gage. "You don't trust me much, do you, Lauren?"

"I don't know you well enough to trust you."

"You have nothing to fear from me as long as you're not out to hurt the Hightowers."

Not believing him for one second, she climbed into her truck. "I'll keep that in mind."

He braced one hand on each side of her door and leaned into the opening, crowding her. She caught a whiff of his minty breath. Her mouth dried and her pulse quickened.

He stopped inches from her face. "Let's get one thing straight. I don't need Trent to pimp for me. If I ask you to dinner, it's because I don't like eating alone. I'm not expecting more. You're not my type."

"Good, because you're not mine, either." She fired the words back automatically. Just because she didn't want him didn't mean his rejection didn't sting.

He straightened, withdrawing from her personal space. "I'll see you in the morning."

He turned on his heel and headed toward a black SUV with long, purposeful strides.

What was Gage's type? The question popped into her head unexpectedly as she turned her key.

Doesn't matter. Forget it. Go home.

But she had a feeling that now that her curiosity had been stirred, she wasn't going to be able to forget it.

Three

Lauren shifted uneasily on the front doormat of the opulent Hightower home. A less-desperate woman would go home without making an already-bad day worse, but knowing Trent had dinner plans with Gage gave her a narrow window of opportunity to talk to her mother before he arrived home.

The door opened and Fritz the butler stood framed in the entryway. "Good evening, miss."

"Hi, Fritz."

"Madame is waiting for you in the salon." He turned and led the way like a butler cliché from an old movie, British accent, black suit, stiff posture and all.

Lauren craned her neck, once again awed and a little intimidated by the soaring foyer with its priceless art collection and grand staircase. Her heels tapped on the marble tiles and the sound echoed off the walls, making her want to tiptoe. Honestly, the place was like a museum or a governor's mansion or something. How could anyone be comfortable here?

Fritz stepped aside and gestured to the open door with its fancy wood trim. "May I bring you anything? Wine? Coffee? Perhaps a light snack?"

"No, but thank you." How could she eat when every encounter with her mother was like an armed truce?

Fritz bowed and retreated, leaving Lauren once more with the surreal sense of being blown off course and landing on a foreign airstrip where you didn't know if the natives were friendly or hostile or even which language they'd speak. The Hightower abode was hardly the kind of place you could kick your shoes off and wander around in your jammies.

"You've come straight from work." Her mother's voice pulled her attention back to the massive room. Jacqui sat in a chair by the fireplace looking almost regal in her black pantsuit, heels and diamonds. "The HAMC uniform looks good on you and makes me quite glad I insisted on skirts instead of pants for our female pilots."

"Um…yeah, thanks. I appreciate you letting me stop by on short notice."

"I'm always happy to see you, Lauren."

Oh, right. Jacqui emitted about as much warmth as an Alaskan winter. There was no shared hug, just a meaningless air kiss. They barely even touched. Her father or Uncle Lou would have swept Lauren up into a big lung-crushing, feet-lifted-off-the-ground hug after a long absence. But the Hightowers weren't the warm and fuzzy type.

"Come in and sit down."

Lauren perched on the edge of a brocade sofa with fancy fringe trim. How could she not have realized Jacqui was her mother sooner? They shared the same build and the same features, although her mother did something to brighten the mousy shade of her upswept hair and her makeup was always immaculate. Jacqui looked good, but Lauren wasn't into high maintenance. She'd stick with her naturally boring hair and soap, water and sunscreen regimen.

"I have some questions about my father."

Jacqui sniffed. "I can't talk about him yet. I miss him too much." Her emotion appeared genuine. But it had been two months—two months with a lot of meaningless chitchat, but no answers.

Lauren was beyond frustrated. "I miss him, too, Jacqui, but I need to understand his state of mind before the accident."

Jacqui rose and went to the wet bar to refill her glass instead of ringing for Fritz the way she had during Lauren's previous visits. "I can't pretend to know what your father was thinking."

"You were the last one to talk to him. Did he seem upset, distracted or depressed to you?"

Her mother faced her but didn't return to her seat. "Depressed? I don't know what you mean."

Lauren took a deep breath. She hadn't discussed the rumors with anyone other than her uncle. "A couple of his friends think the crash wasn't an accident. They claim Dad bragged that if he died, his life insurance policy would pay off Falcon Air's debts."

Jacqui stiffened and paled. She pressed a beringed, manicured hand to her chest. "No. No. Never. Kirk would never voluntarily leave me. Or you. From the moment I told him I'd conceived, you were his life. He planned everything around providing for you."

Emotion welled inside Lauren, tightening her chest. "I don't think he would have deliberately crashed, either. I mean, I can't believe I would have missed him being that upset. He was preoccupied those last few months, but I don't think he was unhappy." But had she missed something? "The life insurance company is refusing to pay the claim until they finish their investigation and rule out suicide."

"I'll give you whatever you need. Tell me how much."

Lauren shook her head. "I've told you before I don't want your money. I just want to know what you and my father discussed that last day before you left him *again*. That conversation could be a key to what happened."

Tears pooled in Jacqui's eyes. Was she faking it? "You believe I had something to do with his crash?"

"How can I know if you won't talk?"

"Lauren…I can't…discuss this."

"But—"

"I know you don't believe me, but I loved Kirk. He is the only man I ever loved, and knowing I'll never see him again—" Her voice broke. Her hand trembled as she set down her glass and covered her mouth.

Lauren hardened herself to the emotion. Jacqui was hiding something. The question was, what? "What about your husband?"

"That was an arranged marriage. My father promised to invest in Hightower Aviation if William married me."

"And you agreed?"

"I was a bit of a…difficult girl. My father wanted me to settle down. He threatened to cut me off without a cent if I didn't do as he ordered. William was quite a dashing pilot at the time. I thought I could grow to love him. I was wrong."

But she was still married to the guy. "Where did my father fit into this triangle?"

"William's only loves were flying and gambling. When my father died unexpectedly, I discovered my husband had gambled us into financial difficulty. I had to learn how to manage HAMC's assets because my husband was too busy having fun elsewhere. Your father helped me. Our…friendship soon became more. I knew it was wrong. But I fell in love with Kirk, and he with me."

Lauren shifted, not wanting to believe her father had knowingly slept with a married woman.

"When I became pregnant with you, your father gave me an ultimatum. Leave William and come to him or we were over. But I couldn't. My father had written into his will that if I left my husband, I'd lose everything. My trust fund. My inheritance. My stock in Hightower Aviation. I had my other children to think of. I couldn't leave them to be raised by that—their father."

"You left me easily enough."

"William pressured me into giving you up. Kirk insisted on adopting you. I agreed, but only if I could visit you. Your father's stipulation was that we not tell you I was your mother. He didn't want you to feel rejected."

But Lauren had always wondered why her mother couldn't love her and didn't want her. "If you loved my father that much, how could you have been happy with only seeing him once a year?"

"That was all William would allow me. I lived for that week."

So had her father. Lauren had experienced a love-hate reaction with Jacqui's visits. On one hand while her mother was there, her father had been happier than she'd ever seen him, but every time Jacqui left he'd been devastated. And nothing Lauren had done had been enough to cheer him up.

She scanned the expensively decorated room. "Yes, it looks like you had a rough time. Living in the lap of luxury with servants at your beck and call when you weren't with Dad and I must have been difficult."

Jacqui cringed at the sarcasm in Lauren's voice. "I would have been with you if I could."

Lauren tried to work up sympathy and failed. Her mother had chosen financial security over a man who'd adored her and would have done anything for her. "So you don't think my father committed suicide?"

Again, Jacqui flinched. "Your father had too much to live for to harm himself. He had such plans, such high hopes."

Lauren wanted to believe her. But there was something fishy in the way Jacqui's gaze kept flitting around the room and never directly engaging with Lauren's.

The front door opened. Male voices bounced off the walls. Lauren stiffened. Gage and Trent. What had happened to their dinner plans? She looked at the archway, praying they'd pass by, but Trent's scowling face glared back at her.

"Mother, I didn't know you were expecting company." An arctic chill radiated from his voice.

"You know Lauren is always welcome here."

Gage said nothing, but his dark assessing eyes lasered in on Lauren. She had every intention of finding out what Jacqui was hiding, but she wouldn't get her answers tonight. She couldn't risk Trent overhearing the questionable circumstances of her father's death. The charter jet business was a small and competitive one. One word to the wrong people and Falcon would be grounded. Permanently.

Lauren rose. "I was just leaving. Good night, Jacqui. Gentlemen, I'll see you in the morning."

* * *

"Any news?" Lauren asked the moment her uncle answered the phone twenty minutes later. She locked her apartment door and set her keys and bag on the nearby table.

"Nothing."

She'd been frustrated by her lack of progress with her mother and needed to talk to someone who understood. "Why is this taking so long? Daddy's been gone two months."

"Lauren, sweetie, your father's case may be number one to us, but it's not to the rest of the world. To them he was just another pilot in an experimental aircraft. He wasn't running from criminal charges or trafficking drugs or anything else that would make him a high priority."

"But Lou—"

"The crashes that have happened since his are higher profile. When are you coming home?"

She unpinned her hair, trying to relieve the slight headache Trent and Gage always gave her. "I don't know. Jacqui's still playing the grieving lover role. I'll try to call the investigators again tomorrow."

"No point. I called today to make sure they had your correct address. They promised the report would be couriered to you as soon as it's done. Just finish whatever it is you're trying to do and get home. I need you here. And I miss you, baby girl."

Her chest tightened. Lou had been a second father to her. Moving to Knoxville on the heels of her father's death was almost like losing both of them. "I miss you, too, Lou."

"Call the minute you get the report."

"I will. Keep your cell phone on."

"I'll try to remember."

She rolled her eyes. "Don't try. Just do it. Love you. I'll call again soon."

And hopefully, by the next time she called she'd have the answers they all needed to be able to get back to life as usual and focus on getting Falcon Air back into the black.

"She's done it again." Trent's angry voice barked through Gage's wireless cell phone earpiece late Wednesday afternoon.

"Who's done what?" Gage's grip tightened on the steering wheel of the sedan he'd rented.

"My mother withdrew almost two hundred thousand dollars from one of her accounts today."

Gage's breath whistled through his teeth. Jacqueline Hightower had always liked her expensive toys. "Has she been car shopping again?"

"I doubt there's a dealership on the island of Anguilla. That's where Mother is now. She flew out early this morning. I'll bet that little leech is connected. Why else would Lauren have been at my house last night? Is she with you now?"

Gage pinched the bridge of his nose, hoping to ward off the tension headache taking root between his eyes. The CEO he'd spent the day with had been difficult and defensive. In the end, Gage had refused the job and walked out.

Turning down work was still difficult for him. He wanted the security each job put in his investment account, but his time was short and the list of clients requesting his expertise was long enough to allow him to choose the ones who truly wanted his help and were ready to accept it rather than deal with the ones who fought his suggestions each step of the way as this one would have.

"No. I just left the job site. I'm on the way to the airport now."

"Tell Lauren to report to my office as soon as she's locked down the plane."

Gage scanned the dense fog outside the windows of his rental car. His headlights barely penetrated the near whiteout. "Check the forecast. Unless she's going to fly blind I don't think we'll be home tonight."

A moment later Trent's curse rang in his ears.

"Don't sweat it, Trent. This could work in your favor. The weather will keep your sister out of town overnight while you track the money trail. I'll use the time to see if I can find out anything relevant to your situation."

It wasn't as if he'd be befriending Lauren. He was simply protecting Trent's interest and digging for facts—something he did every day in his job.

Gage refused to stand by and let someone else's greed derail Trent's years of hard work. Loyalty to his friend wouldn't allow it.

Lauren shifted in the passenger seat of the rental car, glanced down at her HAMC uniform and then up at the restaurant looming out of the fog.

Not again. Why did life keep throwing men who seemed determined to prove she couldn't fit into their world at her? It was probably a good thing her last relationship hadn't worked out. If she'd married Whit— not that he'd asked—she would have struggled against a lifetime of being a misfit. Ditto trying to fit into the Hightower clan.

"Can we go somewhere less…?"

Gage glanced her way as he pulled into the valet parking lane behind three other cars. "Less what?"

"Highfalutin. I realize you're accustomed to places

like this, but I'm more interested in a filling meal than swanky presentation and having to worry about which fork to use."

No matter what her half brother ordered she should never have agreed to have dinner with Gage. But being grounded at a small rural airport by heavy fog had limited her options. Gage hadn't requested in-flight meals, so there hadn't been any food stashed on board, and the airport didn't have a restaurant. She hadn't wanted to waste money on a taxi.

An elegantly clad couple exited the brass-and-glass etched doors and headed for the valet stand, confirming her opinion. "I'm not dressed for this."

Gage inched the car forward. "What makes you think this is my kind of place?"

She flipped a wrist, indicating his tailored suit. He still looked as *GQ* fresh as he had when he'd met her at the terminal sixteen hours ago in the misty morning light. "You're buddies with Trent, which means you were probably born in a suit and carrying a silver spoon. Correction. You probably had a nanny on standby to carry it for you from the moment you took your first breath."

Gage's eyes crinkled with amusement. Lauren jerked back, her breath and heart hitching in tandem. *Wow.* The man was seriously gorgeous when he flashed those pearly whites.

Too bad he was taboo.

But even if he weren't, her life was too complicated for a relationship right now. Besides, Gage had the money thing going, and, compliments of Whit, she'd sworn off rich guys forever. Their sense of entitlement and belief that less-fortunate people had been put on this planet for their use rubbed her the wrong way. Her new family only reinforced that point.

Gage's smile faded. "I wasn't born to money, Lauren. I earned everything I have. But I appreciate a good meal and superior service."

She searched his face in the glow of the dashboard lights. Could he possibly be telling the truth? If not, he lied flawlessly. "Your parents weren't loaded?"

"No."

"How did you go to that expensive university with Trent?"

The broad shoulder nearest her lifted. "Scholarships, financial aid and a job."

He pulled up to the valet station, put the car in Park, released his seat belt and reached for the door handle.

Lauren grabbed his arm, her fingers curling around big, firm bicep. His body heat seeped through his clothing and warmed her palm. She let go and laid her hand in her lap. "Gage, I'd feel more comfortable elsewhere."

He scanned her. "You look fine. No one will turn you away."

Dread curdled in her stomach. She wrinkled her nose and nodded to the couple climbing from the car in front of them. "Do the words *little black dress, heels* and *pearls* mean anything to you?"

He followed her gaze, refastened his safety belt and put the car in gear. "We'll head toward the hotel and see if we can find a restaurant on the way."

"That would be great. Thanks." After two hours of waiting to take off on the runway and being turned back when the airport ceased operation, they'd both been too hungry to check in to the hotel before dinner. Her instrument rating didn't count for beans when the airport shut down before she could get the wheels up. Smaller airports were great when a pilot wanted to avoid traffic, but the downside was some didn't operate when conditions were less than optimal.

Gage pulled out of the valet lane and drove out of the parking lot. "I heard you making a phone call earlier. Something about a bike trip tomorrow?"

He must have eavesdropped while he'd been arranging their hotel rooms. "I needed to let my landlord know I wouldn't be home. She'll relay the message to the neighbors who were meeting me tomorrow morning."

"Your landlord keeps tabs on you?"

"I'm renting the apartment over her garage." Wanting to end the personal questions, Lauren bailed out of the car the moment he parked, hustled for the sidewalk and waited for him to join her. The look he cut her as they entered the building let her know he was on to her.

"What kind of ride did you have planned?"

The smell of grilled fajitas and thick burgers made her mouth water and her stomach rumble. She hadn't had anything to eat since the sandwich she'd packed for lunch.

"I was going on a group motorcycle ride with my neighbors. They're showing me the best of Knoxville on my days off. I was with them when Trent called me into the office to meet you."

He didn't speak again until after the hostess had seated them and departed. "Your neighbors are bikers?"

"Don't say it like it's a bad thing. They're great people. I found them through an online Harley chapter, and when I posted my plan to move to Knoxville they all but adopted me. One even hooked me up with my landlord. Her apartment is ten times better than any complex in the area and half the price. The day I pulled into her driveway my new friends were waiting to help me unpack."

"They were probably checking to see if you had anything worth stealing."

His words said a lot about the company he kept. "Not exactly a trusting soul, are you, Faulkner?"

"Where I came from if something wasn't nailed down, it was fair game."

"Not a nice neighborhood?"

He eyed her as if debating his words. "I spent a good part of my youth on welfare, and part of that living in my father's car."

Shock stole her breath. She didn't want to think of him as a poor, hungry kid or see an approachable side of him. She'd much rather believe he was a spoiled, stuck-up jerk like Trent, Brent and Beth, her three oldest half siblings. Only Nicole, the one closest to Lauren in age seemed to have any redeeming qualities. "I'm sorry, Gage. That's no way to live."

Regret tightened his mouth, as if he were sorry he'd revealed that bit of his past. "I'm not asking for sympathy. The point is you don't deserve anything you don't earn."

His hard tone let her know his barriers were up, and he didn't intend to give her any more peeks into his personal life.

"I agree, and I've worked hard for everything I have."

An expression of disbelief crossed his face.

The server arrived to take their orders. Once he left, Gage looked at her across the table. The probing way he studied her made her uncomfortable. A speculative gleam entered his dark eyes. "You said you grew up around an airport. Regardless of the city, that's not usually the best section of town."

Another personal foray, but given what he'd shared she decided it wouldn't hurt to respond to this one. "We had a small, but comfortable house near Daytona International. We weren't high-class, but we weren't poor, either. I didn't attend private schools, belong to a country club or have servants, a pool, tennis court or any of the other luxuries the Hightowers seem to think they can't function without."

"Does it bother you that your mother's other children had more than you?"

"No. If anything I'm appalled by their dependence on others for even the simplest things. Don't get me wrong. I'm used to people with money. After all, they are the ones who charter jets. But the Hightower's over-the-top lifestyle is like something you'd see on TV. None of them had jobs until after college. Even then, they were hired by the family firm, so there's no chance of getting fired for poor performance."

He sipped his bourbon. "Don't you work for your father?"

He was really determined to see her in a bad light, wasn't he? "I didn't initially. I started with odd jobs for other pilots and owners around the airport. Sweeping hangars, washing and waxing planes and cars. My dad made it very clear that if I did sloppy work, it would reflect badly on him.

"Then from the day I turned sixteen until I was certified as a flight instructor I worked in food service. I realize asking 'Do you want fries with that?' isn't anything to brag about, but at least I learned how to earn and manage money and work with the public."

Despite his relaxed posture his alert eyes assessed her over the rim of his glass. "You didn't go to college, did you?"

"Trent has been sharing stuff from my personnel file again." The rat. "I have an associate's degree from community college, and—"

She bit her lip and studied her hands. She was

working on a bachelor's degree from the University of Central Florida, but if her father's life insurance didn't pay up, she might not be able to afford to finish it. So close, and yet so far from attaining her goal. Getting her degree was more important now than ever. If Falcon Air failed, she'd have to find another employer, and the major airlines required a four-year degree.

And then there was Uncle Lou. At his age he'd have trouble finding another position, and he'd invested all his savings into Falcon. She might need to make enough to support both of them.

"And?" Gage prompted.

She wasn't whining to a stranger about her money problems—especially one who'd probably parrot her words to her half brother. Her situation would only re-inforce her half sibling's opinion that she was here to take a bite out of their inheritance. Time to talk about someone else.

"You seem very familiar with traveling in the copilot seat."

Gage held her gaze long enough that she began to doubt he'd let her change the subject. Finally, he lifted one shoulder. "I used to fly with Trent."

Surprise made her sit up straighter. "Trent has his pilot's license? But he always uses a full crew when he travels. He never takes the controls."

She knew because she'd been cursed with him as a hypercritical passenger on her first dozen flights.

"He works en route."

"If he'd take the controls now and then, maybe he wouldn't be so uptight. I can't imagine being content to sit in the back and let someone else have all the fun."

Gage's eyes narrowed. "You could have a point. He used to love flying."

"You should mention that next time you report in."

The arrival of their salads kept him from replying. After the server left, Gage picked up his fork. "Tomorrow we'll rent a couple of motorcycles from the Harley dealership and tour the area."

Excitement inflated inside her like a balloon. She popped it. Was this like demanding her presence at dinner? She had to comply? "I don't want to spend the cash."

"I'll cover it."

"Renting requires a motorcycle endorsement on your license."

"I haven't ridden in years, but I have it."

She studied him. Gage, with his perfectly fitting suits and immaculate haircut, looked far too sophisticated and uptight to climb on the back of a bike and roar down the roads with the wind whipping at his clothes. Not that there weren't thousands of executives who rode motorcycles, but Gage had an ever-present tension in him that hinted he never loosened up. "I don't believe you."

He extracted his license from his wallet and offered it to her. "I couldn't afford a car in college. I rode an old bike."

She snatched the small card from his hand. Yep. He had the endorsement. She noted his age, thirty-five, then checked his face. The brackets beside his mouth and the groove in his forehead made him look older.

She was about to pass his license back when his address caught her attention. "I know this address. The neighborhood is near my apartment and…not at all ritzy."

"I don't believe in wasting money on frivolous things."

"Like private jets?" The sarcastic quip was out of her mouth before she could stop it. Whoops.

Gage's eyebrows descended. He took the license from her and tucked it into his wallet. "Two of my associates are on parental leave. I'm covering my position in addition to theirs. I'm spending a lot of time in the air, but thanks to HAMC, a lot more time on the job and less time waiting in airport security lines. If I'd been flying commercial today, I would have either missed my flight or had to leave before the job was completed and return to finish my assessment. Either way, that would have cost me money. In the long run flying privately is more efficient since my time and expertise is what people purchase."

She grimaced. "Sorry. I guess I have a bit of a chip on my shoulder. I can't get used to the Hightowers' conspicuous consumption. They throw away a lot of money on extravagant stuff."

"And you don't?"

"I'm pretty thrifty."

His disbelieving chuckle sent a shiver of awareness through her. "Lauren, you own a motorcycle, a truck and an airplane—all three high-performance, pricy models."

Trent again. She smothered a growl of frustration. "Big brother has been talking. Not that it's any of your business, but for the record, I bought my truck from a salvage yard. Dad, Lou and I rebuilt her together. It gets poor gas mileage, but I need it for work, so I started looking for something more economical to drive.

"I got my motorcycle at half price by trading the owner for flying lessons. Consider it sweat equity. My airplane was a similar too-good-to-be-true bargain. The owner was having financial difficulties and needed to unload her quickly. He asked around at the airport to see if anyone might be interested in buying it. My father overheard him and told me. I took out a business loan because I make most of my living with that Cirrus. It's not a toy. It's my office."

A slow smile started in his eyes and spread to his mouth. The combo of gleaming dark eyes and white teeth stole her breath. She leaned back in her chair, putting as much distance between them as possible without actually leaving the table. The odd lightness in her tummy had better be hunger. She couldn't afford for it to be anything else.

"You're a mass of contradictions, Lauren Lynch. I apologize for jumping to conclusions."

In that moment she actually liked him.

He's the enemy, your half brother's spy and wealthy. Three strikes.

The waiter set their meals on the table and departed, but the interruption was enough to allow suspicion to overtake Lauren's brain. Why was Gage suddenly being so warm and approachable if not to set her up and take her down? He and her brother were in cahoots.

"It won't work, Gage."

"What's that?" he asked, looking up from his thick salmon steak.

"Charming me."

One dark eyebrow hiked. "Excuse me?"

"I'm on to the scheme you and Trent have cooked up. I've been burned by one of you rich guys before, and I learned my lesson. I don't care how attractive you are, I won't—"

"You find me attractive?" His eyes crinkled deliciously and a miniature stunt plane did a loop-de-loop in her midsection.

She frowned at him and ignored his question. "I will

not violate HAMC policies by getting personally involved with you. So stop smiling and flirting."

"I'm not flirting."

"Oh, please. Don't bat your lashes at me. I'm not buying that innocent act. And what do you call renting motorcycles and spending the day playing tourist together if you're not trying to get me to let down my guard?"

His expression turned serious. "If I hadn't been late arriving at the airport, we'd have taken off before the fog descended, and you'd be home by now. My overtime cost you your day off. The motorcycle ride is to replace the one I took from you."

Speechless and more than a little suspicious, she stared into his dark eyes, searching for the truth. That sounded fair-minded and almost *nice*. She didn't want him to be nice. She wanted him to be a conceited prick. Like Trent.

But she wasn't dumb enough to look a gift horse in the mouth. She'd always wanted to see the Dutch Amish countryside, and her father had always said, "Take a little of each place you visit home with you." She'd just have to be careful and not fall for Gage's handsome face, his devastating grin or let his sneaky charm worm information out of her that she wasn't willing to share. Of course, that wasn't anything she couldn't handle. Not after the lesson Whit had taught her.

"Okay, Faulkner, you're on. But I'm in charge. Road rules state the most experienced rider leads. That's me. If you can't handle following, speak up now."

One corner of his mouth curled upward. "I can handle anything you can dish out and then some, Lynch. Bring it on."

Lauren's bike engine wasn't the only thing revving as Gage strode across the parking lot toward her.

A muscle-hugging black leather jacket accentuated his broad shoulders and lean torso. Matching chaps framed the denim covering the male package behind the fly of his jeans like a Look Here sign. He paused beside his motorcycle to don his black helmet and pull on his gloves, then he mounted the machine.

She visually traced the line of his straight back, his long legs and the booted feet he'd planted squarely on the asphalt. She told herself she was assessing his form and therefore his skill level, but knew she lied.

He looked good straddling a Harley. Good and hot.

And that was *baaaad*. For her peace of mind, anyway.

Luckily, she'd ridden her motorcycle to work yesterday, and had stowed her riding gear on the plane. Not so Gage. He wore "tags barely off" new everything from the skivvies out—assuming he wore underwear. The biker attire suited him as well as his tailored suit had, maybe better. And thank God he had the intelligence to wear a helmet even though Pennsylvania law didn't require one.

With concentrated effort she forced her attention away from the man beside her to the GPS on the rental rumbling between her legs. After double-checking the route the salesperson had suggested, she heeled up her kickstand.

Gage's gaze scraped her from head to toe. Appreciation replaced the anticipation sparkling in his eyes. Her breath caught and suddenly her neck warmer felt tighter and itchier than a too-small turtleneck sweater. She tugged the stretchy fleece away from her skin and inhaled a lungful of cool air.

He zipped his jacket and flipped down his visor then started his bike and twisted the throttle, making the engine roar. His thigh muscles bunched as he balanced the heavy weight of the bike, making her think of other activities that caused those same muscles to flex. Not something she needed to think about if she wanted to be steady on her wheels.

She cleared her throat. "Ready?"

"Ready." His voice was strong and sure.

Oh, yeah, he'd ridden before and his confidence in his ability to control the powerful motorcycle came through loud and clear.

Damn. Confidence looked good on him. Good and sexy.

Her palms moistened in her gloves and heat filled her jacket and helmet despite the nip in the autumn air. A chilly ride was exactly what she needed to clear her head. A little hypothermia would fix what ailed her. "Follow my lead and watch for my hand signals."

"Just ride, Lauren. I've got your back."

She lowered her visor, put the bike in gear and pulled out of the parking lot. She'd bet her Harley Gage would rather lead than follow, but she'd dealt with hardheaded students before. She knew when to dig in and when to be flexible. Allowing shenanigans could get someone hurt or killed. And one death in the family was all Falcon Air could handle.

Four

Gage's pulse pounded in his ears, and adrenaline pulsed through his veins, energizing his muscles and sharpening his senses. Wind pummeled his leather jacket and whistled through the vents on his full-face helmet.

Ahead of him, Lauren leaned into a curve, her body moving as one with the machine beneath her. He did the same, savoring the power and responsiveness of the well-balanced Harley. It had taken almost an hour for the feel for riding to return, and for him to get comfortable on the bike. As if Lauren had anticipated that, she'd taken it easy on him for the first leg of their trip. Now she pushed him, going a little faster and taking more challenging routes. She leaned farther into each curve.

He hadn't realized how much he'd missed cutting through the air like a missile. He caught himself grinning inside his helmet and surprise sobered him.

In college he'd ridden a motorcycle due to necessity,

not for pleasure, and his inability to afford a car had been an embarrassment and an obstacle to overcome. When he'd sold that old clunker he'd sworn he'd never have another motorcycle. Today's outing made him rethink that decision.

He focused on the curve of Lauren's leather-clad butt. Who was this woman in front of him? Her pleasure in riding the winding roads through the rolling farmlands and roaring through the covered bridges and past silos, horse-drawn buggies, frolicking goats and stacks of hay bales couldn't be more obvious or more contagious. The simple things she pointed out contradicted Trent's certainty that Lauren was a mercenary bitch out to tap the Hightower keg and drain it dry.

In fact, everything Gage had learned about her to this point went against Trent's theory, but Trent had always been a shrewd judge of character. He'd been the only one to warn Gage that Angela was lying about agreeing to forgo children and all she wanted was a meal ticket.

Too bad Gage hadn't been smart enough to listen to his friend and dump Angela instead of marrying her. He'd been blinded by lust and love and bought Angela's pretty little lie that he was all she'd ever need. A year later when he'd stood firm on the no-children issue she'd pleaded and pouted then threatened and finally left him, taking a chunk of his net worth with her in the divorce settlement. If he'd put the no-kids clause in writing, she wouldn't have been able to use it against him. He shook off the negative memory of his ex-wife.

Could Trent be wrong about Lauren? Doubtful. If anything, Gage wasn't seeing clearly due to his attraction to Lauren.

Lauren signaled a left turn and pulled into a rural diner parking lot. Gage geared down and followed her, stopping beside her and killing his engine. The absolute silence of the countryside soaked into him.

She flipped up her visor. "Let's eat before we head back."

"Sounds good." Dismounting, he peeled off his gloves and reached up to remove his helmet. Something felt different. He rolled his shoulders trying to pinpoint the change and discovered the persistent knots that had cramped his neck and upper back for the past year had vanished.

He unzipped his jacket. Cold air bit his hands and cheeks. But it felt good. *He* felt good, and eager for the next leg of the journey. His disappointment over yesterday's wasted hours had vanished.

How long had it been since he'd taken a day off? He couldn't remember. He used to vacation with Trent a couple of times a year, but lately both of them had been too busy to even make their monthly dinners.

After removing her helmet, Lauren turned in a slow circle, scanning the brown patchwork fields surrounding them and finger-combing the tangles from her hair. "Isn't it beautiful?"

She was beautiful. The defensive edge she usually wore had vanished. Her cheeks were flushed and her teal eyes sparkled with joy, vitality and excitement— all of the things that had been lacking from his life lately. If he could have absorbed her energy into his being at that moment, he would have. The temptation to try pulled at him, moving him forward until the toes of their boots touched.

He lifted a hand and cupped her cheek. Her widened gaze bounced to his. Awareness edged out exuberance, expanding her pupils. She shivered.

Her scent, a combination of her leather riding

apparel, the outdoors and a trace of flowers invaded his nostrils and sank heavily to his groin.

Gage's eyes focused on her moist, pink mouth. He told himself to back away. Given Trent's suspicions, acting on this chemistry was a bad idea. Instead, he leaned forward. Lauren's head tilted back. Her lips parted and her gold-tipped lashes descended. A puff of her warm breath teased his chin, and his heart hammered against his ribs.

Contact with her lips—soft, damp lips—zapped him like static electricity, but the spark was far from superficial. He felt it deep in his gut. Hell, the current charged through all his extremities. Eager for more of her taste, he opened his mouth and stroked her bottom lip with his tongue. She tasted of cherry Chap Stick lip balm and…Lauren.

She sighed into his mouth, and her breasts nudged his chest. He cupped her waist, stroked her back, then the tight curve of her leather-clad bottom to pull her closer.

She stiffened. Her eyes flew open, meeting his gaze over their joined mouths. She planted her palms on his chest and shoved, nearly knocking him off his feet.

Wiping her mouth, she backed away. "Nice try, Faulkner. But you're not going to cost me this job."

A sharp gust of wind punctuated her statement and cooled the embers she'd ignited. Gage studied her flushed face.

Who was the real Lauren Lynch? The simple woman who wore Chap Stick and enjoyed the Amish countryside? Or the one out for everything she could siphon from her rich relatives? With two hundred grand unaccounted for, Gage couldn't be too careful.

For Trent's sake, he would find out Lauren's objectives. It was the least he could do to repay his debt.

But sleeping with the enemy wasn't part of the plan. No matter how good she tasted.

The combination of driving rain, a chilly forty degrees and twenty-mile-per-hour crosswinds had added a little extra excitement to Lauren's Thursday-night landing in Knoxville. Those same conditions were going to make her motorcycle ride home from the airport miserable.

She hadn't packed her rain suit when she'd left for work yesterday morning because the cold front hadn't been predicted to dip this far south. Maybe the Fates were giving her the cold shower she deserved for aborting her common sense this afternoon and kissing her brother's spy.

Her pulse skipped just thinking about the firm possession of Gage's mouth, his warm lips and the heat of his hands on her behind. She blew out a slow breath and tried to shake off the arousal prickling her skin like a coarse wool blanket.

Gage would not sneak beyond her fences again. Not today or any other day. But his boyish grin when he'd climbed off that Harley Night Rod had knocked reason right out of her head. The man took himself too seriously. The fact that he'd seemed surprised to have enjoyed the ride had doubled the knee-weakening power of his blinding smile, and those glittering golden-brown eyes had hit her harder than a triple shot of Goldschlager.

Gage Faulkner was dangerous. Probably more so than Whit had been because she'd known what her ex-lover wanted from the moment he'd swept her off her feet with that first fancy dinner. Gage was sneakier and more devious because while the attraction crackled between them, so did the antagonism. But she knew his game plan now. Charm her. Disarm her. Get her fired.

In her logbook, once a fool didn't mean always a fool. She knew better than to mistake herself for Cinderella again. She'd learned the hard way there was no happily ever after for a rich man and a working-class woman. The wealthy took what they wanted short-term then moved on to a more suitable mate for the long haul, one who had connections and social graces. Like the congressman's debutante daughter Whit had married.

That meant Lauren had to get rid of Gage. But how?

She locked the plane then hunched her shoulders and sprinted through the downpour toward the terminal a hundred yards away. She'd dropped Gage off closer to the building where an attendant had been waiting with an umbrella to escort him inside, then she'd taxied the Mustang to her assigned spot on the tarmac.

Cold droplets slipped down the back of her neck, soaked through her uniform and spattered her legs beneath her skirt as she splashed across the concrete. She shook off what moisture she could and debated calling a taxi, but she wanted to send Uncle Lou as much money as she could to cover her father's—now her—share of the expenses, and the ride to her apartment on the other side of town would run at least fifty bucks. The equivalent of a week's worth of groceries.

Drenched and shivering, she opened the door. Inviting heated air welcomed her, but the sight of Gage waiting in the lobby stopped her on the threshold. She'd taken her time locking down the plane hoping he'd be long gone before she came inside.

"Is there a problem?" she asked.

"Park your Harley in the hangar. I'm giving you a ride home."

She opened her mouth to refuse what sounded more like an order than an offer. Other than flying around the storm, the flight home had been calm and enjoyable since, for once, Gage had buckled up in the passenger cabin where he belonged. The last thing she wanted was more time with him. Time to rehash that misbegotten kiss, time to smell his cologne and feel his presence and get her muscles all kinked up again with knots of tension.

But her daddy hadn't raised a fool. She'd rather be warm and dry than wet and proud. "Thanks. Let me turn over the flight log."

"I'll get the car and wait outside."

All too soon she'd handed over the report on the airplane's performance, secured her bike and stood beside the black Chevy SUV Gage had pulled beneath the covered drop-off area in front of HAMC's private departure lounge.

He opened her door. Their fingers touched as he took her flight bag from her, jarring her heart into an erratic beat and almost making her miss her footing as she climbed into the front seat. His steadying hand on her elbow didn't help her coordination any.

The big, powerful vehicle suited him, and the interior smelled like a combination of his cologne and leather upholstery. He strapped in beside her. Maybe she could convince him to talk to Trent about reassigning her on the way home. But within minutes the nasty weather combined with rush hour traffic changed her mind. She'd let Gage focus on getting them to her place without incident.

Water streamed down the windows, isolating them from the rest of the world. Intense concentration furrowed his forehead and stiffened his shoulders. She caught herself contrasting his hard, chiseled jaw with the relaxed and easy smile he'd worn when he'd climbed off the Harley.

Her gaze drifted to his thick dark hair. The neatly combed strands had gotten damp when he'd gone after his car, and the moisture gave the ends a slight curl. He looked more approachable with disheveled helmet hair. He'd probably look even better with bedhead.

The thought made her wince. Oh yeah, she had to get rid of him before she did something stupid. Like risk her job by kissing him again…or worse.

She'd never been a slave to desire before, had never been one of those silly, giggly girls she'd overheard on campus who couldn't wait until spring break to get wild, and she had no intention of getting goofy now. Not that she'd had that many opportunities to get stupid over a guy. But Whit had gotten to her. He'd slipped past her defenses and made her believe for a few short months that she could be more than a jet jockey.

Dumb. Dumb. Dumb. Besides, you love being a pilot.

She squinted and leaned forward to see through the windshield. Darkness and oncoming headlights combined with a fog building inside the car created an awful glare.

She reached for the defrost button and her hand collided with Gage's as he did the same thing. She jerked away, and let him adjust his own controls while she tried to quiet the buzz working through her system like a shorted-out wire.

"Take the next exit then the second right. It's the third house on the left."

He followed her instructions, pulled up to the garage and turned off the engine. Lauren jumped from the car and opened the back door to retrieve her bag. She turned and startled when she saw Gage standing beside her.

He clamped steadying hands on her upper arms.

"Sorry." She pulled free, but the feel of his hands remained after he'd moved out of her personal space. "Thanks for the ride."

"I'm coming up."

"Why?" A chilly raindrop slid down her cheek.

"You didn't leave on any lights."

Something inside her went mushy. She wasn't used to men other than her dad and Lou looking out for her. "I'll be fine."

"I'll see you inside." His inflexible tone warned her arguing would be a waste of time, and she wasn't really interested in getting soaked to prove a point.

Resigned, she led the way up the steep, shadowed stairs and unlocked her door. Stepping inside, she flicked on a glass lamp filled with seashells she and her father had collected on the Florida beaches. Seeing the lamp reminded her why she was here and why she couldn't let Gage blow this gig for her prematurely.

"See. Everything's good. I told you, it's a safe neighborhood. Not all bikers are roughneck gang members."

Gage moved forward out of the rain pounding the landing outside her door and forcing her deeper into her living room. He closed the door as his gaze raked over her belongings as if cataloging and valuing each item. "Nice."

A snort of disbelief escaped before she could stop it. The two-room apartment wasn't big or luxurious, but it was clean and comfortable, and her landlord, a widow, was a sweetie. Lauren had brought only the essential furniture with her since she'd known she wouldn't be staying long, and much to her mother's disgust there wasn't a designer anything anywhere in sight.

Jacqui kept offering to buy Lauren gifts or loan her

money, but Lauren was equally determined to refuse. If her mother had wanted to show her affection, then she should have tried being a parent over the past twenty-five years instead of trying to buy Lauren's love now. The fact that Jacqui had chosen to be a mother to her other children chafed.

Lauren shrugged off the wasted emotion. "The apartment serves its purpose."

"Good night, then."

She glanced at the lamp again and gathered her courage. "Gage."

His dark eyes found hers.

"You need to request another pilot."

A pleat formed between his leveled eyebrows. "Why?"

"Because what happened today can't happen again."

He folded his arms and squared his stance. "It won't."

And yet even as he said the words, his gaze dropped to her lips—lips which tingled in response to his expanding pupils.

"Please ask. Trent won't listen to me."

"And in this case, neither will I. You're mine for the duration of this contract, Lauren. Deal with it." He turned and left, his footsteps pounding down the wooden stair treads.

Lauren groaned in frustration and shut the door.

Nothing good would come of this. Of that she was certain.

She should have called in sick, Lauren decided as she stepped from the plane onto the tarmac.

She'd been tempted to play hooky from work even though she felt perfectly well. But she'd never skipped out on work before, and she wasn't going to let her half brother and his cohort drive her into developing bad habits now.

At any other time the assignment she'd picked up this morning would have filled her with excitement. Three days in San Francisco. Throw in the opportunity to fly a new-to-her model jet, and she was almost in heaven.

Except the fates weren't finished conspiring against her.

She swept a regretful glance over the Sino Swearingen SJ30-2. A sweet, hot little number with a peach of a cockpit. And unless she could find an available mechanic with fast diagnostic skills, she probably wouldn't get to fly her. She expelled a long, disappointed breath. Bummer.

The long layover in San Francisco meant she should have time to finish her economics paper and sightsee, but for that to happen she had to get a different airplane or get the radio fixed.

The terminal door opened as she approached and one of her current headaches stepped out—thirty minutes ahead of his ETA.

Gage's gaze ran over her, taking in her fitted black uniform jacket, pencil skirt and low heels. She'd never considered the HAMC uniform sexy, but the way he looked at her kicked her pulse up a notch. His attention settled on her mouth, and she could feel yesterday's kiss all over again. Her stomach hit turbulence. Wasn't it bad enough that she'd dreamed about that kiss last night? Repeatedly.

She mashed her lips together and snapped to attention, trying to rein in her inappropriate response. "Good morning, Mr. Faul—" His shoulders stiffened and his eyes darkened with anger. "Gage," she corrected quickly.

So much for reestablishing proper protocol between them. "You're early. I still have a few things to take care of. Why don't you wait in the lounge and have a cup of coffee and maybe some breakfast?"

HAMC always put out a continental breakfast for its clients.

If she was lucky, he'd stay behind the bulkhead again today. Passengers, especially this one, belonged in the passenger cabin. She didn't want Gage in the copilot seat and didn't want to have to talk to him and edit every word that came out of her mouth.

"I've already had breakfast." His dark gaze shot beyond her to the aircraft then returned to her. "Is there a problem?"

"The Internet connection is down on the jet. It's probably just a loose wire in the transmitter. I'll get a mechanic to check it out. If it can't be fixed, I'll request another plane. Our Mustang is in for routine service today."

His jaw set in that stubborn angle she'd come to recognize didn't bode well for her. "I won't need the Internet on this trip."

But she would. Her paper was due by eight Monday morning. She still had to verify some research, do a final edit and submit her work to the professor via e-mail. Without the Internet she couldn't do any of those, and she didn't know where they'd be staying or if their hotel had service. She also needed to check in with her mother, who'd suddenly decided to play hard-to-get by taking a trip to the Caribbean.

Playing cat and mouse with Jacqui was getting tiresome. After two months of trying to get answers Lauren still had nothing. She was beginning to think her mother was avoiding her.

"It won't take long." She stepped forward to cut around Gage and enter the building, but he didn't move out of her way. She jerked to a halt, her shoulder touching his. A static shock skipped up her nerve endings, and his cologne invaded her senses before she could back away.

"Did everything else check out?" The minty smell of his breath caressed her face. His jaw gleamed from a recent shave.

"Yes, but—"

"And we both know you're thorough in your preflight check."

"Well, yes, but—"

"Let's stick with what we have. I'm short on time. Trent assures me this aircraft can go the distance without stopping to refuel, and it can land at the smaller airfield we're targeting."

"Yes, but—"

"Lauren, I don't have time for this." He caught her elbow and turned her toward the jet. The heat of his touch penetrated her suit jacket and kicked up a crosswind of sensation, but his high-handedness made her dig in her heels.

"Gage, I'd rather have a fully functional plane. We're early, and we'll make good ti—"

"If this one isn't unsafe—and I can't believe it is since it's your brother's personal aircraft—then let's go." He urged her toward the jet.

She planted her feet. "Gage—"

"Call it in, Lauren. Get it fixed on the other end." He pivoted and strode toward the jet without her.

She wanted to argue, to insist, to bash her head against the fuselage. But she couldn't. Her time was his time. HAMC wasn't paying her to do schoolwork. They were paying her to be a pilot at the client's disposal. They didn't care if she didn't get her degree and couldn't get another job.

The customer is always right unless safety is an issue.

Her father's words echoed in her head once again, reminding her why she was here. She sucked up her irritation and followed Gage to the aircraft, determined to get through the next three days without jeopardizing her job or her education.

Finding a hotel without Internet access in a metropolitan area like San Francisco had been a challenge, but Gage had succeeded—just as he'd succeeded in getting Trent to disable the Internet connection on the plane to keep Lauren from contacting her mother.

Encore, Please, the small bed-and-breakfast hotel in The Haight district of San Francisco had come highly recommended by a former client. It had no pool, no gym, no business center and no Internet—nothing like Gage's usual choice of accommodation. But he had to admit, despite the lack of amenities, the place had a certain charm.

If the property had belonged to him he would have toned down the girlie paint job in shades of lavender, purple and raspberry and eliminated some of the elaborate gingerbread trim and busy spindled railings. Otherwise the Victorian row house appeared to be a valuable, attractive and well-maintained piece of property in keeping with the surrounding homes and businesses.

A guest interested in relaxing would enjoy the postcard-worthy views from each window. But Gage didn't have time to unwind when he was doing the work of three consultants.

"Refill your glass, hon?" Esmé, the proprietress asked. "Another shrimp? Another stuffed mushroom?"

"No, thank you. It's all very good. But if you want me to have room for the delicious-smelling dinner you have prepared, I need to stop." There had been a time when he never refused food because he never knew when his next meal might be. But those days had passed.

When he'd returned from the job site he hadn't been interested in chatting with Esmé, a retired soap opera star with a dramatic flair, or Leon, her sixtysomething-year-old boyfriend, but the couple had somehow managed to bulldoze him onto the front porch and into a white wooden rocking chair and ply him with appetizers and Leon's homemade wine. They'd also put him through a thirty-minute inquisition worthy of the FBI with such subtlety that anyone who didn't dig for details for a living would never have recognized the interrogation. If his evasiveness frustrated them, they never let on. And they never let up.

He couldn't imagine Esmé making a profit running the B and B with the superior quality and high-end food she prepared for her few guests. But then Esmé probably didn't need money. She wore enough expensive jewelry to pay off a substantial mortgage and then some. For her sake, he hoped the gems were heavily insured.

But her finances were not his problem. He had papers to review and accounts to study for the company that had paid for his services, and he needed to locate Lauren. According to the couple, she'd left soon after they'd checked in this morning. Where in the hell had she gone?

"There's our girl now," Leon said.

Gage's abdomen tightened even before he looked in the direction his host indicated and spotted Lauren cresting the hill. A breeze lifted her straight hair away from her face. The setting sun streaked the strands with a copperish hue. Her jeans and zipped-up jacket outlined her slender shape. She paused, shifting her bag on her shoulder then turned toward Golden Gate Park as if soaking up the view one last time before retiring for the evening. Her jeans hugged her backside as faithfully as her leather riding pants had, but had interesting faded spots on each lower cheek. His body reacted predictably, given his recent all-work-and-no-play stint.

Why couldn't he get Lauren out of his head? The memory of that damned kiss and the feel of her pressed against him had disrupted his concentration all day, which was the reason he'd been forced to bring a case of files back to the B and B to work on tonight.

She pivoted and resumed walking toward the house. Where had she been all day?

She must have spotted the wildly waving Esmé because Lauren lifted a hand to wave. He knew the exact second she spotted him because her steps and hand faltered, and her blinding smile dimmed. Her fingers curled and her arm lowered. Even her stride changed from light and bouncy to laborious, as if she were slogging the last hundred feet uphill through knee-deep mud. Her obviously negative reaction nicked him, but he brushed it off. He didn't want to be her friend. Or her lover.

He might admire her confidence, competence and intelligence, but those were merely skills that made her a good pilot and a decent employee for Trent. Without trust none of those attributes mattered.

She climbed the stairs and both Esmé and Leon jumped up to greet her like a grandchild they hadn't seen in months.

Esmé hooked an arm through Lauren's and all but dragged her to the rocking chair beside Gage's. "Did you find the Wi-Fi café and get your paper done?"

"I did. Your directions were excellent. My paper is finished and e-mailed to my instructor days early."

She'd been online again? "What paper?"

Lauren bit her lip and shifted on her feet. "I have an economics paper due Monday morning."

"You're taking a class?"

She hesitated as if debating answering…or making up one. "Yes. Online through the University of Central Florida. You didn't need me, did you? You could have called my cell phone."

Her face looked honest enough, but his goal of keeping her offline had failed. He'd need a new strategy for tomorrow. "No. I didn't need you."

Leon took her bag and pressed a glass of wine into Lauren's hand. "Try this. It's my latest batch of vino."

She smiled her thanks and the old man beamed.

"Why are you taking classes?" Gage asked, recapturing her attention.

"I'm working toward a four-year bachelor's degree in business administration. In this economic climate it's always good to have a backup plan."

Add ambitious to her list of assets. But was she the type to take shortcuts and use others for personal gain? Something didn't add up. The discrepancy between what Trent believed and what Gage saw was too great. Good thing Gage enjoyed solving puzzles because Lauren was a complicated one.

Esmé patted Lauren's shoulder. "Smart girl. And

what about your mother? Were you able to reach her? Did she give you what you needed?"

Lauren hid a frown behind her glass as she sipped her wine and eased into the chair. If he hadn't been watching her closely, he would have missed her slight grimace. So she wasn't a fan of wine. But she smiled at her host and nodded her head as if she loved the subpar stuff rather than hurt Leon's feelings. "It's good."

That was an outright lie, but he could hardly blame her since he'd uttered the same one before she'd arrived. The wine had a distinctly metallic taste.

She tucked one foot beneath her in the chair. "I reached Mom, but she couldn't talk. She claimed she had to be somewhere. I'll try again tomorrow."

The hell she would. A sting of curses silently reverberated through Gage's head. Cutting Lauren off from the Internet had failed, and so had keeping her from contacting her mother.

"What do you need from your mother?" he asked.

She blinked at his unintentionally harsh tone and glanced away. "Answers."

He recognized evasion when he saw it. He'd mastered that particular skill. "What kind of answers?"

Lauren's teal gaze met his again. "She chose not to be my mother for twenty-five years. It would be nice to know why she changed her mind now."

That wasn't all. He could tell by her guarded expression that she was hiding something. What? And how could he uncover her secrets?

"You told me she'd always been a part of your life."

"Not as a parent. She was my father's…friend. She flew in once a year around my birthday and stayed for a week, but she spent most of her time with my father. I didn't mind, because during her stay he was always happier than at any other time of the year. He loved her. Too bad she didn't feel the same."

There was an edge in Lauren's voice that he couldn't quite decipher. She studied the burgundy liquid in her glass then looked up at him through narrowed eyes. "I talked to the mechanic this afternoon. Someone removed the fuse from the receiver that provides Internet access on the plane. It wasn't blown or broken. It was taken. Why would anyone do that?"

"Good question." And one he had no intention of answering since the action had been taken at his request.

Five

The city of San Francisco was waiting and Lauren was eager to hit the sidewalks and explore.

Trying to shake off the lingering tiredness her shower hadn't completely banished, she tightened the belt of the fluffy short white robe the B and B provided and stowed her toiletry items in her bag. She'd slept until six this morning, which was late for her because she usually had to be in the air by then, and given the time difference, she should have been up hours ago.

She blamed her sluggishness on all the tossing and turning she'd done last night. Her bedroom shared a wall with Gage's, and he must have stayed up late. She'd heard him moving around as if he were pacing, and a couple of times his deep voice had carried through the wall behind her headboard. Who had he been talking to at that time of night?

She opened the bathroom door and shuffled across

the landing. Gage's bedroom door opened before she reached her room, and he stepped into the hall. Her muscles locked up. She'd forgotten their single rooms shared a hall bathroom.

Against her will she drank in his mussed hair, sleepy brown eyes, beard-shadowed jaw and broad, bare-chested, seriously well-developed body. The man worked out. Shoulders, biceps, pecs and abs like that didn't happen by accident.

Black trousers, probably from yesterday's suit, rode low on his hips, transecting a dark line of hair that descended from between his nipples to below his navel. His big feet were bare, his toes long and straight. Like her, he held a toiletry bag.

He belonged on a sexy Corporate Hotties pin-up calendar. Her pulse *whumped* in her ears like helicopter blades, and she couldn't seem to suck enough air into her lungs. It took a substantial effort to uncurl her toes. "G-good morning."

His eyes sharpened on her face then slowly descended to the plunging neckline of the wraparound robe and on to her bare legs and feet. Other than the slight expansion of his pupils, his expression gave nothing away. A guy with his money was probably used to models and beauty queens rather than tomboys who wore jeans and no makeup. Not that she cared.

"Morning." The sleep-roughened voice rasped over her, making the fine hairs on her arms rise.

Conscious of her wet hair, freshly scrubbed face and near nakedness, she clutched her travel bag to her chest. "I'm, uh...done. The bathroom's all yours."

To get to the bathroom he had to pass close by her. She caught a faint whiff of his cologne as the air stirred, but mostly she smelled Gage—slightly musky male.

The close confines of a cockpit made someone's scent easily identifiable. Arousal flushed her skin and tightened her nipples, leaving her hot and bothered and wanting to shed the heavy robe. But that would have to wait until she'd shut the door behind her.

"Excuse me." She darted across the hall, not relaxing until she'd closed and locked the wooden panel between them. Knees weak, she sagged against the hard surface.

Why him? Why did Gage Faulkner agitate every feminine particle in her being into a whirlwind of certain disaster? It wasn't fair that the one guy she least wanted to be attracted to would affect her so strongly. But that didn't mean she'd be stupid and act on the bad mojo.

She listened for sounds from the hall while she hastily pulled on jeans and layered a sweater over her T-shirt then shoved her feet into sneakers. After she heard Gage reenter his room, she grabbed her jacket, wallet and computer backpack and jogged down the stairs.

Esmé met her in the foyer. "Good morning, dear. I've set up the breakfast buffet in the dining room. Help yourself."

Lauren debated skipping breakfast. She wanted to be gone before Gage came downstairs, but her loudly rumbling stomach vetoed that idea. "Thanks."

"I'll be in the kitchen if you need anything."

Lauren nodded and headed for the ornately decorated burgundy dining room. Yesterday morning after Gage had headed for the job site, Esmé and Leon had given Lauren a guided tour and history of the house. Her hosts' passion for their restoration project showed the hard work had been a true labor of love.

It wasn't until after Lauren had left for the Internet

café that she'd realized the couple had pried more personal details out of her than she'd ever shared with anyone else, and Lauren hadn't even seen it coming. But that was okay. Her hosts were harmless. They would never use what they'd learned against her. Unlike Gage, who probably used every tidbit of information as a weapon in his arsenal.

Lauren shook her head as she cut through the doily-and-lace-accented living room. Surprisingly, she liked the house. The decor was frilly and feminine and a bit over the top—a huge contrast to the unadorned home she'd shared with her father. There'd been no time, interest or money for superfluities. The Lynch house-hold had been all about practicality and purpose.

Her father's no-nonsense nature was one of the reasons she knew he wouldn't have purposely killed himself…unless he'd truly believed the life insurance money would have paid off Falcon Air's debts.

Oh, Dad, why did you borrow so much against the company?

Suppressing the stab of grief, she grabbed a plate from the sideboard. Worrying and second-guessing wouldn't solve anything, and even if she could eventually get her mother to sit still long enough to fill in the blanks, the FAA's investigation would likely determine whether or not her father's life insurance paid out. If it didn't…

She didn't want to think about that, didn't want to think about losing Falcon Air or what she and Lou would do without the company that had been everything to them. Lou hadn't worked anywhere else since before Lauren had been born, and he was a bit set in his ways. Starting over at sixty would be difficult for him *if* he could find a job.

Her stomach twisted, whether from hunger or nerves or both, she couldn't be sure. But she couldn't resist the delicious-smelling selection on the sideboard. Her mouth watered in anticipation of sampling the crisp bacon, maple sausage, vegetable-filled mini omelets and silver-dollar pancakes topped with cinnamon apples.

Grimacing at the obscene amount of food she'd piled on her plate, she carried it to the table. She'd just lifted her fork when Gage walked in wearing one of his perfectly fitting suits, this one in charcoal with a smoke-gray shirt and a black patterned tie.

He swept her with those dark eyes. "You'll have to change."

She didn't like the sound of that. "Why?"

"Because you're coming with me."

Definitely not what she wanted to hear. She'd only seen a tiny corner of San Francisco. "I thought we weren't flying out until Monday."

"We're going to the computer component plant I've come to assess. If you're studying business management, then you need to view the principles firsthand and see if you've learned enough to apply your book knowledge."

The idea both attracted and repelled her. She was eager to learn anything that might help her untangle Falcon Air's financial issues when she returned home. Yesterday while she'd been sitting in the coffee shop she'd done a little Web surfing research on her passenger. According to three major business magazines, Gage was reportedly one of the best corporate troubleshooters in the country.

Maybe he could help her with Falcon?

No. He was looking for something to discredit her, and he was her brother's spy. Trent didn't need the kind of ammo Falcon's iffy finances would provide to use against her.

The chemistry between her and Gage was an additional complication, especially now that she'd seen him half-naked. Wasn't it bad enough that she relived that kiss every time she closed her eyes? Now she'd see him shirtless, too. She'd bet a tank of fuel that reel would replay in her head.

Spending the day with him was too risky.

"That's an interesting idea, Gage, but I have other plans."

"You'll go." His flat, don't-argue-with-me tone raised her hackles and stirred her temper.

She looked at the breakfast she no longer wanted then at the man she wanted nothing to do with. Was this one of those commands Trent had insisted she comply with? "I take it no isn't an option?"

"Correct." Gage crossed to the buffet. While he filled his plate she debated calling her half brother and screaming at him. It wouldn't accomplish anything. She knew Trent would take sides—and it wouldn't be hers. But venting would make her feel better. Unfortunately, dramatic hissy fits had never been her style.

But damn her half brother for putting her in this position. Shadowing clients was not in her job description. In fact, under normal circumstances, she would have dumped her passenger in San Francisco, gone back on the assignment roster and returned to pick Gage up three days later. HAMC pilots did not sit around and twiddle their thumbs while their clients worked multiday deals. The flight crews filled the hours of their five-days-on-five-days-off schedules flying other customers.

"And if I don't want to go with you?"

"Why would you pass on the chance to see your

textbook theories put into practice unless you're not really interested in learning?"

Something about his tone rubbed her the wrong way. "What are you insinuating?"

"That perhaps you're playing at being a student until a better opportunity comes along."

"What kind of opportunity?"

"A rich mother. A guaranteed job. A wealthy lover."

She gasped. Anger boiled in her veins. "I see my half brother has been digging."

Gage's eyes narrowed. "You have a lover waiting in the wings?"

Okay, maybe Trent hadn't been snooping through her past and uncovered Whit. Just as well. She didn't want to explain how stupid she'd been to believe Whit would marry a nobody like her simply because they'd been long-term lovers. He'd dumped her as soon as the right kind of woman came along.

"My personal life is none of your business unless it affects my ability to keep you safe in the air." She shot to her feet, fists curled by her sides, determined to get as far away from Gage as possible.

"Your accusations are unfounded. I'm a damned good pilot and better qualified than half of HAMC's roster. Ask your buddy Trent. He'll verify that, although he'll probably choke on the words.

"As for not wanting to learn… You're way off base, Faulkner. My father is dead. Falcon Air is now half-mine. I want to learn everything I can about running it, but I don't see how trailing after you will benefit me."

"Because I'm the best at what I do."

A snort burst from her. "Lack of confidence clearly isn't an issue for you."

"Nor you."

She gritted her teeth on the desire to tell him to go to hell. "It's Saturday."

"There are fewer interruptions from employees on weekends. The CEO and a skeleton staff will be on board to provide what we need." He sat across from her and dug into his food. His appetite clearly hadn't been killed by the idea of spending a day with her.

The door to the kitchen swung open and Esmé breezed in with a coffee carafe before Lauren could make her escape. Esmé looked at Lauren's plate. "Oh, good, dear. I'm so glad you have an appetite. I love to cook, and it pains me when the fruits of my labor go to waste. So many of your contemporaries practically starve themselves with that no-fat-no-carbohydrates garbage."

Feeling trapped, Lauren eyed the mountain of food on her plate and resigned herself to forcing it down rather than disappointing her hostess even though she knew the man across from her was going to give her indigestion. A full day of it.

Lauren stared at the pile of purchasing orders Gage had given her and fought the urge to roll her eyes.

Busywork. Nothing your average twelve-year-old couldn't do. She certainly didn't need a business degree to handle what was essentially categorizing and organizing the computer plant's purchasing history. But she wouldn't complain. He probably wanted to make her miserable. The jerk. And that was one payoff she refused to give him.

At the other end of the long boardroom table in the windowless room Gage looked engrossed in something interesting. Fighting the urge to wad up a piece of paper and hurl it at him like a snowball, she swiveled her chair sideways so she wouldn't have to look at him and crossed her legs. Her foot kicked in irritation. She should be out seeing the sights.

Her best bet was to get through this garbage and make him find something else for her to do—preferably something that required brain cells.

She sorted, stacked and tabulated, adding comments on a pad of paper as she worked until she'd finished the pile. Relieved, she shoved it aside and checked her watch. Two hours. Wasted.

"Done."

He hit her with another one of those intense looks, the kind he'd been shooting at her while she worked, the ones she'd been trying to ignore, then he frowned and scanned the neatly paper-clipped piles on her desk. "You're finished?"

"Yes. What else do you have for me?"

He lay down his pen, rose and headed in her direction. "Let me see."

She stood and walked away from the table to stretch the kinks from her spine rather than be near him. The staff had left refreshments for them. She selected a diet soda loaded with caffeine from a mini fridge and popped it open. The cool liquid slid down her throat, reviving her somewhat.

She didn't mind paperwork, not really, but she'd rather be behind the controls of a plane than behind a desk. Her father had been the same way. That's why they'd needed Uncle Lou—who was a whiz with numbers.

"You made these notes?"

Gage's question made her turn. He held the yellow legal pad she'd written on. "Yes."

He flipped through the pages. "You've made a good

point. By not forming a continuous relationship with one supplier our client is paying a wide range of prices for the same products and not benefiting from customer loyalty discounts."

"*Your* client," she corrected. "Every business has its own version of the frequent flyer rewards plan." Falcon always ordered their parts and fuel from the same suppliers.

"I'll get you something else to work on." He crossed to a file cabinet and extracted another manila folder. "You'll find this a little more challenging."

She flipped through the pages. "The company has an investment portfolio?"

"See which ones you think they should keep and which they should unload." He returned to his end of the table.

"Gage, if they need liquid cash, why do they have these investments at all? It's not like the company needs a retirement account. That's more of a personal thing. Besides, none of these brings in big dividends. In fact, some have lost quite heavily."

He met her gaze again this time with respect and admiration in his dark eyes instead of dislike and distrust. "Good observation. When you've finished that, I'll give you the notes I've made on the project thus far, including a transcript of my initial interview with the CEO. Read over them while I finish up for today, then give me two lists. First, the additional data you'd like to see, and second, options you think the company should consider."

Surprise made her eyebrows shoot up. That sounded almost like…teamwork. Was it another test? Or did he actually want to hear what she had to say? She couldn't help but be suspicious. "You want my opinion. Why?"

"You offer a fresh perspective."

"Right. Like that compares to a trained professional."

"Lauren, you think outside the box. You're not constrained by knowledge of what has worked or not worked in similar situations in the past the way a seasoned consultant might be."

That sounded like a compliment.

"Okay." She'd give him her opinion and then maybe she could still get some sightseeing done.

But if he kept looking at her that way, as if he might actually enjoy having her here, then there was going to be trouble, because she didn't want him to like her.

And she absolutely did not want the feeling to be mutual.

He'd underestimated his opponent, Gage admitted as he shoved open the beveled-glass front door of the B and B Saturday evening. "Show me your paper."

Lauren turned on her low heels. "My economics paper? Why?"

She'd worn her black HAMC uniform skirt and a plain white blouse today. The conservative outfit should have made her look prim and stiff, but at some point during the day she'd twisted her hair up on the back of her head and stuck a pencil in it to hold it in place, resulting in a spiky spray. She looked young and fresh and smart. A sexy brainiac.

Gage rejected the idea, but he couldn't get rid of the reluctant respect she'd earned from him today. He'd expected her to be deadweight and a real pain in the ass. He had a packed schedule and no time or interest in babysitting, but he'd had no choice except to drag her along if he wanted to keep her from contacting her mother.

He'd given Lauren busywork to keep her out of his way. She'd dug right in without complaint and come up with several interesting and intelligent observations. She'd ended up saving him time and giving him a perspective he wouldn't have considered otherwise. They'd actually worked well together, but their truce was an uneasy one.

Esmé entered the foyer carrying two glasses. "You're just in time. It's south of the border night. Have a mojito while I put the finishing touches on dinner."

She pressed tall glasses of iced clear liquid into Gage's and Lauren's hands. Green leaves and slices of lime floated near the bottom and white crystals clung to the rim.

"I'll see you two in the dining room. Dinner's in twenty minutes." She headed back to the kitchen, her loose dress floating behind her like curtains blown by a breeze through an open window.

He focused on Lauren who eyed her glass and then him. "I'm not flying you anywhere until Monday, right?"

"Yes."

"Good. Then I can have this. I love mojitos." She pursed her lips and sipped. Her eyes closed and her lips curved upward. "Mmm. Mmm. Minty and sweet."

A crystal clung to her lip. A pass of her tongue wiped it away. He pried his gaze from her mouth and focused on the cold glass sweating in his hand. The sound she'd made had been close enough to a moan to sound almost sexual. An unwanted image of her face flushed, not in the anger he'd deliberately aroused this morning, but in desire filled his brain.

He blinked to clear his head. "I want to see the paper you e-mailed to your teacher."

She took another sip, watching him with a skeptical gaze from beneath her lashes. "Why? You think I lied about it?"

He'd earned her antagonism. "Not after today. You had a keen grasp on the subject. I'm curious to see how far along you are in your studies."

"I have fifteen hours of classes left before I get my degree. I can't go full-time because of work and… well, money."

Another reminder of what she stood to gain from her association with Jacqueline Hightower. But Lauren had shown she was a stickler for following rules. Would a rule follower stoop to shortcuts and swindling?

"I want to see it," he repeated.

Lauren stared at him then sighed and shrugged. "Sure. Why not? Maybe after you read it you can tell my half brother I'm not as stupid as he thinks I am."

"Trent has never called you stupid. And for what it's worth, I don't relay everything to him. What's between you and me is our business unless it directly concerns him."

Gage carefully filtered out the need-to-know facts. Thus far, there had been very few worth sharing. Trent had enough on his plate, and Gage always carried out his end of a bargain.

"You're deluded. The Hightower siblings are convinced I'm a greedy lying witch out to cast a spell on their mother and steal their inheritance."

He didn't bother to deny her dead-on assessment.

"What they don't bother to see is that if I'd really wanted to worm my way into Jacqui's affections or her wallet, I would have moved into the Hightower castle when she invited me. I wouldn't have found my own place."

He filed the info away. "Why didn't you?"

"Because I can't stand the idea of servants hovering around waiting to cook for me or clean up after me as if I was a child. Besides, I like my space and my independence." She pivoted and climbed the stairs.

Following her three treads behind, he tried not to focus on her rear end at his eye level. Tried and failed. Lauren was slender, but curved in all the right places. And she had great legs. Long legs. Whenever she'd been lost in thought today she'd crossed those sexy limbs at the knee and kicked her ankle, garnering far too much of his attention. She'd been a distraction. A delicious, delectable distraction.

He huffed out a breath. What in the hell was wrong with him? Acting on the growing attraction between them would bring nothing but trouble. For all he knew she could have been playing him with every shift of her tight little body.

But he didn't think so. He'd had women in hot pursuit since before he made his first million, and Lauren didn't give off those predatory signals. In fact, more often than not she acted as if she wished he weren't around—a novel, but not pleasant sensation.

Trent's theory was beginning to look shaky. Gage made a mental note to call his buddy to check the status on the missing money. Jacqueline could have simply gone shopping. It wasn't as if she hadn't dropped bundles of money on a whim before.

He knocked back a swig of his drink. Sweet, cold and refreshing after a long day. A little heavy on the rum. Not his usual Knob Creek bourbon, but not bad. He licked a grain of sugar from his lip. The action reminded him of Lauren doing the same downstairs. His body reacted with a physical kick he couldn't prevent.

He yanked his thoughts back to the woman in front of him. "This morning you said Trent had been snooping when I mentioned a rich lover."

Lauren shot a startled look at him over her shoulder as she stopped at her bedroom door. "Excuse me?"

"Do you have a lover waiting for you?" What kind of man would let a woman like her out of sight for months on end?

"I'm not seeing anyone and haven't for…a while." She grimaced as if she regretted replying, unlocked her door and after an awkward hesitation stepped inside. "I don't have a printed copy of my paper. You'll have to read it on my laptop unless you have a portable printer."

"Not this trip." He set his briefcase on the floor by the door and scanned the room. Flowers and ruffles dominated the decor. Not surprising since most of the house looked as if it had been hit by a lace factory explosion. "Boot up."

She shifted on her feet and nibbled her bottom lip, clearly uncomfortable with him in her room. Then she squared her shoulders, crossed the Aubusson rug and sat at the rolltop desk. She opened her laptop and turned it on. Her room, like his, lacked a spare chair. He'd requested suites with bathrooms attached, but he'd booked at the last minute and both of those had already been taken by honeymoon couples he had yet to see, although he had heard some telltale knocking on the wall last night—presumably a headboard. When his assistant played back his dictation he'd probably wonder what in the hell Gage had been doing.

"What exactly were you looking for at the plant today?"

Lauren's question drew him back to the present. He sat on the edge of the pillow-laden bed within a yard of her and tried to engage his brain. Work was rarely a top priority when he visited a woman's bedroom. "Ways to increase efficiency and profitability. Cutting waste is usually the first step."

"Did you find some? You certainly took a lot of notes."

"I'm still assimilating data."

"Ah, yes. Assess, assimilate, communicate and implement," she quoted his earlier words back at him.

"You paid attention during the car ride to the location."

"Yep." Her unexpected smile punched the air from his lungs. "Flying is all about acronyms. All I had to do was make up one to fit your strategy. AACI. Piece of cake. So now what?"

"I'll take the data I gather back to my office, and my team and I will go over it and brainstorm strategies for improvement."

"I would have expected you to fly solo."

She'd read him correctly. "Having a team of specialists allows us to take on more clients."

More clients meant more revenue. More revenue meant more investments. More investments meant a greater chance of financial security if his business failed. Watching his father's financial and mental collapse had taught Gage to always have Plans A, B and C ready to implement at a moment's notice.

Lauren swiveled in her chair to open the file on her computer, revealing the back of her neck and a tiny horseshoe-shaped birthmark just beneath her hairline. Trent had the same one. Gage had noticed it back in college when his buddy had sported a military buzz cut.

Gage couldn't take his eyes off Lauren's vulnerable nape. He tugged the pencil from her hair, letting the strands fall and cover temptation. The urge to test the texture of her hair was an unwelcome one.

Her spine went rigid and then relaxed. "Oops. Forgot about that. I stole a pencil. Internal theft—the curse of the corporate world."

The mischief in her eyes as she looked at him over her shoulder thickened his throat. "Return it tomorrow."

She lifted her glass, sipped and swallowed, once again drawing his eyes to her mouth the way a Dumpster draws flies.

"Tomorrow is Sunday."

"Still a workday."

"Don't take this the wrong way, Gage. Today was very interesting and informative. But I haven't been to San Francisco before, and I'd rather see more of it than the inside of a computer parts plant. My daddy always said take a little piece of everywhere you go home with you even if it's only in your heart, and I aim to do that."

If he turned her loose, she'd go back to that damned Internet café. "We'll work in the morning then sightsee in the afternoon and have dinner at Fisherman's Wharf tomorrow night. That means we'll have to work Monday morning, as well, and leave after lunch."

"We?" Equal parts wariness and excitement warred in her teal eyes.

"I've been here a few times. I'll show you around. But in return, you come to the plant and work with me."

Silence stretched between them. Her ankle kicked. "Another command appearance?"

"This is more of a personal request. I appreciated your assistance today."

"I guess that would be all right." She swiveled back to the computer. "Here's the document. I'll get out of your way."

She made to stand. He put a hand on her shoulder, holding her in her seat. The firmness of her muscles surprised him. It shouldn't have, not with the way she easily controlled her seven-hundred-pound motorcycle or an airplane that weighed several tons. "Don't move.

I'll read over your shoulder. That way if I have questions you can see to what I'm referring."

"O…kay."

Gage set his drink on the desk, braced one hand on the polished surface and the other on the back of her chair and leaned forward. Her scent wafted up to him, floral, but faint enough he suspected it might be her shampoo rather than perfume. It took several moments for him to be able to focus on the words on the screen. As soon as he did she hooked him with her unique premise.

He reached past her to hit the key to turn the page, his forearm brushing hers. Heat scattered through him, but he disregarded it. Or tried to. Ten pages later, he nodded as he read the closing line.

An even deeper appreciation for her intelligence filled him as he turned his head to meet her gaze. "You've argued your theory quite well. Did you come up with the idea or did your professor assign a topic?"

"It's my idea. I like coffee, and I tend to buy a cup whenever I'm out running my weekly errands. I never have to drive more than a half mile out of my way to get it. But a lot of coffee shops don't stay in business long.

"In the rush to have a store convenient to every consumer, most franchises allow branches to open up too close together, thereby sabotaging their revenue base and dooming themselves to fail. Even some grocery stores have coffee shops now. The same applies to restaurants and retail chains. The businesses are their own worst enemy."

She bit her bottom lip as if expecting him to contradict her. But he couldn't. She was right. Too much of a good thing was never a good thing. But seeing doubt instead of her usual cocky confidence revealed a vulnerable side she'd been careful to hide from him up to this point.

Could this woman be the conniving bitch Trent claimed? She seemed too smart, too capable and too willing to work hard. Sure, Trent had been right about Angela, but Gage had become a decent judge of character since his ex-wife's stormy, expensive departure a decade ago. None of the women he'd allowed into his life since his divorce had fooled him.

Lauren dampened her lips again, drawing his attention to her mouth. The memory of the kiss they'd shared ambushed him with sensation and need. She must have read the hunger on his face because she gasped and her eyes widened.

"You're quite an impressive woman, Lauren Lynch. If you weren't such a damned good pilot, you'd make a good business consultant."

"Gage—"

He ignored her warning tone, leaned in and stole his name from her lips. She went rigid. But she didn't pull away. After a moment her mouth relaxed beneath his, and she sipped from him as he did from her. When he stroked her bottom lip with his tongue, she met him halfway. He tasted the sugar and mint of her mojito, but mostly he tasted Lauren. And he wanted more.

Desire raced through him like fire through an abandoned warehouse. He grasped her arms and lifted her from her seat, pulling her forward until her soft breasts rested against his chest and her thighs aligned with his.

Lauren's arms circled his waist, and her short nails scraped a path parallel to his spine, driving a spike of hunger through him. She kissed the way she rode a motorcycle, the way she flew a plane—with one hundred percent commitment. He stroked her hair, then tangled his fingers in the fine, silky strands to cradle her head while he deepened the kiss.

Her mouth was hot and wet and slick, and he couldn't get enough of her, couldn't hold her close enough. The mattress bumped the back of his legs. He wanted her on it. Flat on her back. Beneath him. Naked.

He swung her sideways until they both stood beside the bed. His hands shook as if he had a case of the D.T.'s when he reached for the buttons of her blouse. He freed the first, the second. Her hands covered his and she lifted her head with her eyes tightly closed, then her lids lifted, and she stared at him through her thick lashes. Her chest rose and fell beneath his knuckles, and the sound of their labored breathing filled the room.

Passion darkened her eyes and trembled on her lips, then with one blink uncertainty gave way to purpose. She caught his hands, opened his fingers and spread them over her breasts. The mounds filled his palms, beaded tips raking his flesh as he caressed her. She gasped. Her bra and blouse were in the way. He wanted skin.

Hunger so strong it hurt fisted in his gut. Struggling to regain control, he buried his mouth in her neck and inhaled her fragrance as he thumbed her nipples. He tasted the soft skin behind her ear. Her whimper filled the air.

She felt good and fit perfectly in his arms. He took her mouth again, diving deep with his tongue the way he wanted to drive his body into hers. Lauren responded by pressing her hips hard against his erection. He pushed back and heat detonated in his groin.

A bell tinkled in the distance. He ignored it, spread open Lauren's blouse and cupped the satiny triangles of her bra. His thumbs dipped into the cups, brushing over her tight nipples. She shivered and gave a little frustrated squeak that nearly buckled his knees then she broke the kiss.

"Dinner," she whispered against his mouth, her lips brushing over his with the word.

"Screw dinner."

A shocked laugh burst from her. Shaking her head she disentangled slowly, dragging her nails around his waist and across his abdomen which contracted involuntarily. A naughty grin curved her swollen mouth. "Tell that to Esmé and you'll break her heart."

Lauren's blouse, still tucked into her waistband, gaped open, revealing pale curves above the shiny fabric of her bra. Frustration clawed at him. He stepped toward her, but she retreated and held up both hands. "Don't."

"Lauren—"

"We can't do this, Gage. Not unless you can promise me it won't get back to Trent and cost me my job."

Trent. Duty. Debt. The sobering realization that he'd forgotten all three. At the moment he didn't give a damn. "You want me as much as I want you."

She inhaled deeply and exhaled slowly. Her hand lifted as if to touch his face, but she quickly withdrew it and tucked it behind her back. "Yes, I want you. But that doesn't mean I can afford to follow through."

Six

What were you thinking?

Lauren mentally kicked her own behind as she hurried toward the dining room, running from the mistake she'd almost made. She might be adventurous professionally, but she'd always been cautious in her personal life, her sex life in particular. How had Gage made her forget that?

Surprise stopped her in the dining room entrance when she spotted two other couples already seated at the round table. Gage bumped into her, searing his full body length against her back for one brief pulse-skipping moment. He grasped her waist to steady her, and her breasts and lips tingled, asking—no, *begging*—for more of what she'd sampled upstairs.

The man could kiss. Not even with Whit, the man she'd thought herself in love with and hoped to marry, had she ever felt anything as potent or exciting as the passion Gage had stirred in her.

Desire for Gage still gnawed at her, but that was one hunger she had every intention of denying. She shook off his hands and wished she could blame her loss of control on alcohol, but she'd consumed less than half of her mojito. The guilt rested squarely on her thirteen-months-and-counting celibate shoulders.

"Hi," she greeted the group and then stifled a wince at her overly loud, overly cheerful voice.

Esmé bustled in from the kitchen. "There you are. I was about to send Leon looking for you."

Lauren's cheeks burned like a hot lightbulb, and so did a certain spot below her navel. She hoped the others couldn't read on her face what she and Gage had been doing upstairs before coming down.

"Meet our other guests. Sue and Rob are from Utah." Esmé pointed first at the thirtysomething couple whose arms were entwined like mating snakes then at the fresh-faced couple who looked younger than Lauren. They seemed busy—under the table—if their overly innocent expressions and flushed cheeks were any indicator. "Tracy and Jack are from outside of Austin. Folks, meet Lauren and Gage."

Lauren would have guessed the couples were newlyweds even if Esmé hadn't told her about the B and B's other guests during the tour. The couples' devotion showed in every lingering glance and touch. It was as if the partners couldn't bear to be physically disconnected even though they sat only inches apart.

The only chairs left at the table were side by side. Gage pulled one out for Lauren then took the other spot. Their arms and shoulders brushed as they unfolded cloth napkins, making Lauren's already-agitated synapses crackle like a lightning storm. Another leaf in the table would have given them more room.

The couple across from her kissed, rubbed noses and shared an intimate smile. Their lovey-dovey, touchy-feely antics drove home to Lauren what she could be doing right now if she didn't care about her job, and if she could ignore the fact that she'd disliked the man beside her until sometime today.

She tried to remember at what point she'd realized she no longer hated Gage. It wasn't on the drive to the plant this morning when he'd informed her in a superior tone how he operated and what he expected of her. The change might have started when she'd looked up to find him watching her from across the paper-strewn boardroom table with respect and admiration in his dark eyes instead of dislike and distrust. Or maybe the antagonism had faded when he'd offered her a more challenging task than the busywork he'd initially assigned her, or when he'd started working with her as a partner instead of an opponent.

Esmé served another round of mojitos before Lauren could refuse. Inhibition-lowering alcohol was the last thing she needed when her willpower was already shaky. Leon came in carrying a large tray. He unloaded platters of chiles rellenos, Spanish rice and frijoles charros in the center of the long table. The heady aroma of the stuffed peppers and spicy beans with sausage made Lauren's mouth water. Mexican cuisine had always been her favorite. Esmé added bowls of guacamole, pica de gallo, sour cream and finely shredded lettuce.

"Serve yourselves family style," Esmé said before returning to the kitchen.

Lauren reached for the closest platter. Gage did the same simultaneously.

"Allow me," he said as he grasped the spoon.

Lauren jerked her hands away and stuffed her fists

in her lap. Another round of sparks bounced from her knuckles to her nipples at the near miss.

She fastened her gaze on his hands. Those long fingers had caressed her breasts—breasts currently tingling with a plea for round two. His short clipped nails had grazed her with devastating effectiveness. She hoped he didn't notice the tenting of her blouse when he put a serving of the chiles on her plate.

After spooning his own, he twisted to pass the platter to the newlywed beside him. His thigh nudged hers beneath the table. She moved her leg away, but too late. Heat rushed to the point of contact.

She accepted a bowl of rice from the woman to her right, took a serving then offered the dish to Gage. Their gazes met over the bowl. His fingers covered hers. The promise of passion darkened his eyes to the color of rich cocoa as he took the dish from her. Heat swirled in her belly leaving her feeling a lot like a melting marshmallow. She almost dropped the rice.

He repeated his actions as the remainder of the food circled the table, and each time his thigh and fingers lingered longer against hers. Lauren's appetite for food diminished, while her appetite for the man beside her filled her with an empty ache.

She shot him a narrow-eyed look. Was he deliberately tormenting her? Teasing her? Arousing her?

She'd bet her bike on it. Gage wasn't the kind of man to do anything accidentally. She'd bet each touch above and below the table was calculated for seduction.

Maybe she ought to give in. Go for it. Take the pleasure he offered for however long it lasted. Trent was going to find a reason to fire her sooner or later anyway, and she was beginning to believe she would never get any more out of her mother, who hadn't returned any of Lauren's calls since their chat the other night and had even left the country to avoid a face-to-face chat.

Mayday, Mayday, Mayday, her brain shrieked. *Don't be an idiot.*

One side of Gage's eyebrows lifted in a silent taunt as if he could hear her internal argument.

Oh, man, he should know better than to dare her like that. For pity's sake, hadn't he figured out by now that she thrived on challenges? She hadn't garnered all her certifications by backing down when the hotshot flyboys tried to push her around. She'd learned to fight back. There was no better way to shut up a cocky SOB than to best him. It would serve Gage right if she—

An idea struck her and a wicked chuckle danced in her chest, but she suppressed it. She had less luck curbing the smile taking control of her mouth. He wanted a fight, did he? She could certainly give him one. She could play footsie and tease as well as he could. Let's see how he responded to being bested at his own game.

Beneath the table, she shed her shoe and found his ankle with her toes. His start of surprise repaid her for every irritating jab he'd taken at her expense. Without glancing her way, he shifted his foot out of reach and lifted his fork as if nothing out of the ordinary had occurred.

Disappointed, Lauren mirrored his actions and blindly searched for her shoe. Before she could find it, his foot—now clad only in a sock—covered hers, pinning it to the hardwood floor. Her body went rigid. She almost shoved her fork up her nose and only at the last minute found the target of her mouth.

His heat seeped into her skin and crept up her leg, heading directly toward a recently awakened area. She gently tugged to no avail. He had her trapped. She couldn't escape without an undignified struggle, and she wouldn't give him that satisfaction.

She didn't look at him as she chewed without tasting and debated her next move. A few bites later she wiggled out of her other pump, crossed her leg and dragged the tip of her toe down his thigh. He coughed as if he'd choked on his rice and reached for the napkin in his lap. Only he didn't grab his napkin. He grabbed her foot and held it tightly to his hard thigh.

Her smile died. Lauren scanned the other guests, but the couples were too engaged in each other and dinner to notice the antics going on around them.

Gage caressed her instep with his thumb, firmly sweeping from her heel forward. Good thing she wasn't ticklish.

With his other hand he casually continued his meal. How could he chew and swallow when she could barely think or breathe? Determined not to let him know he'd rattled her, she picked up her fork and fed herself by rote. Conversation buzzed around her, but her mind focused on her captive foot and those caressing fingers. And payback. Oh, yes, there would definitely be payback for his shenanigans.

She tried to extricate herself without luck. He rubbed deep circles on the ball of her foot. She nearly moaned in pleasure. She'd never had a foot massage before. It could become addictive.

The man didn't fight fair.

But then, what man did?

And of course, his lack of fair play meant she could fight dirty, too. She dropped her hand beneath the table and curled her fingers around his wrist. His grip on her instep tightened, but she had no intention of prying him loose. Her goal was to disconcert him as much as he had her. She raked her nails lightly up the inside of his arm. He shivered almost imperceptively, which only encouraged her to repeat the action. Gage cut her a sideways look so blistering hot she almost melted in her chair like ice cream on a Daytona sidewalk in July.

He repaid her by dragging his thumbnail along the arch of her foot, and a ripple of desire washed over her. She never would have considered getting her foot scratched erotic, but boy, was she wrong. Her heart raced and her skin steamed.

Gage challenged her at every turn, making her mentally sharper and more focused and driven. She even kind of liked his confident swagger. Battling with him made her feel more alive than she had since her father's death.

Unless he'd been honest when he said he didn't tell Trent everything, taking their relationship to the next level could cost her her job. Did she dare trust him?

Her gaze fell to Gage's mouth—the one she wanted on her. On her lips. On her breasts. Everywhere.

A quiet breath whistled through his teeth, drawing her gaze back to his. He knew. She didn't know how he'd read her thoughts, but he knew she wanted him. And the sexual promise expanding his pupils and adding a tinge of red to his skin said the feeling was mutual.

He gave her foot a squeeze then stroked up her shin to her knee and down her calf to her ankle. His thumbnail scraped a deliciously light circle around her anklebone, but his gaze fell to her breast. Her nipples received the signal and hardened beneath her shirt. He flicked a fingertip over the point of the tiny bone, but she felt it in her breasts, in her lap.

How could she possibly resist him? He was smart, gorgeous and ambitious—her big three.

Sleeping with Gage was one test flight she yearned to take. Admitting it sent a beehive buzzing through her. *If* she did this crazy thing, she wouldn't fool herself into believing any intimacy between them would lead to forever. They had too much against them. His wealth. His friendship with Trent. Her loyalty to Falcon Air. Living in different states.

She looked at her half-full plate. How long before they could escape? She shoved a big bite into her mouth. The pepper, stuffed with creamy cheese and pork, was one of her favorite dishes, but it wasn't what she craved tonight.

"What about you, Lauren?"

The young newlywed's voice startled Lauren into swallowing in one big gulp. Her cheeks burned from an altogether different kind of heat than the rest of her body. "I'm sorry?"

"Where are you from?" the bubbly blonde asked.

"Daytona, Florida."

"Is your family still there?"

The loss struck again, like a cloud obscuring the sun. "No. My father died recently."

Gage released Lauren's foot. She put it back on the floor and shoved both feet into her shoes.

"What about your mom?"

The inevitable question. "I was raised by my father and his partner."

"Your daddy's gay?" Blondie sounded shocked. Her husband tried to shush her.

Lauren winced. "Sorry. I meant his business partner."

"No revolving door of girlfriends?"

"No. My father only loved one woman in his life, and

since he couldn't be with her, he chose to be alone."
Lauren felt Gage's eyes on her, but didn't turn.

"Why couldn't he? Did she die, too?"

"Tracy," her husband scolded in a whisper. "I apologize. We're from a small town where everybody knows your business."

Lauren waved away his concerns. "It's okay. My mother was and still is married to someone else. Trust me, I didn't miss what I didn't have."

That wasn't completely true. She'd had friends in school who didn't have fathers, but none who didn't have mothers. She'd often wondered why she had to be different. But her father had always said, "Your momma can't be with us, sugar," and that had been all Lauren could get out of him until that day she'd turned eighteen and been enlightened. Too little, too late.

As an adolescent she'd concocted a complicated story about her mother's tragic death in childbirth, but it turned out her girlish fantasies had been just that. The truth was her mother had chosen not to be with her except for a brief visit once each year. Jacqui had preferred her other children. That still stung.

"Are you two—" Sue, the other woman at the table pointed to Gage then Lauren "—together…like a couple?"

"No."

"No," Lauren replied hastily and simultaneously with Gage.

"What do you do, Lauren?" Sue persisted.

"I'm a pilot. Gage is a client of the company I work for." Beneath the table Gage gave her knee a squeeze, then a tormenting caress, shattering her concentration. "I fly airplanes and sometimes helicopters."

Brilliant, Lauren. What else would you fly? Kites?

She couldn't think with Gage drawing circles on her thigh with his fingertip. She shot him a warning glare. He winked and her stomach swooped.

She swallowed and turned back toward the other woman. "Gage is the one with the exciting job. A top business magazine voted him as the man you most want on your side in an economic downturn."

All eyes turned toward Gage. His caressing hand stilled, then withdrew. "I'm a business consultant."

"What does a business consultant do?" Tracy asked.

Two can fight dirty, Lauren decided. She slid her hand to Gage's thigh and lightly dug in her nails. His muscles went rock hard beneath her fingers.

"Consult. Owners. On. Improvement. Strategies." His carefully enunciated words made her lips twitch.

"AACI." She nudged him with her elbow, earning a narrow-eyed stare. Thanking heaven for the long table-cloth hiding her actions, she wiggled her fingers and batted her lashes like an innocent schoolgirl.

He covered her hand with his, flatting her palm against his leg. When she tried to pull free he laced his fingers through hers and anchored her.

"I assess the company's needs, assimilate the data, communicate my findings and help them implement a plan to reach their desired goals—usually financial goals, but some of my consultants specialize in other areas of industrial and corporate management."

"I got to see him in action earlier. He's very good." Lauren added the last tongue in cheek with a brief glance at his mouth.

Fire kindled in his eyes at her double entendre. He didn't look away as he continued, "Lauren is also very…skilled. She's impressed the hell out of me thus far. I can't wait to see what else she has up her sleeves.

Her passion…toward any project is quite extraordinary."

He wasn't talking about flying. Adrenaline rushed through her veins, making her almost light-headed. "Just remember what I told you at our initial meeting. Mastering new…equipment is something of an obsession with me. I'll tackle anything you throw at me. In an airplane it's simply a matter of lift and thrust, and knowing how far you can push your machine before you…break it."

Gage's nostrils flared. Gold glinted in his irises. Challenge issued and accepted.

She had to be out of her mind to contemplate becoming intimate with him. But she couldn't seem to think about anything else. That kind of distraction in the cockpit could be disastrous.

The silence caught Lauren's attention. She broke the simmering connection with Gage and scanned the table to find each occupant plus Esmé and Leon staring at them. From the flushed cheeks and parted lips, she'd bet they'd guessed neither she nor Gage were talking about flying.

Esmé dusted her hands on her frilly apron. "I'll go finish the flan."

Rob, the newlywed who'd been silent until now, cleared his throat. "I… Esmé, I think we'll skip dessert. Right, angel?" He shot his wife a pleading look.

"Yes," Sue piped up. "Dinner was great. Thank you so much. But I think we need to…rest. We have a big day planned for tomorrow." They both rose and bolted from the room. Their giggles as they raced up the stairs echoed to the dining room. Nobody at the table could possibly doubt they were headed for something more active than sleep.

"Um, yes. Us, too," Tracy added with a smoldering look at her husband. "We have an early flight to catch."

Their departure left Gage and Lauren alone with their hosts. Leon shook his head. "Newlyweds. Always the same no matter where they're from. I can barely get them to the table, and when I do they don't stay long enough to finish a meal."

Lauren wished the floor would open up and swallow her. "I'm sorry. I really know how to kill a party, don't I? Folks usually don't run until I start talking about hydraulics or compression ratios."

Gage's expression turned wry. "Run men off often, do you?"

She grimaced. "Let's just say knowing more about a man's car than he does tends to shorten my list of potential suitors."

Leon chuckled as he gathered the other guests' empty plates. "That's all right, sweetie. If a man can be scared off, then you should let him go. Means he's not the one for you."

Esmé nodded. "I'll leave the coffee on the counter and the flan in the fridge. You help yourselves to it whenever you're ready."

"Thank you, Esmé. Dinner was excellent," Gage replied.

The kitchen door swung shut behind Esmé and Leon. It was clear her hosts expected them to dash off to bed, too. Worse, part of Lauren wanted exactly that, even though she was sure it would be a big mistake. Tension invaded her muscles and her pulse quickened.

"You like playing with fire." Gage's deep, quiet voice rumbled over her.

"Apparently so do you."

He turned in his chair, his knee branding her thigh.

"If we go upstairs now I'm going to strip you down, take you to bed and not let you out for flan or anything else before morning."

She gulped at the image he painted with his candor. Should she go against wisdom and take a risk? Or play it safe? Either way, she was pretty certain she'd be damned if she did and damned if she didn't.

Seven

Lauren's heart rose to her throat and pounded as heavily as it had the day she'd stood in the open door of an airplane at ten thousand feet, waiting to make her first solo skydiving jump.

Only the best pilots "flew by feel," trusting their instincts no matter what the gauges told them. She was one of those few, and her sixth sense had never let her down. That same gut feeling told her not to hold back now. But still, going to bed with a near stranger wasn't like her. This was risky business. But a risk she had to take.

Gage Faulkner. Her brother's spy. Her former enemy. And soon to be her lover.

Looking at him, she gathered her courage and took that final step past the point of no return. "I always thought flan was overrated."

Her words ignited a feral passion in Gage's eyes.

A shiver of awareness raced over her, then he blinked and the untamed look vanished. Had she imagined his brief reaction?

He pushed back his chair, steadily, deliberately, and stood then grasped the wooden back of hers and helped her scoot away from the table. She rose on trembling legs.

His palm skimmed down her spine as light as air and settled at her waist. His heat seeped through her clothing, a steaming prelude to what she could expect if she didn't come to her senses in the next few moments.

No. Once she'd committed to a course she followed through. She wanted Gage, wanted to experience the powerful passion only he seemed to be able to summon from her. There was a reason why he'd come into her life now when she was grieving and confused. Her job was to figure out why. And she couldn't do that by running away from what he made her feel.

He guided her out of the dining room and up the stairs with firm pressure. They stopped outside her door. Her mouth dried and her toes curled inside her shoes. She inhaled deeply, but the light-headed, surreal feeling remained. Anticipation made her hands shake as she fished her key from her pocket and slipped it into the lock. She shoved open the door and stepped forward.

Gage grabbed her elbow, halting her on the threshold. "Be sure."

Those two simple words confirmed her decision. That he'd give her an opportunity to change her mind impressed her. Most guys who'd made it this far would push for more whether or not she had doubts. She only had one concern. "This is between you and me? No Trent?"

His unflinching, gold-flecked gaze held hers. "No Trent."

She dampened her dry lips. "Then come in and make love with me, Gage."

The hunger in his eyes entranced her. Unable to look away, she backed into her room and he followed, pausing only to lock the door behind him.

The high mattress bumped the back of her thighs. Pulse pounding, she waited for him to close the distance between them. When only inches separated them she lifted her arms and pushed his suit coat off his shoulders. She caught it as it fell and tossed it on her desk chair. Next, she tackled his tie, loosening the knot until she could pull the silk free and drop it on top of his jacket.

He let her undress him. But while he didn't assist her, she knew he was far from passive. Leashed energy radiated from him. His fists bunched and released by his sides, and his dark eyes watched her, promising passionate payback with every button she freed on his shirt.

She resisted the urge to touch him for as long as possible. She lasted only five buttons before she gave in to the craving to trace the open V of tanned skin with her fingertips from collarbone to sternum to collarbone. His skin was warm, supple, addictive. His scent grew stronger, headier.

His respiratory rate quickened, mirroring hers. She yanked his shirttail free and quickly undid the remaining buttons then spread her hands over his chest, absorbing the warmth of his body and the feel of his heart hammering beneath her palm. She pushed the fabric out of the way, and his shirt fluttered to the floor. Splaying her palms on his chest, she caressed those gorgeous pecs, then his muscled shoulders, biceps and forearms.

The tightening pucker of his tiny nipples fascinated her. She had to touch him, but the nubs teasing her palms didn't satisfy her. She needed to taste him on her tongue. She leaned forward and licked him. His fingers speared through her hair, holding her close, and a groan rumbled from his chest, vibrating against her lips. The vibration traveled down her spine to her core.

His grip tightened momentarily then shifted to cradle her jaw and lift her head. He covered her mouth and devoured her with a barely restrained clash of teeth, lips and tongue. His arms looped around her back, yanking her flush against him. But it still wasn't close enough. Lauren ached for more. Skin on skin. Legs entangled. His body filling the expanding void in hers.

She forced her hands between them and tackled his belt buckle. In a frantic clash of kisses, desperate gasps, fumbling rushing fingers and grazing knuckles she hurried to remove the remainder of his clothing. Her arms tangled with his as he worked on her garments. This I'll-die-if-I-don't-have-you-now urgency was totally new to her.

Her skirt slipped to the carpet. Blindly, she kicked it and her pumps aside. The hem of her blouse teased her bottom like the stroke of a fingertip. Her skin was so sensitive that every shift of her clothing seemed like a caress. She reached for the button at her collar, but Gage broke the kiss and brushed her hands aside. "Let me."

He worked the buttons with more dexterity than she'd shown on his. When he finished, she shrugged her shoulders. For a fleeting moment as her shirt fluttered to the floor, she wished she was one of those girls who liked sexy, daring lingerie. But she'd been born with a practical streak. Her bra and bikini panties were relatively new, but still machine-washable, plain white satin without lace.

If Gage found her lingerie lacking, she couldn't tell by the hungry way his eyes ate her up with first one blistering sweep from her neck to her toes then with a slower, lingering return exploration. Her nipples tightened under his scrutiny. She couldn't wait to have his hands on her. His mouth. The thought stole her breath.

She silently cursed the panty hose required by her uniform. As if he understood her frustration, Gage hooked his thumbs in the unsexy garment and peeled her nylons down her legs. She stepped out of them.

He removed his socks, shoes and pants, and stood before her with his erection straining the silky fabric of his navy boxers.

Eager to touch him she flexed her fingers, but instead, she took the safer option and reached for the hooks on her bra. Gage stepped forward and his chest slapped against hers. He caught her hands behind her back, stopping her short of her goal. The navel to nipple contact and his mild bondage sent a thrill shooting through her.

She undulated against him, trying to get free. "Gage, I want you."

His nostrils flared on a swift inhalation. The line of hair bisecting his belly erotically tickled her stomach. "And I you."

He bent his head. His lips landed beneath her jawbone and worked their way south in butterfly-light touchdowns, brief, shocking, exhilarating kisses down the cord of her neck and over her collarbone. She quit struggling, willing to take whatever route he wanted to pursue. His lips traveled down the slope of one breast and up the other. She arched her back, silently begging him to take her into his mouth, but he ignored her plea.

He transferred her wrists into one of his hands and

snapped her bra open with the other, then dragged one finger forward beneath the elastic, teasing the sensitive underside of her breasts. Her insides tightened as he lifted the cups, freeing her left nipple with a rasp of fabric across her overly responsive skin, then her right. The pad of his thumb grazed each tip, making her gasp. Her eyes closed and her head fell back as pleasure constricted her muscles. A warm gust of breath was her only warning before his hot mouth covered her.

She moaned and tried to free her hands to no avail. She wanted to touch him. His teeth gently gripped a tight tip, warning her to be still and then his tongue flicked her captive flesh sending an even more intense shock of arousal through her.

When he lifted his head she wanted to scream in disappointment, but then he released her and quickly stripped her bra down her arms. Self-consciousness slithered through her as he stared at her, breathing through parted lips. She worked out and her body wasn't bad, but she wasn't lush centerfold material.

She reached for him, her fingers digging into his thick shoulders and pulling him closer. He skimmed his palms up from her waist and cupped her in his hands, his thumbs drawing circles over her aching breasts.

He bent to suckle her again, drawing deeply on one side while his fingers plucked and gently tweaked the other. Heat pooled low in her abdomen, and she squeezed her legs together, shifting restlessly as need pulsed within her with each draw of his mouth.

He straightened and shucked his boxers. Lauren's breath stalled in her chest. She hadn't been with many men, but none of them shared Gage's bragging rights.

Momentarily shaken over the magnitude of the step she was about to take, she turned her back on him to gather her composure while she ripped the covers down the bed. He wound his arms around her waist. His hot body blanketed her back, and his erection scorched the base of her spine seconds before his hands set her breasts ablaze.

His teeth and lips grazed her shoulder, the side of her neck, then tugged gently on her earlobe. He pushed her forward, bending her over the high mattress. The prostrate position startled her. She wasn't used to letting herself be vulnerable. But before she could protest his short nails lightly scored her back, raking over her bottom and plowing a field of goose bumps in their wake.

He dragged her panties down her legs. After freeing them from her ankles, he made the return trip twice as slowly, pausing to tease the back of her thighs with his lips then trace and caress the curve of her bottom. By the time he reached her shoulders again he covered her like a stallion, but without entering her. He pulled away slowly, leaving another trail of kisses down her spine as his body heat eased off.

Confused by his retreat, she faced him in time to see him straightening from the pants he'd dropped on the floor with a condom in his hand.

Protection. She nearly groaned, but assured herself she would have remembered…eventually. She wasn't careless. Ever.

She had an unopened box in her flight bag. She'd bought it last year after she'd broken up with Whit, with the intention of going out and proving with a series of other men that Whit hadn't hurt her. But apparently anonymous sex just wasn't her thing. She hadn't been able to get past the fact that she had to like and respect a guy before sleeping with him. Until Gage, she hadn't been tempted by any other man since Whit dumped her.

She took the condom from him and placed it on the mattress. She'd waited a long time to make love again, and she wasn't going to rush it. First, she wanted to do a little exploring of her own. She lifted his hand and pulled one of Gage's fingers into her mouth, swirling her tongue around the tip. His muscles jerked tight, cording and revealing his perfect physique. He swallowed hard. She moved to the next finger and then the next until he grasped her hand and stopped her.

She curled the fingers of her other hand around his thick erection. His sharply indrawn breath rent the air. He covered her hand with his and stroked his length once, twice, showing her how he liked to be touched. Hot, satiny skin covered a rock-hard arousal, and caressing him triggered a burst of hunger in her belly. She swept over the slick droplet on his tip with her thumb.

"You do like to play with fire." His voice rumbled low and deep like an approaching Boeing 787. He released her, gripped her waist and lifted her onto the bed then positioned himself between her knees. The position put them eye to eye until he captured her hands, lifted them over her head and urged her back on the cool sheets with her legs hanging over the side.

The position left her open and vulnerable, a little uneasy and a lot turned on. He captured a nipple in his mouth and stroked downward from her fingertips to her hypersensitive armpits. His hands mapped her body while his tongue traced the terrain of one breast then the other. Gage's ultralight touch swept her waist, then her belly and thighs, showering her with goose bumps and shivers.

Urgent need coalesced into a tight ball at her bikini line. She wound her legs around his hips and pulled him closer, but he didn't fill her as she craved. He only rested his arousal against her, hot and hard and heavy.

His teasing fingertips dipped closer and closer to her center with each pass until she strained toward his hand. And then finally, finally, when she thought she'd die from frustration, his fingers slid into her curls. He found her slick opening and stroked her. The intense shock of pleasure made her body bow. She cried out. "That… feels…good."

He zeroed in on exactly the right spot, circling again and again, drawing her deeper and deeper into a vortex where nothing else in the world mattered but the way he sucked, nipped and licked her breasts and plied her body. Her legs shook with need as she had never felt before, then she was hurled through a wind tunnel of sensation that pulled her in too many different directions to process. All her neurons seemed to crackle and hiss then explode in a shower of sparks.

When the spasms stopped, she tried to catch her breath. Even before the tingles receded from her toes, Gage's lips blazed a path down her midline toward the place his talented fingers had just vacated. "Gage, you don't have to—"

"I have to know how you taste."

His rough growl rocked her to her core, but that was nothing compared to the first lash of his tongue. Air filled her lungs in a rush. Lauren closed her eyes as every thought and all of her energy zoomed into tight focus on the magic Gage created with his mouth, with his hands. He cupped her buttocks and lifted her to love her with his tongue. The brand of each pad of his fingers burned her skin.

It was too much. Too good. Too fast.

She dug her nails into the sheets and fought to hold off her climax, to stall the shockingly swift ascent. Her senses sharpened, sabotaging her. Gage's scent mingled with hers in her nostrils. She could smell her arousal and his musky aroma. Without effort or intention on her part each of her muscles drew taut. But the coup de grâce, the final straw that snapped her control was the rasp of his five o'clock shadow on her tender flesh as he buried his face between her thighs.

Orgasm snatched her up like the sudden breath-stealing jerk of a parachute opening. Her free fall stopped abruptly and wave after wave of pleasure buffeted her. The hammering of her heart sounded like wind whipping the canvas 'chute. She felt as if she floated, dangled, then touched down with a gentle bump as he laid her on the mattress.

Reality slowly returned. Left weak by the most violent orgasm of her life, she pried her heavy lids open as Gage ascended her body, entangling her in a series of kisses and caresses over her hip bones, her belly, her waist and breasts until his lips reached hers.

He stole the breath she'd barely caught with a ravenous kiss and then eased up to meet her gaze. "You taste delicious."

A fresh gust of arousal blew through her. How had he decimated her that way? Why him? But she had no time to ponder her question. He reached for the condom, tore the packet and rolled it on, then he scooped her up like a limp rag doll and moved her to the middle of the bed, laying her parallel to the pillows.

She snapped out of her lethargy and pulled him closer with her arms, with her legs. The touch of his body at her entrance made her stiffen in anticipation of his first thrust, and he didn't disappoint. With one long, slow glide he filled her deeply, completely.

"Mmm," she sighed against his neck and stroked the bunched muscles of his back.

His whistled inhalation filled her ear. "Damn, you feel good."

"So do you." The weight of him, scent of him, feel of him surrounded her, impaled her. He withdrew. She pulled him back. Impatiently. Eagerly. Hungrily. He set a rhythm and she matched it, digging her heels into the mattress and countering each thrust. She kissed and nipped the cords of his neck, earning an encouraging growl. In return he grazed her ear with his teeth, with his tongue, steamed her neck with his breath and then stole hers with his voracious kisses.

The muscle-quaking tension returned, increasing with each thrust, as another orgasm built within her. She curled her nails into his tight butt and urged him faster, faster. She was close, so close. And then she was there, free-falling, crying out, clinging to him. His pace quickened, deepened, then his own groan of release echoed off the walls.

Heavy heartbeats later Gage eased down on her, bracing the majority of weight on the tripod of his arms and hips. She wound her arms around his waist and savored the feel of his cheek and chest pressed against hers and his breath bellowing near her ear.

Why did Gage have to be the one to destroy her girlish illusions? She'd always believed the kind of magical connection they'd shared would only come with love and trust and commitment. But she barely knew him and she certainly wasn't in love with him. As for a future with him…well, it had never crossed her mind.

Evaporating sweat cooled her body and cleared her head, allowing doubts to edge in. What she had with Gage could never be more than temporary, and she hoped it wouldn't come back to haunt her.

She prayed she hadn't made a mistake in lying with the man who until today had been her enemy.

Gage knew he'd crossed the line by sleeping with his best friend's sister—*half* sister. His personal ethics made his friend's relatives and exes off limits. But he'd broken that rule with Lauren. He hadn't been able to stop himself.

He levered himself off her and lay on his back by her side with his chest still heaving. Their knuckles touched on the mattress, and he had the strange urge to wrap his fingers around hers and hold her hand. Weird. *Damned* weird. He resisted the urge. He wasn't the hand-holding type.

Staring at the ceiling, he tried to work up a twinge of regret for his actions but failed. Maybe once his chest didn't feel as though it was going to explode and his legs had regained a little strength, he'd find a little remorse.

Lauren lay beside him with her eyes closed, but he could tell she wasn't asleep by her carefully modulated breathing and the tension radiating from her.

Her thick lashes slowly lifted and she turned her head. The satisfied expression in her eyes jump-started his slowing heart rate. "That was…"

"Amazing." He finished her breathless sentence when she didn't. He couldn't remember ever having sex that satisfying or intense before.

A smile twitched her swollen lips. She quickly captured it between her teeth. "Yes, it was. But, Gage, I'm not sure it was a good idea."

His thoughts exactly.

Her eyebrows dipped. "Maybe we should forget this ever happened."

What? He wasn't used to women wishing they hadn't slept with him. And he didn't like it. "I dare you."

"I beg your pardon?"

He rolled on his side, his weakened muscles protesting the call to action. She mirrored his move, displaying the curve of her hips and deep V of her waist. One long, slender leg bent, hiding the triangle of dark blond curls from him. But he didn't need to see her. He remembered how she looked, smelled, tasted.

Regardless, he let his gaze travel slowly down her pale body. For a Florida girl she didn't have much of a tan, but she had a nice shape. Slender, curved, delicious. He swept a hand from her shoulder, down her arm and across her waist, settling on her hip. Her shiver brought the blood rushing back to his groin.

"I dare you to try to forget what we just shared." Rekindled arousal thickened his voice.

Her cheeks pinked and her pupils dilated. "Gage, it's not going to be easy to hide an intimate relationship from Trent. He's an ass, but he's not stupid. And I can't afford to get fired."

Damn. He'd never lied to Trent before. He didn't plan to start lying now. "How much longer will you work for HAMC? You said this was a temporary gig."

He wasn't thinking long-term relationship, but he wasn't ready to let her go until he worked whatever it was she'd done to him out of his system.

She reached behind her to snag a corner of the sheet and drag it over her hip. Gripping the pink fabric between her breasts, she glanced away. "I don't know. I don't want to leave until I—"

"Until you…what?"

"My mother has something I need."

That brought them back to the original reason Trent

had called him. Regret climbed into the bed between them. Trent was convinced Lauren was a shyster. What if he was right?

"Money?" Gage spat out the word.

She flinched and met his gaze. "I've told you before I don't want the Hightowers' money. If you won't believe that especially after this, I'll quit wasting my breath."

Her lack of hesitation and the sincerity in her eyes convinced him she was telling the truth. But he'd been wrong before, and it had nearly cost him his home and his company. What if, once again, he'd let his dick do the thinking and been taken in by a beautiful woman?

No. Not this time. Everything he'd learned about Lauren contradicted Trent's summation of her personality.

"I believe you."

If nothing else came of their affair, Gage intended to prove Lauren's innocence to Trent even if that meant spending every possible moment with her and digging for the facts.

Eight

Lauren stared at Gage across the tiny window-side table at the Fisherman's Wharf restaurant. She'd never been more physically in tune with anyone before. But Gage was rich. He was Trent's friend. He lived in Knoxville.

Three strikes.

Four if you counted the fact that she'd only known him a week.

So why did she still want him when there was absolutely no way they could ever make this work?

Girl, you have it bad.

It's just a crush. No big deal.

She hoped.

After an afternoon of playing tourist, riding cable cars and walking the wharf, he was smiling, windblown, a little sunburned and completely relaxed—the opposite of the way he'd been the day she'd met him.

And she was completely smitten.

He looked up from the dessert menu and caught her staring. "I've been to San Francisco a dozen times and eaten on the Wharf half of those, but always at restaurants chosen by my clients. I've probably walked right by this place a few times."

"It's easy to miss crammed between two flashy tourist traps."

One corner of his mouth lifted. "I never would have considered polling the locals to ask who served the best seafood."

She swept a glance over the simple decor of the dining room. The plain wooden furniture and scarred hardwood floors weren't much to look at, but the view of the docks was incredible, and the food had been the best she'd had in ages. This was the kind of place she, her father and uncle adored. Her mother would have been horrified to eat here, as evidenced by the stilted restaurants Lauren had been forced to endure whenever her mother had visited in the past.

She pushed aside the unpleasant memories. "It's a habit I picked up when landing at unfamiliar airports. Locals know where to eat, and mom-and-pop cooks are usually more concerned with flavor than whether the food looks like artwork on the plate."

"After this—" he gestured to his empty plate "—I believe you." As he had after the motorcycle ride, he looked surprised that he'd enjoyed the day. What could make a man afraid to unwind?

They had barely been apart since they'd made love the first time last night. This morning they'd worked together before heading out to see the sights. But despite that, she barely knew him. Most of their conversation had centered around the attractions which he'd missed on previous visits.

"Gage, what do you do in your free time?"

"I don't have a lot of free time," he answered quickly.

"You can't work 24/7."

"I've been building Faulkner Consulting."

No wonder he looked older than his age. "My father had a couple of signs hanging in his office. The first said, 'Making a living is not the same as making a life.' And the second, 'Love what you do and do what you love.' He always claimed that if died—" A knot in her throat squeezed off her voice. She took a sip of her lemonade and tried again. "He claimed if he died living by those simple rules, then he would have had a full life. And he did."

Gage sat back in his chair, his face closing. "Idealism won't keep a roof over your head or food on the table. Sometimes chasing dreams isn't enough."

"I disagree. We should all be lucky enough to pursue our dreams." She had to believe that. Otherwise, her father's life and death were pointless.

Damn her mother. What possible purpose did it serve for Jacqui to refuse to discuss that final conversation with Kirk? Lauren fisted her hands. Enough waiting already. As soon as she got home she was going to corner her mother and make her talk.

"I'd prefer not to have to worry about where my next meal is coming from."

"Like you did when you were a child?"

"Yes. But I prefer not to dwell on the past. It's over and can't be changed." He covered her hand on the table. "Let's get out of here."

The deep rumble of Gage's voice and the sensual promise flickering to life in his eyes quickened her heartbeat and sent heat coursing through her. There was absolutely no doubt in her mind that if they left now, they were going back to the B and B and straight to bed. If she chose to delay and question him further, she'd kill the mood.

Not an option she wanted to take. For someone who'd easily gone without sex for more than a year, she seemed determined to make up for lost time. She was so eager to get back to the B and B and into Gage's arms she could probably run the entire distance back to the Upper Haight neighborhood.

But stellar sex wasn't everything. Watching Gage unwind today had made it very clear she had one more thing to do before she left Knoxville.

Someone needed to tackle the challenge of teaching him how to live before it was too late, and she was the perfect candidate. She'd been lucky enough to have a father to teach her that life was about the journey and not only the destination. There had to be more to life than just work—a concept Gage had missed if his experiences on the motorcycle and as a tourist were any indication.

The moment Gage left the boardroom late Monday morning Lauren reached for the backpack she'd tucked under the table.

They'd been hard at work for hours with Gage pushing her to test her abilities at every turn. While Gage had his wrap-up chat with the CEO she needed to get online and make her airplane payment before they packed up and headed for the airport. She hadn't done it before today because she'd needed to wait for her HAMC paycheck to clear before transferring funds, and her intention of taking care of business first thing this morning...

A chuckle rumbled from deep inside her. Well, Gage had had other plans. In the end they'd had to rush not to be late.

EMILIE ROSE   131

She closed her eyes and rested her head against the back of her chair while the computer booted up. The memory of how he'd monopolized her time flowed through her body like warm oil, tightening her nipples and creating a pool of desire in her belly.

She was exhausted and exhilarated, and she almost hated that this trip was ending. Life and the Hightowers would intrude once she and Gage touched down in Knoxville. How long would their relationship last before Trent found out and fired her?

Grimacing, she straightened, logged on to her computer and pulled up her account to transfer funds from her checking to her loan account.

Balance Due: $0.00

She frowned at the screen. That wasn't right. She still owed almost two hundred thousand dollars. She clicked on her account history. The page claimed her debt had been paid in full on Friday.

No way.

The finance company must have a software glitch or something. But she wasn't going to risk her airplane or her credit rating by skipping a payment and waiting for them to discover their error. She dug her cell phone out of her bag and dialed customer service. A recording greeted her. She hated automated machines, but typed in her account number followed by her security password when prompted. A robotic voice told her to wait for the next available operator.

She checked her watch and tried to block out the annoying elevator music pouring into her ear. Gage would be back soon and he'd be ready to leave.

"This is Rena. How can I help you today, Ms. Lynch?" a pleasant voice said.

Lauren sat up. "Hi, Rena. I'm trying to make a

payment online, but there seems to be a problem with your Web page. It says my account balance is zero."

The tap of computer keys carried through the phone. "That is correct."

Lauren's heart skipped into high gear. "It can't be. I still owe your company money. A lot of money."

"No, ma'am. Your account was paid in full on Friday by certified check. Our offices will mail you the pertinent paperwork within five business days, and you can follow up with the FAA to change the ownership registry. Can I assist you with anything else today, Ms. Lynch?"

"But…that's impossible. I don't have that kind of money. Nobody I know has that kind…of…money." The words sputtered off.

Jacqui.

Her mother had to be behind this. Tension snarled in Lauren's belly and anger stiffened her spine. Gritting her teeth, she forced herself to be polite. It wasn't the customer service rep's fault that Jacqui was trying to absolve her guilt over years of ignoring her daughter with cash.

"Thank you for your help, Rena."

Lauren disconnected then immediately dialed Jacqui's cell phone. The phone rang enough times that she thought her mother was going to ignore her call again. Thanks to caller ID, Jacqui would know if the person calling was someone she wanted to talk to. And apparently, she didn't want to talk to her daughter.

Lauren was debating whether to leave yet another voice mail message when she heard, "Hello, Lauren."

How could Jacqui sound so calm? "Jacqui, did you pay off my loan?"

Silent seconds ticked past. "I wanted to help."

Anger and frustration swelled inside Lauren. Her hand clenched the phone tighter. "We've had this discussion before, and I made my feelings clear. I don't want your charity."

"But, darling—"

"I'm not your darling, Jacqui. I'm not even your daughter. Not in the way that counts. You gave me away. Save your money for your other children. Your *real* children."

She hated the anger and pain in her voice. She'd thought she'd come to terms with the knowledge of her mother's preference for her other children. Obviously not.

"Lauren, you are as much my child as they are, and they already have more than they need. You, on the other hand, are struggling to make ends meet. Your father would want me to help."

The arrow hit its target. Her father had loved this woman enough to accept whatever crumbs of affection Jacqui threw his way. Lauren didn't share that love. In fact, she realized, sometimes she almost hated Jacqui for causing her father so much pain.

"My father taught me to work for whatever I wanted and not to expect or accept handouts. I'll get a new loan as soon as I get home and pay you back."

"I won't accept your money."

Frustrated, Lauren stood and paced to the far side of the room. Why did all the Hightowers think people could be bought? Is that what being raised rich did to a person? If so, she was glad she'd missed out.

"Damn it, Jacqui, we've had this conversation too many times to count. You missed your chance to be my mother."

"And I regret that every single day. I'm sorry I let you go, Lauren."

Too little. Too late. "You know what I want from you, and I'm getting really tired of your stalling tactics. If you won't give me what I need, then I'm going back to Daytona and we're done."

A sound made her turn. Gage stood in the open doorway, his eyes narrowed. How much had he overheard? If he found out what Jacqui had done, he'd believe the worst of Lauren—the way her half siblings did. All of them would be convinced Lauren had weaseled the money out of their mother.

Lauren's stomach churned. She had to repay the loan. But could she even qualify for new financing with Falcon's current financial condition?

"We'll continue this conversation when I get back from San Francisco. I expect you to be in town and available," she told her mother and disconnected.

If you won't give me what I need then I'm going back to Daytona and we're done.

To Gage the angry words sounded like a threat. With whom had Lauren been arguing and why? And why did it bother him that she was already planning to walk away from what they had when a short-term affair had been the agenda all along? Just because they'd had two days of fantastic sex didn't mean he'd break his firm rule against permanent relationships.

His ex-wife and his mother had both bailed when they hadn't gotten their way, proving money was more important and more reliable than love. They'd cured him of ever wanting to try a permanent relationship again. But he had to thank them for the valuable lessons they'd taught him. Take what you want from a relationship and walk away.

He'd based his career on that rule. He took on a company's problems, fixed them, then moved on without a long-term commitment or a stake in the outcome. That meant there were no expectations or disappointments if those involved failed to implement his strategies.

Lauren smiled at him as she crossed the room and closed her laptop, but the curve of her lips looked strained, and her eyes lacked their usual sparkle. "All done with the CEO?"

"Yes. Problem?" He inclined his head to indicate the cell phone she held in a white-knuckle grip.

She lowered her gaze and shoved her phone into her bag. "Nothing I can't handle."

The emotional wall she'd initially kept between them had returned. He didn't like it. An unfamiliar urgency to fix whatever had upset her and get them back on a comfortable footing surged inside him like water pressure building behind a dam. "We need to eat before taking off."

"I'll order your lunch to be delivered to the plane. That'll get us in the air faster." Tension made her movements sharp and stiff as she packed away her computer.

"You'll eat with me."

She looked ready to argue then sighed. "All right."

"In a hurry to get home?"

She slung her bag's strap over her shoulder. "It's a long flight, and we were up early. I'd rather not be too late getting back. Not to mention I'm eager to get my hands on Trent's jet again. That baby's a sweet ride. Can I help you pack your files?"

His hunger for her rekindled at the memory of waking before the alarm went off to make love to her, and then doing so again during their shared shower. Technicolor images of wet bodies, steamed glass shower doors and Lauren braced against the wall in the stall filled his brain. He blinked to clear his head, but neither the pictures nor the heat vanished.

Alarm sirens rang in his subconscious. He hadn't wanted a woman this incessantly in a very, very long time.

"I have it." He swiftly gathered his belongings, surreptitiously keeping an eye on Lauren. She shifted on her feet and stared off into space, her thoughts clearly elsewhere. "Let's go."

Lauren remained unusually silent as the CEO and his PA accompanied them to the lobby. Gage carried his end of the conversation, informing the client what to expect next in the process, but his attention was divided between the job at hand and Lauren. Women never came between him and his work, but he had to admit he'd been preoccupied with Lauren.

They said their goodbyes to the client and buckled into the rental car. Lauren stared out the window. He'd barely known her a week, but he already knew and liked the way she threw herself one hundred percent into everything she did. He liked her analytical mind, the way she relentlessly picked apart the details of an issue until she understood the big picture. Working with her had been easy because he shared the same traits. He liked that she knew how to have fun. She wasn't having any now.

He merged the car onto the highway. "The phone call upset you. What's going on?"

"Gage, it's nothing important." She pulled out her cell phone. "Excuse me for a moment. I need to call the food service people to order our meal and notify the airport that we're on our way."

Part of him admired her efficiency as she quickly dealt with preflight red tape like the pro she was, but her nonanswer frustrated him. He'd bide his time, but he would get to the bottom of what had killed her good mood before they took off.

An hour later he'd made no progress. Any attempts

at private conversation had been derailed first by the need to refuel the plane and complete the ground portion of her preflight check, then once Lauren had climbed on board, the hovering staff serving their meal had made a personal discussion impossible. But finally, Lauren closed and locked the jet's door behind the departing servers, and silence filled the cabin.

Gage positioned himself so that when she turned around she stepped right into his open arms.

Her wide eyes found his. "Is something wrong?"

He rubbed her stiff back. "You tell me."

Her gaze lowered to his chin. "No. I'll have us in the air in twenty minutes."

Not if he had his way. He was determined to discover whatever had her wired, and if that meant getting her to let down her guard by stripping her out of her clothing and communicating the way they did best, then so be it. He stroked a finger along her cheek and her breathing hitched.

"Gage—" Warning filled her voice, but her pupils dilated.

"Ever made love in an airplane?"

She licked her lips. "No."

"Neither have I."

"The, um…mile high club usually waits until the plane's in the air…or so I'm told."

"I'm not interested in flying without a pilot."

"Good. Me, either. The threat of crashing isn't an aphrodisiac for me."

"Let's rock this jet, Lauren." He covered her mouth with his, savoring her soft lips, her taste, her flowery scent. A fragment of his brain wondered if he'd lost his mind. It wasn't like him to mix business with pleasure, and Lauren was definitely the latter.

Her short nails dug into his waist and the stiffness

slowly drained from her. She leaned into him and her tongue twined with his as she returned the embrace. His heart pounded and desire weighted his groin.

Her palms flattened on his chest and she broke the kiss. Her cheeks were flushed, her lids heavy as she looked up at him, but passion glowed in her eyes. "This is crazy. What are we doing?"

Her breathless voice amped up his pulse rate. "We're going to put one of these leather seats to good use before we take off. As you said, once we return to Knoxville, being together will be a challenge."

She bit her lip then rested her forehead on his shoulder. "Everything will change, won't it?"

He lifted her chin and met her worried gaze. "It doesn't have to. Not yet."

But soon she'd go back to Daytona, and his life would return to normal. The knowledge didn't fill him with the relief or satisfaction it should have. He couldn't afford to be sidetracked right now. He was too close to having Faulkner Consulting exactly where he wanted it. He had almost enough invested to make sure he'd never be homeless or go hungry again even if his business folded.

He caressed her cheek, her neck, then traced her ear. Her eyes closed and her lips parted. He kissed her again, a series of brief teasing touches of his lips on hers.

Impatient for the feel of her, the taste of her, he unbuttoned her uniform jacket then her blouse and cradled her breasts in his hands. He tugged the bra cups down until they rested beneath the swells of pale flesh, then he bent to capture one nipple in his mouth, the other with his fingers.

Her sigh filled his ears. She yanked his shirt from his pants and pressed her palms to his chest. Her hands smoothed over his back, waist and belly, inflaming him.

While he sucked and nibbled her breasts, he outlined her hips, then slid his hands beneath her skirt to caress her incredible legs and tight, round bottom. The snug skirt restricted his movements. He worked the fabric up to her waist and peeled her panty hose and panties down for better access. His palms glided over her warm, satiny skin.

"Mmm, I love the way you touch me." Her lips teased his skin as she murmured against the side of his neck. Her hand covered his erection, and she massaged him through his pants.

Hunger racked him. A growl rumbled from deep in his gut. He wanted her *now*. He found the slick folds between her legs. Her whimper rewarded him for hitting the spot he'd learned drove her wild.

Her legs parted slightly, but she covered his hand with hers. He noted she didn't still his circling finger. "You're rushing me."

Her sexy whisper only made him more impatient to be inside her. He grazed her nipple with his teeth then lifted his head and stared into her passion-filled eyes. "This is going to be hard and fast. Got a problem with that?"

Her throaty chuckle vibrated over him. "No."

As he backed toward the nearest seat, her fingers went to work on his belt and pants. She shoved them over his butt, and he sank onto the cool leather. He stripped her panty hose and panties to her ankles then gripped her hips and pulled her toward him.

He buried his face in her curls, savoring her scent in his nose and the taste of her arousal on his tongue.

"Gage, I can't—"

"Hold on," he said against her.

She grasped his shoulders. He licked, sucked and teased her until her legs shook and her nails dug into his scalp. He kneaded her bottom with one hand and her breast with the other. Her breathing turned choppy then her back bowed. Climax shuddered through her, making her jerk against his mouth and moisten his fingers. She sagged into his hand.

He kissed her hip, tongued her navel, then her nipples until the aftershocks passed. "I have a condom in my left pants pocket."

She leaned back in his arms, a sassy smile curving her lips. "Confident, were you?"

"I knew what we both wanted."

"Smart man. No wonder companies pay you the big bucks." She knelt in front of him and bent to dig into the trousers piled on top of the shoes he hadn't removed. Meeting his gaze, she tore the packet with her teeth and wrapped her fingers around him, but instead of rolling on the latex, she leaned forward and took him into her hot, wet mouth.

Gage slammed back against the seat as desire seared him. Her tongue swirled around the head of his shaft, and his control wavered. He gripped the armrests and fought against the explosive need building deep in his gut.

"Lauren." He growled her name in warning.

She lifted her head only a fraction. "You said you wanted fast."

Her warm breath teased his damp flesh. One of the things he liked about Lauren was she didn't play coy or try to hide her desire. She wanted him. He could see her hunger in her eyes, on her wet lips and her pink cheeks. With mischief dancing in her eyes she held his gaze, flicked her tongue over him and stroked him from base to tip and back again. He quaked with need.

"Put the damned thing on and ride me."

Her lips curved into a wicked grin. "Yes, sir. Did I mention the customer's always right?"

She taunted him by rolling on the protection slowly, rechecking the fit again and again by gliding her fingers up and down his length and cupping his nuts. The touch of her hands drove him toward the crumbling edge of his control.

"Witch."

The gutteral word made her grin widen.

He grabbed her wrists and yanked her over him. She stumbled, probably entangled in the lingerie still wound around her ankles. He caught her and urged her forward.

She planted a knee on the wide seat on either side of him. He hit the recline button, laying himself back, then guided her over his erection. She lowered, engulfing him one slow inch at a time.

A seductive smile teased her lips as she eased down until she'd taken his full length, then her breath whooshed out on a half sigh, half moan. "You feel good."

"So do you, babe. Damned good."

He lifted her skirt higher, clearing the view to watch her taking him as she rose over him, lowered, lifted again. He clutched her hips and helped her set a pace guaranteed to drive him out of his mind. Then he found her center and worked her with his thumb. Her legs trembled more with each rise and fall. His muscles clenched as he met each descent with an upward thrust.

He quickened the circles of his thumb and focused on the ecstasy chasing across her face, on the hot, slick glide of her body tightly gloving his. He was damned close, but he wasn't coming without her. Not if he could help it. He arched forward and caught a nipple between his lips.

Her orgasm hit, jerking her with the first wave. Her

internal muscles contracted around him, and he quit fighting. His climax blasted from his extremities through his gut then he erupted like a geyser. Afraid he'd throw her off as the violent spasms rocked him, he grabbed her waist and held on until, drained, he dissolved into the seat.

Lauren collapsed over him with her head on his shoulder and her rapid breaths steaming his jaw. She stroked his cheek, kissed his chin. "Wow."

Her dazed tone startled a laugh out of him. He couldn't remember ever laughing during or after sex before Lauren. But he'd laughed more with her over the past few days than he had in years. She was so real, honest and upfront about her reactions.

Trent was wrong about her. Dead wrong.

"I'll second that wow." Gage caressed her moist back beneath the uniform he hadn't bothered to remove and waited for his heart and breathing to slow.

Lauren eased upright, smiling, disheveled and looking a little bemused. A lock of hair had come loose from the twist she'd pinned on the back of her head. An urge to hug her rolled over him, but he didn't do hugs. Hugs led people to expect more. He settled for tucking the silky strand behind her ear and tracing a finger over the slowing pulse at the base of her neck.

"Lauren, tell me about the phone call."

She stiffened and tried to get off him, but he clamped his hands on her thighs and held her in place.

"You're persistent, aren't you? Don't sweat it. As I've said, it's nothing I can't handle."

He didn't like being shut out. "Problem solving is what I do best. Let me help you."

She held his gaze for several moments. Indecision flickered across her face and her mouth opened then closed. She shook her head. "Not this time. But thank you for offering."

She squirmed again and he let her go. His body slipped from hers, and cool air circulating through the plane replaced her warmth, but it was her mental withdrawal that chilled him. She stood, pushed down her skirt, and turning her back, hastily pulled up her panties and hose, buttoned her shirt and straightened her uniform.

He rose and redressed while she used the onboard bathroom. When she finished he took his turn, discarding the condom and washing up. She was waiting when he returned to the cabin with her shoulders stiff and her chin high.

"I won't be distracted in the cockpit if that's what you're worried about."

"I have complete faith in your flying capabilities. If I didn't, not even Trent's friendship would make me put my life in your hands or your aircraft."

She bit her bottom lip. "I need a favor."

Tension crept into his muscles. Women always wanted something. For them, everything came with a price. "Name it."

"Please don't tell Trent about our...involvement."

"I meant it when I told you I'd keep our private business between us."

"I just needed to be sure. Thank you." She closed the distance between them, rose on tiptoe and kissed him briefly, then rocked back on her heels and took a deep breath. "Let me get this bird in the air and get us home."

She turned toward the cockpit and a heavy weight descended over him. What in the hell was his problem?

And then he knew.

He was falling for Lauren Lynch. Falling hard.

Nine

Emotion grabbed Lauren by the throat Thursday evening. The accident report fell from her shaking hands to the floor inside her apartment door where she'd torn open the package the moment the deliveryman had departed.

Grief, relief and despair twisted inside her like a waterspout. Her father's death hadn't been suicide. His crash had been caused by mechanical defect in the plane's design.

The plane she'd helped him build.

A logical corner of her mind insisted she wasn't an aeronautical engineer, and couldn't have predicted the bolt would shear off or the disastrous results. But she'd practically been raised in a hangar. She knew aircraft structure and maintenance backward and forward, and she'd worked by her father's side on this project for the past ten years.

As many times as they'd dismantled and reassembled

the major components, why hadn't she noticed the faulty part? And how had he flown the plane so many times before without incident?

She stabbed a hand into her hair and circled the room. Maybe if he'd let her fly the plane, she'd have felt an unusual shimmy or lack of responsiveness the failing bolt would have caused. Maybe she could have averted disaster. But her father had never let her take the controls of what he'd called his baby.

She had to call Lou. She reached for her phone, and checked her watch. No one would be in the office this late in the evening. She punched his cell number. When voice mail picked up on the first ring she groaned in frustration. He'd forgotten to turn on his phone again. She left a quick message and disconnected. For a man who could handle any technical aspect of an airplane, he hated what he called modern contraptions like cell phones. She'd only recently convinced him to use the Internet. She'd have to call him at home later after his Thursday night bowling club.

But she needed to talk to someone now, someone who would understand the contradictory guilt and relief racking her.

Gage.

The idea hit her with a jolt of adrenaline. He had a way of looking at a situation from all angles. Maybe he could help her work through the emotions torturing her. She hadn't seen him since a scowling Trent had met them the moment Lauren had opened the airplane door Monday night, and strangely enough, she'd missed Gage the past three days.

Had what they'd shared in San Francisco meant nothing to him? Had he decided to dump her now that he'd slept with her? The idea hurt, and that was stupid because there was no chance of a future between them. But still…

She'd thought him different from the Whits of this world who used a woman then moved on as soon as a model with better perks and more connections came along. If she hadn't, she never would have gone to bed with Gage.

Either way, she didn't want to call him. Because of his connection to Trent, revealing the financial reasons some believed her father had committed suicide wouldn't be a good idea. Falcon's indebtedness would only reinforce every negative belief her half siblings had about her.

That left Jacqui—if Jacqui was back in the country. She hadn't been home when Lauren returned from San Francisco. But Jacqui wasn't a good choice since she was rarely the voice of reason. Still…as much as Lauren had been haranguing her mother for answers, Jacqui deserved to know what the report had uncovered.

Lauren grabbed the papers and her keys and raced down the stairs to her truck. The bite of the cold night air penetrated her sweater, making her realize she'd forgotten her coat. Too bad. She wasn't taking the time to go back and fetch it.

Shivering, she revved the engine and headed for the Hightower estate. If she was lucky, Trent wouldn't be there. Twenty minutes later she hit the doorbell.

Fritz opened the door. "Good evening, Miss Lynch."

"Is she here?"

"In the salon."

"Is Trent here?"

"No, miss."

Good.

Fritz turned and led the way. "Ms. Lynch, for you, Madam."

He stepped aside, revealing Jacqui sitting near the

fireplace, dressed immaculately as always, this time in a dark teal color that brought out the color of her eyes. Lauren couldn't remember ever seeing her mother looking less than perfect. Jacqui's perfection had always been daunting for a rough-and-tumble girl who'd usually had skinned knees, scraped knuckles and hair trimmed by her father.

"Lauren, this is a surprise." Jacqui rose and crossed the room to give her one of those meaningless air kisses.

"I'm sorry I didn't call. I'm surprised Fritz let me in."

"He's been told I'm always available to you."

Nice, but a couple of decades too late. And being physically available didn't equate to being emotionally accessible. "I have the accident report. Dad's death wasn't suicide."

"I told you it wasn't." Jacqui seemed even more tense than her usual uptight self.

"But why should I have believed you when you wouldn't tell me anything else? Like what you and Daddy discussed that afternoon that sent him racing for the airstrip the moment you left. He flew off without filing a flight plan or telling anyone where he was going or when he'd be back."

"That's because I—" Jacqui looked away briefly. "I'm sorry. May I offer you some refreshment?"

Lauren gritted her teeth over the stalling tactic. Jacqui had quite a varied collection of ways to avoid a discussion. "No. Thank you. If we'd known his flight plan, he wouldn't have lain out there in the Glades so long."

Jacqui flinched. "The medical examiner's report stated Kirk died instantly and didn't suffer while waiting for rescue."

"That's the only thing that makes the idea of him dying alone bearable."

Jacqui squared her narrow shoulders as if bracing herself. "What did the report say?"

Words tumbled in Lauren's head—words a nonpilot wouldn't understand. "Without getting technical, the plane's design was faulty. There was too much stress on some parts. Dad hit stall speed during a steep turn and lost control because a bolt sheared off. He was flying too close to the ground to level out and set her down on her belly. That's why he went in wing first."

Jacqui bowed her head, covered her mouth with one beringed, manicured hand and turned away. A muffled sob broke the silence then her shoulders shook.

Watching her mother's grief made Lauren uncomfortable. Unsure of what to do, she picked at the side seam of her jeans and cleared her tightening throat.

Pilots don't cry. Her father's voice echoed in her head.

She inhaled deeply, struggled for composure. *Focus on the facts.* "I should have noticed the worn part when we broke the plane down and reassembled her. If I had, then maybe he'd still be with us."

Jacqui spun around, fists curled, body taut. Her mother's red-rimmed eyes zeroed in on her. "Don't you dare blame yourself for this. You have nothing to feel guilty about. *I* am the one who should have stopped him."

Lauren blinked in surprise at her mother's vehement tone. "How do you think you could have done that?"

"If I hadn't given him the money—" Another sob choked off her words, leaving nothing but the crackle of the fire to fill the silence.

Lauren senses went on alert. "Money for what?"

Jacqui wrung her hands. "The engineering evaluation, the repeated upfittings…"

A knot formed in Lauren's stomach. "Wait a minute. Back up. What engineering evaluation?"

Jacqui's fidgeting stopped. "Kirk didn't tell you?"

"Tell me what?"

Her mother crossed to the wet bar and splashed clear liquor from a crystal decanter into a matching tumbler. After taking a healthy swig, she faced Lauren.

"Kirk contacted me just before your eighteenth birthday. He had designed an airplane that he was sure was going to make him rich. He knew there was something not quite right with it, but didn't know what or how to fix the problem. He asked me to use my connections to get an independent engineering consult. I agreed on the condition that I got to tell you I was your mother and spend more time with you. I had wanted to for years, but that wasn't part of my original agreement with your father or my husband."

Lauren let the information soak in. Her mother had wanted to see her? She found that hard to believe. "About the money...?"

"Your father couldn't afford the engineer's fee. I had chosen the best, of course. So I paid it." She paused to gulp more of her drink. "The engineer found a flaw in the swept-back wing design and told your father it couldn't be corrected. It was something intrinsic in the structure. In fact, the engineer recommended your father not continue to fly the plane. But that airplane was your father's dream, and he wouldn't be dissuaded. He convinced me to loan him the money to keep working on the design. Because I couldn't bear to kill his enthusiasm, I continued to fund the project."

Maybe her half siblings had good reason to distrust her. "How much money are we talking here?"

"That's irrelevant. It was my money to do with as I pleased, and until recently, I covered my tracks well."

"What do you mean *until recently?*"

"Trent's minions have been spying on me. They reported my recent transactions."

No wonder her brother hated her. But she'd deal with that later. "Back to Dad and that day."

"What sent your father off that afternoon was me. *Me*." Jacqui's voice cracked. "I asked him to give up, to admit defeat. I did so, not because of the money, but because I was afraid for him. He kept pushing that airplane harder and harder, trying to prove the engineer wrong. And then Kirk admitted he couldn't afford to quit. He needed to sell and patent the plane's design to cover his debts."

Light-headed, Lauren gripped the back of a chair. Her father had known the plane was faulty and chosen to risk his life anyway. For money. Did everything always come down to money?

"Why didn't you tell me this sooner?"

"Because if I hadn't encouraged him, he'd still be alive. Don't hate me, Lauren. I did what I did because I loved him. I wanted him to be happy."

Lauren shook her head in disbelief. "You funded a suicide mission. That's a strange way to show your love."

A mixture of anger and grief toward this woman and toward her father churned in her belly. "It's likely that he turned to you because he'd already borrowed as much as he possibly could against Falcon Air. We're maxed out. And with the economic downturn of the past few years, business has decreased. We've been struggling to make the payments on his loans.

"If the life insurance company finds out he flew against the engineer's recommendation, they might call his death an act of willful negligence and refuse to pay. And then Falcon will be in deep trouble. We'll have to file bankruptcy or find a buyer."

"I'll give you whatever you need."

The idea repulsed her. "I don't want your money, Jacqui. I've never wanted your money. And what I want now, you can't give me."

"Tell me what it is and I'll find a way," Jacqui pleaded.

"I want my father back."

Lauren had never been one to run away from her problems, but at the moment she ached to be in the cockpit of her Cirrus high above the clouds or racing down the highway on her Harley with the wind tearing at her hair.

She knew better than to operate either machine with her concentration shattered, which was why she was sitting on the side of the road in her pickup staring at the streetlight and trying to gather her composure.

With hindsight, she wished she hadn't pulled over to answer her cell phone when Lou had returned her call because she was too angry to be tactful.

"You knew," she choked out.

Silence stretched through the airwaves. "Yeah, I knew," Lou finally responded.

It was bad enough that her father and mother had selfishly pursued a death wish, but Lou, too? And they'd all kept the engineer's report from her. Hurt and betrayal burned through her.

"Lauren, your dad was a genius with airplanes. I believed Kirk could find a way to reduce the stress on the wing and fix the problem. If anyone could, he could."

Lauren's hands shook so badly she nearly dropped the phone. "But the *expert* said it wasn't fixable."

"And we both know what your daddy did when somebody told him he couldn't do something. He set out to prove 'em wrong. Same as you'd do. You may be the spittin' image of your momma, but you're your daddy's girl through and through. You got his grit, his flying skills and you sure as hell got his mule-headed stubbornness."

She made a face at the phone. It wasn't the first time she'd been accused of being…persistent. But she didn't see that as a fault. "I would never die just to prove a point."

"He didn't do it on purpose, Lauren."

Her father's death seemed like a senseless waste, an avoidable accident. "Didn't anybody care what *I* thought about him risking his life?"

"He didn't think it was a risk. He'd already logged a hundred hours on that plane before he had the engineer look at it."

"Turns out he was wrong. Lou, I gotta go." Before she did something stupid like bawl her eyes out.

Pilots don't cry.

Heart aching, Lauren disconnected. She couldn't go back to her empty apartment, and she couldn't keep driving aimlessly around Knoxville.

Gage. Gage would help her put this into perspective.

To hell with what her siblings thought. If her father's life insurance refused to pay up, Falcon's financial woes would be in the airline news soon anyway when its assets went on the auction block.

Gage's muscles ached with fatigue, and his eyes felt as if someone had dumped a bag of sand into them. Spending the past thirty-six hours without sleep by his father's side had left him wanting food, a hot shower and a comfortable bed.

He considered ignoring whoever was ringing his doorbell, but he still had a business to run. He'd been incommunicado since his cell phone battery died two days ago, and he'd forgotten to check the message machine when he'd dragged himself into the house.

The smell of the hospital still clung to him, but he reached into the glass cubicle of his shower and shut off the inviting steamy spray. He dragged on a bathrobe and slowly descended the stairs to his foyer. Who would be visiting at almost midnight? He checked the peephole.

Lauren. His heart jolted into a faster rhythm. He hadn't spoken to her since Trent had greeted him at the airport with news of his father's hospitalization. Afterward, while his father had lain in intensive care hovering between life and death, calling anyone had never crossed his mind.

His exhaustion vanished. His formerly leaded limbs suddenly felt lighter. He opened the door.

With her arms wrapped around her middle, she stood shivering and pale on his porch without a coat. Her hair was disheveled and a worried pleat creased her brow. She didn't look like she'd been resting during her days off.

She stared up at him. "I'm sorry. I know it's late, but can I come in?"

"Of course." Because he wanted so badly to take her into his arms, he stepped out of the way instead. She passed by, leaving a hint of flowers in the air. He closed the door. She shifted on her feet looking ill at ease. "What's wrong, Lauren?"

"I received the accident report on my father's crash today, and I…I need you to help me make sense of it."

Having been through hell and back with his father in the past few days, her unusual vulnerability pulled at something familiar deep in his chest. He took her hand in his. Her fingers were as cold as ice. He led her to his den. A flick of a switch ignited the gas logs. He sat on an ottoman in front of the fireplace and pulled her down beside him.

A shudder racked her. He put his arm around her shoulders and pulled her close. The action felt eerily natural and comfortable. She pressed her face into the open V of his robe. The shock of her cold cheek against his skin contrasted with the warmth of her breath on his flesh. Thoughts of bed returned, this time not involving the eight hours of uninterrupted sleep he needed. But sex wasn't what Lauren needed right now. And hell, as tired as he was, he wasn't sure he was capable. A humbling thought.

He rubbed her stiff back. "What did the report say?"

"My father didn't commit suicide. At least not intentionally."

Unintentional suicide didn't compute. "Explain."

"He—*we*—built an experimental aircraft, my father, Lou and me. Dad planned to patent the design and sell it. But—" she inhaled shakily "—the design was flawed. Dad knew it. My mother knew it. Even my uncle knew. But Dad flew the stupid plane anyway. He pushed it beyond its limits…and it killed him."

Her words echoed his concerns about his own father who seemed hell-bent on following a dream regardless of the costs. "Go on."

"Gage, I spent almost as many hours working on that plane as he did. I should have seen the flaw."

Self-blame. Another familiar refrain. He understood and had experienced the same helpless frustration numerous times. His determination to fix his father's life had caused a rift between him and his dad that seemed unbridgeable. They'd barely spoken in the past few years.

"Lauren, the accident wasn't your fault."

Her eyes beseeched him, and he wanted to sweep in like a superhero and fix her problems.

"He never asked what *I* wanted. I would much rather have my father alive and with me than have a damned airplane named after me. I'm a better pilot. If he'd let me fly it—"

A crushing sensation settled on his chest. "Then you might be dead instead of him. My father also has an apparent death wish, and he's more than willing to die for what he believes in. Helping others might sound like an admirable goal, but not at the risk of his personal safety.

"I realized years ago that I can't control him. Not that I haven't tried. But he's not a child. What he does is not my fault. The best I can do is be around to pick up the pieces."

She leaned back, her eyes brimming with questions. "What happened?"

He hadn't intended to share his past with her, but he'd already shared more with Lauren than anyone else except Trent. And Trent only knew because he'd lived through some of it with Gage. An urgent need for her to know who he was and where he'd come from rose within him.

"I told you I lived in the family car for a while." He waited for her nod. "Before that my father was a successful real estate developer. His dreams were always larger than life, and we lived the high life. Not on the Hightowers' level, but close. By the time I turned ten he'd overextended himself, taking on more debt than he could handle. Then the real estate market tanked. He hadn't prepared for that, and he lost everything, including our home. We lived in the family car for six months. My mother bailed after three.

"Dad never regained the drive to try again. We were

in and out of public housing projects and shelters after that because he couldn't hold a job. He wasn't cut out for taking orders or being anyone's subordinate. He was too used to being the boss."

The sympathy in Lauren's eyes almost dammed his words. "What about your mother?"

He shrugged. "I never saw her again and haven't looked for her."

"Not knowing you is her loss, Gage." Her fingers squeezed his. "Is your father still alive?"

"Not for lack of trying to kill himself. Seven years ago I bought him a house, but he insists on hanging out at the local homeless shelter. He claims he's found his true calling in helping others.

"It's a rough inner-city crowd, and Dad doesn't hesitate to step in when fights break out. He's been hurt a few times, but this week—" Knowing how close he'd come to losing his father made his throat close up. "This week he tried to break up a knife fight and got sliced up. By the time I reached the hospital he'd already flatlined once, but they'd brought him back. I've been there since we landed."

"That's why Trent was waiting for us—for you?"

"Yes. Tonight they moved Dad out of intensive care. He's going to pull through. That's the only reason I came home. For a shower and some sleep."

"Gage, I'm sorry." Her sincerity shone in her eyes and his lungs took a siesta. He wasn't used to someone caring for him. And then he realized he'd never allowed anyone to. He'd kept his acquaintances at a distance and never let them see behind the wall he'd built around himself. Only Lauren had blasted through, by refusing to back off when he threw up barricades.

Head reeling at the discovery, he tried to remember

his point. "I wish I could believe this would teach Dad a lesson, but it won't. Lauren, our parents make choices over which we have no control. You can't beat yourself up over it. You have to let them live their lives the same way you want them to let you live yours."

Her wide gaze held his and he saw acceptance slowly seep in followed by gratitude then regret. She mentally pulled away before she stiffened in his arms. "Thank you for helping me make sense of this. I should get out of here and let you rest."

The idea of her leaving repelled him. "Stay."

"You need sleep."

"I need you more." The minute the words left his mouth he knew they were true. After seeing his father's failure and his mother's and ex-wife's fickle natures, Gage had sworn he'd never allow himself to need anyone again. But Lauren made him want more than just a financially secure future. She made him want someone to share it with.

And allowing himself to want something he couldn't control scared the crap out of him.

Ten

The warmth of the fire at Lauren's back couldn't compare to the heat in Gage's eyes. Her heart blipped wildly and her mouth moistened as Gage lowered his head.

His lips swept hers so tenderly, emotion welled up in her throat. Choking back a sob, she broke the kiss, buried her face in his neck and wrapped her arms around his middle, hugging him as tightly as she could.

Gage soothed her with long strokes down her spine and soft kisses in her hair, on her temple, along her jaw. The tumultuous feelings inside her morphed into something altogether different, and by the time his mouth returned to hers, Lauren ached for him and for the passion and momentary oblivion he could offer.

She tunneled her fingers into the opening of his robe, gliding her hands over his warm, supple skin and savoring each hiss of his breath. She wasn't supposed to feel this close to him, this emotionally bonded to him.

He was supposed to be temporary, a plane that passed in the night-dark sky.

He rose, pulling her to her feet, then with one powerful kick he sent the ottoman skidding out of the way. He peeled away her clothing with economical precision. Her sweater, bra, pants and panties landed in a pile on the floor. He stepped back, his eyes devouring her as he stripped off his robe and spread it on the rug in front of the fire.

He scooped her into his arms, startling a gasp out of her and knelt to gently lay her on his robe. Thick velour fabric cushioned her back. Seconds later his hot body blanketed her front, before he slid to her side, freeing his hands to map her body with devastating, bone-melting thoroughness.

In the past they'd made love feverishly, but this time Gage lingered, painting languorous circles over her breasts, belly and thighs alternately with his palms and fingertips, making her core shudder with every pass closer and closer to her center.

Hungry for him, she captured his face in her hands and brought his mouth back to hers. His tongue plunged in, sweeping, stroking. His fingers mimicked the action, delving into her curls, finding her moisture, caressing her most sensitive spot until her back bowed as pleasure twined ever tighter inside her.

She tore her mouth away to gasp and grip his shoulders as release shuddered through her like the rise and fall of turbulence, and then drained, she melted into the floor.

He pulled her into his arms and soothed her with gentle kisses. She forced her heavy lids open. Banked hunger still raged in his eyes and in the erection pressing to her hip, but he made no move to drive inside her the way she wanted him to.

"Your turn." She tried to push him onto his back, but he resisted.

He brushed his lips over hers. "This time was all about you, baby."

She stroked her fingertips down his chest until she reached the rigid flesh between them and coiled her hand around him. "Gage, let me make you feel as good as you made me."

He caressed her face. "You do that by being here."

Her heart and lungs contracted as if a giant fist had squeezed them, and Lauren knew she was in trouble.

This wasn't just about sex or two people finding comfort and pleasure in each other.

She'd fallen in love with Gage Faulkner.

Run, run home to Daytona. You have your answers. Now you can go.

She mentally dug in her heels, even though she'd already lived through the rich man–working girl scenario once before and knew a happy ending was unlikely. The ugly finish of her relationship with Whit had nearly broken her, and she hadn't felt nearly as connected to him as she did to Gage. That had been a Cinderella fantasy.

This...this was love. And it was terrifying and exhilarating. And she was not going to run from it.

Her life was a mess. She had no business dragging Gage into it. But if she wanted even a slim chance of a future with him, she had to tell him the whole truth, and hope he believed her and not Trent's poison. And maybe if she was very, *very* lucky, Gage would help her find a way to save Falcon Air.

She opened her mouth, but the words wouldn't come out. She wouldn't tell him, not tonight. Tonight he was tired, and she wanted to sleep in his arms knowing she loved him.

Tomorrow would be soon enough to find out if he was going to break her heart.

Gage absently stirred the eggs while he tried to figure out what about the way he and Lauren had made love this morning bothered him. The prolonged episode, while still hot and extremely satisfying, had felt like a goodbye.

Everything in him rejected the idea. He wasn't going to let her go. Lauren tormented and tested him, but she'd also made him feel more alive than he had in years. Having her in bed beside him when he'd awoken this morning had felt *right*—like a habit to which he would like to become accustomed.

How could he make it work when her life was in Daytona and his business was here? It would be business suicide for her to move Falcon Air onto High-towers' home field. But he'd worked long and hard to build a Faulkner Consulting team he could trust. He wouldn't break them apart. The past few weeks had proven that with a jet and a pilot on call he could get anywhere faster. Would a long-distance affair last?

"Gage," Lauren called from behind him. The quiver of her voice caused the fine hairs on his nape to prickle with unease. "There's something I need to tell you."

He knew before he turned off the burner and faced her that whatever she had to say would likely blow his good mood to smithereens.

She hovered near the entrance of his breakfast area, her long legs bare beneath the hem of one of his white T-shirts. He could see the shadows of her areolas and the points of her nipples through the fabric. Desire pulsed in his groin even though he'd made love to her barely an hour ago.

Worry clouded her eyes and furrowed her forehead. He nodded, indicating she continue.

"I learned more from my mother than about my father's crash." She pleated the hem of his shirt between her fingers, flashing him glimpses of her upper thigh.

He forced his gaze from her sexy legs to her face. "Go on."

"Please hear me out before you jump to conclusions."

The burn in his stomach intensified.

"Jacqui has been funding my father for years, beginning with paying for the aeronautical engineering study then for improvements to the plane."

That answered Trent's question about where the money had been going. "How much?"

"I don't know exactly. She wouldn't say. And then…" She bit her lip and glanced away. Her breasts rose and fell on a deep in- and exhalation before her cautious gaze returned to his. He braced himself.

"She paid off my airplane loan."

Her words hit him like a sucker punch. The missing two hundred grand.

"I found out while we were in San Francisco when I tried to make my payment online."

If you won't give me what I need, then I'm going back to Daytona and we're done.

Lauren had been furious and insistent with the person on the other end of the phone. Looked as if she'd gotten her way, and her way was little better than extortion.

"Gage, I didn't ask her to pay it."

He didn't believe her. He'd heard the argument.

"I've told her a hundred times that I don't want her money. I've never wanted her frilly dresses or dumb dolls or useless manicures. All I wanted was a mother who'd braid my hair, kiss my boo-boos and teach me about boys and makeup. Things money can't buy. And all I wanted when I came to Knoxville was answers. Until last night she withheld those."

Her words gushed like water from a broken mainline, pouring over each other in a tumbled rush. Was she protesting too much? In his line of work he'd learned that those with something to hide always gave more information than the situation required. They talked fast and avoided eye contact—exactly the way Lauren was doing now.

"I intend to get a loan and pay her back. If I can. But—"

"But what, Lauren?"

She fidgeted uneasily with fussy fingers, wiggly toes, shifting shoulders. "Falcon Air is in trouble. Before my father approached Jacqui for money, he borrowed heavily against the company to finance building his plane. If the insurance company finds out he knew the plane was faulty and chose to fly it even though he'd been warned against it by the engineer, they may not pay. If that happens, I might lose Falcon Air..." Her pleading gaze met his. "Unless you'll help me."

He recoiled. Trent had been right. Lauren had been trying to get her hooks into the Hightower fortune. Gage felt like a fool for once again being taken in by a woman's lies.

What was his problem? A little sexual attraction and his brain ceased to function? He'd be damned if he'd let her humiliate him the way Angela had—Angela, who'd strung him along with her professed adoration, her duplicitous nature and her betrayal.

"What you're telling me is you and your father have been milking Jacqueline for cash for years, and now you want to tap into me, too."

She paled. "No. *No.* I want your business consulting expertise to help me turn Falcon around. I've seen you work, Gage. I know you can do it."

"You want to hire me?"

She bit her lip. "I'm not sure I can afford you. But I'm sure we can work out something."

"Like what? Sex for services rendered?"

She flinched and then her chin lifted and her shoulders squared. "How can you say that?"

"Seems obvious. You want something from me, and you're willing to sleep with me to get it."

Dots of angry color appeared on her cheeks. "I was trying to barter with you in a way that would benefit us both. I was thinking more along the lines of trading my piloting skills for your business acumen. You need to travel. I have a plane. I want to save my company and the jobs of all Falcon's employees. Gage, I don't want your money. You have to believe me. I love you."

A jolt from a defibrillator would hurt less. The pain jarred his body. Her declaration was a perfect example that women would say and do anything to get what they wanted. How many times had his ex sworn she loved him? How many times had he looked into her eyes and believed her lies? How many times had he been a fool?

And then Angela and her lawyers had screwed him over. He'd almost lost Faulkner Consulting. As it was, she'd stripped him of every liquid asset he had, and he'd had to start rebuilding the security he'd worked so damned hard for from scratch because of her greed.

But he wanted to believe Lauren, ached to believe her, and his weakness disgusted him. "No."

"No? That's it? No?"

"You're on your own. I no longer need a pilot or you. Goodbye, Lauren. You know your way out."

She stared at him for ten full seconds, her bottom lip quivering until she caught it between her teeth, then she turned and staggered from the room. He was a little surprised she didn't argue. He had to fight the compulsion to go after her as he listened to her climb the stairs then descend moments later. The front door opened then closed. Lauren's big V-10 engine roared in the driveway then the sound faded away.

He congratulated himself on averting another disastrous mercenary relationship.

But the relief he'd expected to feel was nowhere in sight.

Lauren stared at the life insurance check in her hand and recounted the zeroes.

She looked up at her uncle Lou. "This is enough to pay off everything Dad borrowed against Falcon Air and give us a nice cushion. Our financial problems are solved."

So why didn't she feel better?

"Hallelujah. Now if we can get your personal problems fixed, we'll be right as rain."

She stiffened. She thought she'd done a better job of hiding her broken heart by diving right in and assuming her dad's old duties in addition to hers. "I don't have any problems."

"Bull. You've been moping around here for three weeks. If your face gets any longer you'll run over your bottom lip with your landing gear."

"I'm pulling my weight."

"Yes, baby girl, you are. But like the sign behind you says, 'Making a living is not the same as making a life.'" He pointed to the sign hanging on the wall behind her father's—now her desk. "You're running on auto-pilot and logging too many hours. I'm guessing you have unfinished business back in Knoxville. And I don't mean with your momma."

"Then you'd be guessing wrong. Without trust you have nothing. And that's what I left in Knoxville. Nothing." Too bad her heart hadn't signed off on that plan.

She rubber-stamped the back of the check with For Deposit Only then rose and gathered her gear. "I have a lesson to teach. Send Joey out to the Cirrus when he gets here."

She slapped Lou in the belly with the check as she passed. "Take this to the bank when you leave for lunch."

"Lauren, it hurts me to see you like this."

Lou's gruff, but gentle voice stopped her in the doorway. Her aching heart swelled for love of this man. He and Falcon Air were all she had left. "Don't sweat it, Lou. It's like a cold. I'll get over it."

She pivoted and strode out of the office. Her stupid stinging eyes started watering again. Damn Florida's fall grass and weed pollen.

She shoved on her sunglasses then walked around her newly refinanced airplane, doing her preflight check even though she knew she'd make her student repeat the process. The routine soothed her.

As soon as she'd returned from Knoxville, she'd applied for a new loan. When the loan had come through last week she'd mailed a check to Trent with a brief explanation because she'd known her mother wouldn't accept her money. Her half brother hadn't bothered to reply. Said a lot about what he thought of her. But that was just as well. She wanted nothing to do with the Hightowers, either.

Tomorrow when the life insurance check cleared, she'd pay off the rest of Falcon's debts, and she'd once again be free and clear except for the Cirrus.

Life was good.

So why didn't it feel like it?

The last time Gage had found Trent waiting for him outside on the tarmac at the bottom of the airplane stairs, the news his friend had delivered hadn't been good. Judging by Trent's drawn face and tight lips, what he had to say today wasn't going to be any better.

Whatever the current catastrophe might be, Gage wasn't sure he had the energy to deal with it. In the three and a half weeks since Lauren had left, he'd been running around the clock. He worked and slept, woke and showered on an airplane, then reported to the client's office only to begin the entire process again on the flight to the next destination. He couldn't go back to his empty house without picturing Lauren on the rug in front of his fireplace or in his bed.

Trent stood by silently as Gage descended the stairs and thanked today's crew for a good flight. When Gage returned his attention to Trent, his friend held a slip of paper in his extended hand. Curious, Gage took it.

His bleary eyes scanned a certified check for two hundred thousand dollars made out to Trent Hightower, then he zeroed in on the signature of the payer. Lauren Lynch.

A burst of adrenaline kicked up his heart rate. A cold knot formed in Gage's gut and a heavy weight landed on his shoulders. "What's this?"

Trent's exhaled breath clouded the frigid air between them. "Lauren sent the check with a note saying our mother would never cash it, but she trusted me to handle getting the funds back where they belonged. And she promised to make payments of a thousand a month on the remainder of the money our mother gave her father over the past seven years. It's a substantial sum."

Thoughts slammed around Gage's head. His tired brain couldn't begin to sort them out or even find a starting point to making reparation.

"You okay?" Trent asked when Gage said nothing.

He'd been wrong about Lauren. "I was afraid to trust her or the power of what she made me feel. I called her a liar and ordered her out of my house, believing she'd screwed me over the same way Angela had by lying and setting me up to bleed me dry. Instead, I'm the one who wronged her. How in the hell can I apologize for that?"

"Wait a minute. You and Lauren? You never said anything."

"It was none of your business." He raked a hand over his gritty eyes while guilt burned in his stomach like acid. "I treated her badly."

Trent grunted. "You're not the only one. I thought she was a money-sucking leech. I perceived her as a threat, and I did everything I could to run her off. Bottom-of-the-barrel jobs. Obnoxious clients. Our worst planes. Hell, any other employee would have sued me for harassment.

"Mom's a hysterical mess because Lauren's refusing to take her calls. She's threatened to fly down to Daytona, but Lauren's uncle warned her she wouldn't be welcome and that he'd have her escorted off the property."

Gage knew Lauren had to be hurting to take such drastic measures.

"I love her. Lauren. Not your mother." The words burst out before he could stop them.

For the first time in Gage's memory, Trent looked flabbergasted. "Shit. You should have said something."

"I have to find a way to fix this. I can fix this. Fixing things is what I do. And I'm good at it." Who in the hell was he trying to convince? He'd be lucky if Lauren didn't throw him headfirst into a spinning propeller.

He deserved it.

Trent clapped a hand on Gage's shoulder. "My jet is the fastest one we own. It's yours whenever you want it."

"How about now?"

Trent startled and glanced at his watch. "It'll take me a couple of hours to find a pilot."

"What about Phil?" He jerked his thumb over his shoulder to indicate the man who'd just flown him back from Seattle.

"He's maxed out on his hours in the air for the week."

"You fly me."

Trent shrank back. "I haven't taken the controls in twelve years. I'm not risking both our necks."

"C'mon Trent, Lauren says that plane practically flies itself."

"Flying's not like driving a car, Gage. You can't just climb back into the cockpit. All the computerized components are different. Lauren just lost her father to a plane crash. I'm not costing her you, too. Besides, my plane's too damned pretty to break."

The last was clearly a forced attempt at humor. Gage swallowed his objections. "Find me a pilot. Get me to Daytona."

"You've got it. Now go home and clean up. You look like a mangy dog. She won't let you in the house if you show up like that."

Eleven

Lauren's senses went on alert when an unexpected aircraft turned from Daytona International's taxi runway onto the ramp in front of Falcon's hangars.

Her stomach did a loop-de-loop and her pulse stuttered when she identified the make and model as a Sino Swearingen SJ30-2. Her half brother's plane.

No. Couldn't be.

Her gaze shot to the tail number, hoping she was wrong. Her mood nosedived at the familiar sequence she'd relayed into the radio when she'd flown the jet. Her anger stirred.

Trent Hightower had invaded Falcon territory.

What did *he* want? She knew he'd received the check four days ago because she'd sent it by registered mail and he'd signed for it.

The jet came to a stop. She didn't want to talk to him. On second thought, she wouldn't mind if he'd flown to Daytona to apologize and grovel. Especially grovel. The jerk.

Or maybe it was her mother. She didn't want to talk to her, either. They had nothing left to say.

"Sweet ride," her student said. "One of Falcon's?"

She forced her brain back into instructor mode. "No. Check the call sign. All of our N-Numbers end in *FA* for Falcon Air. That one's *HA,* registered to Hightower Aviation. Let's finish your postflight inspection. Where are you on your checklist?"

Her student returned to his task, but he was as distracted by the flashy jet as Lauren. Her ears picked up every sound from behind her, but she kept her eyes focused on her beloved Cirrus. She heard the trespassing aircraft's parking break engage and involuntarily cataloged each step of proper shutdown procedure thereafter.

When the jet's door opened her spine went rigid, but she didn't turn around. If Trent wanted to talk to her, he'd have to cool his jets—the way he'd made her wait outside his office so many times.

When she couldn't stall any longer she signed off on her student's logbook. "That's it for today. You did well. Study for your solo flight next week, and don't forget to wear a shirt I can cut off you. I don't want your mom screaming at me for ruining your best dress shirt."

The postsolo shirt-cutting ceremony was the highlight of her students' lessons. Hers, too. Most of the shirttails hanging on the hangar walls of Falcon's office had come from her students.

"Cool. Can't wait." The seventeen-year-old almost skipped away, leaving Lauren with a memory of having once been that carefree back in the day when she didn't know about debts or her other family—one of which had decided to curse her with a visit.

Taking a bracing breath she pivoted to face her unwelcome relative. Gage stood beside the open cabin door. Gage. Not Trent. Her muscles seized. She couldn't breathe, couldn't move.

Dark sunglasses shielded his eyes, but that thick, glossy dark hair, perfectly shaped body and his purposeful stride were unmistakable. He wore his leather motorcycle jacket unzipped over a black T-shirt, jeans and his black biker boots. Her pulse got as wild as a Mardi Gras parade.

Why was he here? Dressed like that. And where was his obnoxious sidekick? She glanced past Gage to the plane but only saw one of HAMC's pilots circling the aircraft doing his postflight. No sneering half brother waited in the plane's open door.

Her gaze ricocheted back to Gage only thirty feet away and closing, his heels hitting the concrete with a brisk pace. Lauren's heart hammered. Her mouth dried and her hands moistened. With colossal effort, she rallied her anger. His lack of trust had cut deeply. She'd given him her heart, and he'd given her the boot.

Hugging the clipboard to her chest, she wished she could come up with a snarky insult. But her brain refused to cough up any witty words, so she remained mute.

Gage stopped a yard away. "Hello, Lauren."

His deep voice tugged at something buried inside her. She nodded. "Gage."

"We need to talk."

Right. So he could insult her some more? Tear another chunk out of her heart and crush it beneath his shoes? Nope. "I'm working."

"Tell me a convenient time. I'll come back."

Wow. That didn't sound like him. He was usually pushier. "Never sounds pretty good."

He took a quick breath and ripped off his sunglasses. The pain and regret in his dark eyes made her gasp. "I'm prepared to camp on your ramp until you and I have talked."

"Go home, Gage. You're wasting your time." She had to get away from him. The pollen was burning her eyes again. She turned toward the office.

"I have something for you."

She stopped. He held out an envelope. She kept her arms folded over the clipboard.

"It's from Trent."

Probably her final paycheck. She wouldn't have been surprised if her butt-headed half brother had refused to pay her, since she'd left HAMC without working out her two weeks' notice. Since landing in Daytona she'd tried to work up a little guilt over that, but she'd failed. Trent had wanted her gone, and in her opinion, she'd done him a favor by granting his wish.

But hey, if he wanted to throw money at her to ease his conscience for being a prick, she'd take it and donate it to the local Bikers Against Drunk Driving fund. She plucked the envelope from Gage's fingers, tore it open and pulled out the check inside.

A cashier's check for two hundred thousand dollars shook in her hand. Her check. Uncashed. She shoved the paper back where it had come from and thrust the envelope back at Gage. "This isn't mine."

He made no move to take it. "Trent says it is. Either you use the money to pay off your new loan, or I'm to shred the check in front of you. Either way, Trent says to tell you he's not cashing it."

"He can't do that."

A smile twitched one corner of that delectable mouth. "Trent can do pretty much whatever he wants.

Most of your Hightower siblings can. Get used to it. You're one of them now."

"I am not. So you're acting as his delivery boy now?"

Gage's lips compressed. "I offered to return your money, since I was coming down anyway."

She scanned his clothing. "Bike week's in March."

"I'm not here for bike week. I'm here for you."

Her lungs did that lockdown thing they usually did when he touched her—only this time he stood a yard away. "Too bad. Because I'm not available to you."

She did an about-face and hustled toward the hangar. His footsteps followed, deliberate and firm. "Lauren, I made a mistake."

"That's not news," she called over her shoulder without slowing.

"I'm here to help you save Falcon Air. And if I can't come up with a revitalization strategy, then I'll become a silent investor."

Not knowing what to make of his declaration or whether to trust it, she slowly turned. "Thanks, but I no longer need your help. Dad's life insurance paid up. Falcon is back in the black. Besides, you should know by now that I'm no one's charity case. I pay my way."

"Then maybe you'll help me."

What was he trying to pull? "With what?"

"I'm looking for property in the area, and I don't know my way around."

"A vacation home?"

"Two properties. The first is commercial. I'm relocating Faulkner Consulting to Daytona. The second is residential. I put my house on the market."

Her mouth dried. Whatever game he was playing, she didn't have time for it. She resumed her path to the office. He kept pace beside her. She glanced at him. "What's the matter? Knoxville's cold weather getting to you?"

A smile eased over his lips and the gold flecks in his eyes glittered with warmth. "No. I fell for a Harley-riding pilot chick. She lives here."

Lauren tripped over the threshold and would have fallen flat on her face if Gage hadn't caught her arm and hauled her back onto her feet. He swung her around.

"I've been miserable since she left me. Can't eat. Can't sleep. Can't concentrate. Hell, I can't even go home. I've been living on an airplane. My only option if I don't want to go crazy is to chase her until she lets me catch her."

Panic made her heart pound, and a surreal floating sensation took over. Crashing into reality was going to hurt. Bad. "If you think that's funny, then you have a sick sense of humor, Faulkner."

"There's nothing funny about me being blind and not seeing what was right in front of my face. There's nothing funny about hurting the woman I'd fallen in love with because I was too scared to face the truth."

Dizziness swamped her. She clung to the door frame. "You fight dirty."

His smile widened and his eyes glinted with mischief. "You haven't seen anything yet. Give me a chance to regain your trust, Lauren. Let me prove I love you."

She identified the weightless sensation as hope and tried without success to snuff it. "How are you going to do that?"

"I'm not sure, but if I keep trying new strategies for the next fifty years or so, I'm sure I'll hit on a winning combination sooner or later."

He cupped her cheek, stealing her breath and making her eyes sting. "I love you, Lauren. I love that you're genuine and honest. You don't pretend to be someone you're not. I love that you appreciate the simple things instead of going for the bling. I love that you have enough pride to insist on earning what you have, and that you're stubborn enough to stick to your guns when you know you're right.

"But most of all, I love that you're generous enough to share your gifts with me."

Her cheeks burned. She swiped at them and found tears. *Pilots don't cry, damn it.*

Gage caught her soggy hand in his. "We haven't known each other long. We'll take it as slow as you want. I want to learn everything there is to know about you. But I already know the important part. That I love you and want to spend the rest of my life with you. Promise me you'll give me that chance."

Emotion welled up in Lauren's throat. She wanted to laugh. She wanted to cry. But more than anything she wanted to smack Gage for putting her through missing him.

She yanked her hand free and slugged him in the upper arm, not hard, but enough to show her frustration. "If you'd figured this out sooner, I wouldn't have had to live through almost a month of hell."

Gage's laugh boomed out, echoing off the metal hangar walls. "I hope our kids are as spunky as you."

"Kids? Getting ahead of yourself, aren't you?" Then the smile she couldn't contain burst free. "How many?"

"A hangar full."

He yanked her into his arms and kissed her hard once and then his mouth opened over hers. Lauren opened to him, opened her mouth, opened her heart, opened her life. He tasted so good, so familiar, so welcome, and she couldn't get enough of him.

Her clipboard clattered onto the concrete floor. She wound her arms around Gage's neck, tangled her fingers in his hair and poured her love into the kiss.

When dizziness threatened to make her faint in his arms, she lifted her head and cupped his cheeks. "I love you, too. And nothing would make me happier than spending the rest of my life with you."

* * * * *

Don't miss the conclusion to Emilie Rose's
THE HIGHTOWER AFFAIRS!
Look for
His High-Stakes Holiday Seduction
Available November 2010 from
Mills & Boon® Desire™.

2 in 1
GREAT VALUE

HIGH-POWERED, HOT-BLOODED by Susan Mallery

CEO Duncan needs an image change. His solution: a sweet kindergarten teacher who will make him look like an angel...

WESTMORELAND'S WAY by Brenda Jackson

After a mind-blowing night of passion with the raven-haired beauty, this Westmoreland has decided he's the man destined to satisfy *all* her needs...

MILLIONAIRE UNDER THE MISTLETOE by Tessa Radley

After unexpectedly sleeping with her enemy and secret benefactor, Miranda's taken by surprise when he proposes a more permanent arrangement!

HIS HIGH-STAKES HOLIDAY SEDUCTION by Emilie Rose

Forced to pretend a past relationship he never had for the sake of his twin, this CEO finds himself caught in the middle of a passionate affair based on mistaken identity.

THE TYCOON'S SECRET AFFAIR by Maya Banks

Impending fatherhood is not what Piers Anetakis wanted from one blistering night of passion. Still, he insists on marrying his lover... but a paternity test changes everything!

DEFIANT MISTRESS, RUTHLESS MILLIONAIRE by Yvonne Lindsay

Bent on ruining his father's company, Josh lures his assistant away. But the one thing he never expects is a double-cross! Will Callie stick to her plan?

On sale from 15th October 2010
Don't miss out!

Available at WHSmith, Tesco, ASDA, Eason and all good bookshops

www.millsandboon.co.uk

MILLS & BOON

are proud to present our...

Book of the Month

Proud Rancher, Precious Bundle
by Donna Alward
from Mills & Boon® Cherish™

Wyatt and Elli have already had a run-in. But when a
baby is left on his doorstep, Wyatt needs help.
Will romance between them flare as they
care for baby Darcy?

Mills & Boon® Cherish™
Available 1st October

*Something to say about our
Book of the Month?
Tell us what you think!*

millsandboon.co.uk/community
facebook.com/romancehq
twitter.com/millsandboonuk

All the magic you'll need this Christmas...

When **Daniel** is left with his brother's kids, only one person can help. But it'll take more than mistletoe before **Stella** helps him...

Patrick hadn't advertised for a housekeeper. But when **Hayley** appears, she's the gift he didn't even realise he needed.

Alfie and his little sister know a lot about the magic of Christmas – and they're about to teach the grown-ups a much-needed lesson!

Available 1st October 2010

www.millsandboon.co.uk

M&B

FIVE FABULOUS FESTIVE ROMANCES FROM YOUR FAVOURITE AUTHORS!

A Christmas Marriage Ultimatum by **Helen Bianchin**
Yuletide Reunion by **Sharon Kendrick**
The Sultan's Seduction by **Susan Stephens**
The Millionaire's Christmas Wish by **Lucy Gordon**
A Wild West Christmas by **Linda Turner**

Available 5th November 2010

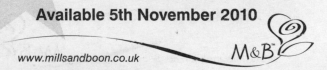

www.millsandboon.co.uk

M&B

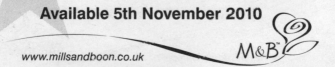

Three glittering Regency stories!

SCARLET RIBBONS *by Lyn Stone*

CHRISTMAS PROMISE *by Carla Kelly*

A LITTLE CHRISTMAS *by Gail Ranstrom*

Available 15th October 2010

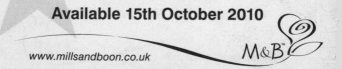

www.millsandboon.co.uk

M&B

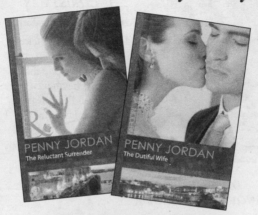

2 FREE BOOKS
AND A SURPRISE GIFT

We would like to take this opportunity to thank you for reading this Mills & Boon® book by offering you the chance to take TWO more specially selected books from the Desire™ 2-in-1 series absolutely FREE! We're also making this offer to introduce you to the benefits of the Mills & Boon® Book Club™—

- **FREE home delivery**
- **FREE gifts and competitions**
- **FREE monthly Newsletter**
- **Exclusive Mills & Boon Book Club offers**
- **Books available before they're in the shops**

Accepting these FREE books and gift places you under no obligation to buy, you may cancel at any time, even after receiving your free books. Simply complete your details below and return the entire page to the address below. You don't even need a stamp!

YES Please send me 2 free Desire stories in a 2-in-1 volume and a surprise gift. I understand that unless you hear from me, I will receive 2 superb new 2-in-1 books every month for just £5.30 each, postage and packing free. I am under no obligation to purchase any books and may cancel my subscription at any time. The free books and gift will be mine to keep in any case.

Ms/Mrs/Miss/Mr _____ Initials _____

_____

Surname _____

Address _____

_____

_____ Postcode _____

E-mail_____

Send this whole page to: Mills & Boon Book Club, Free Book Offer, FREEPOST NAT 10298, Richmond, TW9 1BR.